D1572591

Montana Reunion

Also by Caroline Fyffe

Montana Reunion

A McCutcheon Family Novel

Book Eleven

Caroline Fyffe

*For families and family reunions, and the love
and connection we find there.*

List of Characters

Montana McCutcheons

Flood & Claire
Matthew & Rachel
Mark & Amy
Luke (Half Cheyenne) & Faith
John & Lily (Live in Rio Wells, Texas)
Charity (McCutcheon) & Brandon Crawford (Sheriff of Y Knot)

Texas McCutcheons

Winston & Winnie
Dustin & Sidney
Chaim
Madeline
Becky
*Wendy Knutson (Friend from Rio Wells)

Mail Order Brides

Chance & Evie Holcomb
Hayden & Heather Klinkner
Tobit & Kathryn Preece

Chapter One

Arizona, May 1888

Gusts of gritty wind whipped off the Arizona horizon and peppered Chaim McCutcheon in the face as he squinted into the sun. His cheeks, dry and darkened from too many hours in the harsh climate, felt like old boot leather. Any vestiges of humor remaining inside his soul after Emmeline's betrayal was gone, left behind in Rio Wells the night of Dustin and Sidney's wedding—when he'd ridden away and hadn't looked back. Chaim remembered the conversation with clarity, as if it had transpired yesterday, not eighteen long months ago.

"I'm not going for good. Just need to get out of town for a while. Maybe I'll head up to Montana. See Y Knot for myself."

"Don't do this, Chaim!" Dustin begged.

"I lost her, Dustin," he'd whispered. "Tell me you'd sit around doing business as usual if Sidney went back to Santa Fe. Somehow, I don't see that happening."

"What was her reasoning?"

"Does it matter?"

Dustin shook his head. "Guess not. But I'll go with you. Sidney and I both will."

Chaim forced a smile for his brother's sake. "Your destiny is here." Chaim stared Dustin in the eye. "Making Ma and Pa happy with all the little ones you and Sidney will have. They've waited a mighty long time for grandbabies. You can't follow me over hill and dale."

"Have you told 'em yet?"

"Nope. Didn't want to spoil their time." Without warning, Dustin pulled him into a strong embrace, making Chaim's throat squeeze closed.

"You be careful," Dustin choked out. "Don't get yourself hurt, or worse."

A dust devil swirled effortlessly along the sunbaked ochre horizon. The small twister tossed small rocks and twigs as it zigzagged this way and that. Emmeline's duplicity—her departure a month before their wedding all those months ago, never to return, write, or contact him in any way—had left him a man adrift. Chaim had set out immediately to ease his troubled heart. Once he'd found Arizona, the perfect place to scourge his soul, he'd sent Brick Paulson, his traveling companion and ranch hand, back to Rio Wells. With no demons of his own to exorcise, Brick had no reason to remain.

Since then, Chaim had called Arizona home. The magic of the desert challenged him. The hardness, too. He'd needed the pain the harsh climate inflicted. At times, he'd been close to insanity with grief. The scorching heat, giant saguaro, spiky prickly pear, and abundance of rattlesnakes was his medicine. To teach him a lesson he'd never forget. And it had—in spades.

"Almost a year and a half since I've seen Texas," he whispered to the landscape. "I wonder what's changed. Did they build the new barn? Has Rio Wells hired a new sheriff?"

Dustin came to Arizona, intending to bring Chaim home but failed. His brother used every tactic to guilt him back to Texas, the ranch, their parents, and sisters. When nothing worked, Dustin's patience gave way to anger. Back when they were boys, Dustin could strike the fear of God in Chaim, but not anymore. When a man had nothing to lose, nothing much frightened him.

The dust devil now gone, Chaim raked his arm across his sweaty brow, feeling the ever-present sand that seemed to appear out of nowhere and coat everything. When Dustin's anger hadn't worked, his brother had begged. Something Chaim had never seen before. Chaim didn't want to cause strife to his family. He just wanted to be left alone.

Shaking off his thoughts, he took in the broken-down ranchero he'd purchased for pennies. His small herd grazing the sparse pasture were a far cry from the beefy, well-fed steers produced at the Rim Rock. Tired of his musings, he gathered his hammer and shovel and started for the barn.

Scottsdale, or so the area had been recently dubbed, possessed potential. New folks looking for a dry, healthful climate arrived daily. And where people congregated, there were mouths to feed. Where mouths needed feeding, beef was a prime commodity. Chaim's knowledge of the cattle industry had already been an asset to the growing stockyard in town.

Stripping off his sweaty shirt, Chaim trudged toward the house. The place must have been something special in its time, but now it just looked old and tired. He stopped at the lopsided rain barrel, ladled out a dipper of water, and poured it over his head. As if on cue—*lest I forget*—grit again peppered his body.

The sting felt good. Grounding. Escaping the granite rigidity of this land wasn't possible.

Emmaline's face wavered before him. Her silky-soft skin, made even more attractive by her dark, alluring eyes, mesmerized. Her kissable lips were drawn down in a seductive little pout.

Always the same!

Pain gave way to resentment. How long before her ghost left him? He'd vowed months ago he was done. Over her. Her memory would inflict no more pain...

I have a life. The one here and another back in Texas, if I decide to go home.

Angrily, he stomped into the structure he now called home. He went to the dilapidated pie cabinet and withdrew a handful of letters, mostly from Dustin. Taking the top envelope, he extracted the missive he'd already read and looked it over again. His extended family was planning a surprise birthday party for Uncle Flood up in Y Knot.

Last year, on his uncle's fiftieth birthday, the party was postponed following the hellacious winter which took cattle and people alike, or so the invitation stated. But this year, they were proceeding. Aunt Claire and his cousins planned a historic gathering of the two McCutcheon families and wanted him to come.

Everyone in Texas planned to go. His cousin, John, who moved to Texas after medical school and was now the doctor in Rio Wells, would make his first trip home, bringing his wife, Lily, and their new daughter.

He turned the letter over in his hands. It had arrived last month. He'd telegraphed Dustin he wasn't going, then stuck the correspondence in the drawer and hadn't bothered since.

But now...

Am I prolonging my pain by staying here and mooning over Emmeline? Didn't I swear I was finished with that part of my life? Don't I need to begin to live again? Put my declarations to work?

Chaim set the letter on the table and paced to the window. Far off, a deep brown line wavered on the horizon. A dust storm headed their way. He needed to get the steers into the shelter of the barn.

Shouldering back into his sticky shirt, he returned his gaze to the invitation, thinking of the young rancher who owned the spread next door. He'd approached Chaim a month ago about buying the place. The fella had a wife and son not yet four years old and couldn't afford to pay much. And that's about how much this ranch was worth. The fact cattle could survive on such barren lands still amazed him. Arizona was not Texas.

Was he ready to go home? Or, at least, to Montana? After the reunion, he could make the final decision about Texas. If he departed in a few days, and made good time, he'd arrive in Montana around the same time as Dustin and the rest of the family. Perhaps a change would finally vanquish Emmeline from his heart and soul. For the first time in many long months, the corners of his mouth pulled up. He'd go. The time had come. Yanking open the door, he ran toward the lowing cattle, plans tumbling around in his head.

Chapter Two

Y Knot, Montana Territory

Charity McCutcheon Crawford galloped into the ranch yard of the Heart of the Mountains, where she'd grown up, and slid to a stop, dispersing a plethora of hens amid loud squawks and cackles.

Hickory hurried from the barn.

"Good morning, Hickory." Charity dismounted and handed the boy the reins of her palomino mare.

A cinnamon hue rose to Hickory's cheeks. His shaggy, sun-colored hair was tied back in a ponytail. Her brother, Luke, had brought the orphan home from the neighboring town of Waterloo about two and a half years ago. Since then, he'd grown a good five inches on the plentiful food of the bunkhouse. Now nine years old, he was polite and did his best to work as hard as any grown man.

"You want her unsaddled, Miss Charity?"

"No, thanks. Don't think I'll be here for long. Just loosen her cinch and give her a handful of oats as a treat for the early morning gallop." Charity glanced around the yard. The bunkhouse was quiet. "Have you seen my father this morning?"

His face brightened. "Sure have. Was talking with Lucky about an hour ago. I think him and a couple of hands rode over to Luke's place. I believe they was going to the upper pastures."

Charity didn't correct his English. The foundling had taken to reading and numbers since coming to the Heart of the Mountains but was still somewhat behind. On school days, he rode in with the other children and attended school where Ashley Wells, the ranch hand Francis's wife-to-be, was the new teacher. Charity loved this little fellow and couldn't imagine the ranch without him. "Why the upper pasture? Do you know?"

Hickory shook his head. "Naw. Sorry."

Charity debated making a quick stop in the bunkhouse before going inside to speak with her mother but changed her mind. Spring had arrived, and with the season came a sign of normalcy. After the huge snow of eighty-seven, the world seemed a little righter this year, especially with plans for the big surprise for her father. This reunion was just what they all needed—as well as the town. "Thanks for the information, Hickory. I think I'll run inside and speak with Mother."

"Miss Sally's inside with the baby. She and Roady came for a visit last night and decided to stay over."

"Perfect! I haven't seen little Gillian for days." Charity hurried for the door, her mind swirling. Mr. Tracy's telegram was burning a hole in her pocket.

When the door opened and closed, Claire looked up. The baby sleeping in her arms stirred and made a few mewing noises. Now eleven months old, Gillian had stayed as petite and pretty as the day she was born. "Good morning, Charity," Claire said softly, as not to wake Gillian.

Charity tiptoed up and kissed the top of her mother's head.

Claire was so thankful her only daughter finally married and settled down. Charity and Brandon were a perfect match, and most of their back-and-forth sparring before marriage disappeared once they'd said their *I do's*. That wasn't to say they didn't have their differences, because they did and were only too happy to disagree, sputter, and spark, only to make up within moments and kiss. They did so much kissing and making up, Claire was a little surprised Charity hadn't conceived. But that blessing was in God's hands, and she'd not worry one little bit— *yet*. Everything in its season.

"Good morning, Mother," Charity whispered, peeking down into Gillian's sleeping face and then up at the stairway. "Where's Sally?"

"I sent her back to bed for a few hours of peace and quiet. This little angel has been waking up every night for the past week. And when she's up and pacing, Roady is, too. He's not one to allow his wife to do all the work."

Charity fingered the golden curls atop the infant's head. "Aww, the poor little thing."

Gillian's cheeks were chapped and ruddy from all her crying. As if she could feel she was the topic of conversation, the child breathed out a deep sigh and snuggled farther into Claire's lap.

Charity pulled up the ottoman and sat by their side. "Is Roady out with Father? Hickory said he and some men rode out early."

"No, he was up at one o'clock this morning, walking the halls with Sally, trying to get Gillian to settle down. She's teething and can't seem to rest once darkness falls." She glanced down at the eleven-month-old cuddled on her lap. "Flood told Roady he didn't want to see him until noon."

Charity laughed softly, somewhat surprised. "I can't believe Roady complied. In the old days, nothing kept him from what needed doing. He puts his family first now. As it should be."

"Flood insisted. And he didn't even argue. Just took Sally's hand and disappeared upstairs. I've had this little angel ever since." She motioned toward the empty child's bowl on the coffee table. "She ate and finally fell asleep."

Charity's eyes dimmed just the tiniest bit.

Claire needed to choose her words carefully. Charity never mentioned anything about not conceiving, especially since both her brothers' wives had relatively new babes under their roofs. The ranch had no lack of toddlers to hold and play with. But Charity might be doing a good job of hiding her feelings. Claire silently admonished her insensitivity. She laid a hand on Charity's arm. "I'm delighted to see you. What brings you out so early? Let's have some coffee and pastry. I'm famished. Esperanza is busy in the kitchen now."

Charity nodded. "I accept. But first…" she reached into her pocket. "I have some news!" She pulled out a folded yellow envelope. "All the way from Rio Wells. Dustin says everyone is on schedule to leave tomorrow, but more importantly, he received a telegram from Chaim. He's coming, as well. This truly will be a party to remember."

Deep emotion squeezed Claire. They all knew about the sad happenings with her nephew Chaim and his bride-to-be, Emmeline Jordan. The same young woman had traveled to Rio Wells to marry her son, John. When that relationship ended, she and Chaim fell in love, but she deserted Chaim a month before the wedding and never returned. One didn't recover from such heartbreak overnight. Chaim left Rio Wells and hadn't been back since. "That's fantastic news, Charity. Perhaps we can help Chaim get over his loss."

At the sound of footsteps, they both glanced at the stairway. Roady and Sally joined them in the front room.

"Mornin' again, Claire," Roady said with a lopsided smile. "Charity." He was dressed and ready for the day.

Sally was still in her robe.

He kissed her and sat her in the chair on the other side of the crackling fire. "Don't think I've ever slept this late in my life. Feels wrong."

Claire laughed, enjoying the sight of young love. Roady, with his lean countenance and vivid blue eyes, was like another son to her and Flood. And Sally was as dear as she could be. "Don't be so silly," she said, keeping her voice low. "The time's nowhere near noon. You should take Flood up on his offer. May not come around again anytime soon. You're both worn to threads."

Sally smiled dreamily, eying her sleeping daughter but making no move to take her. She nodded her greeting.

"You two look like snuggly bears just out of hibernation." Charity's smile pushed up into her eyes.

"Just as soon as Gillian's tooth breaks through, you'll have some relief." Claire nodded. "I remember these days well."

The baby stirred.

Roady quickly kissed his wife's cheek, gathered his hat by the door, and was gone.

"Are you planning Flood's party?" Sally asked.

"We are. And I brought Mother the good news the others are setting out tomorrow. Plus, Dustin received word Chaim will be traveling on his own from Arizona."

Sally's eyes lit with pleasure. "I know you all were praying for a miracle."

Esperanza came into the room with a tray and set it on the coffee table. "Coffee, Miss Claire. As well as some cinnamon rolls and biscuits warm from the oven."

Both Sally's and Charity's eyes lit up.

"Thank you, Esperanza. Everything looks delicious. Come on, girls, we have more organizing to do. Thanks to Shad and your brothers, Flood will be gone most of the morning, and we don't have to worry about being interrupted. He won't be allowed to return until noon. Now, it's time to put the finishing touches on his party."

Chapter Three

Two days after the sandstorm, Chaim sold his small ranch for less than the property was worth. If he'd held out until fall, when he'd planned to take the cattle to market, he'd have turned a handy profit. But with the reunion, waiting made no sense.

Once he'd made the decision to attend, he was all fired up to get there, excited to be reunited with his family, and meet the ones he didn't yet know. After visiting the bank, he settled up with the few shopkeepers who had extended him credit. That left enough money for a stage ticket of nine dollars, a hotel room in Prescott, the forty-six dollars he'd need for the train, and sixty-seven left over. Not much to show for all the blood, sweat, and tears he'd given to his small ranch, but better than nothing. He was used to existing on a shoestring. After settling in Arizona, he'd learned to be frugal. He'd survived these eighteen months on the sweat of his own brow, with no help from home.

Until Chaim rode out of Texas, he'd been blind to how much he took for granted. He'd practically grown up with a silver spoon in his mouth, having had a housekeeper and cook, plus a cut in the Rim Rock's earnings. Sure, he'd made coffee over a campfire now and then and opened a can of beans. Or cooked up a prairie hen or a haunch of venison. How different from running a household, even for a single man. After a long day's work, supper needed to be cooked. And laundry. And changing the bedsheet at least a couple times a year. His eyes had been opened. He cringed, remembering how long he'd put off necessities to avoid the chore. Dust crept inside every time he opened the door. Housework, if he chose not to live like an animal, was *never* done.

He paced the Scottsdale boardwalk feeling antsy. The stage would reach Prescott in a day. There, he'd board the Pacific Railway taking him through New Mexico and then head up north, eventually connecting to the line headed to Waterloo, Montana. If things went to plan, that's where he'd meet up with the rest of his family. Y Knot was another day by stagecoach or quicker on horseback.

He glanced at his satchel and saddlebags resting against the porch post. He had a lot of making up to do for staying away so long. Would his mother and father forgive him? That worry gave him pause. His old chambray shirt was clean and pressed, but a bit too hot for the climbing Arizona temperature. He'd repaired a rip in the pocket last night by lamplight. He'd buffed his boots and even ironed his royal-blue bandanna which was knotted around his neck.

This morning, when he'd been in the mercantile perusing the aisles and killing time, he'd spotted a cream-colored Stetson in the men's section. Twenty-two and three-eighths inches, a perfect fit. He'd been looking for a hat this color for years. On a whim, he laid out the money. He'd been gone so long he wanted to make a good first impression. It felt mighty nice on his head.

Sweat trickled down his temple, but he resisted the urge to wipe it. Figuring he was as ready as he'd ever be, Chaim relaxed against the post and waited.

"McCutcheon!" a voice rang out. A moment later, the telegraph operator arrived, a yellow square of paper in his hand. "You got a reply. Saw you standing out here and thought I better bring it over before the stage arrived." He handed the telegram over.

Excitement brought a smile, a near-forgotten expression. "Thanks. I appreciate your dedication."

"Happy ta help, young fella. Have a safe trip. It's been nice knowin' ya."

"It's been nice knowing you, as well." Chaim meant the words.

The man tottered away.

Everyone delighted you're coming STOP Our family and the folks in Y knot too STOP You've made me a happy man, Brother. Can't wait to see you STOP Safe travels STOP Will try to meet up in Waterloo STOP Leave a message at the telegraph office if you go on to Y Knot STOP We will do the same STOP If you go on to Y Knot check in at the sheriff's office STOP Brandon is expecting you STOP

Dustin. A warm feeling filled Chaim's chest. He tucked the correspondence into his shirt pocket. *I guess I'm going home.* First to Y Knot, and then Rio Wells? *Feels like I am, but one never knows for sure. We'll see how things work out.*

Looking up the street, he wondered about the stage. A middle-aged man dressed like a salesman sat in the shade of the overhang. A travel case sat at his feet. Chaim grinned. *Only him and me. We'll have a wide-open coach. Plenty of room to stretch out.*

"Excuse me," a female voice said from behind.

Chaim turned. A young woman gazed into his face as if she knew him. She was pretty, with wide-set blue eyes and shapely brows. She held a sleeping baby in her arms. Surprised, he took a small step back, unsure for the first time in months. "Me?"

"You're Mr. Chaim McCutcheon, aren't you?"

She swallowed and her brow wrinkled into a frown. Thankfully, the baby slept peacefully, a knitted pink blanket covering half of his or her face.

Flummoxed, he took another step back giving them space. He didn't know this young woman. He didn't know *any* young women in Scottsdale, except the ones who worked in the saloons, and those only on a "thank you, ma'am" basis. All these months, he'd kept to himself and was glad to do so. Emmeline's memory wouldn't allow him anything else.

This woman was of medium height with hair the color of honey-nut cookie dough showing beneath a yellow sun bonnet. She looked to be about his age, or a few years younger. He'd already noted her pretty face and alert eyes. Her dress was quality and clean but didn't look overly expensive. No reason in the world existed why she should know him or seek him out. None. Whatsoever. Her intensive gaze made the bandanna around his neck feel as if someone had just yanked it tight. "Yes, I'm Chaim McCutcheon. Is there some way I may be of help?" *I can't imagine how. And anyway, I'm set to depart as soon as the stagecoach arrives. You better talk fast.*

She nodded, looking briefly down the street for the stage. "I just learned this morning you stayed in town last night and are departing today. I arrived three days ago and intended to search you out before, but this little girl has a severe bout of colic, only now able to sleep. Lugging her around in the hot sun when she wasn't feeling well wouldn't be kind." A light sheen glistened on the woman's forehead as she regarded him nervously. She glanced at the sleeping child for all of one second and then back at Chaim. "Thank God, I caught you before you left."

What in heck could this be about? "I'm sorry to hear she's not been well, ma'am." He looked again at the baby and raised his brows. "But my stage is arriving any minute. Once it does, I'll be gone. What's this all about?" He resisted the urge to withdraw his pocket watch and open the lid. Something inside told him his world was about to change.

Chapter Four

San Antonio, Texas

Steam poured from behind the black iron wheels as Dustin handed his mother onto the first step of the passenger car assisting her ascent. People dressed for travel bustled about amid the calls from the conductor, hugging their goodbyes and kissing crying faces. Excitement filled the air.

Next, he handed up his sister, Madeline, and her good friend, Wendy Knutson. The two were close, and he rarely saw one without the other. When Madeline shared their travel plans, Wendy had professed how much she'd always dreamed about seeing Montana. After consulting her parents, Wendy received permission to go. The young woman, oldest of the Knutson sisters, was reserved, but intelligent. Did her coming along have anything to do with seeing Chaim again? He'd have to question Madeline the next time they were alone. Chaim's long absence was a good indicator he was not yet over Emmeline's betrayal. "Up you go." He took Becky's hand. His youngest sister was a bit glum, having left her intended back in Rio Wells. She was followed by Lily and his own wife, Sidney.

Once they'd crossed the badlands without incident, Dustin released the anxiety over watching over the large group. He hoped the ranch hands, who'd ridden guard over the precious cargo here, had the same good luck on their return trip to the ranch.

Leaving the Rim Rock felt strange. But his mother had put her foot down. The Texas McCutcheons would present a united front. She'd wanted a trip to Montana for as long as Dustin could remember. This surprise birthday party for his uncle was the perfect time to make up for all the years lost.

John appeared at his shoulder holding baby Clara in his arms. "This is it, cousin." The eight-month-old slept peacefully, even amid all the loud talking and clamor of loading the luggage car only a few cars down the line.

"That it is." Dustin liked the feel of his unusually good mood. "Have you seen my father in the last few minutes? Don't want him to miss this train. We need all the help we can get watching over all these females." He gestured toward the baby. "Even pintsized females. Changing trains could get tricky, plus outlaws and drunken cowboys to avoid. Last time I saw him, he was standing in line at the giftshop."

John laughed and gripped Dustin's shoulder. "Stop worrying. He wouldn't miss this train for the world. He hasn't seen my father since before Luke was born. That's thirty-one years." John shook his head and smiled. "This'll be some reunion. Can't wait to introduce Lily and Clara!" He stopped and studied Dustin's expression. "Even better now too, since Chaim's decided to come."

Dustin's throat tightened. He'd cried tears of joy when Brick Paulson brought the correspondence to him at the livery where he was collecting his horse. Luckily, he'd claimed a sliver of hay had lodged in his eye, causing the moisture. Dustin hungered to see his younger brother's face. Witness with his own eyes and feel with his own hands that Chaim was alive and well. The telegram hadn't specified he'd be returning home to Texas after the party, but Dustin was determined to make that happen.

"There's Uncle Winston now," John said. "Behind those old ladies. His satchel looks full to bursting. I guess he feels the same as you." He raised his eyebrows at the carpetbag at Dustin's feet.

Dustin laughed at himself. It was true. He'd been a bundle of nerves since they'd begun to pack. So many things not to forget, like one of his sisters. Thank goodness for Sidney's passion of making lists. His wife kept him sane. Then, just yesterday, he'd gotten the blessed telegram from Chaim—which was the icing on the cake.

"Stop fretting," John chided. "Manolito and Brick have been at the ranch for years. They know how to run the place. The Rim Rock won't even miss you."

Now that Winston was almost upon them, Dustin thought John right. "You're not such a big talker, cousin." He raised a brow. "Old Doc Bixby said you've been like a tornado around the office with all your notes and lists. He said the place feels like a post office instead of a medical building. Have you forgotten he was the doctor of Rio Wells before you arrived? He doesn't need to be told every little thing."

John shook his head and laughed. "Forget? Not possible! Bixby still cuts me out of some of my cases. He'll never completely retire."

Dustin stepped away from the entrance to allow two thick-shouldered fellows to pass by and board the train.

John's chuckle caused Clara to stir in his arms.

The baby murmured, smacked her lips a few times, and settled back into a peaceful slumber.

"I suppose you're right. Step aside, and I'll take this little princess aboard and give her to her mommy. It's time to begin this holiday. Can't wait to get home to Y knot. I wonder if the place will look the same?"

Dustin hefted his bag, and John's, too, since his cousin was holding his daughter. They followed Winston up the stairs and through the passenger car to the last few seats before the connecting door. He claimed the empty aisle seat Sidney had saved for him. She looked fetching in her new blue dress and bonnet. Since she ranched with him day-in and day-out, it wasn't often he got to admire her all gussied up in a feminine dress and shawl. She didn't need those things to be the most attractive woman he'd ever seen, but he was enjoying the sight just the same. Her soft perfume drifted his way.

Sidney flashed him an excited smile and laid a hand upon his leg.

"About time you got settled," Becky said quietly, touching his shoulder from behind. Her voice was laced with anticipation, as well. "I was getting a little worried. I think we're about to pull out."

She, Madeline, and Wendy were seated behind them. John, Lily, and the baby were across the aisle. Mother and Father had the seat in front of John and Lily. When they reached the first transfer, they'd have a sleeper car all the way to Waterloo. For now, they'd have to make do.

"All aboard!" the conductor called loudly from the outside platform.

In a flurry of movement, the few travelers still milling around outside in the boarding area hurried to the train. The platform cleared out in an instant.

"All aboard!" The conductor looked up and down the train.

A hush of excitement settled in the passenger car. Everyone sat quietly in expectation of the first *chug-chug-chug* of the locomotive. The whistle blared once, twice, and then the long metal conveyance began to crawl slowly down the tracks. Expectation sizzled through Dustin. Seeing his brother again. Going to Montana for the first time. Reacquainting himself with the family he knew and meeting the ones yet unknown. And finally meeting *Luke McCutcheon.*

The third eldest Montana McCutcheon was somewhat of a legend in Montana and had become one even in Rio Wells. With the arrival of Luke's brother, John, in Rio Wells, and the short visit from his sister, Charity, the intrigue grew. Dustin didn't know why Luke fascinated him so much, except that the two were the same age, and Luke was half Cheyenne. The history of Aunt Claire's abduction, and Luke's heritage, was hush-hush in his household for as long as he could remember. As a boy, he'd had his mouth washed out with soap more than once when his pa overheard him calling Luke a half-breed. Facts were facts. Dustin couldn't deny being overly interested then—and now.

Well, I don't have long to wait until we meet face to face, the famous Luke McCutcheon and me. Imagine that. Reaching down, he lifted Sidney's hand from his leg and folded it into his own, wondering what the coming weeks held in store.

Chapter Five

The top of Chaim's head felt like an egg in a frying pan as he waited for the woman to spit out what she had to say. If she didn't look so distressed, he'd usher her to the overhang a few feet away where there was shade from the glaring Scottsdale sun. Just as she opened her mouth to speak, the stage rounded the corner in a clatter of hooves and jangle of harnesses and bits.

A look of panic filled her eyes.

She stepped closer. "T-This baby is your *daughter*, Mr. McCutcheon," she stammered softly.

Her statement was only loud enough for his ears. Her arms tightened infinitesimally around the sleeping child as she gazed up into his face.

"I'd planned to speak with you the moment I arrived, but, like I said, she's been fussy, more so than usual, and I've been worried about her."

The words took several seconds to register. Thunderstruck, Chaim blinked, wondering if he'd misunderstood what he'd just heard, or *thought* he'd heard, over the rumble of the arriving stage.

"Mr. McCutcheon?"

"I'm sorry," he sputtered. "What did you say?"

"I said, this child is your daughter. I'm from Boston. A close acquaintance of Emmeline Jordan."

Emmeline! Chaim ran a hand over his mouth and jaw, struggling to make sense of what was happening. Could that last night in San Antonio, the night before Emmeline was to board the train back to Boston, be the reason? Fully intending to marry the following month, they'd made love for the first and only time. Passed most of the night in each other's arms, professing their undying devotion to each other, after which he'd gone quietly to his own room in the silent hotel. The next morning, they'd shared breakfast and then sweet, teary words on the station platform as they waited for the train. Emmeline had boarded and never returned. Or even written any letters.

And now this?

"Mr. McCutcheon?"

The stagecoach clattered to a halt alongside the boardwalk, the horses dripping with sweat.

He turned to the driver. "How long do we have?"

"Fifteen minutes, tops," the wiry, whiskered-faced driver replied as he climbed down. He opened the door, and two men exited the stage and dispersed in opposite directions.

Wranglers rushed forward and began unhitching the spent team.

"All aboard, everyone! As soon as these horses are changed, and I get a cup of coffee, we're pulling out."

"Please," the woman begged, lightly touching Chaim's arm. "I can explain *everything*, but not in so few minutes."

Anxiety laced her voice. She gave the sleeping child, who looked much too large in her arms, a long, heartfelt look.

"Please. We've come so far."

The exhausted team was led away in their traces, and others were brought out already harnessed together. They were backed to the stagecoach, and the wranglers began hitching them up.

My baby? Where's the proof? Is Emmeline pulling another fast one on me? "I know nothing about this, Miss, uh…"

"Webb," she finished for him.

"Or about babies."

"I see the disbelief in your eyes, and that's totally understandable. You don't trust she's your child. In Emmeline's first tender realization she was in the family way, she revealed a very intimate moment the two of you shared the night that, uh…" She glanced away, and her cheeks grew pink. "Well, let's just say, when you hear it," she went on, "you won't have any doubts who this little darling belongs to."

Anger stirred and fueled his words. "If what you say is true, why didn't Emmeline return to Texas? To me? Or write to me? This story has too many unknowns. And even if she did try, I'd never trust another word Emmeline said. She wouldn't know the truth if it jumped up and bit her in the face."

Miss Webb glanced at his boots, her bottom lip clenched in her teeth. "I'm sorry to hear you say that about Emmeline, Mr. McCutcheon. She passed away a month ago, leaving this child, for all intents and purposes, an orphan." Her lips wobbled. "I've hardly come to terms with the shock myself."

Emmeline dead? Pain ripped through Chaim's chest. The thought was too much to bear. He didn't like what she'd done to him, and for a while, he'd hated her for it. But he'd never wish her dead. He couldn't conceive of the notion. What was he supposed to do now? This woman knew the whole story and, if he wanted to know more, he'd have to speak with her, possibly believe her claim. That meant staying behind. Or did it? "How?" he heard himself asking.

"She became seriously ill with an extremely high fever. The doctor could do nothing. She succumbed after a week of delirium."

The driver ambled out of the stage office, a cup of coffee in one hand and a fist of papers in the other. "We're leaving just as soon as I down this here brew," he called loudly, even though Chaim and the other man were his only riders. "Climb aboard if you're coming. Get settled. Pull straws to see who gets the forward-facing seat." He chuckled and watched as the employees of the stage line finished harnessing the new team, checking the buckles, and yanking on straps. He stretched his back. "Kiss the baby and be done with your goodbyes. Your stage is pulling out…"

A thousand feelings squeezed Chaim's chest. He couldn't believe what he'd just heard. Was this woman telling the truth? Could no one in Emmeline's family write him a letter about Emmeline's passing? Was doing so too difficult?

What in the hell was he supposed to do now? He'd sold his rickety ranch for a pittance. How would he care for a baby? They needed things, didn't they? Like a home and a mother! Still, this whole notion could be a trick. How, though? This woman had traveled a long way. Or so she said. Maybe she was lying. Trying to turn a fast dollar. "If you're from Boston and knew Emmeline, why don't you sound like her? I don't hear the same accent."

"My family was not originally from Boston, so my mother had no accent. I didn't do much socializing until I was older."

He rubbed his forehead, feeling the Arizona heat. "Like you just said, I'm leaving town. I sold my ranch." He reminded himself not to be moved by her expression. She was probably an actress. But if so, how did she know about Emmeline?

Her breathing quickened. "You're her father, Mr. McCutcheon. I promise it's true. She needs you."

Chaim was over a barrel and had little time to sort this crisis through. Doing the only thing he could, he made a hasty decision. "If I hire you to care for her, can you travel to Montana Territory with me? See to her needs until I'm able to hear the whole story. I'm not sure I can trust the word of Emmeline Jordan. This has dropped out of the sky like a falling star." He felt himself squint. "I don't know what to think."

She stared into his face.

"Once we arrive in Waterloo, my family will be there. I'll have funds to pay you for your time, as well as all your past traveling expenses both ways and home again, and any expense you've incurred along the way for the child and yourself...if you're telling the truth and she really is mine. I hate to doubt your word, Miss, but there's nothing else I can do." He studied her intently.

Why would this young woman go to such expense and effort for someone else's child? Makes no sense. Unless she's hoping for a large payout now. "If you're expecting compensation today, I'm sorry to disappoint you. I don't have those kinds of funds here."

If she was there just to extort money from a rich McCutcheon with a wild tale and a baby she'd taken from an orphanage, she wouldn't travel to Montana, would she? She'd run from the fraud now. Far away, where she wouldn't be caught. "I'm fairly certain you can understand my position." As if realizing what a monumental idea she was asking him to believe, her face softened, and her arms tightened ever so slightly again around the child.

"I can go to Montana, if I must. I wouldn't want her to suffer with someone who is ignorant of her care."

She means me. "One last question. How did you find me here in Scottsdale? As far as I know, Emmeline never knew I'd left Rio Wells."

"She did know. Your sister, Becky, wrote to her saying you'd left home with a broken heart. She begged Emmeline to go to Arizona, to a town called Scottsdale, and find you. Your sister said, if Emmeline made the effort and the two of you made up, she was sure you'd return home."

She knows my sister's name? "Did Emmeline write back to Becky?"

The woman shook her head.

Tossing the last of his coffee into the street, the stage driver stretched his back again and then climbed onto the front seat. The other traveler had already boarded minutes ago.

Chaim glanced around wildly. "Do you have other things? Your clothes, and a rig for, you know—" He glanced at the sleeping child, the little face peaceful and quiet. "For the baby."

"I do. In the hotel."

The Borderland Hotel was conveniently stationed directly across the street. Chaim did a quick mental calculation. Another ticket for the stage, plus the extra train fare, would take almost every penny he had, leaving little for food and unexpected purchases. "Hurry and grab your bags, Miss Webb. I'll get the ticket."

She chewed her bottom lip. "I have some money."

"I'll take care of it. Do you need help retrieving your belongings?"

She shook her head.

The driver scowled down at them. "What's this?"

"I need five minutes to buy another ticket. And Miss Webb needs time to retrieve some things from the hotel. She's coming along."

The driver yanked out a pocket watch and flipped it open. "And the baby?"

Chaim nodded. "Her too."

"Five minutes, and not a second more." He snapped the watch closed. "Have a schedule ta keep."

Miss Webb pushed the baby into Chaim's arms. "I can go faster if you hold her."

Chaim fumbled, his breath coming fast. "You *are* coming back!"

She smiled. "Yes, Mr. McCutcheon, I'm coming back. Now, we ought not to anger this good driver any further." She shushed the fussing baby, who was now awake and gazing about. A tiny, well-worn pink bonnet dotted with yellow flowers appeared in the woman's hands like magic. She quickly covered the baby's head and deftly tied the bow. "I'm afraid he might leave us all behind if we do. Have no fear, I'll be quick." Turning, she darted away and crossed the road.

The baby squirmed, trying to sit up in his arms.

Being totally unfamiliar with children, Chaim juggled the cumbersome-feeling infant as he tried to find a position she liked. With her pretty, sky-blue eyes and wispy blonde hair she resembled him more so than she did Emmeline. He looked for some likeness to his late fiancée but didn't see a one.

"The ticket?" The displeased driver held the lines to the fresh horses.

The shotgun messenger sat beside him.

Now content in his arms, the baby focused on his face. Almost instantly, her lips wobbled, and her brows scrunched together. With lightning speed, her hands came up, and she pushed against his chest, wailing so loudly Chaim couldn't hear himself think. Her head turned this way and that, presumably looking for Miss Webb. He never knew a baby so small could make so much racket.

"The ticket!"

Unable to do anything else, Chaim lifted his satchel and saddlebag and made for the stage office while cringing from the pain piercing his eardrums. Thankfully, the room was empty. He strode to the counter. When he rang the small, silver bell, the child stopped crying for one instant, her eyes glassy with tears. "Shh, shh, there you go," he said softly, liking how the quiet felt. He gently bounced her in his arms, smiling into her face. "See? That's not so bad."

Her lips pulled down. When she blinked, two fat tears trickled down her cheeks. She opened her mouth to cry again, but before she could, Chaim tapped the bell a second time.

She glanced around, stifling her whimpers, and looked down at his hand.

The old man who'd sold him the first ticket stuck his head out from a back room and glared. "Patience, sonny! I'll be right there."

At the man's gruff rebuke, the baby, whose name he realized he didn't even know, whined and resumed her sobbing, compelling Chaim to ring the bell in one long, continuous string.

Ring-ring-ring-ring-ring-ring-ring-ring.

The man stomped out, a cigar clenched in his teeth, but the look Chaim gave him stopped any reproof that may have been on the tip of his tongue.

"What's wrong with her?" the man asked around the cigar, smoke drifting around his face. "Why's she screeching like a stuck pig?"

Chaim lifted a shoulder, all the while bouncing her in his arms. "Heard tell she's colicky."

Shaggy white brows arched, and he gave a small nod. "Know all about that. Have six grand young'uns of my own. Now, what can I help ya with?"

The baby's mouth trembled, and she let out a whimper, growing louder and longer at the end of each complaint.

Ring-ring-ring-ring-ring-ring-ring-ring.

"Another ticket to Prescott," Chaim said loudly, his hand hovering above the bell. He talked fast to beat the coming storm he saw brewing on the baby's face. "For *this* stage. The one pulling out as soon as we board."

The man opened the money drawer.

Chaim fished his money clip out of his pocket.

The attendant smiled at the baby and gently poked her belly. "There, there, sweetie. Don't cry no more."

Her lips quivered again, and she began to sniffle.

"She's cute. What's her name?"

"Don't know. But I have one more question."

The shotgun messenger knocked loudly on the window.

"How much do you want for the bell? It's a long way to Montana. Please keep in mind, I don't have much in the way of cash."

The man eyed his new hat and smiled.

Chaim stifled a groan. "Fine." He removed the Stetson, but he didn't hand the hat over. "I just paid six dollars for it this morning in the mercantile. It's brand new."

The man chewed his cigar, eyeing the prize. "I've been wanting a new hat for over a year. I'll give ya two dollars and the bell."

"That's robbery! How about five and the bell?"

The man folded his arms and rested them on his potbelly. A stubborn line appeared on his tall forehead. "I can go to the mercantile and pick my own."

"This is the only cream-colored one." Chaim ran his hand lovingly around the brim. "The rest are black. Four dollars and the bell." He'd need every cent he could come up with.

The fella nodded.

The baby seemed interested in the negotiations, glancing from one face to the other.

Chaim handed the hat over and pocketed the bell. The payment and ticket were exchanged.

The man chortled at his good luck, fitting the much-too-small hat on his bison-sized head. "It'll be perfect, once I get my overdue haircut."

Chaim didn't think so.

"Nice doing business with ya, sonny. Don't worry. Things'll get easier once you're on the stage and there ain't no place for her ta go." He grinned at the baby. "Nothin' like new fatherhood."

"Thanks." Chaim lifted his bags, quickly crossed the floor, and stepped out into the baking sunlight. Would things get easier? He tended to doubt it, recalling the baby's piercing cry. Montana was a long way off.

Chapter Six

Inside the Heart of the Mountains' bunkhouse, Luke straddled the table bench as he listened to Flood laying out the work for the next few months. All the ranch hands were present, except the ones out with the cattle. Matt and Mark hung back by the window.

The hot cup of coffee felt good in Luke's hand. Now that the plans for his father's surprise party had fallen into place, all was right with the world. And the fact Mrs. Lambert, their neighbor on the bordering lands, had accepted their offer to buy her out was icing on the cake.

Her land increased the holdings of the Heart of the Mountains by twenty-five hundred acres. Nothing to shake a stick at. The previous hard winter had all but crushed her husband of forty-five years. Then, three months ago, he took sick and died. She wasn't staying on to shoulder the rebuilding of their herds alone. The McCutcheons offered to help her get back on her feet, make repairs, and restock her herds, but she was determined to leave. She hadn't seen her family in forty-four years. With that decision firm, Flood offered top dollar for the once-prosperous ranch. The settlement made her an extraordinarily rich woman. She wouldn't want for anything in her twilight years. The last time Luke had seen her, she'd been the happiest he could remember. Exactly how his father looked now.

"Jonathan will take up residence at the Lambert place until it's fully repaired and functional." Flood looked around the cozy room. The fireplace stood dark because summer was only a month and a half away. "Ike, you'll come and go every few days with a list of supplies for the renovations. Nick and Tanner'll work there, too."

Nick and Tanner Petty, sitting on either side of their older brother, Shad, nodded. *The young men had grown up since they'd hired on at the Heart of the Mountains. Become responsible.*

"With some men away, we'll be a little shorthanded around here," Flood went on. "But we'll manage. We always have."

"We don't mind working hard, Boss," Smokey called through the gray trail winding up from his cigarette.

Hickory squared his shoulders. "I can start punching cows," he said in all seriousness. "I can work wherever you need me."

Luke's little friend still wore his hair long, and Luke doubted if it would ever see a pair of scissors. The difference now, though, from when he'd found the boy cold and hungry on the streets was that his hair was washed and tied back neatly with a leather strip. Hickory walked to the beat of a different drummer, not caring what others thought of him. Luke admired the boy greatly for that.

Flood nodded. "Thanks, Hickory. I'll keep that in mind. You're growing up."

Luke hid his smile, as did everyone in the bunkhouse.

Flood paused and placed his hands on his hips. His brow creased. "How come you're not in school today with the rest of our menagerie?"

Hickory cocked his head. "Menagerie?"

"Group of wild monkeys," Lucky barked. "A word you'd be learning in school, iffen you was there."

Hickory lifted the honey crock from the center of the table, scooped out a spoonful and stuck it in his cup. "Woke with a bad throat. I'm having tea and honey."

Flood made a deep, dubious sound in his chest.

Lucky circled the room, filling the empty mugs from his large metal coffeepot. "Been years since I've been out there. Gertrude used to like my cinnamon cake right well," he reminisced. "Those were happy times. Hard to believe Brian's passed and Gertrude's gone back to Virginia." He shook his head.

Luke remembered Lucky had been good friends with Brian and Gertrude Lambert.

"Will we be bringing the remaining head of beef over here?" Francis asked. "What was the last count? Forty or fifty?"

"That's right. We'll hold 'em separate in the upper pasture for the time being until we check 'em over. Can't have them infecting our herds with any pestilence."

"What needs doing at the ranch?" Jonathan asked. "You bought the place pretty much sight unseen. The house? The barn?"

Flood rubbed his palms together, his smile quick. "I won't kid you, there's a lot of work to be done. Mrs. Lambert said they let the place go the last few years. The barn, parts of the log house, and some of the outbuildings. Anyway, getting the spread back into shape will take plenty of effort, and twice as much money. But we've never let something small like hard work stop us before. It's the land that makes this purchase so valuable.

Having another spread as a complement to the Heart of the Mountains will come in handy, too, especially during the winter months."

Nods and murmurs went around the room.

"Sounds good," Roady threw out. "When do we get started?"

"Jonathan and Ike'll set out as soon as the buckboard is loaded with items they'll need to live, tools, and anything else they can think of." Flood looked at Francis, who nodded.

"The rest of us will head out tomorrow to evaluate the repairs. What needs doing first. Or what needs tearing down."

"I'm long overdue for a new adventure." Jonathan chuckled. "I think one's just bitten me on the backside."

The men laughed, all of them, even Hickory, in on the big surprise.

Satisfaction slid through Luke's blood. He glanced at Mark, and then Matt, whose return grins said they were feeling the same. Flood would be knocked off his feet when his brother, Winston, and the rest stood before him in the flesh. This surprise would be one to remember for all time. And they didn't have long to wait.

Chapter Seven

Charity gazed over her husband's shoulder as he sat at his desk in the sheriff's office in Y Knot, a piece of paper laid on the top.

"Dustin and Sidney will stay with Luke and Faith," she said, anticipation zipping through her body. The arrival day was drawing near.

Brandon glanced up, his unshaven jaw rugged and handsome. "With all those children underfoot? Don't you think Dustin and Sidney will be happier somewhere else?"

Charity pulled back. Of course, Dustin would stay with Luke. They were cousins and the same age. They had to get to know each other sooner or later, so her cousin could see Luke was honorable, goodhearted, and strong—much like himself. In Texas, Dustin hadn't even tried to hide his unwarranted bias against her half Cheyenne brother. What better time to smooth over the rough spots than with their wives by their sides?

She gave Brandon a knowing smile. "Yes, Brandon, I'm sure. Colton doesn't count as a child any longer because he's thirteen and helps out just like an adult. Dawn is almost five and Holly two. Dustin and Sidney will be charmed. And, don't forget, it's only for a few days until the party. After that, they can move over to the big house if they want, with Mother and Father, as well as Uncle Winston and Aunt Winnie. I know Dustin and Luke will find common ground and become fast friends. There's no two ways about it."

Brandon nodded and dutifully recorded the names in his nice handwriting.

She loved so much about Brandon. Even his penmanship was exemplary for a man's, let alone a manly-man sheriff. Must be due to the daily log of town activities he painstakingly documented each night. Sometimes, she thought he loved that journal more than he did her. She rubbed his shoulders as he worked. "Thank you. Now, John, Lily, and baby Clara are with Mark and Amy. I can't wait to meet my new niece," she said on a gush of breath. "I hope she looks just like Lily. Cinder is two and a half and can be a help. Little Zach will enjoy having someone younger than he is to play with."

Brandon began writing. "That puts an eight-month-old together with Zach, a little over a year and a half. You know how loud Zach can be. He has a set of iron lungs. Won't be much napping over there."

Charity ignored a little slice of hurt threatening to bubble up. Why hadn't she and Brandon conceived? It wasn't fair. They'd been married almost two years. "Babies are everywhere, Brandon. They can't be avoided. If the hotel were to fill up without cause, my father would be sure to hear about it. You know old Mr. Simpson. That sweet-hearted storekeeper couldn't keep a secret if his life depended on it. He's so forgetful, he'd ruin the surprise by accident. Keeping everyone hidden with family and friends will be much safer."

"If you say so."

"I do say so. Mr. Herrick, too. Trent's father at the leather shop enjoys passing on news, and I can't fault him. Other than rocking on his porch, what else does he have to do? But keeping Father's party—and more, his brother and family from Texas—a secret are all important. That's why I'm so thankful for the purchase of the Lambert ranch. Father is occupied with assessing the new land. Plus, the repairs on the homestead will keep him out of town for some time to come. The timing couldn't be better."

Charity let her hands drop from Brandon's warm shoulders. She walked to the window to look out on the street. Y Knot was quiet.

Justin Harrison, Brandon's deputy, exited the bank. The sun shined below the brim of his hat and lighted his face. He strode one building over and disappeared into the Hitching Post Saloon.

Chance and Evie Holcomb were directly across the street in front of Berta May's Sewing Shop, their son, Garth, cuddled in his father's arms.

"Who's next?" Brandon asked. "Seems you've slipped off somewhere and left me behind."

She turned to face him, taking in his gaze. Did he ever wonder about the things she did? If so, he by no means let on. "Never, my love." She returned to her spot behind him.

"Uncle Winston and Aunt Winnie will stay with Matt and Rachel. Their extra bedroom is nice and large, and they'll be comfortable there. Billy and Adam don't count as little ones anymore, and Beth is almost five."

"But Heath isn't yet a year and a half. Another set of McCutcheon iron lungs, if you ask me."

"It's the McCutcheon blood that makes them holler so loud." She squeezed Brandon's shoulders as he did her bidding. *Our child will be the same...* "Won't seeing them all again be fantastic? I'm so happy we went to Texas. Got to know them. Love them. Saw the Rim Rock Ranch. Befriended the townsfolk of Rio Wells." She sighed, remembering. "I'll never forget...wasn't it lovely?"

Brandon paused. "Lovely? Me paying fifty dollars for your box supper didn't feel lovely!"

She knew the anger in his voice was pretend. Many times, before they made love, he'd tease her about the Rio Wells fundraiser and how another man bid up the cost of her box supper. But then he proclaimed the money was well spent to win her love. Those were such amazing days. She leaned over and kissed his ear.

He turned in his chair, gathered her into his arms, and pulled her close until his lips found hers. "I remember feeling like I'd died when those Comancheros abducted you, Charity," he said against her lips after they'd kissed. "That was the most terrified I've ever been. Promise you'll never take such chances ever again."

She ran her fingers through his thick, brown hair. She loved his hair. His eyes. His mouth. Everything about him. "I promise." She straightened and turned him back to his job. "Now, Madeline and Becky will stay out at the mill with the Klinkners. Ina is over the moon she gets to put up some of our relatives. And I know my female cousins will adore her and Norman, as well as Heather and Hayden."

Brandon made the note and patiently waited. "And Chaim? Amazing he's decided to show up, too. We didn't expect him."

"I know. What a fabulous turn. Being a bachelor, he can stay just about anywhere. Have any ideas?"

"With Chance and Evie?"

"Hmm." Charity tapped her lips, thinking. "Their place is pretty small. It's a little far from town, but what if he holed up at the Preece farm? Tobit and Kathryn have the large farmhouse. Isaiah always likes a new face to share all his tried-and-true memories with. And Poppy is away right now, traveling with the Sanger children to Nebraska." Sadness rippled inside. What if the Sanger children didn't return? She'd miss those little ones. Rubbing Brandon's shoulders, she watched him write Chaim's name. "What do you think about Chaim staying out there?"

"Perfect. We'll supply a horse so he can get away when he wishes."

"And Father's never met Chaim, so we don't have to worry too much about him being spotted. Yes, we'll put him with Kathryn and Tobit, and I'll be sure to check with them today to ensure his staying won't be an imposition."

Brandon glanced up. "You haven't forgotten Kathryn's expecting, have you?"

"No. But not far along. Same with Heather. They won't mind having a guest or two."

"Good." Brandon set his pen on the desk, eyeing his handiwork. "Finished, for now. I feel my stomach calling."

"So do I. If our new home was built, we'd have room to join the fun." She let out a deep breath.

He shrugged. "Actually, I like our small house here in town. When I'm hankerin' for a kiss, the two rooms make finding you a snap." He scraped back his chair and stood, taking her hand. "And it's an easy walk to the sheriff's office. Come on, honey. Let's go home."

Chapter Eight

The baby cried for the first hour out of Scottsdale, and no amount of bell ringing helped. The stage was hot and stuffy, so Chaim couldn't blame her in the least. He'd been anxious to question Miss Webb, wondering if he'd made a huge mistake. She could be anyone and seemed too prim and proper to have made the long journey all the way from Boston unchaperoned. She'd yet to tell him anything that calmed his suspicions about Emmeline and who the baby really belonged to. He was waiting for the right time to question her more fully. If they were to talk now, he couldn't hear himself think, let alone catch Miss Webb's replies. The child's wails reverberated around the small walls, piteously needing something. The sound did wrench his heart, if he were honest.

The other gentleman, Mr. Hohenstein, introduced himself right away out of Scottsdale as a salesman of women's fine underclothes, geegaws, and unmentionables, after which he'd turned to stare out the window the entire extent of the trip.

They'd stopped twenty miles out to change the horses, and he'd hoped to get a few minutes alone with Miss Webb then, without the howls of the infant, but that had not transpired.

Chaim glanced across the coach to where Miss Webb was seated next to the salesman, enabling her to face forward. The baby dozed in her arms, having consumed half a bottle of milk, only to directly spit the contents of her stomach up all over herself, which Miss Webb cleaned up the best she could with water from his canteen. He'd never seen a flattened bottle with a rubber tube from which the baby sucked.

Miss Webb called the contraption a nursing bottle and brought along extra rubbery tubes because she refused to reuse one until it was boiled in water at least twenty minutes.

The exhausted baby was drenched in sweat. Her crumpled bonnet sat on top of the overburdened carpetbag, looking like a wet dishrag. The aroma of the curdled milk spoiling her clothes was made worse by the stuffy, warm Arizona air.

The stage slowed, and they started a gradual incline.

The child whimpered and stirred in Miss Webb's arms.

With her fussing, he'd been unable to speak with Miss Webb about anything important. Chaim thought, if the baby truly was his daughter, he should feel some sort of pull toward her, but that wasn't the case. The infant spooked him more than a Texas rattler.

Realizing he was staring at the child, he lifted his gaze to find Miss Webb studying him with a wrinkled brow. He shifted uneasily. Compelled to say something, he offered, "Your arms must be tired, Miss Webb. Would you like me to take her? Give you a rest?"

At their conversation, the baby stirred.

Mr. Hohenstein looked their way. The salesman regarded them both a few seconds and then turned back to the window.

Miss Webb searched Chaim's face. "You're sure?"

He nodded.

She hesitated briefly, inched forward, and then held out the baby in her soiled gown. The coach was much too warm for any blankets.

He settled her in his arms and leaned back against the seat.

"I'm sorry about her clothes," Miss Webb said softly. "If I can find fresh water at the next stage stop, I intend to give her a quick birdbath and redress her in a clean diaper and clothing. She's so warm, cool water will help with her crankiness."

"Birdbath?"

"Just sponge her off to the best of my abilities. Doing so helps with the heat. She'll feel better after."

The diaper under his arm felt soggy and full. An unpleasant odor wafted up to his nose. He must have reacted because the worried V between Miss Webb's brows grew larger.

"I would change her now, but it's a bit difficult in the rocking coach." She allowed her gaze to stray stealthily to the side, where the salesman gazed out the window. "To my calculations, we're within a mile or two of the next stop."

He couldn't stop a small smile at her non-verbal communication. "She's no problem, Miss Webb. But I've never asked her name, and you've never said."

"That's because it's related to the personal moment Emmeline told me about—the one I mentioned earlier," she whispered. "I'd rather we be alone when I share it." She glanced at Mr. Hohenstein again. "If you don't mind waiting a little longer."

Chaim was all too aware of the tiny girl in his arms. If what Miss Webb claimed was true, and this baby girl really *was* his daughter, he'd be the first in their family to give his parents a grandchild, something they'd been desiring an extremely long time. His mother and father had been overjoyed when Dustin and Sidney married and said so many times leading up to the day. Then he and Emmeline were supposed to be next to the altar. The days waiting for Emmeline to return to Texas were excruciating. His sisters and mother were giddy with excitement, planning the wedding that never transpired. Remembering, he glanced down into the sleeping face, and below it, the long yellow stain running the length of her soft, burgundy dress.

Poor little thing. Starting out your life without a mommy or daddy.

The stage reached the top of the incline and leveled out. The horses slowed even more.

"Feels like we've reached the stage stop," he said quietly. The last thing he wanted to do was wake her and start her crying again. *Should I give her back or carry her inside?*

Beyond the window was a corral filled with horses and mules. An old cabin with an outhouse behind stood to the right of the corral. Some ten feet farther was a small barn, several outbuildings, and the station. The sun at the top of the sky beat down mercilessly, making everything stark and foreboding.

The driver opened the door and placed a stool below.

Still holding the baby, Chaim went first and then offered his hand to Miss Webb.

"We'll be resting here a short while," the driver said. "Use the facility and grab some grub. The food ain't too bad since they got a new cook."

The salesman made straight for the building.

When Miss Webb reached for the baby, Chaim took a small step back and shook his head. "I'll keep her and walk you to the outhouse. Check for snakes, lizards, and other scaly creatures. My sisters don't cotton to uninvited guests. When you're finished, you can tend to the little one then."

"Thank you. I can't say how helpful it is having a second set of arms. They do come in handy."

Chaim couldn't envision how she'd managed thus far without him.

She gave a small laugh and nodded. "Things always work out, Mr. McCutcheon. When someone trustworthy wasn't available to hold her for a few moments, I'd have to set her on a blanket inside the filthy outhouse with me or leash her with one of my scarfs to one of her feet just outside. That said, she didn't like being tethered one little bit. She's crawling now, which makes everything significantly more challenging." She took a moment and smiled into the tiny face. "Isn't that right, sweetheart?" she whispered and then looked up. "But we found you in time, and that's all that matters. I threw the horrible blanket away when we arrived in Scottsdale." She turned to reach back inside the coach for the carpetbag, but he beat her to the punch.

With the outhouse checked out and Miss Webb inside, Chaim walked slowly back to the stage station and stepped inside, being careful not to wake the baby.

At the table, Mr. Hohenstein was eating a thick stew with plenty of meat. A generous basket of biscuits, a platter of crispy bacon, and a large water pitcher filled to the brim sat on the table. Two other places were set for him and Miss Webb.

Mr. Hohenstein wiped his mouth with a napkin. "She sure likes to cry."

Chaim nodded, feeling a bit protective. "She has colic."

"The heat can't help."

A crotchety-looking fella limped over to look at the baby. His wrinkled face softened. "Don't get many like her coming through," he whispered. "She sure is a cute little bug."

Chaim took in the sleeping face. "She is—now that she's napping."

They chuckled.

The baby stretched and opened her eyes.

Miss Webb came through the door and glanced about. "She's just now waking up?" she asked, sounding surprised.

The unspoken praise felt nice.

"I'll take her."

He placed the baby in her waiting arms.

She turned to the man. "Do you have some fresh water I can use to quickly bathe her? Preferably cool."

"I'll fetch you a pan from the barrels around back. Come from the creek this morning, but it ain't too cool."

"That's fine." Her gaze wandered between the men. "Do you think I could use your back room? I don't need much space."

Mr. Hohenstein's head jerked up. "Will washing make her cry some more?"

"No, she likes baths, and she'll feel better when I'm through. Happier. She's never this cranky. It's the Arizona heat." She glanced at Chaim. "I promise."

With Miss Webb and the baby closed away in the back room, Chaim took care of his needs and then wolfed down two bowls of the tasty food. He wasn't sure if his great hunger made the meal so appealing, but he'd not question his good luck.

The fella, who was both cook and station keeper, limped forward and replaced the empty plate of biscuits with another and refilled the crock of butter. "Don't look so surprised," the fella said on a chuckle. "I've got a cow in the barn. Around here, she's more valuable than gold. Most passengers think highly of the fresh butter."

Such luck. "Can I get a few jars of milk?"

"You sure can. And I won't even charge you. Take some extra biscuits, as well. That little sprite has brightened my day."

Not even sure if the baby ate solid food, Chaim didn't think twice. He shook out his mostly-clean handkerchief and filled it. He was nervous Miss Webb wouldn't have a chance to eat and was just figuring out how to transport some of the stew on the stage when the door opened. Miss Webb stepped out, holding the baby, whose soft cheeks were rosy from the heat. Her lips were drawn up in the first smile he'd seen.

He stood and reached for her. "Eat, before the driver tells us to load up. I've some jars of milk on the way and a few biscuits in here. Does she eat solid food?"

"Oh, yes, for some time now. But she'll enjoy the milk very much. Thank you. Finding a cow has been rare."

The station keeper set two Mason jars of milk on the table. "Fresh this morning."

Without the soggy diaper, the baby felt lighter. And she smelled much nicer, too. He chuckled as she gazed inquisitively into his face. Bouncing her in his arms, he walked to the window to check on the progress of the stage. The fresh horses were harnessed. "Only a few more minutes," he called over his shoulder. "See the horsy?" he asked the baby, pointing out the window. When her playing stopped and she stared at him, he repeated, "Horsy." He hoped to have a moment to speak with Miss Webb before they climbed inside with Mr. Hohenstein again.

"If you'll bring her here, Mr. McCutcheon, I'll see if she'll have any of this stew."

Chaim hadn't thought of that. Of course, the little one needed to eat as well.

Miss Webb withdrew a bib from the carpetbag and tied the bright fabric around the baby's neck.

Then, seated in her lap, the baby hungrily took bite after bite of potatoes, meat, and carrots, all cut into small portions with Miss Webb's spoon.

Chaim was mesmerized.

Now finished, Mr. Hohenstein used his napkin, excused himself, and headed out to the stage.

Several minutes later, the driver leaned inside the station. "You three 'bout ready to go?" His tone had softened, probably a result of listening to the disheartening sobs emanating from the coach mile after mile.

Miss Webb glanced around, a look of relief on her face. "We certainly are. Thank you so much for your kindness," she called to the stage keeper. "Your stew was delicious. Its heartiness will last us." She glanced at the milk jars on the table. "And for the milk. I'll not forget you any time soon."

The fella blushed.

Back out at the coach, Mr. Hohenstein was settled on the top with the luggage. With a nod, he called, "I think she's all napped out, and I can imagine she might just start crying again once we pull out. Hope you're not offended."

"Not in the least," Chaim called back before assisting Miss Webb and the baby inside.

As soon as the door closed, and the infant took in her surrounds, she began to whimper, which soon turned into her insistent crying.

With disappointment, Chaim realized his questions would once again have to wait. Would he ever get to the bottom of this mystery? And before he came face to face with his parents?

Chapter Nine

Tessa Webb did her best to appease Michaela, but no amount of pattycake or singing consoled the worn-out child.

She cried, and whined, and fussed.

If only the stage had a place to set her down where she could play. The scarred floorboards were splintered, jagged, and marred with dirt. Not fit for tender baby skin. The upholstery was ripped in several spots, and one stain even looked like blood.

Normally, Michaela was such a good, agreeable baby, and she had been content for most of the trip from Boston. She'd done her best to sleep, eat, and play when asked to do so. But her little body could only take so much. She was tired of the rocking stagecoach where she couldn't get down and crawl around. She had to miss her garden back home, filled with all kinds of grasses and flowers, as well as her tabby, Sasha.

When they'd arrived in Scottsdale only three days ago, Tessa believed she had all the time in the world to let Michaela adjust to the Arizona heat and allow her colicky tummy to settle, before she approached her father. She hadn't wanted to introduce Mr. McCutcheon to a screaming daughter he didn't know existed.

But, to her horror, just this morning, when she'd gone down to the hotel lobby to find a cup of coffee, she'd overheard a conversation proclaiming Chaim McCutcheon had sold his ranch and was on his way out of town for good. She'd nearly swooned. And she would have, except doing so would have taken too much time. Instead, she'd gone directly to the stage office to check the timetable. From there, she'd flown back to the room and awakened Michaela, to the poor baby's distress. Tessa bathed and dressed her quickly.

Ever so astute, Michaela had picked up on Tessa's angst and had barely stopped crying since.

"Shush, my sweet girl," Tessa crooned next to her cheek, nervous for all the noise she was once again making.

The baby seemed not to hear a word she said. Her mouth was frozen in a large O shape, tears running down her soft cheeks.

"Shh, shh, shh. All is well, my love, don't cry. Shh, shh, shh." Tessa's words melded with the hammering of the horses' hooves as they galloped down the hard-packed road, her hand patting, patting, patting Michaela's back.

Nothing seemed to calm her. Anxious, Tessa chanced a fleeting look at Mr. McCutcheon, who appeared oblivious to the noise as he gazed out the window.

He's a handsome man, she thought, remembering how his gaze touched her on the Scottsdale boardwalk, warm like the sun overhead. Strong profile, jaw, and nose. His shoulders were a crossbeam, his legs powerful and strong. His thick, sandy blond hair brought out the blueness of his eyes. He was everything Emmeline claimed, and more. But there the similarities stopped. Emmeline described his sunny disposition as infectious. He radiated humor and goodwill. Tessa assumed his hesitant manner toward her and Michaela was understandable, given the circumstances. She'd yet to give him the proof he needed to accept what she claimed was true. At the last stop, when he'd been holding Michaela, he'd seemed to soften somewhat toward her. Still, at any time, he might get fed up and put them aside.

"Shh, shh, shh, sweetheart." She pressed her lips to Michaela's forehead. "We'll be there soon. No more tears, please." She caressed the damp, downy hair as each unhappy cry pierced her heart. "I'm sorry she's carrying on so," she raised her voice to be heard. "It's the rocking and noise. She's tired of being cooped up and wants to play, outside on some soft grass, or a clean rug somewhere."

He turned their way, his gaze touching them both. "The crying doesn't bother me. You needn't worry."

She glanced out the window at the scorching sage and sand hoping what he said was true. This area was plentiful with tall cacti and brush. So different from house after house in Boston, as well as tall office buildings and throngs of people. This land was wild. The stately plants looked mysterious, and she'd been told they were filled with water for anyone who knew how to extract it.

Glancing back, she gave a wan smile. "I had hoped this would be the perfect time for us to talk," she called. "Since Mr. Hohenstein chose to ride on top."

He nodded but didn't reply. The coach bumped and jiggled on an unusually rough stretch of the road adding to the tumultuous mood inside.

"She's usually such a sweet child. Not fussy at all." If Michaela didn't stop, Mr. McCutcheon just might decide he didn't want such a nuisance in his life. That wouldn't surprise her in the least after what Emmeline's husband, Jason Whitmore, had planned to be rid of her.

Mr. McCutcheon's gaze went from her face to Michaela's. "Like I said, I don't mind her crying, Miss Webb," he called over the baby's howls.

Miss Webb leaned forward. "I'm sorry. I didn't catch that."

"I said, my eardrums feel like a dartboard."

His eyebrow peaked, and then a smile appeared. "No worries. This is the last leg to Prescott. We'll talk over supper." He lifted a brow and gazed at Michaela. "And *she* can get some crawling done."

His tanned face was weathered from the sun. After visiting Arizona, she could understand. She wondered how different his life was since he'd left Texas over his broken heart. Could he ever be the happy-go-lucky man Emmeline described? Or was *this* Chaim McCutcheon someone totally different? A changed man. Did he plan to sneak away once they'd reached Prescott, now that he'd listened to Michaela crying for hours on end? What man would want a baby, one he never knew existed, dropped in his lap?

She reminded herself Mr. McCutcheon had traded his hat for the little silver bell. He'd presented the shiny object and dinged it for a good five minutes. When his scheme hadn't produced the outcome he'd expected and Michaela had cried all the harder, he'd honestly seemed disappointed.

The stage hit a rut, and the whole conveyance jerked like a slingshot, eliciting a howl from Michaela. A moment later, the baby began another bout of tears.

Mr. McCutcheon turned back to search out the window.

"You can go up top with Mr. Hohenstein if you'd like," Tessa called over to him. "You won't offend me in the least."

He turned back, a different look in his eyes, softer, lighter...and maybe even with a trace of humor. "And miss all this? I wouldn't think of it."

Chapter Ten

The only hotel in Prescott was a broken-down fleabag. The floors were dirty, and the windows were brown with grime. A musty odor permeated the walls of this room and everything inside. If Chaim had been alone, he'd camp out under the stars instead of staying here.

The baby, now bathed and dressed in a clean-but-rumpled sleeping gown, dozed on her tummy with her thumb in her mouth, her tiny lips softly working.

Miss Webb covered her with the tattered sheet.

He hoped the bedding had been changed after the last guests. He didn't care so much for himself, but for Miss Webb and the baby.

"There," she whispered softly, turning to face him. "I pray she sleeps through the night. She used to at home, before we packed up and left."

His brow rose. Back home? Who *was* Miss Webb? He was anxious to find out. Chaim glanced around. His room was through the connecting door, which now stood ajar. "Will she be safe here? What if she wakes up and crawls over the edge of the bed?" Probably nothing. The bed was low to the floor.

"I'll have to stay where I can see her."

He gestured to his room with a sweep of his arm. "I can bring your chair into my room where our talking won't disturb her, but you'll be able to keep watch. Will that work?"

She nodded a smile. "Indeed. Thank you."

Before coming up to retire for the night, they'd shared a meal of chicken, rice, and beans in the restaurant across the street. After the baby ate some of the rice and quite a bit of chicken, she'd sucked down the last of the warm milk they'd gotten at the stage stop. Then Miss Webb had allowed the baby to crawl around on the dusty floor, all the while keeping a close eye she didn't put anything into her mouth. He'd wanted to question Miss Webb about Emmeline and the baby then, but he felt the timing wasn't quite right with her following the child here and there.

Now is the time. He'd finally get answers. If this was a huge deception, he'd rather find out now, before he presented his parents, as well as his sisters and the rest of his extended family, with a fake illegitimate granddaughter. He hoped to hear concrete information to alleviate any doubt either way. *I just want the truth.*

Going slowly so as not to make any noise, Chaim carried the extra chair through the connecting doors and arranged the furniture so they'd both have a clear view of the bed in the other room.

Miss Webb was doing something in the carpetbag.

How had she carried everything? Did she do laundry along the way? She mentioned the need to find and purchase diapers.

Chaim couldn't imagine the expense this woman had incurred to bring him his daughter.

If, indeed, she is mine.

What other motive could Miss Webb possibly have? Perhaps she would prove the baby's fatherhood and then present him with a huge bill for the last three months' care. *Or longer.* She'd said the baby was about nine months old. Maybe Emmeline turned the baby away as soon as she'd been born. Maybe she wasn't Emmeline's at all, but Miss Webb's. Anything was possible.

For a moment, Miss Webb stepped out of his view to her dresser where there was a pitcher and a mirror. He heard water pouring and felt like a Peeping Tom. Going to his own mirror, he looked at his reflection.

Darker. Harder. Lines he hadn't seen in Rio Wells fanned out from the corners of his eyes. He finger-combed his hair and then poured musty-smelling water into a glass and gulped it down before inspecting it too closely. He'd wanted a beer at supper but, when Miss Webb had ordered tea, he refrained.

Chaim thought of the last night in San Antonio with Emmeline. They'd stayed out late, consumed several glasses of wine with their dinner. When he'd walked her back to her room, she'd invited him inside, saying she wanted to stay up all night because she'd miss him so much once she left.

One thing led to another. Soon, they were on the bed, kissing passionately. Surprising him, Emmeline began unfastening the buttons on the front of her dress. Chaim was in no condition to stop her. He didn't want to stop her. What would it hurt? Their wedding was the following month. If she conceived, the timing was so close, no one would be the wiser.

He heard a sound and turned.

Miss Webb stood at the door.

"Please," he said, gesturing to the chairs.

She nodded, rubbing together her hands.

This must be her Alamo. She'd brushed her hair, which was now out of the messy, fist-sized bun she'd worn all day and it lay across her shoulders like a silky cape. She'd also washed away a smudge of grit she'd had on the side of her chin for most of the day. If he'd known her better, he would have mentioned it. His sisters always said doing so was the decent thing to do.

She sat and Chaim took a seat. She raised one brow and touched her now-clean chin. "You should have told me, you know."

"In light of everything that's happened, a little smudge didn't seem important."

She glanced around and took a deep breath. She reminded him of a groundhog circled by a hawk. "So," Chaim began. "You said you have information for me. Something Emmeline shared with you."

She fluffed her skirt. "Yes, well, where to begin…?"

"How about at the beginning? I want to know every detail."

She nodded. "When Emmeline wrote home from Texas about no longer being engaged to John McCutcheon, her father, Mr. Jordan, had been elated."

Chaim held up a hand. "Tell me how you know this," he interrupted. "What's your relationship to the family?"

Her gaze momentarily searched his face.

She was debating something. What? He didn't know.

"I've been employed by the Jordans for most of my life. I know them all very well."

That was believable. Nothing was kept secret in a house with servants. They were always the first to know everything.

"The Jordans hadn't wanted Emmeline to go to Texas in the first place. They believed marrying a country doctor was beneath

her. They tried everything to change her mind, but she would
have none of it."

"I hadn't realized that. She always made her family sound so
friendly. Accepting."

"Emmeline was strong willed. Difficult to control. By the
time Mr. Jordan got to the end of the letter I mentioned, his
elation over Emmeline breaking her engagement to John
McCutcheon had soured. She explained she'd fallen in love with
a different McCutcheon, John McCutcheon's cousin." She studied
his face. "*You.* And the two of you planned to be wed in the
coming months."

Chaim knew the side of Emmeline Miss Webb described.
Her uncompromising strength when she wanted something. Her
many harmless manipulations to get her way. But, at the time,
head over heels in love, he'd thought everything about her was
charming and attractive. He'd happily gone along with anything
she'd said or wanted.

"I actually saw the letter the next day. After her
announcement about her *new* wedding plans—same sacrament,
different groom—the letter went on for several pages with
questions about the news from home. The Boston fashions.
Which shops were selling what? Who among her friends were
engaged, and to whom? Were the matches well thought of? She
was a social butterfly through and through."

Yes, Emmeline was a social butterfly, all right. That was a
perfect description of her—and one of the reasons his mother
and sisters had taken to her so well. She was irresistible when she
turned on the charm.

An old, familiar pain sliced through Chaim, one he'd thought
the Arizona sun had burned out of him, along with all other
emotion. He'd been wrong. Hearing this hurt more than it should
after all the months that had passed.

Miss Webb blinked and looked away for a moment before regaining his gaze. "As you know, Emmeline returned to Boston because she'd been told her father had taken ill. When she arrived, she found he was being treated in another apartment they owned, one which was closer to the family doctor. The report given her said he was recovering nicely and would soon be home. While she waited, she visited old haunts. Enjoyed the grand department stores she'd missed so much while in Rio Wells. Dined with her mother and friends at the finest restaurants."

Chaim ignored the punch to his gut. He'd felt all along the ploy to get Emmeline home was false. He leaned forward in his chair. "Her father wasn't sick at all, was he?"

Her face colored, and she shook her head. "No, he wasn't. The old fox deliberately stayed away so she could reacquaint herself with all the things she loved and had missed while she'd been away. So she would realize how sweet life was in Boston and how unsuited she was for a rugged Texas town."

He clenched his fists, angry Emmeline had fallen for her father's trickery. So much so she hadn't written to him once, replied to his telegrams, or extended even one small courtesy.

Miss Webb reached out but let her hand fall away. "This is upsetting for you. We can finish tomorrow morning."

He relaxed his hands. "No, go on."

"When the time was right, Mr. Jordan returned home. Emmeline soon learned her family was in ruinous debt. Everything her great-grandfather accumulated and passed down was at stake. Mr. Jordan allowed her to suffer for a whole night, thinking her mother and father would soon be living in a small apartment on the bad side of town." She shook her head. "But then he revealed all would be restored if she married a nice young gentleman Mr. Jordan met at his club. The man intended to marry an upstanding young woman with connections in Boston. His mother, being Italian, was a stumbling block for him. Jason Whitmore favored her dark coloring, which made his acceptance into genteel English society difficult. All he needed was a wife who already knew the right people and could ease him into the circle of influence—which Emmeline did." She shrugged and took a breath. "He was rich beyond anyone's wildest dreams. Her father painted a fabulous picture of his newly acquired home in Boston, and another of their family home in England."

Emmeline was married? Never in his wildest dreams had Chaim expected this. With the surge of bewilderment inside, he worked to take the next breath of air. "Jason Whitmore," he mumbled.

"Yes. An Englishman. That's why Emmeline never returned Becky's letter. She was already married."

With a loud squeak, Chaim forcefully sat back in his chair. "With a family like that, I'm surprised she got the letter at all."

"She was at her parents' home the day it arrived, otherwise she might not have."

Suddenly, Chaim had heard enough. He didn't want to know any more about Emmeline's marriage. He needed to make decisions. From here, he could just as easily put Miss Webb and the baby on a train headed east and be done with it, if he decided this whole story was a lie.

"What about the baby, Miss Webb? The night is getting away, and I want to be sure to hear the part you claim will persuade me she's mine. She could wake up any moment and begin to cry—as I now well know." He looked through the doorway. The baby hardly made a lump in the bed.

"Yes. I'm sorry. I'm sure you want to get to that. I was with Emmeline the night before her wedding."

She said that quickly, as if she knew talk of the nuptials, which were supposed to be his, caused him pain.

"She'd been home almost three months, and with all the goings-on, how busy she'd been socializing, she hardly realized her monthly..." She blushed and looked at her hands.

"You don't have to mince words with me. I'm a rancher."

She nodded and gave a rueful smile. "Well," she went on, "she was trying on her dress after a minor alteration and noticed the garment was unexpectedly snug around the middle. Other parts of her anatomy had become highly tender, as well, achy like she'd not felt before. In a burst of awareness, she realized she must be with child."

Had Emmeline already picked out a dress for their wedding before her father had changed her mind? Was it one and the same she'd wear for Jason Whitmore? He worked to picture her, long white dress and a veil covering her face, but couldn't now. He'd blocked out everything except her deception. "She still had time to call off the wedding and return to Texas, if she'd wanted..."

"That's true. But the wedding was a huge expense. Everyone who was anyone in Boston was invited." Miss Webb tilted her head. "Please don't think too harshly of her. She was extremely distraught. Once she realized she was carrying your baby, Emmeline was inconsolable. Guilt ridden. So sorry things turned out the way they had. Still, she carried the enormous weight her father placed on her shoulders to save the family fortune. He was counting on her marriage to fix the mess he'd created."

Chaim pulled back his shoulders. A surge of love and pride filled his chest. "My family owns the largest cattle ranch in Texas. We aren't exactly poor."

"No. But you're cowboys. And live out west. Uncultured, according to him."

He clenched his jaw. "You said Emmeline told you something."

"She did. We were alone at the dressmaker's. After her first gasp of surprise, she caressed her tummy and lowered herself to the sofa, her eyes brimming with love and tears. Shocked, I rushed to her side, fearing something was wrong. I couldn't imagine what. I didn't know if she had become sick or was in pain. I was wrong. She was ecstatic, glowing with the thought of your baby growing inside her. The story tumbled out how you'd spent your last night together in San Antonio. She'd never looked as beautiful as when she retold the memory. Then she said the two of you talked. If she was pregnant with a girl, she wanted to name her Michaela because that sounded so nice with McCutcheon. And if the child was a boy, she'd name him McCauley Chaim McCutcheon, for the nice look of the McC names together."

The memory crashed over him like a tidal wave. He'd been delirious with love that night, praying the morning would never arrive. Chaim stood and quietly entered the adjoining room. Stopping at the bed, he gazed down at the sleeping child. "Her name is Michaela," he said through a tight throat. "Michaela McCutcheon." He felt Miss Webb standing at his shoulder.

"Yes, Mr. McCutcheon. Meet Michaela, your daughter."

Chapter Eleven

At nine o'clock the next morning, Luke, his father, brothers, and several of the ranch hands approached the newly acquired Lambert ranch, feeling excitement growing within. They'd started out at sunup after filling their bellies with hot coffee, flapjacks, bacon, and mush Lucky had prepared.

Flood was riding Ace, the buckskin gelding he'd favored for years. His father looked young and fit, much stronger than he should for his age. This project was exactly what he'd needed to take his mind off all the devastation and heartbreak the territory suffered during the past winter. Nothing like hard, backbreaking labor to make a man grateful for his blessings.

Flood halted and sat straight in his saddle. "There she is. I haven't been out this way for years. Amazing how some things never change."

Luke reined up beside his father.

Shad Petty stopped alongside.

Shad's specialty on the ranch was starting the two-year-olds and getting the three-year-olds out on the trail. The gelding he rode today, a muscular bay with a wide blaze and four stockings, was a handful, and then some. The moment he'd reined up, his impatient mount pawed the ground, ripping the boot-high grass from the earth. When Shad gave a sharp squeeze to distract him, the unruly bronco took a sweeping sidestep and thumped into Luke's gelding.

Luke's horse pinned his ears in warning at the youngster.

Luke smiled and shook his head.

Shad grinned. "Sorry, Luke. He has an attitude a mile high. But he's gonna get a long, roundabout gallop back to the ranch on our return. After that, he'll be nice and cooperative—and thankful to be home."

Shad would have been married by now if he and Poppy Ford hadn't twice postponed their nuptials. First, because Poppy wanted a spring wedding, and then again for her parents, who'd taken a last-minute overseas business trip which couldn't be cancelled or rescheduled.

At the moment, Poppy was out of town with the three little Sanger orphans she and Shad planned to adopt. Surprisingly, a distant aunt, unknown to the children, had replied to an announcement in a Nebraska newspaper. Crushed by the news, Poppy took the children and was meeting her father in Nebraska to meet the next of kin. Whatever the outcome, her and Shad's wedding was now set for early July.

"No problem," Luke replied, taking in the sight of the new ranch. Prime grazing pasture as far as the eye could see, but the weeks of work needed on the homestead was evident, even from this distance.

Matt and Mark arrived, reining up on the other side of Flood, followed by Roady, Francis, and Smokey. Nick and Tanner were coming along in the early afternoon, after their chores were completed.

"Well, boys, what do you think?" Flood asked, pride ringing in his voice.

The original log cabin predated even the Lamberts' purchase. They'd enlarged the home structure, adding several more rooms, intending to grow their family. But that never happened. Now, the clapboard rectangle looked old and tired. A large barn with several outbuildings dotted the ranch yard. A windmill creaked slowly in the breeze, pumping a trickle of water into a manmade pond with a holding tank. The tarp-covered buckboard he'd sent out the day before sat beside the barn stacked with a multitude of tools the men would need to accomplish the work before them, as well as a large order of lumber, nails, and plaster.

"The land looks mighty fine," Luke offered, wanting to say something nice. Hadn't his ma taught him, if he couldn't say something nice, don't say anything at all? "Not overgrazed in the least."

Flood glanced over and chuckled. "Always the diplomat. I know the land is good, that's why we bought the spread. I'm talking about the homestead." He made a sound in his throat. "Appears pretty dilapidated to me. Look, there's Jonathan and Ike exiting the barn. Wonder how they fared last night."

"What are we waiting for?" Mark queried. "Let's go find out. I'm anxious to see the place."

Matt nodded. "Agreed."

Halfway to the house, Jonathan spotted them descending the knoll and lifted an arm in welcome.

The men stopped and waited for the group to ride in.

"Howdo?" Ike called when they were within hearing distance. "Welcome home."

Even before dismounting, Luke noticed missing blades on the windmill, and the ones that remained appeared cracked and brittle. The roof of the barn sagged like a stretched-out clothesline with too many sheets. Shutters on the house hung at odd angles, straining their few hinges, and bottle-green moss, wedged between the shingles, made the roof look like a mouth full of crooked teeth. Ten or more chickens scratched around the yard, and a henhouse to the left of the outhouse listed dangerously to the right.

That Mrs. Lambert lasted out here as long as she had was amazing. But, on the bright side, a nice plume of welcoming smoke chugged from the chimney. The day hadn't yet warmed to the fullest, and he was sure Jonathan and Ike missed Lucky's usual ample breakfast and the snug bunkhouse where they'd lived for years.

At Jonathan and Ike's side, Flood stepped off his horse, looking as proud as a peacock.

Yes, this ranch is exactly what Flood needs. Luke dismounted. How delighted he'd be when his brother showed up.

Fully absorbed in the new sights, Flood absentmindedly handed Ace's reins to Luke and then did a full circle. Finished, he glanced at Jonathan and the rest of the ranch hands. "So, what have you discovered?"

"Barn roof is shaky," Jonathan said, looking in that direction. "Must have been the heavy snow last winter. A passel of racoons were nested in one of the stalls where the Lamberts stored their grain. The critters were none too happy gettin' run out. The male is the largest I've ever seen. Keep an eye out. He's vicious."

"I think putting on a whole new roof would be easier than repairing what's there," Ike added. "Not much left to save."

Flood nodded. "We'll send for more lumber. We'll keep the Klinkner mill humming for months."

"Water's good and plentiful. No problems there. Ike and I scouted out the source this morning. The waterways are clear. I don't think this place will ever have a shortage, even in the hottest of summers."

Flood grinned. "Good work, men. What about the house? I can see the shutters are practically falling off. Any problems inside?"

"No indoor pump, so we've been fetching water from the holding tank," Jonathan said. "There's some settling on the northeast corner. Dry rot in the root cellar. If you can call it that."

"What? The dry rot?" Francis asked.

Ike chortled. "No, the root cellar—well, the one in the original log cabin. Don't know what they were thinking when they dug it out. A large man just might get stuck. I can barely turn a circle. Not worth much for storing. But Lambert built one in the remodel and left the other alone."

"The log cabin was built long before the Lamberts bought the land," Flood said. "It's been here even before I arrived in Montana." He sucked in a deep breath and slowly released it. "I'm damn happy to have something new to work on. To think about. This'll make a fine place for one or two of our hands to live once our herds populate these lands. God has been good to us again, boys. And in the process, we were able to help Mrs. Lambert out of a desperate situation she'd found herself in. Can't get much better than that."

Flood clapped his hands together and grinned, reminding Luke of his father's younger years. Building the upper bridge, the pole barns in the higher pastures. Each and every one of his and his brothers' homes.

"Let's get to work and unload the buckboard so we can send Francis back to Y Knot for more lumber. Stack the timber inside the barn, as well as the tools." He grasped Mark by one shoulder and Luke by the other as they headed for the barn. "I can hardly wait to get started."

Chapter Twelve

The wooden floorboards rocked under Dustin's feet as the train began to slow. Only a few minutes remained until they arrived at the next stop. The passengers would disembark and take their morning meal at a railway restaurant built close to the station. He was hungry. Besides eating, he'd have to carve out some time to find extra foodstuffs to buy. The hamper they'd brought along to nibble from needed replenishing.

After three days on the train, the women were doing as well as could be expected. Lily had plenty of help with the baby, walking her or playing, singing silly songs to make her laugh. She was a sweet little thing, and his cousin, John, was as proud as a father could be. Dustin looked forward to the day he'd be holding his and Sidney's child.

"Dustin?"

At the sound of his wife's voice, he glanced around. Sidney made her way down the rocking aisle in his direction, carrying the wicker picnic basket. "That was my exact thought," he said, taking the container from her arms. "I'll go in search of foodstuffs while you get a table and order my meal." Her shoulders slumped. He leaned forward and kissed her forehead. "Tired?"

"Yes. Changing trains in Denver was hectic. I'm thankful we didn't leave anyone behind."

Towards the back of the passenger car, a baby began to cry.

She lifted her head and looked back. "That's Clara, in case you don't recognize her cry yet. She's almost as exhausted as the rest of us."

Outside the window, signs of Grand Island, Nebraska, dotted the landscape. Houses and people began to appear. A production plant of some kind pumped gritty black smoke into the air from several towering smokestacks. Farther on, a steepled church with glistening white paint was a contrast to the ebony smoke of the factory a half a block away. The wide-open, double doors welcomed people inside. Buggies, carts, and wagons traveled in both directions on the road. Pedestrians were everywhere.

The train slowed down to a crawl.

Sidney's face brightened. "Looks like a nice day out there. Did you hear the porter? We'll have a little longer at this stop to eat and stretch our legs. A whole forty-five minutes. That'll feel like Christmas."

The train jerked, then chugged slowly.

Dustin put a steadying arm around his wife's shoulders. "Forty-five minutes? Praise God. I'm hankering for some solid ground beneath my feet. When we disembark, you get a table for all of us. I'll get there as soon as I can."

The train shuddered to a stop. Passengers stood and gathered their belongings. Some stepped out into the aisle, preparing to depart for their breakfast. With his hand on her lower back, he aided her along as the passengers began to bump and move about.

They descended the stairs into the sunshine. He walked with her to the door of the red, clapboard eatery.

She gasped. "Look!"

At her frightened tone, Dustin jerked around. "What?" All he saw on the other side of the tracks was a small church in need of tending. A cemetery lay to the west, and weeds grew up around the headstones. A few broken tree branches littered the ground.

Sidney gripped his arm.

"What has you spooked?"

"Didn't you see the flock of crows? Look up." She pointed. "Crows in a churchyard means something terrible will happen. They covered the headstones and the top of the church."

He smiled and gently took her chin. She was shivering. "Sidney, sweetheart, that's just superstition," he said patiently. "I know you cherished your dear, beloved Carmen, but that old housekeeper did you a great disservice, filling your innocent head with all these worries when you were so young. She had a superstition for everything." Still seeing the worry in Sidney's eyes, he kissed her forehead. "*Nothing bad* is going to happen. We're traveling to Montana for a special get-together. It'll be mighty nice to see Charity and Brandon again and meet the rest of our kin. I can't wait to show off my wife."

"I feel it, Dustin." She gave his arm a shake. "Something, *something* is on the horizon. And it's not good."

"The last time you pointed out a crow you said it was *good* luck! You can't have it both ways."

Sidney smiled a bit sheepishly. "That was different. A *dead* crow in the road brings good fortune. I know what I'm talking about."

He arched a brow.

Now fully recovered, Sidney went up on tiptoe and playfully tweaked his nose. "And don't you ever forget it, Dustin McCutcheon. Mark my words."

"And *I* know what *I'm* talking about. You have nothing to fear. And, if by some odd *chance*, something *does* come along, I'm right here at your side to protect you. You have nothing to worry about. Unless I don't get a seat at a table inside. Or if the restaurant runs out of food. If *that* happens, your crow premonition might just come true."

Sidney turned with a smile and followed a family of broad-shouldered farmers, by the looks of their clothes.

Alone now on the landing, Dustin stretched his frame to full height, enjoying the cool air and the feel of extending his muscles. The train didn't have much leg room. He glanced back at the passenger car.

John gave a wave. They were getting close to the exit door.

With a nod, Dustin strode away, stepped off the platform, and made quickly for Grand Island, a good-sized town, at least compared to Rio Wells. Several shops already bustled with business. Excitement made him smile at the sun. He'd never been this far from Texas before. A big, wide world existed out here for the taking.

He walked down the boardwalk in front of the blacksmith's shop when a deep-throated curse made his step falter. The sounds and smells of the forge—iron, charcoal, and sweaty horseflesh—took him back to his boyhood. He recalled the son of the Rio Wells blacksmith, a bully who had broken Dustin's nose. The boy, who stood a head taller and outweighed him by a good twenty pounds, was slurring his Aunt Claire and his half Cheyenne cousin, Luke McCutcheon. The boy must have heard the information from a ranch hand at the Rim Rock. Dustin stood up to him and told him to shut his mouth. After giving

Dustin a harsh beating, the boy gleefully insisted Luke's tainted blood marred the McCutcheon name, and when everyone learned the truth, Dustin wouldn't be quite so high and mighty.

For months, the two boys quarreled. Every time Dustin went to town, the blacksmith's son demanded a quarter to keep quiet. Pay up, or he'd spill the beans. When Dustin's father punished him for fighting, Dustin never revealed the true reason of defending the McCutcheon name. One blessed day, Dustin learned the blacksmith was gone. He'd pulled up stakes and moved out of Rio Wells, taking his family. The relief was instant, but the confusing feelings the situation had caused lingered. Dustin was ashamed he'd allowed himself to be blackmailed. And bloodied. Anger for all the scuffs and bruises he'd suffered were leveled on Luke, his cousin. The mention of Luke's name brought a smoldering resentment, instantly followed by humiliation. The way he felt was unfair to Luke, and he knew it, but controlling his animosity took work. Charity saw the truth when she'd come to Rio Wells, and she'd chastised him for his probing curiosity about Luke then. Now he'd have to do the work for himself.

A surprisingly slight man for the blacksmith trade ambled out, wearing blackened chinks and a sweat-covered shirt. "Can I help you, mister?" he asked, a ready smile on his face. "I saw you stop and glance inside, but you didn't come in or move on."

Dustin snapped himself out of his reverie. "I'd be obliged if you'd direct me to a place where I can pick up a few supplies for my family traveling on the train. I don't have much time."

"I'll be happy to. Go down my alley to the next street, and you'll find a mercantile with everything you could need."

Dustin nodded. "I best get to it. Thank you." And he'd best remember Luke was not responsible for all the disharmony between Dustin and his father back then. None of the tension had been his cousin's fault then—and it wasn't now.

Chapter Thirteen

Chaim stared out the train window, not seeing much of anything. Miss Webb's revelations were tumbling around in his head like a cup of dice. His many unanswered questions could fill a book. But all he had to do was look across the way at the young woman holding his daughter and his voice fell away. That baby girl was his child. His and Emmeline's. When Emmeline realized she was pregnant, why hadn't she called off the wedding to Jason Whitmore and returned to Texas? To him? They'd been engaged. Her parents, if not supportive, would have at least understood.

Because she didn't want a life tied to a Texas rancher in a rustic town void of all the things she loved. She hadn't loved me enough.

The baby, Michaela, seemed less fussy today. The three of them boarded the train after a brief breakfast in the same restaurant where they'd eaten the night before. Since then, not much talk had transpired between them. Michaela was sitting in

Miss Webb's lap, playing with the ribbons from Miss Webb's yellow bonnet.

"Say, ba ba ba, black sheep..." Miss Webb said softly, speaking directly into Michaela's face. She captured Michaela's hands in her own and patted them together then kissed each palm, pretending to nibble at the ribbons with her teeth.

The child giggled and tugged on the tails of fabric, making the bonnet flap in and out around Miss Webb's face.

Chaim knew he should feel something. Some tender fatherly ache somewhere inside his heart. He searched for it, for something, but came up empty. The information Miss Webb shared removed all doubt in his mind. Still, he felt numb all over coming to grips with the news Emmeline was dead. And the other astounding news, she'd married another man before that. The realization was unimaginable. Had he ever really known Emmeline at all?

Yes, his mind whispered. The memory of her, rumpled in the sheets after their lovemaking, pierced him. Yes, he'd known her, and in doing so, perhaps he'd doomed their future together. She'd been an innocent. Maybe she'd regretted their actions. Knowing the truth now was impossible. "What happened after Emmeline began to show?" he asked. "Surely, her husband became suspicious." At his words, Miss Webb started and looked up, wide eyed. She'd seemed to be content on tending the child and pretending he wasn't there—or that their talk last night hadn't changed his life forever.

"I'm sorry, Mr. McCutcheon?" she asked. "I'm not sure I caught what you said."

The baby yanked on one of the ribbons and almost pulled the bonnet from her head.

Unruffled, Miss Webb smiled and straightened it, ever polite and patient with Michaela.

"What happened when Emmeline's pregnancy began to show?" he asked again. "And why doesn't Jason Whitmore want Michaela? Does he know her true paternity?"

With Miss Webb's full attention now on him, Michaela began to fuss and squirm on her lap, trying every which way to get down to the none-too-clean train aisle.

She was a handful when she wanted to be. Chaim decided to try the silver bell again, since the poor little thing wasn't so colicky. Reaching into his bag, he drew out the bell and tapped the ringer several times.

Michaela stopped squirming and turned to see what had created the sound. She carefully took the offering and brought it directly to her mouth.

Alarmed, he glanced at Miss Webb. "She's biting the bell?"

Miss Webb smiled and nodded. "There're no small parts that can come off and choke her."

"No. I checked that right away. Everything is screwed on tight."

Somehow, maybe with her tongue, Michaela made the bell ring. The baby pulled back, her eyes wide. And then she cooed.

"You asked about Emmeline. Yes, she went ahead with the wedding, even though she knew she was with child. I'd like to say the only reason was because of her father's desire for her to do so, but I do know how much Emmeline enjoyed the finer things in life, too."

Miss Webb cast a sad glance out the window, making Chaim wonder how well the woman knew his late fiancée.

"She was enamored with expensive clothes," Miss Webb went on. "Her future husband's estate was grand, even by Boston's measure. He lavished her with gifts and promised a number of extravagant trips all over the world once the marriage transpired."

"You've mentioned that before. But how... surely, someone noticed."

"Mr. Whitmore's schedule was busy, and he traveled extensively. With the pregnancy to hide, Emmeline claimed reluctance to go along since she'd so recently returned from Texas and also stressed her father's fictitious ill health. Wanting to keep her happy, Mr. Whitmore complied. She believed concealing her growing waistline wouldn't be difficult with him away. As weeks passed, she declined most invitations. After a time, she'd say she'd conceived on the wedding night, and the baby came early. That's not uncommon." Her cheeks darkened to a rosy hue.

How would he explain to his parents? Dustin and his sisters? Guilt for worrying over their reaction rather than the hardships Miss Webb had gone through to bring Michaela to him pushed at Chaim's chest.

The baby rang the bell again, this time with her hand. She giggled.

"Good girl," Miss Webb praised softly, smiling into her face. "That's a smart little bunny. You're getting the hang of it."

"Please. Go on."

"What Emmeline didn't plan on was her mother-in-law. The woman came from England for the wedding and stayed. Mr. Whitmore was her only son, and, in her eyes, no woman was good enough to kiss his boots. Especially someone who'd just returned from a broken engagement. From the start, she despised Emmeline and watched her every move. She didn't trust her in the least."

"How do you know all this, Miss Webb? For a servant, you seem to know quite a bit."

Miss Webb tensed.

Something wasn't quite right with her story.

"When she married, Emmeline brought me to her new home. She wanted someone nearby who she knew and trusted. A companion to pass the long days while her new husband was traveling. The arrangement wasn't optimal from the start—but for her needs, it was perfect."

The whole scheme sounded farfetched. Marriage availed two people to live as one, to love and share. Grow together—and grow old together—like his parents. Not live apart for monetary sakes and to keep the truth from being discovered. "Mr. Jordan is a coldhearted..." He left the sentence unfinished. "He sold his daughter's happiness for profit. But I'm not stupid. Emmeline was ultimately responsible for what happened; she could have refused at any time. Written to me and I'd have come for her. Or just boarded a train and returned to Rio Wells on her own. Still, the idea began with her father, who valued his rich lifestyle over Emmeline's happiness. That family has no idea what love means," he gritted out. "Family bonds, being truthful. Someday, I hope I meet him so I can give him a piece of my mind."

Ashamed, he stopped and lifted a placating hand. "Please, continue. There's more to this story, and I'd like to hear everything now. We'll arrive in Waterloo early tomorrow and perhaps meet my family. I'd like to know everything beforehand."

"I understand."

Her voice was soft. The empathy in her eyes made him feel as if she did, indeed, understand.

"Emmeline's waist began to thicken somewhat after the wedding, which she blamed on the cook's delicious cuisine. In reality, she ate very little. Mr. Whitmore was gone much of the time but, in turn, her mother-in-law's scrutiny increased. I never learned what the arrangement was between Mr. Jordan and Mr. Whitmore concerning finances."

Miss Webb adjusted the baby on her lap.

Chaim nodded her on.

"About two months after the wedding, I overheard a confrontation between Emmeline and her mother-in-law. The angry conversation carried out to where I was arranging a vase of chrysanthemums on the entry hall table. I could tell Emmeline was in tears. The woman threatened to expose her to her son. She said, when he learned the truth, any agreement between him and Mr. Jordan would become null. Then the conversation lowered, and I was unable to hear anything else. After that, Emmeline was emotional and anxious all the time."

Michaela began to fuss and cry, the bell forgotten in her hand.

"I'm sorry, I think she's getting hungry, and I know she needs to be changed. Do you mind?"

Miss Webb was using the back of the passenger car for changing, where some privacy could be found. She hadn't said anything, but he could tell her travel bag was becoming quite light. She must need additional diapers and supplies. She'd kept the wet diapers and did her best to rinse them out when possible but threw the soiled ones away. "Take your time," Chaim replied, feeling anything but patient.

"I'll give her a bottle back there, too, and maybe she'll fall asleep. Then I'll be able to continue."

Chaim watched them walk away, not liking his thoughts. Emmeline stopped eating to keep the pregnancy from showing. She'd hidden the truth, to her own emotional distress. What a mess. Even through his anger, empathy for her situation won out. After everything, he still would have married her. If she'd only returned.

Chapter Fourteen

Flood McCutcheon took a deep breath, letting the fresh air fill his lungs. The warmth of the morning sun felt good on his chilled skin. Earlier today, he and his men removed their shirts for the heavy lifting. They'd painstakingly hoisted up all the cumbersome lumber needed to replace the barn roof.

Jonathan and Smokey hammered the two-by-fours into place.

The other ranch hands fanned out, dispersing to other chores needing attention.

A good start. Flood took in the new ranch. The few days had gone by in a blink of an eye. What they'd name this new addition to the Heart of the Mountains had yet to be decided.

A new purpose. A new lease on life.

Was feeling this way unfair? He possessed everything a man could ever want. Four outstanding sons—strong, moral—who were building legacies of their own, as well as keeping the Heart of the Mountains the most admired ranch in Montana Territory.

Their heritage would live on long after he'd passed away. And he had a daughter who was just as strong and able as his sons and the apple of his eye. A plethora of daughters-in-law, a son-in-law, and grandchildren to bounce on his knee when the snow drifts piled up.

And Claire—a wife like no other. Still a beauty to this day. She was there for him through thick and thin. Her never-ending love and support ran in his veins like blood. They'd loved and cried together through the whole shebang. Through miracles and calamities, through heartbreak and blessings. She was his rock and always would be. If he wasn't blessed, then there wasn't a man anywhere who was.

Still— something feels missing.

Winston, his older brother, came to mind.

The two hadn't seen each other in decades. Flood left Texas before he was twenty, returning only when Claire was abducted by the Cheyenne, and he'd needed the stability of his brother and sister-in-law to look after his small sons while he searched for her. Flood didn't trust his little boys, only Matthew and Mark, at the time, with anyone else. Could be, he'd get killed and never return. He needed to know his sons were with family. If the worst transpired, and Claire was never found or Flood was killed, his brother would raise his sons as his own. No, he didn't see Winston often but believed in their iron-clad bond.

But what about his other brother? Gideon McCutcheon?

Are you beleaguering my mind, Gideon? Where are you? Where did you go, little brother? I would surely like to know if you're still alive.

Gideon would be forty-nine this year. Flood found himself wondering more often about Gideon and his life. Had Flood caused his brother's decision to set out on his own? Would he ever know the truth?

A shout went up from inside the cabin where Jonathan, Luke, and Francis shored up the sagging wall.

Francis appeared in the doorway. "Come quick." He waved him on. "We've discovered something interesting."

Feeling younger than he had in years, he hurried his footsteps. "What's the excitement about? What've you found?" He stepped into the dimly lit cabin end of the house. Even with three small windows and two lanterns burning, the area was shadowy and dark. The place smelled musty and old and of hidden secrets. He wondered about Mrs. Lambert living in such a primitive home.

Francis hurried to the narrow stairway leading to the root cellar.

Flood hadn't given the storage area more than a cursory glance before because of what he'd been told. The sound of Luke's voice came from below.

He turned to Francis. "I thought Ike said the root cellar is barely large enough for one person. I hear Luke and… Jonathan."

"That's what we've found." Francis gave him a long look. "And that's not all. Are you going down to see?"

A challenge shone from the younger man's eyes. "You're darn right, I am." He took the candle Francis held out. Just like Ike claimed, the way was barely wide enough for his shoulders. At the bottom, the clammy scent of earth assaulted his nose. A stream of cold air flowed from a small, darkened passage he'd have to bend over to travel. "How long's the tunnel?" He waited for a reply. "Hello?"

"Come on in, Flood," Luke called. "It's not more than four or five feet long but bends so you can't see our light."

Hunched over, Flood slowly made his way along the corridor. The path dipped, going deeper into the earth. The air became heavy. He arrived at the glow of Luke's and Jonathan's candles.

"What have we got here?" He let his eyes adjust. "The true root cellar? This is plenty big."

"Could be, Boss, but come closer. And steel yourself for a shock."

"I hope it's a treasure chest of jewels," Flood joked.

"Not hardly." Luke's tone was serious.

On the floor before them were human remains. A skeleton draped in rotted clothing.

Flood started. "A man?"

"Think so, by his height," Luke replied.

A large boulder had crushed both the man's lower legs.

Instantly, Flood's gaze went to the ceiling above. "Is the roof stable? I don't want to end up like him."

"Looks to be a fluke accident." Luke felt along the ceiling above, dirt and grit falling onto the bones. A large crater indented the area above the man. "Seems just this widow-maker was loose. Poor fellow."

The skull was turned to the side, and the mouth gaped wide. Maybe he'd been calling for help. Then again, maybe his jaw just opened when the muscles rotted away. "Looks ancient," Flood stated. "I'd say a hundred years or so. Much older than the Lamberts' residence. From the looks of this, they never even knew he was here."

Jonathan rubbed a hand across his mouth. "Maybe they discovered him at some time and didn't say anything. Allowed this place to be his tomb." He shuffled his feet. "You know how superstitious people are, sometimes. Others might think the place cursed and not buy their beef."

They stared for several silent seconds in thought.

"And with how badly the ranch fared through last winter, just might be the truth," Francis whispered from behind.

Flood jerked straight. Francis walked so silently, no one heard his approach.

Luke harrumphed. "For some reason, couldn't get the boulder off after his legs were crushed. Not the way I'd want to die, I can tell you that." The flame of Luke's candle swayed, creating moving shadows on the earthen wall. "But who walled him in?"

"Let's not let our imaginations run away with us, boys," Flood cautioned, pushing away his own skittishness. "How'd you find the passage?"

"Don't know why I came down again," Luke said. "Just started tapping around with my hammer. When I heard a hollow sound, I dug with my claw end and discovered the wood. Someone must have known he was here and closed him in, packing the wooden door with clay. After all these years, it easily fell away."

"A disgruntled wife, maybe?" Jonathan asked.

Flood took a step away, anxious to be above ground. His hunched back was beginning to ache. "Well, fellas, we have a mystery on our hands. How about we go topside and discuss this further? My back's not what it used to be."

They turned and shuffled in single file toward the stairs.

"The records for Y Knot are few, and I wonder how far back they go. I'd like to know who he was. Tomorrow, before I come out here, I'll head into town and see what I can discover. The possibilities have my mind spinning." He grinned at Luke, who suddenly didn't look quite as excited about the find as moments before. "What's the matter?" Strange too, Francis and Jonathan looked the same. "Is there something you're not telling me?"

Luke held up a palm. "Nothin' at all, Flood. Just wondering who this poor soul could be. And how long he's been trapped down here." He snapped his mouth closed and headed up the steps, leaving Flood to wonder about his son's and ranch hands' strange response.

Chapter Fifteen

Tessa came awake slowly. A rolling ache slithered up her back and radiated out into each arm. When she tried to lift her chin to glance out the sooty, frosted window, a crick in her neck sent a jab of pain down her side. A foggy memory of Mr. McCutcheon taking Michaela from her last night when she was unable to hold her eyes open a moment longer filtered into her mind.

"Good morning."

His deep voice was a whisper. She turned her head.

Mr. McCutcheon stood in the aisle, still holding Michaela, who'd yet to awaken.

Alarmed, she realized the train wasn't moving. "Good morning." The passenger car was empty. Dismayed at sleeping through their arrival, she straightened and went to stand. A loud moan issued from between her lips, and she plopped back down.

Without a word, he put out a hand and helped her to her feet.

She was rumpled and gritty. What she wouldn't give for a hot bath and a soft bed to pass out on. "What time is it?"

"Seven o'clock."

"I see we've arrived. You should have awakened me."

"Only just now."

"Your arms must be tired. Did you hold her all night?" She pushed through the pain and then stretched her back.

"My arms are fine."

Still no smile. What would happen now? They'd arrived in Waterloo, their destination. Would he never soften to his baby's plight?

"I'm glad. She can get heavy. Did Michaela awaken in the night? Did you have to feed her?"

"Yes, and yes. I'll tell you everything as soon as we get off, unless you want to continue northward." His gaze fell to Michaela, still in his arms, and a ghost of a smile pulled his lips.

Tessa fingered her drooping hair, realizing nothing could be done to help. She glanced around the seat for their things. "I'm sorry. I meant to take her from you last night. Did you get any sleep at all?" His red, bloodshot eyes said he had not.

"Please hand me your carpetbag." He glanced at the bag at her feet.

The routine was one they'd been doing since they'd begun the trip she realized after he'd ignored her question. He carried the baby and her heavy carpetbag, and she carried his small one and his saddlebags.

"Of course." When she bent for her bag beyond her by the window her back protested. She stuffed in the loose cloth she'd been using for a burp rag, the baby's bonnet on the floor, and a small container of crackers she'd been sitting on, and then handed the carpetbag over. Was there any possibility of getting a room for a few hours where they all could get some *real* sleep, on a *real* bed?

By the time they reached the platform, most of the other travelers had cleared out. From the elevated position of the train station, she could see the L-shaped layout of the small town of Waterloo. A sign said *Welcome to Waterloo*. Yellow daffodils and purple crocus grew up around the legs of the sign and along the road. A sweet scent of spring tickled her nose. But the clear blue of the Montana sky, sweeping from one horizon to the other, was what stole Tessa's breath. The exhibition was gorgeous, like nothing she'd seen before in Boston or beyond. Possibilities swirled inside her.

When she'd begun this dubious journey, the unknowns were numerous. She hadn't known what to expect. And she still didn't. Had the Jordans been alerted to her taking the baby? Could they be following? Had they alerted the law? All she knew for sure was that Michaela McCutcheon belonged with her true father. Not in an orphanage. Not with Jason Whitmore. And not with the Jordans, people who would never love or accept her.

Chaim stepped over to a porter. "Excuse me. I'm not from around here. What time does the stagecoach leave for Y Knot?"

"That usually departs around eleven in the morning every day, but today, it's been cancelled. Darn thing broke an axle. Tomorrow'll be your next chance." He offered a kind smile. "That is, if the coach ain't already full of passengers who were put off today. If that's the case, the following day."

His gaze swept around. "I suppose there's a hotel in town?"

"Of course. The Oyster." He pointed. "Right down there on Main Street, across from the stage station." Brow furrowed, the porter glanced at the baggage car's open door. "Did you and the missus have any trunks? Everything has been unloaded and taken."

Chaim didn't flinch at the mention of their mistaken marital status but adjusted Michaela in his arms. The breeze ruffled his messy, dark blond hair over his forehead.

Feeling her face heat, Tessa glanced up as if she were interested in the comings and goings of the birds in the sky. What she wouldn't give to belong to a man like him.

"No, we travel light," Chaim responded. "Thanks for the information." He stepped closer to the man and whispered something Tessa couldn't hear.

The porter responded.

Chaim nodded then stepped away. He started for Main Street, Michaela in one of his arms, her carpetbag in his other hand as if the weight meant nothing to him.

As she'd done before, Tessa fell into step after she slung his saddlebag over one shoulder and carried his other bag in her hand. After making her way by herself from Boston, his carrying the bulk was a great relief. Right now, she had no idea what he planned. Michaela was sure to be hungry the moment she awakened. Tessa's own stomach begged to be fed, but she felt shy to broach the subject.

When they reached Main Street, they paused and took in the town.

Chaim's gaze bounced from the prosperous-looking establishment called the Oyster Hotel and landed on a smaller building a few doors down. "This way," he said, not unkindly, but still aloof.

She was surprised when they passed the hotel, and then a restaurant exuding a delicious aroma. They stopped at a small, brown pawn shop. Jewelry, household objects, a couple guns, and even some clothing items were displayed in the window.

Chaim's face reddened. "Can you wait out here for a few moments? I'll be quick."

"Of course." She glanced inside, but the interior was quite dark.

He passed Michaela to her without waking the child and disappeared inside.

Tessa glanced up and down the street, waiting. Did she have time to buy something small in the restaurant? When he didn't return, she put her hand to the glass and peered inside.

Mr. McCutcheon stood alongside a man who must be the shopkeeper. Chaim reached into his pocket and withdrew something. A money clip? He removed the paper money and offered the clip to the man.

The shopkeeper turned the item over several times and then bounced it up and down as if evaluating the weight. Finally, he nodded and preceded Mr. McCutcheon to the counter. After money was exchanged, Chaim paused, dug something more from his pocket and the process was repeated. What else had he pawned? She'd seen him look at a watch a time or two. Her heart stuttered. Pawning his possessions *had* to be difficult for a man like him.

When they shook hands, she turned away, not wanting to be seen prying, and adjusted Michaela in her arms.

He appeared at her side and put out his arms for the baby.

"I can carry her for a while," Tessa offered. "I don't mind."

"You've done all the carrying since you left Boston. I don't know how you managed. I have two more stops I need to make before we eat. Can you last that long? You must be as hungry as I am."

Warmth filled her. "I can."

"Good. We best be off. Once Michaela awakens, there won't be any more errands." He looked up and down the street once more and started off.

Inside the telegraph office, Chaim, now empty handed, studied a large bulletin board mounted on the wall.

Miss Webb was busy changing Michaela's diaper in the chairs on the other side of the vacant room.

Feeling tense, he searched for a message from Dustin and the others amid all the notices. This situation hadn't felt quite so enormous when he was still hundreds of miles away. Now, within a day or two, he would come face to face with his family—and his mother and father. He'd need to explain everything to the best of his ability. What had transpired in the year and a half he'd been gone? Was coming to Montana a mistake? Would working this out on his own for a few months have been a sounder way?

Shaking off his disquiet, Chaim concentrated on the job at hand as he read through the notices. Someone looking for a sober ranch hand with a clean mouth. Free kittens for the taking. A girl seeking employment as a domestic—to an employer who could see past her tainted past and not take advantage. *Good luck with that.* A management position at the bath house. Scores of men looking for wives. Rooms for rent and land to lease. Wagons, horses, and furniture to buy. Stud service for bulls and stallions. Fresh-baked pies delivered to your home with a smile. Mending of all kinds.

But nothing from Dustin. His family had yet to arrive. At the bottom, one advertisement stood out in large, bold print. Wanted: woman, between the ages of fifteen and fifty. Must be able to cook and clean and manage six young'uns all under the age of seven. Referral fee will be paid upon hiring.

His gaze slid over to Miss Webb and lingered for only a second. She certainly took good care of Michaela. She cared for his daughter with kid gloves—as well as love. The baby's happy gurgles were easy to hear all the way across the room.

Michaela nibbled on a cracker Miss Webb had taken from the carpetbag.

She'd be able to handle a family of six, he was sure. Chaim went to the counter and cleared his throat.

The man sitting at his desk looked up. "Need somethin'?"

"I'm Chaim McCutcheon. Have I received any telegrams in the last three days?" Dustin may have tried to contact him from one of the towns they'd been traveling through.

The man stood. He glanced at Miss Webb and Michaela and then back at him, his face full of questions. "McCutcheon, you say? I know all the McCutcheons up in Y Knot, but I don't know you. Relative come to call?"

Chaim felt himself smile. He should've known the name would draw attention, but circumstances had him off balance. "That's exactly right." He'd not say anything about the party for Uncle Flood. He didn't want to be the one to wreck the surprise. "I'm a cousin from Texas."

"You're darn tootin' you are! I see the resemblance in your eyes and mouth. Smile, too." He looked Chaim up and down. "And, of course, the build. Seems all the McCutcheon men are fine-looking, manly specimens."

Feeling awkward, Chaim shuffled his feet as his face heated.

At the man's none-too-quiet voice, a woman came out of the back room. She looked Chaim up and down, too—then smiled.

"I'm expecting the rest of my family tomorrow or the next day. We're meeting here in Waterloo before proceeding to Y Knot. I looked over the bulletin board but didn't see anything. My brother, Dustin, will check here on his arrival. Can I purchase a piece of paper so I can leave a message? We'll be staying at the Oyster Hotel."

The man reached under the counter and produced a half sheet of paper. "I usually charge a penny a sheet, but for a *McCutcheon*—it's free."

The woman came to the counter and stood next to the man, not hiding her curiosity. She stared at Miss Webb and Michaela, adoration shining in her eyes.

Chaim felt a niggle of unease slide through his veins.

"And I'll be on the lookout, too," she said, extending a hand toward Miss Webb. "They won't go on without you. I'll make sure of that. Can I get you something? Anything you need? I can see you just came off the train."

Chaim shook his head. "No, thank you, ma'am. We're fine. Soon enough, we'll get a bite to eat and settle into the hotel. It's been a long trip." Everyone he'd spoken to so far believed he and Miss Webb were a married couple and Michaela their daughter. He didn't know how to correct the misinterpretation without going into a long explanation which was nobody's business but his. *And my daughter's,* he quickly corrected. Once his family was here, he'd do his best to explain the complicated situation and make them understand. But would they? This homecoming could have been different. Him a proud new father presenting his parents with their first grandchild—something they'd craved for a long time indeed. How would they react? And what should he do if they rejected both him and his daughter?

Chapter Sixteen

With the trip to the telegraph office complete, surely Chaim would consider their need for food. Michaela was hungry and chewing on her fist. If they didn't feed her soon, tears would spill. As Tessa imagined a stack of pancakes topped with melted butter and maple syrup, she dug in the carpetbag for a cracker and handed it to Michaela.

Chaim took the baby from her arms, and they started off away from the Oyster Hotel and the couple of restaurants close by.

Surprised, Tessa tamped down irritation. "Where to now?" She was exhausted and famished. They all needed something to eat—even if just tea and toast.

"Trust me. We're almost there."

His voice held a deep, rich quality she hadn't noticed so much on the rattling stagecoach or the loud train. Being out in the open air after so many days of travel was nice.

He glanced at a scrap of paper in his hand. "828 Lindor Street."

What on earth?

Now that she had a cracker to chew on, Michaela seemed completely content in Chaim's arms. When she noticed a tiger-striped cat sitting on a low tree branch outside of a dress shop, she squealed. They stopped for a few moments and let her view the animal until it climbed away from Michaela's reaching hands.

"She had a tabby back home," Tessa said. "Sasha was identical to this cat, and even had the same black-tipped ears. The two would sit in the sunshine, with Sasha rumbling loudly. I've never seen such a patient cat."

Chaim's expression fell.

Immediately sorry, Tessa scolded her insensitivity. Fatherhood was new to him. Any mention of home would bring back the hurt of losing Emmeline. The wound was again fresh. Coming to terms would take a long time. More than a few days or weeks. Her betrayal. Then marriage. And now, her death. The fact she'd had his child and didn't tell him was unforgivable. Tessa still couldn't believe it herself—especially now that she'd met Chaim and understood him on a deeper level.

They proceeded away from buzzing businesses and continued until they reached Lindor Street. Houses lined both sides of the road, some finely kept while others appeared in want of care.

"There," Chaim said, raising the carpetbag to point. "Up ahead. The man said to watch for a two-story with a white picket fence, gate, and maple tree with a swing." He glanced again at the note.

"The man?"

"The proprietor of the pawn shop."

He held the gate for her, and she preceded him through.

Tulips and hyacinth bloomed in a small flowerbed beneath the windows. A three-foot-tall wooden stature of St. Francis stood in a shady spot, a small bunny nosing about near the hem of his robe. The sight brought to mind the prayer her mother had taught her when she was little about sowing love where there was hatred, pardon where there was injury, and faith where there was doubt.

At the door, Chaim used a shiny silver knocker in the shape of a rose. After a few long moments, the sound of a slow thumping beyond the door grew louder and louder.

An elderly lady answered, a cane in one hand and a smile on her pleasant face.

Even leaning on a cane, Tessa could tell she was tall. She wore a nicely pressed blue dress with a rounded, white color and white cuffs at her wrists.

"May I help you?" When she noticed the baby in Chaim's arms, her eyes lit with pleasure. "Oh, what a darling child. She's adorable."

Even without her pink blanket or dress, Michaela looked all girl. Then again, she was wearing her old pink bonnet.

"I hope you can, ma'am," Chaim replied. "Are you Mrs. Mary Margaret? We've just come in on the train from…" He looked at Tessa with a furrowed brow.

Tessa shrugged and gave a weak laugh. "We've been through so many towns; I can't remember which was last. All I know is, the trip was long, the benches hard, and we started in Arizona."

The woman's hand flew to her mouth. "Oh, my word. That's many days' travel. You must be exhausted. Please, come in and rest."

Chaim shook his head. "That's kind of you, but no thank you. These two young ladies have yet to have any breakfast. I'll rectify that as soon as we're finished here."

At the mention of eating soon, Tessa almost swooned with relief.

Mrs. Margaret gave a quizzical look.

Chaim went on, "Ernest at the pawn shop gave me your name when I asked where I might purchase some clean diapers. They've been a challenge to obtain along the way, and I believe we're down to our last one."

Chaim must have discovered the truth when he'd tended the baby last night while she slept. "I didn't know if I should mention anything," said Tessa. "I'm thankful you noticed."

"The pawn shop, you say?" Mrs. Mary Margaret's gaze assessed their travel-worn clothes, and probably the look of hunger in their eyes. "Well, yes. I do have diapers I can *give* you, and much more. Anything you need for the little one. Are you leaving on the eleven o'clock stage today?"

"No, ma'am. Tomorrow, if there's room." He shifted his weight from one leg to the other. "And I have money to pay for the diapers, but thank you for your kind offer."

Money *now*. Her admiration for Chaim McCutcheon grew exponentially.

The woman nodded. "I'm glad to hear you're staying until tomorrow. That means you have plenty of time to come in and rest. Scandalous, you might believe, I run a home for unwed mothers. I know that's not the case with you, but I cater to babies." She reached forward and tickled Michaela under her chin, making her smile. "Please," she said, her voice softening. She stroked Tessa's arm. "I can see you're both worn out. I have a playroom filled with many delightful toys. I'm sure this little one would like some time on the ground to stretch her arms and legs. I'll be happy to look after her while you rest. And I can replenish your supply of diapers, as well as anything else you might need. I have everything you can imagine." She laid a wrinkled hand over her heart. "How about a clean dress for this princess and a new bonnet? No worries, I make them all from donated remnants from the mercantile."

Tessa looked longingly toward Chaim, praying he would agree. He'd make the final decision. How fortuitous to find this Godly woman who would gladly give them a small rest.

"And it just so happens, there's water heating on the stove right now. I'm sure a nice bath and cup of tea could be of use to you both. I'll not take no for an answer. But, before that, how about a nice bowl of stew and bread still warm from the oven?"

A bath. And stew. Oh, how good that all sounded. And some sleep on a real bed? She'd give her right eye if he'd say yes.

Not waiting for his answer, Mrs. Mary Margaret took hold of Chaim's sleeve and gave a gentle tug. "Follow me, dears. You both look dead on your feet." She started away, leaning on her cane as she proceeded into the warm house.

The postage stamp sized room was as neat as a pin. A small brown sofa sat on one side, and two mahogany armchairs, with tufted burgundy upholstery, sat on the other. Between them, a round accent table held a lamp burning low. A crucifix hung on the wall above. At the scents of cinnamon and simmering meat, Tessa's mouth watered.

Mary Margaret stopped in the kitchen. "There's the stove and the water. Cups are directly above. Tea, that canister. Mrs. …uh," she glanced at Tessa, "I have several pap boats of goat's milk in my icebox that only need warming. Place one in the pan of shallow water."

Tessa gladly opened the woman's icebox to see a tidy row of bottles.

"Two mothers live here now, so I like to stay prepared. They're out picking up a few needed items in town but should return shortly. Please, don't worry."

Chaim hung back, looking immensely uncomfortable, but relieved, as well.

"What shall I call you?" the woman asked. "You know my name, Mary Margaret, but I've yet to be enlightened."

Tessa cut her gaze to Chaim.

His cheeks darkened. "I'm Chaim McCutcheon, ma'am." He looked to Tessa. "And this is…"

"Tessa," she said quickly.

A moment of surprise crossed the woman's face, but she quickly blinked it away. "McCutcheon? What a small world this is, indeed. I know the McCutcheons in Y Knot. But you are travelers? Are you related to them? Another brother I've yet to meet? Or is this some strange coincidence?"

"Not a coincidence. Cousin from Texas. More relations are on the way, as well."

Tessa could tell he was choosing his words carefully. The woman would learn nothing more from him unless she asked a direct question. Chaim seemed honest. Lying wouldn't come easy for a man like him. He reached in his pocket and pulled out some coins, she suspected were in payment for the diapers and milk. He placed them on the counter.

"Well, I'll be. Last year, Luke McCutcheon took in a little friend of mine named Hickory. The boy lost his parents as a small tyke and was homeless. Mr. McCutcheon, a fine figure of a man, and charitable, too, offered Hickory a job at their ranch in Y Knot."

"Luke's my cousin. We've not met, but I'm looking forward to the time even more now."

Her head tipped. Tessa realized the woman was putting two and two together in her mind. Surely, from what Tessa had heard, the Montana McCutcheons were very well off. Like the McCutcheons in Texas. Mary Margaret was now wondering why they looked like beggars, without food or even diapers. Had even visited a pawn shop. Tessa glanced at Chaim again, who looked ill at ease. What he wanted to share with others was his decision.

"I see," she responded without missing a beat. "Well, that door leads to a bathing room when you're ready. The door on the far side of the parlor is the playroom. As soon as you're set, I'll take the little missy in to play. But first," she began ladling out three bowls of stew. Two large and one small. "We fill the bellies."

Chapter Seventeen

Mary Margaret stuffed them all with as much beef stew as they could eat, and then afforded all with a bath. Chaim felt like a new man. Soon after, he set out to inquire about availability of the stage if his family arrived the following day. He also needed to check into the size of the coach. Perhaps the men of the group would need to rent horses to make the trip on the same day.

Striding along, he pictured his daughter as she'd been set on the clean rug with a plethora of toys. Mary Margaret graciously gifted her a calico dress with a matching bonnet. She'd looked as cute as a pin. The woman had taken a soft chair on the wall with a cup of tea. She assured him this was where she spent most her days, watching babies. In the exact same spot doing the exact same thing.

Waterloo was busy. Riders and wagons moved along the street. Merchants swept boardwalks in front of their shops. Here in Montana, the air was fresh and light.

Perplexed, he stopped on the boardwalk by the tree where they'd met the cat. The animal was now gone. What would leaving everything familiar do to Michaela? She was so young. Would she remember Sasha? More importantly, would she remember Emmeline?

He should have considered things more carefully before he bundled everyone up and started off on this journey. Should he have cancelled coming to Montana? But he'd already sold his ranch. If he'd stayed in Arizona, he'd have no home or way to support her. A man alone was one thing. A child, now that was different. How could he work, let alone run a ranch, caring for Michaela at the same time? He knew nothing about babies. No one in his family had yet given birth. The only child he knew within Rio Wells was Candy, Martha Brown's little girl, and she must be six or seven years old.

Now everyone who saw him with Tessa and Michaela assumed they were a family. And why shouldn't they? They fit together perfectly.

And that's exactly what my family will think the moment they lay eyes on us.

A woman stepped out of the dress shop behind him, a baby in one arm and holding the hand of a little boy.

Chaim would have doffed his hat if he'd owned one, and since he didn't, he respectfully dipped his chin. The baby looked much younger than his. His whole life, he'd been trying to live up to his big brother's image and failing. His leaving Rio Wells after Emmeline's departure and refusal to return hadn't helped. Back in Arizona, when he'd contemplated the coming reunion with Dustin and his family, many days still far off, the event hadn't felt quite so life changing. Even though he didn't know Michaela well, he'd be a liar if he said he wasn't proud as a peacock to call her his own. And, yes, he loved her, too. He'd tried to keep a detachment these travel days as he worked through what her arrival would mean to him. His future.

Chaim pushed his longtime feelings of inadequacy aside. This wasn't about what was right for him. Or even what was right for his family. What they thought was no more important than a grain of sand. Michaela was his only concern now, and doing what was best for her.

What would Tessa's leaving do to Michaela? She hadn't said as much, but to him, it seemed Tessa had been caring for Michaela since her birth. Surely, Michaela thought of her as her mother. No one else could easily step into the young woman's shoes in the eyes of the child. If he hired someone else once he was back in Rio Wells, the rug would be pulled from under Michaela, so to speak. She'd be in a strange place with strange people. Was she old enough to be frightened about those things? The thought pierced his heart.

Will Tessa stay on if I ask her?

She'd caught him off guard on the day of his departure. And since then, he hadn't thought that far ahead. Seemed his days were filled with finding milk, clean water, and a private place for changing a diaper…

What *were* Tessa Webb's plans after they reached Montana? She'd never said. And he felt shamefaced he'd never inquired. He'd been so caught up in hearing about Emmeline, and her exploits after she'd left him brokenhearted in Texas, he'd not only not asked Tessa, but he'd not given it a thought.

In all honesty, he knew little about her except that she'd worked in the Jordans' household for years and seemed to know quite a bit about everything. Did she have a suitor waiting in Boston? Would bringing Michaela out to him make her lose her job? What were her aspirations in life? He had no idea. He'd squandered all the time dwelling on his own troubles and licking the wounds inflicted by Emmeline.

A buggy went by carrying a young family, much like they would look.

What if?

No, he couldn't even contemplate such a thing. Doing so was wrong. Tessa was young. She had a life of her own. Just because he'd never fall in love again didn't mean she wouldn't—or perhaps she was already involved with someone back home.

This was *his* problem—and Michaela's. But Michaela loved Tessa like a mother.

Chapter Eighteen

When her father walked through the doorway of Brandon's office, Charity almost fell off the chair. His chestnut hair, flecked with gray, was windblown. His shoulders still appeared a mile wide, just like when she was a little girl. He wore the worn-out buckskin chaps her mother had been trying to replace for years.

Quickly tucking her list under a book, she took a deep breath and stood. What was he doing in town? Their relations were set to arrive any time. Today? Tomorrow? All the places they'd be hidden away were on alert. She met him halfway across the floor. "Father," she said, trying for a breathy, carefree voice. "What're you doing in town this morning?" She leaned into his embrace for a hug and kiss on his cheek.

He chuckled and pulled back to examine her face. "Can't I come into town without an invitation?" He glanced around. "Where's that husband of yours? He's never here when I need him."

She waved a hand toward the window, smiling. "He went down the street for some such thing, I can't remember. Should return anytime."

Since she'd been busy with the final details, Brandon offered to check with Mr. Lichtenstein at the mercantile about her special orders for the party, being they were overdue. From there, Brandon was stopping at the telegraph office for any news from Uncle Winston and Dustin and their travel progress.

Mr. Tracy, the telegraph operator, was in on the secret as well—as was most of the town—and had been careful to keep everything under wraps. As the number of people who knew grew, so did the possibility of the secret being spoiled.

She cut her glance to Brandon's desk and saw the telegram from the Twilight Singers, the traveling group from Pine Grove, accepting their request to play at the party. She'd gotten the message an hour earlier and irresponsibly left it out.

Flood crossed the office and went to a bookshelf by the iron stove. He ran his finger along the titles.

"What're you looking for?"

"History of Y Knot. First settlers and such. I know the basics, but I'm ashamed to say, not near enough."

"What's got your interest now?" This was strange, coming from her father.

"We made an astonishing discovery out at the Lambert place. A skeleton in the root cellar."

She jerked straight. "What?"

"The room was blocked off, and a new root cellar dug. A boulder crushed the man's legs and trapped him. But that doesn't explain how and why he was left inside. Someone walled him in."

While he studied the books, she crossed to the desk and carefully put the telegram in the pocket of her split riding skirt.

"A skeleton? I can't imagine. And, most importantly, did the Lamberts know?" *Were our neighbors guilty of murder? Hiding a body?*

"The bones appear to be incredibly old. Most likely have been there for years. Before the Lamberts bought the place. I'd like to see what Brandon knows or if he's ever heard any rumors. He speaks with Sheriff Huxley in Pine Grove from time to time. That old timer's been around longer than any of us."

With everything now hidden, Charity forced herself to relax. She didn't want to be the one to spill the beans by acting suspicious. "Anything to do with official business wouldn't be kept there, Father. Brandon locks those books up in the house where they can't be stolen. Do you want me to go see if there's a ledger that dates back that far?"

"No need. I can wait for Brandon." He turned and gave her his full attention. "It's been nice having the Lambert place to work on." He grinned. "I'm enjoying the toil. The challenge." He picked up the coffeepot and gave it a gentle shake.

"Oh! My manners have flown right out the window. Would you like a cup of coffee while you wait?"

"Yes, Daughter, thank you. How've you been? Keeping busy these days? I haven't seen much of you at the ranch. I miss our rides out to check the herd or ride fence." He winked, looking much younger than his fifty-one years. "Your perspective is refreshing—different from my boys. You've always been the apple of my eye, you know. Even with all my grandbabies. Don't you forget that, Charity."

She handed him a cup of coffee, wondering where this sentimentality was coming from. She was certain of her father's love. He was always kind and affectionate. She never doubted him. But today, he seemed a bit different. "Thank you, Father. I miss those days, too. And getting into trouble with you and my brothers."

"Ahh, your brothers." He drank from his cup and then shook his head. "How I miss John Jake. I wonder if he'll ever make the trip home, or if Texas is now in his blood so much he's forgotten us."

John? What a time for Father to think of John. If he only knew his youngest son was en route to Y Knot and would arrive any day. "He's married with a new daughter. We can't expect him to drop everything there."

"And being a doctor, the residents of Rio Wells depend on him," her father said. "He might never return. I know he has a right to his own life, but the reality makes me sad. That's all. Have you heard from him? Has he written? You're the one who always gets his letters."

"That's because I write him first. Have you written to him lately?"

Flood shook his head.

"Well, therein lies the problem. Take the first step." She felt sad for her father, but excited, as well. "I haven't heard a thing, of late. I always let you know when I do, of course. But I was talking about Luke and how he always chided me to act like a lady. I just didn't have it in me." She looked down at her split riding skirt and well-worn boots, which hadn't been shined in too many days to remember. "Guess I still don't."

Flood studied her over the rim of his cup. "You're more than a lady, Charity. You're a princess."

At that moment, Brandon came barreling through the door, his head buried deep in the newspaper. "Everything is set at the mercantile. Mr. Lichtenstein said to stop worry—" He pulled up short and snapped his mouth closed.

"What's this?" Flood turned toward Brandon. "About Lichtenstein's? And not to worry?"

Charity blinked. An uncomfortable number of seconds passed before she gathered her wits to answer. "Just girl talk."

"But it came from your husband. About Lichtenstein. Is something going on that I don't know about? I can keep a secret."

She had to do something fast. The first person she could think of was Sally. She hoped Roady's wife wouldn't mind too much being used as a diversion to save the surprise. Charity closed the distance between them and put her hand on her father's arm. She dropped her voice. "This is a *huge* secret, Father. If I tell you, you have to promise not to breathe a word until I say it's all right."

He dipped his head. "I'm captivated. Go on…"

"Sally's expecting again," she whispered. "I'm planning a little surprise get-together with the girls. You know, Evie, Kathryn, Heather." She ticked off her fingers as she named every woman she could think of. "Rachel, Amy, June, Ina, Mother…"

His bushy eyebrows shot to the ceiling and a happy grin split his face. "Sally? In the family way again? How come I haven't heard anything about it yet?"

"Because *Roady* doesn't know yet, either. That's why it's important you don't mention anything to *anyone*, even Mother. Sally's waiting, you know, to be sure. What she doesn't know is I want to throw her a little tea party of sorts, maybe at the Biscuit Barrel or Cattlemen's Hotel." He pulled back and stared so hard at Charity she wanted to laugh.

"But *you* know?" he said incredulously, and then cut a look to Brandon. "And *Brandon*? That makes no sense at all."

"You're right. Sally and I were together the other day in the Biscuit Barrel, and she accidently let the exciting news slip. She got all hot and queasy while eating a slice of gooseberry-raisin pie. I promised I wouldn't say a word."

Shaking his head, Flood placed his empty cup on the desk, scooting things around to make room. "So, you told your husband?"

Charity let go the breath she'd just gulped. "Brandon heard me talking in my sleep. He practically forced the secret out of me. That's when I decided to have a party for her, so I ordered some special items from the mercantile. I wanted to be ready when she made the announcement."

Brandon winked from behind her father's back.

"Well, I guess that makes sense," Flood replied. "Gillian's about a year old. I'm sure Roady is ready for a son. Except that, you have a whole nine months to get prepared."

She gripped his arm. "You know me. I don't like to procrastinate. Nothing good ever comes of it. Now, *promise* me you'll not tell a soul. Sally will have my hide if someone congratulates Roady before she has a chance to tell him herself." She gave her father her sternest look.

"Well, *this* doesn't feel right, us knowing but not Roady, but you have my word. And I'll do a darn better job of keeping my lips closed than you've done. Brandon, myself, *and* Mr. Lichtenstein?" His eyebrow peaked. "Who else? I have to say, this feels like tomfoolery, if I've ever heard it."

"I know. I feel plenty bad already. You can't make me feel any worse than I already do."

Flood grinned wide again. "A new baby. No news I like better than that."

Her father's comment hit a mark without him even intending to. He didn't know how she'd been feeling. Nothing anyone could do but wait and pray.

"Where's Ace?" Brandon glanced out the window. "Don't see him at the hitching rail."

"Threw a shoe on my way into town so I left him at the livery. June'll have him fixed in a jiffy." Leaning back, he crossed his arms over his chest. "Say, what do you know about the spread we bought from Lambert, Brandon—and previous owners? Any history at all? That's what I've come in to find out. I'll be heading back there in a little while, to stay overnight."

Charity returned to the desk as her father filled Brandon in on the discovery out at the new ranch. Their voices blurred into a soft drone as she contemplated holding Brandon's baby in her arms, aching with longing. She'd yet to dredge up the nerve to speak with Dr. Handerhoosen about any possible problems, but the fabrication she'd just shared about Sally being pregnant had stirred her yearnings.

Maybe, after all the fun of the surprise party calmed down and her relations returned to Texas, she'd ask Brandon to take her to Waterloo, where two doctors resided. Broaching the delicate matter with one of them felt more palatable than Dr. Handerhoosen, her life-long friend. She'd ask for a little time away. A holiday, so they could be alone somewhere, just husband and wife, instead of an on-guard sheriff.

Justin, his deputy, was solid and smart. He was always asking for more responsibility, so why not?

Yes, once the surprise had come and gone, and everyone went home, she'd address her problem. She'd not stick her head in the sand any longer.

Chapter Nineteen

The tables of the opulent Oyster Hotel's dining room were dressed in white linen and adorned with a short, dancing candle and a small vase of flowers. The room was semi-full, even at the early hour of six. The food was delicious. Chaim thought the quality matched that of the Lillian Russell Room back in Rio Wells, minus the multitude of paintings of scantily clad women.

Tonight was the first grand dinner he'd treated himself to since riding out of his home state almost a year and a half ago. Since then, his life was one long self-punishment, void of any luxury or vice to make time pass more easily.

The funds his money clip and watch had produced were enough for this treat, as well as the much-needed diapers and a few nights' lodging in the hotel in the event his family didn't show up tomorrow or the next day. The money clip had been part of the McCutcheon family for generations, beginning with his great-grandfather. It was passed down to him on his twentieth birthday.

As difficult as parting with the keepsake had been, the money was needed, he thought, gazing across the table at the two sleepy-eyed girls.

I'd make the trade again in a heartbeat.

Michaela looked comfortable, nestled in Tessa's lap. During supper, she'd sat primly in a highchair and been exceptionally good. No crying tonight. And when she'd laughed, he'd finally seen vestiges of Emmeline. Her delicate cheeks pressed up into her eyes, making them smile, as well, and a tiny dimple appeared at the corner of her lip, looking exactly like his late fiancée. There was no doubt about Michaela's true mother.

As much as seeing the resemblance hurt, it also bolstered him. Michaela was *his* daughter, created out of his *and* Emmeline's love. The revelation brought such a rush of tenderness he cut his gaze away, lest his eyes fill.

And the baby had eaten well, too. Bits of Tessa's steak and green beans, with a preference for the mashed potatoes and gravy. *And* the bread. He'd never seen her eat so much. But then, they'd never sat down to this kind of fare, either. He and Tessa both splurged on a glass of wine each and even enjoyed two small slices of vanilla bean cake.

This evening was a night to remember. How it ended was yet to be seen. "Did you get enough to eat?" He knew full well neither of them could take another bite. The small smile he'd come to know over the last few days appeared on Tessa's lips.

"Yes. Thank you. Everything was delicious. And this little girl has become roly-poly. I think she'll sleep for days, if we let her."

His daughter was far from roly-poly, but lean and long. He'd bet she'd end up being quite tall when she was grown. Tessa had been attentive to Michaela throughout the meal, the baby laughing at her silly faces as she spoon-fed her, careful of her new clothes. The truth couldn't be clearer. Michaela considered Tessa her mother. They looked like mother and daughter, as well.

He glanced away again, conflicted. He didn't know what to do about the situation. What he *did* know, was his family was set to arrive soon. The moment they saw the three of them together, they'd think them a family. He'd run out of time and perhaps options, as well.

"Mr. McCutcheon?"

He turned his attention back to Tessa. "I think you're right," he offered, feeling embarrassed. "I've never seen her like this. So quiet. So happy."

Tessa nodded. "The long nap and playtime at Mary Margaret's did wonders. Especially after the other mothers returned and their children joined in. What a generous gift she's offering to those young women."

"I agree."

"Actually, this is how Michaela usually behaves. Sweet. Playful...*quiet*." She smiled. "That's why I was frightened when you first met her. With all her crying, I feared you might..." Her voice lowered, and she looked away.

He sat back, a bit surprised at her directness. "You thought I might not want my daughter?"

"I didn't know. I hadn't met you. Your decision could have gone either way." When the baby lifted her hand to touch Tessa's face, Tessa glanced down to see her eyelids drooping with exhaustion.

He studied her, wondering if the time was right to discuss tomorrow and beyond. Would the baby stay quiet for a bit longer, or should they wait until Michaela was tucked into bed for the night?

Tessa Webb was a strong, determined woman. Intelligent too. He'd barely noticed her beauty when she'd first approached him, but then had been blindsided by her proclamation about the baby in her arms. Then his hurt over Emmeline's betrayal, even after she discovered she was with child—*his* child—kept him preoccupied. But he'd noticed on the train, when things settled down and Michaela hadn't been quite so cranky. The golden streaks in Tessa's hair glimmered whenever they were out in the sun. The way her eyes smiled along with her lips when she was particularly pleased with something. Her graceful neck and soft hands.

And maybe, too, he could only notice after he'd internalized all the information about Emmeline. So much pain offset by the goodness of this young woman.

Tonight, Tessa's hair was newly washed from her bath at the Mother's Home and was swept up on her head in an attractive French twist. An abundance of lashes, matching her honey-colored hair, framed her pretty eyes. Her lips were finely shaped and, at most times, pulled up in an agreeable expression.

This trip was a difficult journey for her, traveling alone with a baby. His debt of gratitude was endless. He shouldn't use her for his own good, or for his daughter's, he reminded himself. She could offer a lot to a man.

Waterloo was the end of the line for them in more ways than one. This was the ending point she'd agreed to travel to. Was she expecting to leave them here, catching a train heading east when he went on to Y Knot? Once he got funds from his father, he intended to pay her way, as well as the wages she'd accrued tending to Michaela. He needed to make plans for tomorrow.

The baby's eyes fluttered and then closed.

"She's asleep," he whispered. He took the last sip of his coffee and smiled.

She nodded, her teeth nibbling her lower lip.

Did she anticipate the coming conversation? "I guess we have a few things to discuss tonight. Will she be all right sitting there like that? Or should we wait until you put her to bed?"

Tessa rocked Michaela farther back in her arms, making her more comfortable. "I think she'll be fine here if we speak quietly. It's nice the maître d' chose this table in a private corner. And these seats are extremely comfortable. I think we should stay here."

"I believe the man was looking out for his other customers."

Her smile widened. "You're probably right." Her smile faded, and she turned serious eyes on him. "I've been thinking about the future, too. And what this day might mean."

His fingers absentmindedly rolled the edge of his napkin laid beside his plate as he wondered how to proceed. "This situation happened so suddenly. I'm embarrassed I haven't inquired about you before now. Do you plan to go home to Boston directly after my family arrives?" He wanted her to have an easy way out, if that's what she wanted.

The waiter approached with a light step. "Will you or the missus need anything else?" he asked softly.

He'd been exceedingly conscientious of the baby throughout the meal. Chaim didn't flinch. He'd gotten used to others assuming he and Tessa were husband and wife. The mistake was logical. "I think that's all." He looked at Tessa.

She nodded.

"Very good. I'll bring the bill. But, please, there's no hurry." He smiled at the sleeping baby and hurried away.

They stared at each other.

Chaim sat back. "We have several options and a decision to make. Tomorrow, or the day after, when the rest of my family arrives, if you'd like, I can pay you for your services and purchase your tickets and you can be on your way. I'm sure my mother and sisters can assist me with Michaela until I become more proficient with her care." He glanced at the baby, and his heart gave a gentle thump he'd come to recognize.

Tessa looked stoically calm. He had no idea what she was thinking. Feeling. She'd be good at poker. He wished she'd say something, help him along. The next few moments would determine so much. "Or, if you don't have any responsibilities waiting, and you have the time, and it's your desire, you can continue on with me."

She swallowed. "I've cared for Michaela since her birth. I feel more like her mother than a nanny."

Her words came out in a whisper, but they were hard and crisp. He'd have to be blind to not see she was scared to death. He recalled their first meeting when she'd told him Michaela was his daughter. Her arms had instinctively tightened on the sleeping child as if she couldn't bear to let her go. "I'm not going to give the long, drawn-out explanation about my daughter to everyone I meet, but I do plan to be truthful with my family. There'll be questions. Some confusion. But going back to Rio Wells on a pretext of untruth after being gone for almost a year and a half would be wrong. The reality is, I wasn't man enough to face up to my family and the town after Emmeline rejected me. I needed to punish myself for giving my all to someone, heart and soul, who didn't return my feelings."

She blinked several times and then glanced down at Michaela's face. "Are you happy you have Michaela, Mr. McCutcheon? Is she a joy to you?"

Surprised at the question and the conviction in her voice, he just stared.

She raised her gaze back to his. "Sometimes, I wonder."

That hurt, although the assessment was fair. At first, he'd been frightened out of his head to hold Michaela—or feed her.

Her cries alone made him want to step away for air. But now, only a few short days later, she'd wormed her way into his heart. He was more than glad to have her. He *loved* her. Looked forward to her sweet little smile every morning and her drowsy cow eyes each night. His world had changed for the better since she'd come into his life.

The waiter was back.

Chaim quickly looked at the amount, gave the fellow five dollars, and told him to keep the difference.

He went away with a smile.

"You don't have to worry. I'll not give her up or send her away. I'll raise her as my own—and be proud to. I'm not saying it'll be easy, the way people like to talk, look for the bad in situations, but that's the way of life, and there's no changing it for me or anyone else. Just look at the home Mary Margaret started. She saw a need. Children shouldn't be punished for things they had no control over. Michaela is my daughter, and I'll raise her as such."

Chapter Twenty

The rapid beat of Tessa's heart made twinkles dance before her eyes. Lightheaded waves swished through her mind, and nerves skittered up and down her spine like an army of ants. With a shaky hand, she reached for her water glass and took a small sip to wet her throat. Could Chaim see her jittery nerves?

All she could think about was the worst possible outcome of the conversation to come. The scenario played over and over in her mind. Still, she was no child. She'd made up her mind months ago, traveling mile upon mile from Boston to meet Michaela's father. Such a journey was no small feat. She'd come to do what she'd planned, and no number of nerves roiling in her stomach would keep her from her target. The day she'd met Chaim, he'd mentioned Waterloo as their destination. Now here they were, sitting across from each other in an extravagant restaurant, having taken a fine supper like husband and wife. "So, that's what you'll do, Mr. McCutcheon? Raise Michaela yourself?"

Thank heavens he was facing this difficult moment tonight and giving her an opening to voice her idea. Her opinion, hopes, and fears about Michaela's future. He could have just as easily paid her what was owed when his family arrived and said goodbye. Put her on the train, never to be seen again. That had always been a possibility, *and still was*. Nothing in life was guaranteed—and especially not happiness.

"Yes. As I said, my family will help. I have two younger sisters, as well as my mother. She's wanted grandchildren for some time. We also have a kind woman who does the cooking and cleaning. I'm sure I can hire others, if need be…" His words trailed off as he looked at her intently. "Find a nanny until she's older."

Had he stumbled over the last few lines as if he were waiting for her to put up a fuss? Or was she imagining things? She lifted her chin. "Have you considered how difficult your daughter's life will be if you raise her yourself—having never been married? The taunting and shame she'll endure? It won't be easy for her. Or you, for that matter. When she comes home crying, you won't be able to make her reality better, because, in fact, those insults will be true." Tessa still heard the mocking slurs she'd suffered as groups of children passed the little place where her mother rented a room on their way to school, calling her a fatherless pauper, and worse. They'd laugh and then run off, not giving their heartlessness a second thought. The memory stung bitterly and made her blink.

"I've thought about it," he replied. "More than you could know. It's *all* I think about. It's kept me up every night since we've met, considering what's best for Michaela. Her happiness is all that matters. I don't care about what anyone thinks of me. But I do care how that will affect *her*." He glanced at his daughter with a furrowed brow. "Life will be more challenging for her than most children. But I guess there's no help for it. I can't change the past."

"Easy for you to say. You come from a fine home, a prosperous family, mother and father, siblings…"

He stared with raised eyebrows.

"By all intents and purposes, up until you left Texas, you'd lived a perfect life. A charmed life. I'd bet you haven't known a day of difficulty until the last year and a half." He opened his mouth as if to contradict her, but then snapped it closed. Had she pushed him too far before she was able to voice her plan? If he got up and walked out, then where would they be?

"No, not easy to say, at all," he finally responded firmly. "I realize how fortunate I've been. Apparently, you have more to say about this subject than you've let on, Tessa. Please, don't be shy."

Well, this was what she'd wanted, wasn't it? What she'd prayed about every night? She couldn't back down now. She needed to be strong, for Michaela's sake. She shifted the sleeping baby in her arms. "You're right. I do have more to say. And I won't mince my words. Michaela's future is too important for that."

He folded his hands on top of the table.

"You must have wondered how and why I came alone to bring your daughter to you."

He nodded. "I've been expecting you to tell me sooner or later. I didn't want to rush you."

Tessa's throat tightened painfully, but there was no changing her mind now. "My mother never married. I carried the stigma of being an illegitimate child all of my life. I know how Michaela will feel and what will happen. How she'll smile to hide her pain from *you*, so *you* won't hurt. Even though she pretends otherwise, her grief will be there, like a knife, always twisting, twisting." She mimed the motion with her free hand. "She'll feel like an outcast, even among her family, her cousins. They'll be kind to her, of course, but their actions won't keep *her* from feeling different. Lesser in every way. I don't want such a life for Michaela. It's not easy and it's not fun." She recalled the sympathetic looks, and, too, the sly, whispered remarks.

He remained silent. His thoughts unreadable.

"My father, Theodore Jordan, *Teddy*, is Emmeline's uncle. He met my mother, a woman many classes beneath him, where she worked at a department store. It was a good job for her. Because she was attractive, he showered her with attention. Bought her small, inappropriate gifts. She should have known better, but she had stars in her eyes—hopeful she'd make a good marriage. He gave the impression he was in love and wanted them to share a life together." Pausing for a moment, she glanced across the room, reining in her agitation. "When she told him she carried his child, he never contacted her again."

Chaim straightened abruptly. "You're Emmeline's cousin! Named for Theodore Jordan?"

"Cousin and friend. That's why she confided in me. When my mother's pregnancy began to show she was dismissed from the department store without a reference. The only work she could find was that of a maid. But that only lasted so long, as well. After I was born, she brought me to the Jordans' home, hoping they could help in some way, but they turned her away. Said the only thing they would consider for me was employment in the house when I was of age. Until then, we lived off the few things my mother had to sell, as well as laundry work where she could take me with her."

Chaim's brows drew down over his troubled gaze.

"When Emmeline was dying, fearful Michaela would have a life akin to mine after she was gone, she begged me to find you. Convince you to accept your daughter and raise her as your own. Her mother-in-law did share her suspicions with her son but, wanting to avoid a scandal, the man turned a blind eye. But, Emmeline firmly believed he wouldn't raise another man's child after she died. She feared for Michaela. And, too, because of Michaela's illegitimacy, Emmaline suspected her own parents might treat her unkindly. The way they'd treated me over the years—as a servant living in her family's home."

"And what about your mother? Is she alive?"

Oh, how I wish she were. "She's not." Tessa tried to keep the sadness from her expression, but she'd never been a good actress. "She passed when I was thirteen. One year after I went to work at the Jordans'. I miss her every day."

"And there was no other family to take you in? Thirteen is so young…"

"My grandparents migrated from Canada to Boston when my mother, an only child, was just an infant. When they passed early in a wagon accident, she was truly alone. Their death was a few years before she met the man who would become my father."

A long silence hung between them.

"You said Emmeline feared for Michaela. Do you share her concern?"

"I've since discovered Jason Whitmore has met someone else and plans to marry and move to Georgia, where she and her family resides. Michaela would only slow him down. Ruin his chances with her."

Chaim's frown deepened. He leaned forward placing his arms on the table. "How do you know all this?"

"I'm friends with the maid who works for Whitmore's mother. She heard them talking. On their way to Georgia, they planned to leave Michaela in an orphanage somewhere along the train route under a different name. That way, no one could ever find her or know what truly happened. They'd intended to claim Michaela became ill and died along the way. They don't want anyone to discover his late wife was pregnant by another man." The pain on Chaim's face was tangible. Tessa took a sip of her water, wetting her throat.

Getting through this was not easy. "Because of Emmeline's request, I'd been trying to locate you and decide how I could fulfill her appeal. Learning what Whitmore planned for Michaela, I offered my services to go with them. Michaela knew me. The circumstances would be easier on her with me, her nanny, by her side. About halfway there, Mr. Whitmore told me his mother wasn't well, and they were staying over a day or two. I panicked. I wasn't sure what they would do or tell me. I didn't wait to find out. That night, in the hotel room I shared with Michaela, I bundled up our things and crept out into the night and never looked back. I have no idea how they reacted."

"What about the Jordans?" he bit out angrily. "Did they ever find out?"

She shrugged. "They believe Michaela was moving to Georgia with her father, and that's all. They had no say in her life, and no idea what was planned. I didn't go to them because of Emmeline's wishes that you raise her. That your daughter would have a better life with you and the McCutcheons."

Anger drained from his face and was replaced with sadness. Pain glimmered in his eyes. "I can't imagine how frightened you must have been. If you'd been caught, you didn't have anyone to vouch for your story." He studied her closely. "I can never thank you enough."

"I don't want your thanks. I want a good life for Michaela."

"Did anyone know your plans? Could they be trailing you?"

"Not that I know of."

He again drummed his fingers on the table for a few seconds and then stilled. "What then are you suggesting, Tessa? Put Michaela up for adoption so she'll have a mother and a father? If that's your aim, I'm sorry to disappoint you." His gaze again fell to the child sleeping in her arms. "She's all I have left of Emmeline. Even after everything you've told me, all Emmeline could have done to rectify the situation after she found out she was with child but didn't...I still love her. Most importantly now, I love Michaela, too. I did the moment I set eyes on her, even if my actions said different. She's a McCutcheon and will remain a McCutcheon until her dying day."

"Adoption is not at all what I'm suggesting," she said on a whisper. Tessa glanced down at Michaela's peaceful face and gathered her courage. She was opening herself up, putting everything on the line. She took a deep breath and then slowly released the air. "If so, I would have allowed Whitmore to succeed in his endeavor and not put Michaela through such an arduous journey—especially one where the outcome was unknown. There's another solution you've not considered. One where she can have both a mother she's known since birth and her true father."

Chaim's eyes widened.

She nodded. "I'd do *anything* for Michaela. She was placed into my arms mere moments after she was born, and I've been seeing to her needs ever since." A deafening silence surrounded them. Oh, how she wished he'd realize her intention and pick up the conversation. Save her the embarrassment of saying the words aloud. She couldn't look him in the eye and focused her gaze on the vase of drooping violets dividing the table. "Mr. McCutcheon," she finally said slowly, "*Chaim*—I'm asking you to marry me."

When he didn't respond immediately, she glanced up and met his gaze. "So Michaela will have her *true* father and, as her mother, a woman she's known all her life." Her face heated, so she rushed on. "Emmeline *was* a good mother when she tended Michaela, but I cared for her just as much as Emmeline did. Our union will legitimize Michaela. She'll never have to know the truth, unless you think she should when she's older. Established. When her past means little to her compared to her future. Preferably after she's married and has the love of a strong man to help her through the shock. Because, no matter how you slice it, the truth will come as a blow, regardless of the loving family who's raised her. There will always be questions."

His purposeful gaze gave her hope. He hadn't scoffed and rejected her suggestion as rubbish. He hadn't stood and stomped out of the room. And proving her worst fears groundless, he hadn't laughed in her face. On the contrary. He was carefully listening to each word out of her mouth. "I understand you still love Emmeline, and probably always will," she hurried on. "I *understand* that—I do! She was a lucky woman. I'm not asking for your affections. I'll be a wife in name only, so you needn't worry about my expectations." Embarrassed, she paused and fingered her napkin. "I won't have any hopes for anything more except a roof over my head and the child I already consider my daughter." She swallowed nervously, praying he'd say something—*anything.* "After we return to Texas, and a sufficient amount of time has passed, and if you find the situation intolerable, I can say Texas doesn't suit me, and I'm unhappy. I'll leave and go home back east somewhere. Not to Boston, where I'm known by some. I'll start fresh in a new place. You can have a divorce, so you'll be free to marry again when the time is right. Whatever the outcome, Michaela will be perceived as a product of *our* union in everyone's eyes. I hope, in time—"

Chaim held up a hand.

"Oh," she hurried on. "I don't expect alimony, if that's what you're thinking. I'll leave with what I came with and not one thing more. I promise you. I have money saved. Having lived with the

Jordans for all the years they've employed me, I didn't have many expenses. I guess I have *that* to thank them for." She gave a confident nod, but he didn't look convinced. Her heart sank. "I've saved for years. I'll be fine."

"Nothing could be further from what I'm thinking. What about you? Don't you have someone back in Boston waiting for your return? A beau? A suitor? You're a beautiful woman."

She again dropped her gaze to the flower vase. *A beautiful woman? I hardly consider myself that.* "Not any respectable man, but plenty of the other kind. Until Emmeline's passing, I was determined never to marry." She paused. Gathered her thoughts. Was she speaking too quickly? "But, please know, I'm not suggesting this marriage for me, not by any stretch of the imagination. It's so Michaela can grow up with her father and to ensure she won't have a stigma hanging over her head."

"How would you take care of yourself? A divorced woman is shunned in some circles. What's in this for you?"

She couldn't stop her response and felt her face brighten. He was actually considering her proposal. "What's in it for me? First, my being able to sleep at night, knowing I've done everything in my power to make Michaela's life better." She paused, thinking. "But in it for me personally? I've never had a true surname before. You'd be giving me that. I'd be careful with the McCutcheon name and not bring scandal to it in any way. For me, a surname is more precious than a diamond, to be cherished and guarded." A moment of embarrassment made her pause and collect her runaway feelings. "And concerning employment, I'd get a job in a library, a bookstore, or something of the sort. I'm very well read, and the Jordans *did* give me time to take the courses I'd missed as a child. I'll do very well, indeed. Once I depart, you won't have to give me another thought."

Chapter Twenty-One

Chaim took several long minutes, considering Tessa's words. The crazy idea had merit. He'd long ago decided he'd never marry. Not after Emmeline, and all the pain she'd put him through. And an arrangement like this would certainly be best for Michaela. Taking her from Tessa now would be like snatching her from her mother. Cruel and heartless. She'd be crushed. They both would be. And, on a lesser note, his having a wife would keep his family off his back. Knowing them as he did, as soon as they returned home to Rio Wells, his mother and sisters would be throwing women at him left and right, to mend his broken heart. And to mother Michaela. All with good intentions, of course. With Tessa along, he could skip all the awkward meddling and having to turn away nice, eligible young ladies. All aspects of returning home he dreaded.

And, to be perfectly honest, I considered the option for a moment or two, myself...

"Mr. McCutcheon?" She swallowed hard. "Chaim?"

Tessa stared as if she thought he was about to stand and storm off.

Michaela stirred. One arm reached out and stretched.

"Your idea makes a lot of sense—*for Michaela*. I should have thought of the solution myself. Actually, I did, for a moment, but I didn't know your situation and obligations. This is giving up all your freedom for the sake of a baby."

"Not *a* baby. Michaela. As I said before, I'd do anything for her…"

What would life be like married to Tessa and caring for his child? Seemed this rollercoaster he'd boarded a year and a half ago was just getting started. "We don't have much time left to arrange everything before my family arrives," he replied. "So, we better get cracking."

She blinked several times and a small smile appeared. "You're absolutely right."

He glanced at the far wall by the stairway that led to the second floor where an elegant grandfather clock marked each half hour with a resounding gong. "It's still somewhat early. I'd say a town this size must have a church."

"I saw the spire as we walked to Mary Margaret's," she responded enthusiastically. "I believe it's only a few streets over."

"I'm sure Mary Margaret knows the minister, too," Chaim added. "She seems like a God-fearing woman. She could set up what we need with few problems, I'd think." Was he going off without thinking this through? *This is my life. And my daughter's. Tessa's too.* He didn't know Tessa well, but what he did know of her, she was a fine, soft-spoken, but spunky young woman who had put his daughter's well-being before her own. The journey here hadn't been easy. No doubt she was pretty, and Dustin and the rest would believe wholeheartedly he'd fallen for her.

"Why don't you return to your room and do whatever women like to do before getting hitched? I'll go speak with our old friend. See if she can persuade the minister. He might not like such short notice." He paused. "There's one problem."

Tessa shifted the baby in her arms. "Yes?"

"The timing. Michaela is nine months old. That would mean you and I, uh, well, got together almost immediately after Brick Paulson, the ranch hand of the Rim Rock I was traveling with, returned to Texas after I settled in Arizona. At the time of his departure, I was devastated over losing Emmeline. He'd have to believe I pulled myself out of my heartbreak in a few short weeks and fell for you." He rubbed his palm over his mouth, thinking. "My brother, Dustin, might not be so easily fooled."

"You could say our feelings were sudden and leave the rest to his imagination," she replied. "Love at first sight does happen, at times—although I believe it's rare. Sometimes, the less one says, the more believable they are."

Chaim reached across the table to Michaela, who was now awake.

She took his finger and struggled to pull it to her mouth.

He chuckled. "I'm not sold on keeping the truth from everyone. Doing so goes against my gut. Truth finds a way of sneakin' out. That's why it's always best to be upfront right from the get-go." He smiled. "The words of my father."

"I guess I understand," she replied. "I'll honor your decision, if you're set. Still, I feel strongly that the fewer people who know what really happened, the safer Michaela's future will be." Tessa glanced down as Michaela now played with the ruffled collar of Tessa's dress.

Having had a nice nap, she seemed wide awake. A line creased one side of her rosy-pink cheek where she'd been pressed up to Tessa's bodice. She began to fuss.

With the bill paid, Chaim stood and circled behind Tessa to assist with her chair.

Michaela smiled.

His heart warmed. "True. And it's no one's business but ours. I'll decide on what to tell the family later. Right now..." He walked her to the stairway leading up to their two rooms. "We have a wedding to attend. I'll return as soon as I can."

Chapter Twenty-Two

The next morning, attired in the dress she'd worn the evening before, Tessa waited beside Chaim on the train platform.

Several other people waited, too. A lone man, dressed in coveralls, held a small bouquet of flowers she recognized as the ones growing plentifully along the road to town. Across the platform was a woman with two small children gussied up as if going to Christmas service.

Who were they waiting for? Their father or grandparents?

The woman saw her looking and sent a shy smile.

The station manager stepped through the door of the depot. He wore a long-tailed blue coat adorned with four silver buttons and a matching round hat with a shiny black bill. He looked like a character from a Dickens novel. He glanced up the track in the direction the train would approach and checked his watch.

A man reading a newspaper glanced up from his seat on a bench, stood, folded his reading material, and tucked it under his arm. He ambled closer to the tracks.

Tessa's blood hummed through her veins. She worked to keep her breathing from galloping off. Chaim, *her husband*, held Michaela, who had been most agreeable this morning, allowing Tessa to give her a warm bath and attire her in the pretty blue calico dress and matching bonnet Mary Margaret had gifted her the previous day. The blue fabric made her eyes appear even more vivid, rimmed in an abundance of long lashes. She was, by far, the prettiest baby on the face of the earth.

Chaim looked at her and smiled. "Don't be nervous."

Don't be nervous? She felt like throwing up. In fleeting moments she'd be face to face with Chaim's parents. Butterflies swirled in her stomach as she recalled the candlelit ceremony last night, attended by the minister, his wife on the piano, and Mary Margaret holding Michaela in the first pew. The sacrament was brief. The deep sincerity of Chaim's voice vowing to love and honor her all the days of her life resonated in her heart, regardless of their marriage of need, a marriage in name only, nothing more.

Hooot hooot hooooooot.

A gleaming black engine appeared at the bend in the track. The horn sounded again, making Michaela glance around with wide eyes.

Chaim pointed and whispered something into her ear, calming the coming storm of tears.

If the McCutcheon family was on this train, they'd be here in seconds. Chaim's mother and father. His brother, Dustin, and two sisters, Madeline and Becky. As well as his married cousin and his family. Last night, after the wedding, they'd sat together as Michaela slept peacefully on the big bed. He'd given her a brief history of everyone, the ranch, and about the town of Rio Wells, where they'd all settle after they returned home.

A possibility existed the clan wouldn't be on this train and would arrive tomorrow, or the next day, but she didn't think so. Her heart said this was it.

As the train chugged closer, a charcoal-colored column of smoke pumped out in billows from the towering smokestack, smudging the sky with a long, black tail. Streams of white steam shot from a vent on the engine with a hiss.

Michaela squealed and wriggled in Chaim's arms.

He glanced over to Tessa again with a reassuring smile, his own flushed face handsome.

He hadn't seen his family in a year and a half, and here she was, sharing the reunion with him—like a real wife. When they'd met in the hallway this morning, he'd been quiet and introspective. Did he wonder how this would play out?

"Ready?" he asked.

"As ready as I'll ever be." That was all she had time to say before the tall engine arrived, steam hissing and spitting in every direction.

Chaim turned back to the train.

She fortified her courage.

The passenger car halted directly in front of them, and people poured off.

Tessa closed her eyes and said a small prayer. Would Chaim's family believe their story? Would they like her? If they knew she was Emmeline's cousin, they certainly wouldn't. Not after the way Emmeline had hurt Chaim—and the rest of them. Chaim said his family had welcomed Emmeline with open arms, even after she'd so recently been engaged to his cousin, John McCutcheon. Surely, his mother, at least, wouldn't be so understanding this time around. Especially if she knew the truth. At the sight of the very tall older man resembling Chaim, the confidence she'd felt last night when she'd proposed evaporated in one swift puff.

When he saw the man, Chaim straightened.

"Son!" the man called in a hoarse voice.

A mixture of hurt and excitement etched his face. The love in his eyes nearly dropped Tessa to her knees. After Chaim left Rio Wells, nobody knew if he'd ever return. She tried to put herself in their shoes. To feel what they were experiencing at this moment, after long last—but couldn't. The sensation was just too intense.

A moment later, the man engulfed Chaim and Michaela into his embrace.

"Pa, I'm sorry," Chaim said in a strangled voice, still clenched in his father's embrace.

"Shh, don't say anything. A man does what he feels is right. And that's just what you did, son. No apology needed. We're simply happy to have you back. Coming home to Texas."

Michaela began to squirm for air between them.

Another fellow, who couldn't be anyone except Dustin McCutcheon, Chaim's older brother, descended the narrow steps. He turned and offered his hand to an older woman, and then several younger women.

They could be none other than his mother and sisters, of course. Others crowded around, as well. All laughing and talking excitedly. Taking their turns to hug and kiss Chaim. She could tell he was very well loved, even after his time away. Seemed no one in the McCutcheon family held a grudge. She was glad for him. And for Michaela. Curious glances were cast her way every few seconds and at the baby. Everyone was bursting at the seams to find out their identities.

Michaela began to cry from all the confusing excitement.

Tessa stepped forward with outstretched arms. "Let me take her, Chaim." His name rolled sweetly off her lips as if they'd been married for years.

The gathering grew quiet.

Chaim handed the baby to her and then, with his arm around her back, ushered her more fully into the group. "Father, Mother, Dustin, and the rest, I'd like you to meet Tessa McCutcheon, my wife. And this is Michaela Rose, my daughter."

Chaim was a particularly good actor, since the joy in his voice was impossible to miss. His grin was nothing but delighted.

Dead silence descended, making Michaela's cries sound all the louder. All gazes shifted quickly from the baby to her.

"I'm sorry, son, what did you just say?" Winston McCutcheon tilted his head. "So much going on, I must be confused."

"You're not confused, Pa," Chaim replied with confidence. "I said this is my wife, Tessa Webb McCutcheon, and my daughter, Michaela. I know this comes as a shock to you all, but I hope you'll welcome my family with open arms."

"Of course, we do!" his mother exclaimed, moving closer to admire the baby, whose lashes were still wet with tears. "What a little sweetheart. Oh, Chaim, I'm so happy. And look how closely she resembles little Clara." She waved her arm over to the others. "It's astonishing."

Everyone took a moment to glance between a pretty infant a young woman held and her and Michaela, smiling and nodding.

The two babies were both blonde-haired and blue-eyed, and so adorable. They were almost identical. Tessa thought they must be close to the same age.

"Tessa, this is Winston and Winnie, my father and mother, Dustin, my brother, and Sidney, his wife. John and Lily, my cousin and his wife, and daughter, I see, who *does* resemble our Michaela.

Congratulations, John and Lily." He swept his arm wide. "That's Madeline, my oldest sister, and Becky, my younger." He paused. "And you brought along a friend. If I remember correctly, this is Wendy Knutson." He smiled at the slender young woman.

The group murmured their hellos.

"Welcome to the family, Tessa dear," Winnie said warmly. "We're delighted to meet you." She leaned forward between the squirming baby and pressed her cheek to Tessa's.

At the endearment, Tessa's heart warmed. Her own mother used to greet Tessa the same way. Winnie McCutcheon smelled of violets and talcum powder. After searching Tessa's eyes for a quick moment, her gaze turned to Michaela, a look of adoration on her face. "Welcome, Michaela, my charming, beautiful, sweet granddaughter." She glanced between Chaim and Tessa and then, for a brief moment, over her shoulder at Winston, joy shimmering in her eyes. "May I?" She held out her arms.

"Of course!" Tessa prayed Michaela wouldn't burst into tears as she passed the baby over. Tessa kept a smile plastered to her lips and murmured hellos to Chaim's sisters and their friend.

Lily huddled around Winnie McCutcheon, holding Michaela.

Dustin, John, and Winston stood with Chaim, talking and slapping him on the back with congratulations.

Every few seconds, she felt their gazes on her. Tessa couldn't have been prouder of Michaela if she tried. The bright-eyed baby smiled and responded to all the cooing and tickles as if she knew she was meeting her Texas relations for the very first time and needed to make a good impression. The sunshine made the curls at the rim of her bonnet glitter like liquid gold. Her smile was infectious. She was the star, and Tessa was thankful the spotlight was away from her. While she watched Mrs. McCutcheon holding Michaela, Tessa listened to Dustin and Sidney welcoming—and questioning—Chaim. Tessa recognized the glint of suspicion in Dustin's eyes.

"Why didn't you write to tell us?" he asked, a bit gruffly. "Or introduced me to Tessa when I came out to Arizona? You never said a thing."

His wife, Sidney, buffed Dustin's arm. "Now's not the time for questions." She rolled her eyes at Chaim and then smiled. "It warms me to see you, Chaim. You stayed away much too long." She glanced to Tessa and smiled. "You should have brought your family home sooner. I should be annoyed with you."

Tessa had just begun to feel left out when Chaim put out his arm, calling her to his side. An unaccustomed thrill pierced her, and she closed the few steps between them.

"I guess I just wanted some time for us, Sidney," he replied. "I knew these few months would be our only time alone together." He smiled lovingly at Tessa. "To live a semiprivate life, and I just took the opportunity. We'd planned all along to come home to the Rim Rock."

Dustin's eyebrow winged high.

Chaim was right. Dustin would be the one to win over.

The other fellow, the cousin, came forward and engulfed Chaim in a bear hug. "So good to see you, Chaim. We were all so pleased when you decided to join us to Y Knot. The reunion'll be better because of you."

"Thank you, John. I feel the same."

John turned to Tessa. He smiled and said hello, then added, "You look familiar, Mrs. McCutcheon. I don't think it's possible, but the moment I saw you, I knew we'd met before."

She shook her head and smiled. "Please, call me Tessa. And many people tell me the same," she said softly. "I must have a common face." But that wasn't true at all. In all the upheaval of finding Chaim and getting him to believe Michaela was truly his daughter, she'd totally forgotten she'd met John McCutcheon once when he'd been to the Jordans' home to meet Emmeline's family. Tessa had been dressed for church, not in the dress and apron she usually wore. Emmeline introduced her as a friend, not a cousin who worked in the home. Would John McCutcheon remember her from Boston? Did he already, and was covering for them?

John gave a little laugh and then winked at Chaim. "A common face? Sorry, that's not possible. When I figure out the mystery, I'll let you know."

Tessa's smile wobbled. "All right, I'll be waiting."

The young woman named Lily approached, placed her daughter in John's arms, and turned to Tessa. "I'm delighted to meet you. Having another Mrs. McCutcheon in Rio Wells will be interesting," she laughed. "You'll make four of us. And when we reach Y Knot, several more will be there. Just think of the confusion we'll create." Her eyes glowed with affection. Her soft German accent was endearing. "Our daughters look remarkably close in age. Petite and pretty. We named Clara after John's mother, Claire. She's eight months old. How old is Michaela?"

"Nine months."

Tessa smiled and nodded as Michaela was passed from Mrs. McCutcheon to Madeline. Tessa scanned the group and, although she shouldn't be, was startled to find John regarding her intently. Even though everyone was studying her, which was to be expected, his arched brows and smile gave her pause. He might not remember her yet, but he would. And when that happened, the warm welcome into Chaim's family would fly right out the window. Being related in any way to the woman who broke Chaim's heart was not a place she liked to be.

Chapter Twenty-Three

"What do you make of it?" Dustin asked his cousin from the interior of the livery as they waited for the five horses they'd rented to be saddled. He and John had volunteered to fetch the mounts they'd reserved when they'd arrived this morning. With Tessa and Michaela, as well as two other travelers, the stagecoach was overcrowded. Dustin wasn't one to resign himself to cramped torture if an alternative was available.

John rubbed his chin, looking as puzzled as Dustin felt. "Anyone can fall in love and marry, Dustin, *and* have a baby right away—but *Chaim*? I'm a bit surprised, as well, after what happened with Emmeline. I still feel responsible for that, me being the reason she came to town in the first place." He glanced up at Dustin with deep lines marring his forehead.

"Don't blame yourself for her misdeeds, John. What she did wasn't your fault."

"Hard not to. Without me, Chaim and Emmeline would never have met. If anyone is culpable for what took place, it's me."

Dustin gripped the back of his neck, bewildered. "Maybe I could see him moving on. He *has* been gone a year and a half. A lot can happen in that amount of time. But with the age of his daughter, *that* moving on must have occurred the moment Brick Paulson pulled up stakes and headed back to Rio Wells. Brick said Chaim was still a shattered man." He shook his head. "Tessa's pretty, though. I can see her catching Chaim's eye. Being shy and reserved, she's the complete opposite of Emmeline, who enjoyed being centerstage at all times. Maybe that's what drew him."

"She just met a slew of in-laws for the very first time, Dustin. Knowing they weren't even aware of her existence. Give her a few days to get to know everyone. She might be an entirely different woman by then. Anyone would feel intimidated with our crew."

Perplexed, Dustin turned and gazed through the barn doors at the hotel where the others were refreshing themselves before the coming journey to Y Knot. "I don't know…"

John laid a hand on Dustin's arm. "Don't look for trouble, Dustin. We don't know the facts. There's always more to a story than what meets the eye. Maybe, well…" His voice trailed off, and he closed his mouth.

"Yeah, you're thinking the same thing I am. Maybe she's a saloon girl he got in trouble and felt obliged to marry. Or maybe she's a friend who found herself in trouble by someone else and turned to Chaim for help. Stranger things have happened. My brother's the most soft-hearted man I know. Never could turn away a person in need. There're a thousand different ways this could have happened besides the one they're spoon-feeding us."

John drilled him with an icy stare. "Be warned, Dustin, you've just got your brother back. Don't run him off by wanting to know the details so badly you forget everything else. It's not worth it. And really, it's none of your business. Let them settle in. Become easy with the family. I know you think of him as your *little* brother, but he's a grown man—and doesn't need you to help with every situation. He has a right to his privacy—even from you!"

Dustin harrumphed and kicked a dirt clod across the barn aisle. "I know you're right. I just don't like seeing my little brother taken advantage of."

"You know nothing of the sort!"

The wrangler walked their way leading three horses. He handed the reins to Dustin and went back for the other two. Sidney had volunteered to ride with the men, since she ranched with him every day and much preferred being on the back of a horse instead of squished inside with too many people.

John looked at his watch. "We better get moving. Not long before the stage pulls out. I'm sure everyone is set to go."

"With the big meal we just had, I'd rather be taking a nap."

"No time for that." John took the reins of two more horses and headed for the livery door.

"Be sure to leave the horses at the livery with June Pittman," the wrangler called. "My man'll be by in a day or two to pick 'em up. You'll get charged two bits a head every day they're late."

"Did you say June? A woman?" Dustin asked, surprised— and then amused. He'd never heard of a female livery owner before. He wondered if she could arm wrestle with the best of 'em.

"Yes, sir. And she runs her livery as good as any man. You'll see when you meet her." He gave a friendly nod.

The stage was loaded by the time they arrived. Their trunks were strapped to the top of the coach and two other travelers were already seated inside. His clan still clustered around where Tessa and Lily held the babies.

Spotting him and John approaching with the throng of horses, Chaim and their pa strode out to meet them. His brother looked happier than he could remember. He was damn glad to have Chaim back, whatever the circumstances. But this other mystery prickled his nerves. He wished he could let the feeling go like John suggested, but he wasn't ready just yet. And he'd have to be blind to miss how Miss Wendy Knutson watched Chaim walk away. Was that the real reason why Madeline invited her along? To mend her brother's broken heart? Maybe Miss Knutson confided in Madeline about liking Chaim at one time. Well, she was a little too late for that.

"All set?" Winston looked over the two bays, the sorrel, the buckskin, and the black.

Dustin nodded. "Any reply from Charity or Brandon? They know we're headed their way today?" He'd telegraphed as soon as they'd hit town this morning. Said they'd arrive sometime late this afternoon or early evening.

"Sure did." Chaim grinned and placed his hands on his hips. "We've already spoken to the stage driver. He's letting us off at a well-known landmark just before town. That's where someone will be waiting with transportation. We're being split up to keep us hidden until the party. They'll take us to individual homes where we're to lay low. Sounds interesting."

Dustin laughed and shook his head. "They sure know how to plan a surprise." He'd been admiring the beauty of Montana. The green rolling hills and lush grass. And, just as they said, the sky looked as if it went on forever, but that was nothin' out of the ordinary for where he was from. He was a Texan through and through and would never leave Rio Wells.

Sidney strode forward, having changed into her split riding skirt. She took the reins of the buckskin mare from John. "I've always been partial to a pretty buckskin," she said. "And this one sure is a sight. I wonder what she's doing being rented at a livery." She slowly ran her hand over the horse's muscled chest and then patted her flank. "I'll hold out my final opinion until after I ride her, but I think she'd make a fine addition to my string."

Dustin shook his head and chuckled. "Your string of horses is the longest at the Rim Rock. You collect horses faster than a spider catches flies." He slung his arm affectionately around his wife's shoulders and pulled her close.

She craned her neck and looked up at Dustin, a smile playing around her lips. "Are you complaining, husband of mine?"

"No, ma'am, not a chance of that. Just stating a fact. I prefer a wife who collects horses to a wife who collects gowns."

"But that's the horse I wanted," Chaim said, stone faced at her side. "Caught my eye as soon as I saw her."

Startled, Sidney turned to face him, her smile gone.

The disappointed slant on Chaim's mouth Dustin knew all too well. He was pulling Sidney's leg and wanted to see how far he could take it.

"Oh, well...in that case..." Sidney stepped forward and slowly held out the long, leather reins, stained dark with use.

Instead of taking them, Chaim laughed and slung one arm over Sidney's shoulders and the other over Dustin's, pulling them into a hug. "I'm just messing with ya, Sister-in-law. Wanted to see how you'd react." He winked playfully. "You passed the test with flying colors."

They all laughed, including Winston and John.

What a joy to have Chaim back. And he did seem much improved since the last time they'd met, which was in Arizona when Dustin visited with the intention of dragging Chaim home by the ear. By Dustin's calculations, Chaim would have been married at that time, and yet Dustin hadn't seen one speck of evidence a woman lived in the small, ramshackle house his brother called home. Or around the ranch. He'd never said a thing, either, and still looked miserable and brokenhearted. Something wasn't right.

Standing across from him, John caught his gaze and shook his head the teeniest bit.

All right, cousin, I'll let the subject be, for now, so I don't upset the applecart before the party. But I'll not close my eyes to any shenanigans. I aim to know the truth.

Chapter Twenty-Four

Tessa took a calming breath, all the while keeping a pleasant smile plastered on her lips. The stagecoach rocked and rumbled along, doing little to quell her growing panic. Had she done the right thing? Since Emmeline's death, all she could think about was Michaela and what would become of her. About saving her from the shame and abuse she'd endure growing up as an illegitimate child, *especially* a girl. People always considered Tessa loose and fast because that's what they thought of her mother— getting in the family way without the benefit of a husband. But nothing could be further from the truth. Now, seated across from Chaim's family, she wasn't sure she could pull off the duplicity.

Positioned next to the window of the rattling stage, she gazed at the countryside and attempted to relax. An abundance of trees, streams, and sometimes even wildlife appeared along the route. They'd frightened a small herd of deer and a bevy of quail. This landscape was remarkably different than the brick buildings towering to the sky she was used to in Boston.

Becky pointed out two coveys of quail and a sage grouse, the latter identified by its thick white collar and speckled tail. Chaim's little sister seemed pleased to share about both of her brothers. "They love to hunt together," Becky gushed, appearing delighted to have everyone's attention. "They leave before sunup and spend hours before returning home with a feast for Maria to cook up. Coots are their favorite. Father's, too."

"Coots? I'm not familiar with the bird." Tessa tried to sound like she knew at least something of wildlife. She'd spent her whole life in the city. Montana and Texas were as foreign to her as the moon.

Becky lifted a brow. "Coots are mostly black with a white bill. They have strong, large feet they use to attack each other if their territory is in danger of encroachment. I've seen it, and the sight is rather funny. They're waterbirds."

Tessa blinked wide. "You hunt, as well?"

"Not anymore." Becky shook her head but had straightened proudly. "When I was younger, they allowed me to tag along—as long as I was quiet."

Maybe she and Becky could become friends. She could learn a lot from her. Now the land beyond the rutted road fell away, and in the distance was a tall ridge of purple mountains, a sight she'd not seen in her travels. Their beauty calmed her somewhat, and she took a cleansing breath. She wished Chaim were inside, instead of riding in front of the stage with the others. At least, with him by her side, he'd field some of his family's questions.

Beside her, Clara on Lily's lap, reached over and tugged the ribbon of Michaela's bonnet. On the other side of Lily was a married couple. They hadn't said much but nodded and smiled as she and the rest had piled into the stagecoach, amidst much scrunching and shifting, doing their best to get comfortable without jabbing each other with an elbow or knee. They hadn't seemed disturbed in the least to be crowded together with a gaggle of women and two babies.

As much as the babies' antics pleased Tessa, she was still all-too-aware of the four women opposite taking her measure. They'd been polite and not asked how she and Chaim had met, or when they'd gotten married, but she was sure those questions would come eventually. It was only a matter of time. She glanced up at the uncommonly quiet group.

Directly across, Chaim's mother nodded a small smile as the coach jiggled her from side to side. She was a handsome woman of middle age. Her brown hair was peppered with gray but didn't distract from her youthful appearance. Must be the ranch work that kept her fit as a fiddle. Beside Winnie was Becky, who had Chaim's fair coloring. Now, after a few hours of travel, she appeared rumpled and tired. Between Becky and the friend, Wendy, Madeline, Chaim's dark-haired sister, older than Becky but younger than Chaim, studied her with coffee-colored eyes. Tessa guessed the young woman to be in her early twenties. She'd been kind, as well, but standoffish from the start. Tessa hoped they'd become friends.

An astounding realization made her glance from their faces to the world outside the window. In truth, this was her family now. And would be for all time—even if and when she and Chaim divorced. A marriage in name only was still valid. When she'd begun this journey, she'd never expected such a turn of events.

Feeling as if she was drowning in the middle of a lake, Tessa glanced down at the top of Michaela's head as the babies babbled and laughed at each other.

"They're darling together," Winnie said, a sound of adoration in her voice. "Imagine my surprise to learn I was a grandmother." She caught Tessa's eye. "I can't tell you how happy you've made us." She reached across the short distance. Michaela took her proffered finger, trying to tug it into her mouth.

Even though the words were spoken with affection and caring, Tessa felt them as criticism. *Why didn't you let us know? Why didn't you telegram when you and Chaim married? Did you keep him away from home all this time on purpose?*

"Claire's granddaughter and my granddaughter, only a month apart...may I hold her again? I've been itching to since leaving Waterloo."

"Of course, you can. Anytime. I enjoy sharing her."

"And I'll take little Clara," Becky said. "So they don't cry when separated. She made a funny face at Clara as she brought the baby onto her lap.

Clara giggled and snuggled in.

Wendy nodded, openly adoring the babies as they babbled and played.

Once Clara was settled on Becky's lap, Becky glanced at Tessa. "Madeline and I watch this little one three days a week, since Lily has her shop to attend to. Or more, sometimes, if she's really busy."

With her hands and lap now free, Tessa fluffed her dress a little and scooted around, adjusting her position. Michaela was being so well mannered. The baby smiled sweetly at her grandmother, who glowed happiness. Seeing how much everyone in this family loved Michaela, Tessa felt greatly confident she and Chaim had done the right thing. "Lily, you have a shop?"

All the women glanced her way.

What was she thinking? Chaim would have talked about his family in Rio Wells after all the months they were supposed to have been together. She needed to choose her words wisely.

"A dress shop," Lily replied, as if she hadn't noticed the mistake. "Lily's Lace and More."

"She's incredibly accomplished," Becky added. "And sells lots of dresses. I love all her creations."

"Of course." Tessa smiled calmly and then clamped her mouth closed. To keep her hands busy, she reached over and removed Michaela's bonnet.

"Tessa, did you have an easy birth?" Lily asked. "Was Michaela late or early?"

Tessa had been frightened when Emmeline went into labor. She'd bathed Emmeline's brow with a cool cloth and held her cousin's hand throughout the ordeal. "This little one was right on time." Remembering the love she'd felt that day witnessing the birth, Tessa reached out and fingered Michaela's hair as she sat in her grandma's lap. "And she didn't give too much trouble. Only twenty hours. Not exceptionally long for a first birth."

"Oh!" Becky exclaimed. "Twenty hours?"

"The time goes quickly, Becky," Lily responded. "For me, in the blink of an eye. Or, at least, that's what I remember. John was busy with Tucker Noble, that's one of his partners in his healing salve business, packaging orders to ship. I didn't think the pesky pains jabbing my tummy were enough to alert him." She laughed, and her eyes crinkled in the corners. "By the time he returned home, I was ready to deliver. He barely removed his hat and washed his hands before Clara made her appearance. He was quite annoyed with me."

"I can't imagine John upset with anyone," Madeline objected. "Especially you, Lily."

All gazes turned to Tessa.

Did they expect her to go on? She didn't want to spin stories for entertainment, ones she might have to later retract. She glanced at the only man in the coach and smiled.

Chaim's mother gave a slight nod. "I'm thankful for the stops we've made to stretch our legs, but now I'd like to arrive. I hope wherever they put me tonight has a nice, soft bed. The train trip has worn me out."

Tessa felt worn out as well. Not in body but in spirit. Would Winnie's warm gazes turn to frost if she knew the truth? And Chaim's father, Winston, had welcomed her with an almost holy adoration—like the father she'd never had. As right as the intention to conceal Michaela's true parentage had seemed before, now Tessa wasn't so sure. Meeting them today, the dishonesty seemed darker. She felt as if she were ice-skating on a mountain pond as the sun was about to top the ridge, bringing disaster and heartbreak.

Chapter Twenty-Five

Chaim rode at an easy lope alongside his brother as if the last year and a half hadn't transpired. The two had picked up exactly where they'd left off. One thing about Dustin, he was faithful, if not a bit suspicious. Chaim was touched by the welcome his family had given him, despite the way he'd deserted them. He didn't deserve their loving words and tears. Still, he was moved and grateful.

Did I really expect anything different?

No, not in his heart. And they'd accepted Tessa and Michaela with open arms and love. And a good dose of curiosity, which he'd expected. Thinking about Dustin, Chaim almost chuckled as he enjoyed the sunshine warming his back. The wind felt good on his face, and he felt as free as a bird. Amazing, because he'd just gotten married.

Married.

Once he'd paid for the small ranch in Arizona, he'd all but consigned himself to a life of bachelorhood, vowing never to marry. But when it came to his daughter's happiness, denying her the woman who'd cared for her for her whole life would be cruel. He took a deep breath and let the horse's stride ease his mind. Tessa knew exactly where they stood. They were of one mind. There would be no mixed messages between them. He'd provide for her, give her his name and daughter, so to speak, and she'd help him give Michaela the best life possible. The plan would also keep his family off his back by trying to mend his heart. As soon as he'd seen Wendy Knutson, he'd known he'd made the right decision. If he and Tessa kept a clear mind, and knew where they stood in their relationship, they'd be fine. A marriage in name only. He was good with that. And she was, as well.

Charity tried to be patient. She fidgeted on the hard wooden seat of the buckboard next to Brandon, excited John and the rest would arrive any time. John hadn't been back to Montana in years—not since he'd left for medical school in Boston. And she'd yet to meet his baby girl. Father would be shocked speechless.

Nick and Tanner Petty relaxed in two buggies beside them, holding the lines.

Brandon reached over and took her hand.

Several extra benches had been added to the bed of the buckboard to accommodate more passengers.

Charity checked her watch one more time. The length of the trip depended on how hard the driver pushed the animals, or if the stage needed to stop for any given reason. Sometimes a horse or mule pulled up lame, or threw a shoe, slowing the progress considerably.

"You all right?" Brandon smiled down at her. "I felt you tremble. Shall I reach back for one of the blankets?"

She hugged his arm and laid her head on his shoulder. "No, thanks, I'm fine. Just breathlessly excited. John's been away so long. I wonder what he'll think of Y Knot now, since he's lived in Boston for a time. And also Texas. As much as I'm excited for father and his party, I'm more so to have my brother home. I wish they'd extend their time or stay for good. I know this is just a visit, but I can't help but dream."

Brandon put his arm over Charity, snuggled her to his side, and leaned his cheek on the top of her head. "I know you do, sweetheart. But John's carved out a new life for himself in Rio Wells. We're just lucky he has family there to look after him for us. Keep in mind, he left because of the accident all those years ago. No one in Texas knows his history."

"The accident?" She sat straighter, his arm falling away. "He was just a boy—only nine years old when he shot Bob Mackey. Nobody can hold that against him. No one even remembers anymore."

"I'm on your side, Charity, no need to convince me. No one might remember, but John does. I hope I'm wrong, but I think he still carries some guilt. A man of good conscience doesn't easily forget about taking another man's life, accident or not. And, the fact the event happened inside the ranch house doesn't help." He picked up her hand again and laced his fingers through hers. "But I might be mistaken, so don't fret."

Father was at the Lambert Ranch today. Roady had promised he'd cook up some reason to keep him there overnight so they wouldn't run into anyone while delivering the out-of-town guests. "Did Father find the town log he was looking for?"

"He did. I keep anything significant pertaining to Y Knot in the 'important file cabinet' in our bedroom. Flood wanted to take the book home, but you know I can't allow that, not even for him. Depending on who the sheriff was at the time, some years have no entries, at all. It's truly a shame."

"From my husband who keeps a detailed town journal. You should be proud of yourself. I am."

He chuckled. "You'd be proud of me if I raised pigs. If Flood wants to study Y Knot in depth, he'll just have to come visit more. Spend the evening." He playfully jiggled her hand and wiggled his eyebrows. "You could cook him dinner."

She gave a small laugh. "You'd have to do the cooking. He knows me too well."

"What're you talking about, silly girl? You're a good cook."

"Fine at boiling water…"

"Fine then, he can come spend the day with me and read to his heart's content in the sheriff's office. We have so few records of the beginning of our town; we can't chance them going astray."

She again hugged his arm. "Going astray? Surely, you trust my father."

"Without a doubt. But if I allowed him to borrow, I'd have to permit the next person who inquired to do the same. That's a risk I'm not willing to take."

"You know best, Sheriff." At the sound of rumbling wheels, she bolted to her feet.

The stagecoach appeared around the bend. The Texas McCutcheons were about to arrive!

Chapter Twenty-Six

Chaim lifted a hand when he spotted three rigs parked next to a rickety fence in the waning light. He glanced at his father, cousin, and brother, as well as Sidney, riding at his side, to see their wide grins. Why'd they wait so long before making this trip? Seemed a shame, all the time they'd lost. His generation was grown and working on families of their own.

In a clatter of hooves, the scent of sweaty horse flesh, and broad, welcoming smiles, Chaim and the rest pulled up. Not far behind came the stagecoach, which rumbled to a stop in the middle of the road.

"John!" Charity climbed from her perch without the help of her husband and ran to meet the horses. As soon as John dismounted, she vaulted into his waiting arms. "We're so happy you're here! With Lily, and the baby," she cried. "You've finally come home." She leaned back, smiling into John's face. Then she turned to Chaim. "And Chaim! You made it, too. We're all so pleased..." Her smile wobbled and then vanished as her gaze searched his face.

Ignoring the implication he was so delicate he might shatter to pieces, he picked her up and swung her around, as well. "Hello, young cousin. It's darn good to see you. I'm happy I came, too. It's about time my senses returned."

Her brow creased together again, and she studied him in silence.

That must not have been the welcome she'd expected. Well, she was about to get the surprise of her life. "Before you say anything more," he said with a chuckle, "let's let the others disembark from the coach before we start introductions."

"Yes, of course," she said, her lips puckering.

Brandon and the ranch hands joined them, shaking hands all around.

The women appeared from the stage in a flutter of excitement. Cries of joy and tears transpired as they hugged.

Chaim couldn't stifle a chuckle at the ranch hands and the stars in their eyes at the sight of so many young women in one place.

His father introduced their group, and then Brandon did the honors for the Montana family. Chaim watched Charity and Brandon closely as Winston didn't miss a beat saying Tessa and Michaela were Chaim's wife and daughter. Charity's eyes widened. And he was darn proud of Tessa. Unless somebody asked directly for the date of their wedding, appearances said they were an old married couple. He reached out and Michaela, now completely comfortable with him, leaned into his arms and cooed as he lifted her into the air.

The driver lowered their bags to the ranch hands and then climbed back onto his seat. Goodbyes were said, he flapped the lines, hawed the team, and the stagecoach rumbled away.

The luggage was divided between the wagon and buggies, depending on the destination of the occupants. The women were helped up. Excitement zipped through the air. Not until Charity turned to face him did he realize the extra people he'd brought might present a problem. "We'll be happy to stay at the hotel, Charity, if lodging is tight. Or a boardinghouse. I should've let you know about Tessa and Michaela before we arrived, but I wanted their appearance to be a surprise." He glanced up at Tessa, who was already seated.

"There's no problem. I'm just thinking. I have you at a farm a couple miles out of town with a nice couple named Tobit and Kathryn Preece. Their farmhouse is quite large, and I'm sure they won't mind having two more guests. Actually, they'll be delighted."

For all her protestations, her tightly clasped hands and furrowed brow indicated she wasn't convinced at all.

She turned to the others. "You'll only have to hide for two days, so please, be patient. Your hosts are thrilled to have you and would have been here on your arrival but doing so might have drawn suspicion. I'll send word with any news." She spread her arms wide. "Welcome to Y Knot! On behalf of my mother and the rest of the family who aren't here, thank you for making the long, tiring trip north!"

Chapter Twenty-Seven

Chaim leaned against the upstairs bedroom wall of the Preece farm, watching Michaela play. He'd been sent up to the bedroom, out from underfoot, with Michaela while Tessa helped Kathryn finish dinner preparations and set the table. His job was to watch Michaela and keep her entertained.

At the moment, Michaela waved the small doll his mother purchased in Waterloo before boarding the stage for Y Knot.

As soon as she'd held Michaela for a few minutes, kissed her cheek and hugged her, her first duty as a grandmother, before she'd even taken a bite to eat, was to find a toy for her granddaughter.

Chaim was touched. And so was Tessa.

Twenty minutes later, his mother returned with the toy made from pink calico fabric. The doll's face was stitched with black thread. Ringlets of golden embroidering ribbon constituted her hair.

Michaela was entranced.

His mother remembered Tessa, as well, presenting her with an elegant lavender shawl made of wool. Speechless, the two embraced.

Seemed everything was off to a good start. He hunkered down by Michaela and the baby stopped playing and looked at him. "You like dolly, do you?" He adored her with his gaze. "You're putting her through her paces. Reminds me of your Uncle Dustin and how he tests me." He chuckled at his own joke.

Michaela glanced at him, her play only fleetingly interrupted. She happily gummed the doll's arm, a drizzle of drool slipping down her chin. The baby's eyes smiled.

"It's from your grandma." He rubbed her soft hair. "Who loves you dearly." His mother's eyes had glittered with emotion, as had his father's. Chaim had felt a flash of happiness at that moment, being the one to give them their first grandchild. Seeing their pleasure and delight was icing on the cake. After today, he was sure they'd forgiven him for leaving Rio Wells for so long.

Chaim's heart stuttered at the realization. Michaela was *his* child. *He* was a father. He'd sired this tiny human being. The feeling was quite remarkable, and nothing else compared. He hadn't found much time to really ponder the amazing fact to any extent before this, with the journey, his wedding, and then the arrival of his family.

The crib on the far side of the room was added after they'd arrived. Tobit Preece and his elderly father, Isaiah, lugged the furniture down from the attic.

Kathryn insisted she would need it soon, anyway. Without missing a beat, she dressed the crib in fresh linen and assured Tessa the room was thoroughly cleaned, and the rug beaten outside on the line.

The whole Preece family seemed delighted to have them.

The doll now forgotten, Michaela started across the rug on her hands and knees.

Chaim stood and followed. He'd only been alone with her twice and wanted to keep a close eye out.

Michaela reached the crib and rolled onto her bottom, looking especially pleased with herself. She glanced up at him and smiled. A moment later, she grasped the bottom slat of the crib, which was within her reach, and struggled to her feet. Wobbling unsteadily for a few seconds, she plopped back to the floor.

"Very good! You'll be standing soon enough. Be patient." He let his gaze wander the room and landed on the bed covered with a patchwork quilt of bright colors. Here was where things could become tricky.

Tobit and Kathryn's bedroom was at the end of the hall. Isaiah mentioned he slept below, close to the kitchen, where he enjoyed the warmth from the stove when the weather grew cold. Chaim and Tessa hadn't yet discussed what they'd do about sleeping arrangements, either here or when they returned to Rio Wells. How was this marriage-in-name-only to work, while keeping the truth from his family?

Tessa appeared at the open door. She smiled at Michaela, who was again back on the braided rug where she'd left the doll. "It's so quiet up here, I came to check on you two. I see you both have everything under control."

This was their first private moment since the arrival of his family. Last night, in the hotel, they'd kept the separate rooms. Was she having the same thoughts? Her face was a deep shade of pink as her gaze skittered away from the quilt-covered bed. "Please, come in." He tried for a normal smile, but it felt off. "This is your room, too."

"Indeed."

Fiddling with her skirt, Tessa approached and squatted next to Michaela. She lifted the doll and made her dance.

The baby smiled.

Chaim shifted his weight from one foot to the other. He'd been contemplating sitting on the bed but changed his mind with Tessa's arrival. "I noticed a chair at the top of the stairs. Perhaps I can sneak it in after everyone else is asleep."

Rocking Michaela into her arms, she glanced up at him. "Or you could say Michaela needs to be cuddled before falling asleep, and a chair makes the task easier."

His wife-in-name-only was bright *and* sensible. "Good idea. I'll mention it at supper."

She murmured to the baby.

Michaela climbed up to stand in Tessa's arms as she looked up at him.

"I think she's getting used to me," Chaim remarked, feeling a pinch of pride.

"I agree. She's usually shy with men. The fact there hasn't been any crying up here says a lot." She tipped her head and studied the baby, smiling when Michaela leaned forward and gave her an open-mouthed kiss. Tessa laughed. "The day's been long and stimulating, though. She didn't nap, and now she's past her bedtime. Tonight might be a long one for you."

"Don't worry about me. I'll be fine. You survive in the stagecoach? Or did my family pepper you with a thousand questions?"

"Everyone was exceedingly kind. They'll ask their questions later, when we've become better acquainted. And that's totally understandable. I'd have questions, too. Your little sister entertained us with stories about you and Dustin growing up. Shared the story of the honey-filled beehive."

Chaim frowned. "Not a good memory. I received over ten stings and couldn't sleep for almost a week. I learned my lesson, though."

"I heard about Lily's dress shop. How she's put Rio Wells on the map with her sewing." Tessa tipped her head and smiled up at him.

Michaela crawled off her lap and went to investigate the legs of her crib again.

"Lily is so soft spoken," she added. "I'd never guess she'd be a successful businesswoman."

"There's a lot for you to learn, concerning my family. I hope you don't regret our decision yesterday."

Seeing Tessa gather herself to stand, he put out his hand and helped her to her feet.

At a light tapping, they both turned to the threshold.

"Dinner is served," Tobit said, one hand on the doorjamb as he leaned into the room.

Chaim lifted Michaela off the floor, warmed by the comfortable feel. How things had changed. He chuckled to himself as he followed the others out the door. Maybe the only thing worse than a baby crying at night, was no baby crying at all.

Chapter Twenty-Eight

Oh, the joy Charity felt was difficult to contain. After the pickup, Tanner with Chaim, Tessa, and Michaela headed for the Preece farm. The rest of the group started for the Klinkner Mill. Their two-story, clapboard home was large and had plenty of room for the three young women. Madeline, Becky, and Wendy promised to stay out of Y Knot until the shindig. Afterwards, they'd do their fair share of shopping and sightseeing.

Charity marveled at the revelations. Chaim's happiness. Dustin said he'd refused the invitation for the last couple of months. And now he turned up, married with a baby! All that time, he'd never said a word? Something about the situation didn't feel quite right. Still, she was thrilled. Tessa was beautiful and nice, and Michaela was stealing hearts faster than a cat caught mice.

After a brief visit with the Klinkners, the rest of the group headed for the Heart of the Mountains. First, they dropped Uncle Winston and Aunt Winnie at Matt and Rachel's. They went there first so Matt and Rachel could say hello to John and Lily before they reached their destination at Mark and Amy's. The reunion of brothers produced many tears all around.

One more stop to make.

The wagon felt empty with only Dustin and Sidney sitting behind. They pulled into the yard at Luke's home. Several lanterns burned in the windows, welcoming the travelers. By now, all the shadows were gone, and a silvery moon shined over the mountains in a splash of milky white clouds.

Charity felt a ping of nervousness. She remembered all too well her first days in Rio Wells defending Luke to Dustin. Dustin was overly curious about Luke's Cheyenne heritage. Almost disdainful. Dustin had asked what Luke was like, how he *looked*— as if his Indian blood made him so different. Charity, always ready to rise to Luke's defense, had wanted to take Dustin down a few notches. And told him so, in not so many words. But that was before she'd come to know her cousin better and indeed come to love him, too.

Now the two were about to meet face to face.

The door opened, and Luke strode outside, followed by Faith with two-year-old Holly in her arms.

Dawn, just shy of five, held Colton's hand, standing on the doorstep. Colton was now as tall as Faith and was a handsome boy, so dear to all the family's hearts. No one ever thought of him as Luke's stepson. He was true family.

Brandon jumped out of the wagon and helped her down. Their gazes touched briefly. Was he thinking the same things she'd been only a moment ago? He'd been in Rio Wells, too.

"Welcome," Luke called. "You can be none other than my cousin, Dustin McCutcheon, and his wife, Sidney, from all the descriptions Charity and Brandon have given us. Welcome to our home."

Luke waited as Dustin helped Sidney to the ground. A moment later, the two cousins stood together, equal in height, equal in breadth, and equal in curiosity.

The image was profound in the moonlight.

"Luke McCutcheon," Dustin barked, offering his hand. "It's a pleasure to finally make your acquaintance. After all these years wondering about you, I'm glad to be here and staying in your home. From what I've seen of the ranch so far, the Heart of the Mountains is a formidable place. You all should be proud."

Land's sake. Charity never heard so many words come out of Dustin before all in one breath. And what did he mean with his first comment about wondering about Luke? He could have saved that for later. Even in the moonlight, Charity noticed a flicker of something cross Luke's face. An expression she'd seen before, but never with family or friends. Had she made a colossal mistake bringing Dustin and Sidney here? Charity wanted everyone to get along, love each other, like she and Brandon did when they'd gone to Rio Wells.

Faith moved to Luke's side and threaded her arm through his after he took Holly from her. The women said their hellos.

Luke's brows drew together. "Thank you, Dustin. It's a pleasure to meet you, as well. And you, too, Sidney. We're proud of the ranch, as I'm sure you are of the Rim Rock. Brandon and Charity shared many complimentary aspects about your home and town in Texas." He flashed a half smile in her direction.

His reminder of the days he'd been furious with her for sneaking off without telling anyone she'd planned to take the stagecoach all the way to Texas alone. A dangerous trip for any unaccompanied young woman. She'd taken several tongue lashings from her brothers over that escapade.

"Thank you for taking the time and expense to make the trip special for *my father*," Luke said in a measured tone. "He'll be knocked off his feet when he sees you all."

When her husband stepped closer and took her hand, Charity looked up at Brandon. Did Luke just emphasize the words "my father"? Had things escalated so quickly?

"Meet Faith, my wife, Colton, our son, Dawn, and Holly." Luke chucked Holly under her chin, making her smile. She'd shyly tucked her head under Luke's chin and snuggled close as soon as Faith handed her over. "But, please, come in and get comfortable. Supper is ready. Faith has cooked up a feast in your honor."

"Colton," Brandon called. "Help me with these trunks. We'll take them upstairs."

The boy jumped into action.

Inside, as Brandon and Colton lumbered up the stairs, Dustin and Sidney oohed and aahed over the spacious rooms. Luke and Faith had furnished their home with a carved wooden coffee table and sideboard. A mixture of leather and fabric made a sophisticated rancher's dream. The large pinewood dining room table was decked out lavishly for the important guests.

Love for her brother and Faith bubbled over. Wanting to smooth the awkward beginning, Charity blurted, "You'll never believe the news. Chaim has a wife and nine-month-old daughter! No one knew, not even Dustin or his parents. Isn't that remarkable? I was practically speechless when I met Tessa and Michaela."

Luke, finished assisting Faith with a hot platter of pot roast to the trivets, turned to join Dustin and Sidney. "That *is* a surprise. I was under the impression Chaim was still broken up over the young woman who jilted him. He never wrote to you from Arizona? I've yet to meet Chaim, but this news has me curious."

Jilted? Charity chomped down on her bottom lip. When Dustin's forehead furrowed, Charity realized her mistake. Dustin would go to any length to defend his brother. Luke probably knew that instinctively and was poking at the bear.

A muscle in Dustin's jaw twitched. "Chaim wasn't exactly jilted."

"Emmeline changed her mind about the wedding when her father took ill," Sidney filled in quickly as the wince that appeared at Luke's description of Chaim slowly faded away. "We're all delighted about the developments." She reached for Dustin's arm and ran a soothing hand along the fabric.

Yes, Sidney knew her husband well.

"Well, it still feels a bit inconsiderate to keep Uncle Winston and Aunt Winnie in the dark. Especially since this baby is their first grandchild." Luke fingered his chin and then shrugged.

"I'm so happy to finally meet *you*, Sidney." Charity rushed forward. "I'm sure you've heard Brandon and I spent some time in Rio Wells a couple of years ago. We found your town genuinely nice. I actually taught school for a short time."

"A *very* short time." Brandon clomped down the stairs with Colton trailing behind. "Those days feel like ancient history. Come on, we best get the buckboard to the ranch and then beat it back to Y Knot. We're not out of the woods yet with your father. I'll not rest easy until the day after the party."

"Yep, you're right. You all have fun getting to know each other." She waved with a huge smile on her face. "We'll see you later. Remember not to show your faces anywhere Father might see you. Not that he'd know either of you, but one of the townspeople might say something."

Luke and Dustin stared at her like granite statues.

"Enjoy your dinner," she babbled on, hiding a grimace. Their frowns pinned her as if she'd just grown a third eye. "Smells delicious. Faith makes the best pot roast this side of the Rockies."

Brandon placed his hand on her back and propelled her out the door.

Tonight was one strike against Dustin. Another for Luke. She'd let them both know how she felt when she could speak with them separately. Now was not the time for disagreement or fighting. If Dustin got on Faith's bad side by slighting Luke in any way at all, even the tiniest, she'd not come around soon. And what was Luke thinking, attacking Chaim? One thing Dustin wouldn't stand for was belittlement of his brother.

The last thing Charity or the others wanted was a family feud at the surprise reunion. That would not do at all.

Chapter Twenty-Nine

"Stop worrying, sweetheart," Brandon said into the dark room.

Charity was beside him, her head propped on his bare chest, and her warm body curled to his side.

"Everything'll be fine. You're torturing yourself for no good reason." He ran his hand down her back and played with her loose hair, a movement second nature since they'd wed.

"How'd you know I was still awake?" she asked into the darkness of their small home.

Her breath stirred across his chest, and he pulled her closer. Someday, they'd have their new house built on the land Charity's family gifted them for their wedding. They'd been meaning to start construction, but several factors delayed the course of action. For now, they still lived in the small bachelor home behind the town jail—and Charity hadn't complained once. "You breathe different when you're asleep. But more, your agitation is seeping through your skin and into mine." With a finger, he tipped her face up and kissed her. "Let Dustin and Luke work out their differences themselves. They're adults." Charity always carried the weight of the world on her shoulders. And nothing he could say or do would change that. He let his lips linger on hers.

"Mmmm, that was nice," she whispered. "Thank you."

"But not nice enough to shift your line of thinking."

She huffed and pulled away. "I'm sorry, Brandon, I should have listened to you. I never should have put Dustin and Luke together. I knew better. *You* knew better. I remember Dustin in Rio Wells asking all those questions about Luke and his Cheyenne heritage. The two standing face to face was enough to freeze my blood. They should be hugging and kissing, not sizing each other up."

Brandon chuckled softly and kissed the top of her head. "Hugging and kissing? That would be a sight I'd like to see. Strange but interesting."

She lifted her face and looked up at him in the darkness. "You know what I mean. I'm going to box their ears when I have a chance. Shame on them both."

He pulled her closer wanting to relieve her fears. She always felt perfect in his arms. This was where their best conversations happened. "Just stop, Charity. I can't abide you being so upset. You'll do no such thing. Just let it go. They won't fight. They're both too afraid of their spouses for that. They'll be fine once they get to know each other. They need to work this out on their own. You'll see."

"I'm also worried about Chaim and Tessa staying at the Preece farm." Charity sat up, swung her legs over the bedside, and lit the lamp.

The tiny room glowed golden.

"I wish I'd ridden out to the farm with them. Explain to Tobit and Kathryn why they were getting three guests instead of one. What if they don't have a place for Michaela to sleep? Or what if they're annoyed with me for putting them in a tight spot? I have a hundred and one different outcomes rolling around in my head."

"How about this one...*they're thrilled* Chaim came with a family. Kathryn spent the whole night holding the baby and playing with her. And you remember how easygoing your cousin is, don't you? Chaim charms everyone. He's funny and gracious. If Tobit and Kathryn don't have a place for the baby to sleep, I'm sure Chaim and Tessa will put her between them in the bed. How do you think they've managed on the trip here?" Brandon sat up, too. He wouldn't get much sleep tonight until Charity talked out her fears. "They've been dealing with the baby for nine months. It's second nature to them by now."

"Dealing with? You make Michaela sound like a broken arm or something. She's a tiny person, Brandon, with feelings."

Something much larger than her family's welfare was bothering Charity. Was Chaim showing up with a baby in his arms the reason? Or perhaps the problem was the lack of one in *theirs*? He'd begun picking up little clues for the last few months. He'd not given their lack of conception a thought, really. Seemed like only yesterday they said their *I dos*, not almost two years. He didn't think a problem existed, but *she* might. God gave you a baby at the right time, that's what he'd always heard. Maybe they weren't ready yet. Wasn't much you could do to hurry the process along, except keep trying.

In a flash of awareness, he realized they hadn't made love for almost two weeks, an incredibly long time for them. Just shy of that, he'd been summoned to Pine Grove by ol' Sheriff Huxley. The codger's telegram claimed he needed assistance with an issue, being he was hard of hearing. Brandon hadn't the heart to turn him down. The fella was getting so ancient, sometimes he just needed another lawman to chew over old cases, which made him feel young again.

Problem was, halfway through the day of checker playing, Huxley asked him to help move a bulky file cabinet from his storage area. In wrangling the thing, Brandon pulled a muscle in his back. The painful ache was like a badger, hanging on to the bitter end. He was still a little sore when Charity began feeling a bit puny. Enough so she'd not been interested. Then came the pre-party planning, which kept her preoccupied. Now the Texas McCutcheons had her distracted in a hundred different ways.

Had she noticed their lack of intimacy? The only way to help her was to be ready and willing. *Which I am!* The baby-making process—although a woman's business—began with him. He inched closer and tiptoed his fingers up her spine, the thin gown silky beneath his touch. "Come to bed, Charity. Your side's getting cold."

"Tomorrow, I'll run out to Kathryn's first thing in the morning," she replied. "I'll take a pie from the Biscuit Barrel, so they won't think I have ulterior motives. I'll rest easier if I see they're set up and Chaim and Tessa are comfortable. I don't want Father's birthday surprise to turn into a hardship for anyone."

Brandon didn't reply but edged closer. He moved her hair to the side and kissed the back of her neck feeling her shiver. "Come to bed, Charity," he whispered again.

With a low sound in her throat, she leaned back and fell into his embrace.

Slouched in the upholstered chair he'd brought into the bedroom, Chaim sat quietly, wishing he could doze off. Tessa and Michaela were fast asleep in the bed.

After a delicious supper of roasted chicken with all the fixings and apple pie for dessert, Tobit showed him around the farm. The barn, sunflower patch, and even a walk out to the fields. Tobit's first alfalfa crop was poking through the soil. He'd shared that, after last winter, free-range grazing was a thing of the past in Montana. Ranchers were fencing off their land to keep their stock close. He and his business partner, and soon to be brother-in-law, Shad Petty, planned to cash in on the new trend. Their first crop of hay would be harvested this October.

Trying to get comfortable, Chaim yawned and pulled at his blanket, causing the chair to squeak.

At the sound, the baby stirred and whimpered.

He still struggled with the amazing fact he was a father. Michaela was the prettiest baby he'd ever seen. And so alert. Nothing got past her. Tessa was amazing, as well, willing to forgo her own life to try and make Michaela's better.

His thoughts meandered to the coming party. How did he really feel about going back to Texas? Would Tessa like Rio Wells? What if she grew tired of a marriage in name only? What if she found Rio Wells too small and rustic for her liking, as Emmeline had? Would Tessa walk out on him, too? Taking Michaela? Would she ask for a divorce? With all the many uncertainties, Chaim rubbed a weary hand over his stubbled jaw.

One day at a time, he told himself. That's all a man could do. One day at a time.

Chapter Thirty

Flood relaxed back in his chair, a bit fatigued from all the heavy lifting he'd done over the past few days. He'd not complain. A little pain in his back was proof he was still alive. And that was a good thing.

"Why must you go back to the new ranch so soon, Flood?" Claire assessed her husband over the rim of her coffee cup at the dining room table. At any moment, Esperanza would appear with a hearty breakfast of eggs, potatoes, and flapjacks. "You just got back this morning. I was under the impression you were taking a few days off. Staying home. And with the ranch hands living out there for the time being, you aren't needed night and day. They're keeping watch. None of this makes any sense. What is the draw? I can't even begin to imagine."

Flood didn't miss the exasperation in his wife's voice. Still, he couldn't explain the lure. For some unknown reason, he was meant to be out at the old Lambert place. That's all he knew—

no, felt. "Don't know, sweetheart. I'm sorry. I'd tell you if I could." Claire was a patient woman—she had to be, to put up with him for so many years. That said, he was surprised at all her questions—and veiled complaints. Life on the ranch was full. Sometimes, they went from dawn to dusk without seeing each other. "I like working out there. Testing my strength makes me feel young again. I'm sorry if that upsets you."

"You're *still* young, Flood."

They both knew her assertion wasn't true, but he appreciated her effort. "I can't put my finger on any other reason."

She took a sip of her coffee and nodded. "Did you hear me? I said you're still young—and can even outwork your sons."

Another fib, but sometimes he did.

"And…your working there doesn't upset me. I'm just curious, is all."

Right…

"How did you pass the night?" she asked immediately. "Was the bed full of fleas?"

He crooked a brow. She knew very well he didn't sleep in any beds but used his bedroll under the stars. Took him right back to his youth—until morning dawned and he tried to crawl out of his blankets. Then his old bones loudly screamed their protest at his stupidity as he painstakingly straightened each limb. They felt as brittle as an old branch ready to snap. "The ground wasn't softer than it ever is, but I enjoy sleeping outside with the coyotes and owls. I can't remember the last time I did. The sight of the shimmery heavens always takes my breath away. It's God's miracle all over again every single night."

"You could sleep out here, with your grandchildren. They'd enjoy hearing your old ranching stories around the campfire. Cattle drives. Breaking the new colts. Even building a growing Y Knot." She reached over and placed her palm on his arm.

Enjoying her sudden loving attention, he marveled at how a hand so small could get so much done. He shrugged. "Ride back with me today and stay over. We'll set up our own little camp, far away from the others." He lifted a brow knowingly.

"Flood!"

"What? I'm not dead yet. I might be old, but this seasoned horse still has some races left to win. You'll feel a draw to the place, yourself." He really wasn't sure if she would. Somehow, he believed the poor soul who'd perished in the root cellar might be the key. Then again, maybe not. Regardless, Claire looked very pretty this morning with her hair braided down her back like a girl. Her cheeks turned a pretty shade of pink at his sensual proposition, and he thanked God he continued to affect her that way after all these years. Feeling more virile than ever, he hid a smile. They still had a spark.

Esperanza appeared with a platter of bacon and another of eggs.

The portions were more than they could eat, but more times than not, someone walked through the ranch house door and helped them partake.

Esperanza hurried back to the kitchen and returned with flapjacks, biscuits, and fresh whipped butter and jam.

"This looks tasty, Esperanza," Flood said. "That fresh air stirred my appetite like when I was twenty." He glanced at Claire, who'd yet to reach for any of the plates. He dished her a scoop of scrambled eggs and then served some to himself before reaching for the bacon. "Do you remember how much I could eat when I was young, Claire? Especially after a long day of work?" He laughed heartily, setting several slices of thick bacon on his plate.

"Do I remember? I was the one doing the cooking. You worked for a year just to support your food purchases at the mercantile. Land's sakes, Flood, I don't think even any of our boys ever ate as much growing up."

They both took a flapjack and smeared the fare with a generous portion of butter.

Claire refilled their coffee cups from the china coffeepot. A smile replaced her expression of amazement.

"Those were good times, weren't they?" she said. "I remember everything. I hope you do, as well…"

"Of course, I do. We've had a good life. I wouldn't change a thing."

With her eyes full of stars, she rubbed his arm a second time.

He wondered again at her attention. He was lucky. She was an affectionate woman who enjoyed being loved. But today felt different. Something had her distracted. Making her sentimental and temperamental at the same time. He didn't know what that might be.

Did she know about Sally being in the family way? Claire was good with keeping a secret. Maybe he should tell her. Or maybe she already knew. "Have you heard the good news?"

Her arm jerked, and eggs fell from her fork to her plate. "Good news?"

He leaned in. "I heard it yesterday morning. From Charity."

"What's this about?"

He had her full attention. "Sally's expecting."

"*What?*"

"Charity said you didn't know yet, but understanding our daughter the way I do, I thought she may have ridden out to the ranch and told you. Charity swore me to secrecy because Roady doesn't know yet. Now you'll have to keep the secret, too."

"What on earth?"

"What's so surprising about Sally being pregnant? The second child is always easier to conceive than the first, and Sally caught almost immediately the first time around." He laughed, enjoying her consternation. "You can close your mouth now, dear wife, before you catch a gnat. Sally must be as fertile as the barn cat. Just like *you*. There's no revelation here."

Claire straightened and then smiled. "I hadn't heard. I'm incredibly happy for both her and Roady. They have a good marriage. So in love. If Roady hadn't found her in the hunting cabin when she was snowed in, the outcome could have been disastrous. Roady's mentioned several times he'd like a large family. And Gillian is almost a year old. It's best if they're not too far apart." She patted her mouth with her napkin.

Claire always loved babies. He winked. "Guess we'll be in for more babysitting—not that I mind."

"Why should you? I do all the work, and you get all the fun."

"As it should be," he teased and bit into his bacon. "If you don't want to go back to the new ranch with me later and stay over, maybe I'll ride over to Luke's—not right away, mind you," he added quickly. He'd just gotten back after an overnight trip. With the way she'd been talking, he didn't think she'd stand for him riding off again without good reason. "I think a night in his bedroll will do Luke good, as well. With all those children under his roof, he rarely gets a minute of peace to think. Men need to get away, sometimes." He grinned.

Her mouth puckered up as if she'd just bitten into a lemon.

"You leave Luke alone! You know he indulges you more than he should, no matter the request. I heard Faith saying she wanted him to..." She blinked and reached for her coffee cup.

He crossed his arms over his chest and waited. She was acting as squirrely as a fresh colt. What had her buggered up?

The door banged open.

Colton rushed inside. Seeing them at the table, he jerked his hat from his head and dangled it in his fingers. His face was flushed. "Pa's taking me hunting," he proclaimed and puffed out his chest. The boy glanced around the room with a narrowed gaze as if he expected someone to jump out from behind a chair and refute his statement. Then a noticeably wide smile was directed at his grandmother.

Flood narrowed his eyes. What was going on?

"There. You see?" Claire blurted. "Luke is busy. He's taking Colton hunting. Faith said so the other day. Luke doesn't have time to pal around with his pa over hill and dale. He has a family to attend to." She returned Colton's smile and gestured to the biscuits. "Won't be long before Dawn will want to go hunting, as well."

Flood crooked his eyebrow. "Dawn's just a little girl, honey. Have you been in the locoweed?"

Claire fiddled with the napkin in her lap. "She's *almost* five, and I've never seen such a tomboy in my life. If you thought Charity was wild and bold as a child, you better prepare yourself, Flood McCutcheon. Your darling granddaughter will be hunting with the boys before you know it; you mark my words."

"Grandma's right. Dawn's taken over my first horse. Pa brought Firefly in from pasture last week and put her in a stall so Dawn can brush and love on her. She's been riding around the yard nearly every day."

Flood chuckled. "That old mare will teach all my grandchildren to ride. Good for her." He pointed at Colton, who was wolfing down a biscuit slathered in butter and jelly.

A glob of blueberry hung on his bottom lip before he licked it away.

"I hope you're taking your cousins hunting, too. Billy and Adam will be sore put out if you don't."

"'Course we are. Pa's over there now, doing the asking. I came over here to let Grandma know, so she don't come *looking*." He snapped his mouth closed. "You know, make a trip for nothin'."

"Only Grandma? What am I, chopped liver?"

Colton's chuckle sounded just like Luke. "You know you're not chopped liver." Colton circled the table and gave Flood a hug, a poignant display out of character for him. "You're usually busy doing something, Grandpa. Everyone has—"

"Skedaddle, Colton!" Claire sharply interrupted. "You're talking like a magpie. You don't want to keep the others waiting." She stood and pointed toward the door.

Something had Claire riled—or, if not riled, acting strange. If he was suspicious before, now, he was sure of it. First, her annoyance with him for being gone, and then her displeasure when he'd mentioned going back. That wasn't like her. She usually let him come and go unfettered. He thought back. Maybe she was hitting one of those markers when women's biology changed. Or, more likely, she was lonely after last night, thinking about this big, empty ranch house and had romantic plans in store today. They rarely slept apart. Perhaps she'd missed him more than he knew. What else could it be?

"You listen to your grandma, Colton. And good luck hunting. I'll expect a nice haunch of venison when you return. Deer or elk, makes no nevermind. Either sounds perfect for a night under the stars." He was teasing her again. And by the look of her, he'd better stop soon, or he'd never find out what she had in mind.

With a sheepish smile, Colton plopped his hat back on his head, turned, and headed out the door.

Chapter Thirty-One

When she heard Kathryn Preece ask for her assistance baking pies for the party, Tessa jumped at the chance. Early morning light streamed through the farmhouse window, muting her memories of the night before. Chaim across the room, sleeping in a chair. Her snuggled in the bed with Michaela. Yes, she'd traveled with him by stagecoach and then by train, but sleeping in the same room while wearing her nightgown was new. A nerve-wracking experience she'd need to get used to quickly, lest they give their secret away. She'd lain awake for hours, listening to his breathing. Was he also pondering what their life held in store?

"How did you and Chaim meet?" Kathryn asked, wrapped in a red-and-white polka-dot apron, her hands messy with piecrust. She mixed the pastry gently, as if touching spun glass instead of pie dough—to keep it flaky, she'd explained.

Mouthwatering scents filled the spacious farmhouse kitchen. Over the stove and doorway, the buttercream-colored walls were decorated with porcelain molds brightly painted in warm golden crimson to a soft, cool, cerulean blue. Happy, blue-and-white gingham curtains adorned the large window. The spice rack was filled to overflowing with jars and containers. A framed painting of a farmyard and the surrounding fields with square borders reminded Tessa of a patchwork quilt. Six finished pies stood on the open windowsill.

"Tessa?"

She and Chaim told everyone they'd fallen in love in Arizona, and in actuality, that *was* where they'd met. But what did she know about Arizona? Not much. "Chaim and I met on the street quite unexpectedly. His vivid blue eyes startled me, and then he smiled at my surprised expression. We began to talk. No man should be gifted with such gorgeous eyes." *Where had that come from? I'm not sure, but it's true.*

Kathryn smiled her approval. "Was it love at first sight?"

Tessa felt uneasy about fibbing. This deception had painted her into a corner of no escape. But she could do nothing else but go forward. Keeping to her job, she sifted flour over the crust Kathryn had rolled out as her mind circled how to answer such an innocent question. She and Chaim should have taken the time to talk through the finer details. "Not actually love at first sight, but compared to others I've known, I guess you'd say our relationship developed quite quickly."

"I don't know if you've heard…" Kathryn carefully lifted the finished crust and laid it into a pie dish. She pressed the rim with her fingertips, creating a pretty edge. "…but I was a mail order bride. Tobit sent to Philadelphia for me after he met Heather Sandford, the mail order bride who married Hayden Klinkner." She looked at Tessa and raised a brow. "You don't know Heather and Hayden yet, but you will soon. And there's another mail order bride living in Y Knot, as well. Evie Davenport Holcomb. She was first to come to Y Knot to marry, then Heather, and then me."

Tessa stored the names away, trying to keep everyone straight.

Kathryn set the pie dish away and plopped a second popcorn-ball size of crust on the counter. She waited for Tessa to sprinkle an ample amount of flour over the top, as well as the surrounding surface. Afterwards, Kathryn began moving the rolling pin in short pushes, turning it this way and that with a *clomp-clomp-clomp.* "We met at the matrimonial agency in St. Louis, and we're all very close friends."

"I've heard of the concept, of course, but I've never known anyone who actually became a mail order bride. When you arrived, was it love at first sight for you and Tobit?"

Kathryn laughed, her cheeks turning a bright pink. "Hardly. The only reason he sent for me was to give him a child before his grandfather passed away! Can you imagine?" She caressed her tummy lovingly. "Isaiah's true heart's desire was to bounce his great-grandchild on his knee before he died. Since Isaiah gifted the farm to my husband, being the good man he is, Tobit wanted to fulfill his grandfather's dream—*before he passed on*—and without much conversation with his wife-to-be. Thing was, Tobit had explained everything to me in a letter before we agreed on the marriage, but the correspondence went astray and has never been found." She leaned into the rolling pin, moving forward and back.

Her arm and back muscles worked in the process and the small, butter-yellow crust grew large and round, emitting a delicious scent. Tessa's mouth watered.

"Needless to say, I was quite shocked when the truth came out—as it always does. I felt like an old brood mare, but he had no idea why I was acting so distraught."

"Oh, my stars." The exclamation shot out of Tessa's mouth before she knew what she was about. "I'm sorry—I didn't mean to…well, I can't imagine what I'd do under those circumstances." *I guess my journey to the altar isn't that shocking, after all.*

"And you don't know the half of it. On my way to Y Knot, before I boarded the stagecoach in Waterloo, a travel case fell off the top of the transport and hit me on the head. When I finally arrived, I didn't remember a thing. Not the letters from Tobit. Not why I was traveling to an unknown town. Not even my dear friends Evie and Heather. The doctor forbade them from telling me anything about the past, who I was, and why I was here, because doing so, he said, might worsen my amnesia." Kathryn began to giggle and was soon doubled over in laughter, tears running down her cheeks. "I'm sorry, I've just never quite expounded on our strange courtship before."

The kitchen door opened and Tobit, followed by Chaim carrying Michaela, stepped inside.

"What's so amusing?" Tobit asked. "Dare I ask? Kathryn, I've never seen you so full of laughter."

Chaim sought Tessa's gaze, and a half smile appeared.

The sight of him holding Michaela warmed her, as it always did, and she knew bringing the child to her father was a decision she'd never regret. But tying Chaim to herself…

With a hand on her middle, Kathryn gasped for air. "One minute," she eked out, between gulps. "Let me catch my breath. I just told Tessa how we met, after she shared about meeting Chaim." She glanced at Chaim. "Yours is such a romantic story, Chaim. Your vivid blue eyes captured Tessa's attention and stopped her on the street." She touched Tessa's arm. "I see what you mean and totally agree."

"Not quite like our story?" Tobit deadpanned. "Amnesia and letters gone astray? Before we could say "I do" you let me know *you didn't* and left the farm to live in town."

Kathryn crossed the room, went up on tiptoe, and kissed her husband right in front of everyone. "I do—and I *still* do, Tobit Preece. I only have eyes for you."

Tobit didn't seem to mind her pie-crusted fingers splayed on his crisp blue shirt for balance. All the couples she'd met seemed incredibly affectionate and not the least bit shy about displaying their feelings. So different from the Jordans' household. She couldn't remember hearing their laughter or witnessing a kiss.

"Tessa, did Kathryn mention she was married in a pair of paint-splattered overalls with a kerchief on her head?" He glanced at his wife and pointed at her kerchief. "Quite like the one she's wearing today. Actually, if I remember correctly, it *is* the one she's wearing today."

Feeling conspicuous standing alone on the other side of the room, Tessa crossed and stopped beside Chaim, his presence keenly felt.

Michaela leaned from his embrace with outstretched arms.

Tessa gathered her close. "Overalls? I can't imagine. Why?"

"That's another story Kathryn can share later," Tobit said. "Right now, we came in to see if you'd like to take a short break from your baking. The foals are frisky this morning, and their antics have Michaela laughing up a storm." He winked at Tessa. "I'm sure you'll like the show, too."

Chaim must have felt pressured from Tobit and Kathryn's display, because he put his arm around her shoulder and pulled her closer, which caused Michaela to smile up into his face with the most endearing expression. The baby had come to love her daddy in the short time they'd been together. "I'd love to see,"

Tessa said. "As long as Kathryn agrees. She's the one in charge of the pies. I'm only the helper."

Kathryn removed her apron and washed her hands. "No pies in the oven to worry about. That makes my decision easy."

Tessa noticed Kathryn's gaze tracked between her and Chaim with a slightly lifted brow. Did she have any suspicions about their relationship? If she did, she kept them well hidden.

Chapter Thirty-Two

Outside, Chaim lounged against the fence of the Preece farm pasture with one eye on the three foals romping in the thick, boot-tall grass and the other on Tessa and her wonder at the sight. Growing up in the city couldn't have provided much time for relaxation or enjoyment with her mother being the only breadwinner. Empathy filled his chest. She'd missed a lot as a girl. The smile on her face made her appear innocent and impressionable. The sunlight made her blonde hair glitter.

"Look," Tessa pointed, a V pulling her brows together. "The tallest is such a troublemaker. It keeps nipping the other two and chasing them around. The smallest wants to taste the pocket of grass by the trunk of the tree and isn't allowed to."

"That's because the tallest is a colt and the other two are fillies." Chaim felt certain from her upbringing she knew little about animals.

"Thank you, Husband," she responded in a teasing tone. "Chaim knows I'm a city girl," she said to Kathryn. "That young horse might be a colt, but he's *still* a troublemaker in my book. The fillies are minding their own business, nibbling the grass, and he won't let them. *Shame* on him."

When the small roan filly Tessa referenced lashed out lightning-fast with a hind leg and connected with the muscular bay colt's chin the two women burst into laughter.

He pulled up in shock and pain, shaking his head.

"Oh, that must smart," Kathryn added, between laughs.

"She takes care of herself just fine," Tobit exclaimed. "She may appear smaller, but I've noticed she usually gets her way."

The three grown mares and two geldings also grazing in the pasture ignored the people.

"That's a handsome colt," Chaim remarked to Tobit. The horse did have nice lines, but his thoughts were more on last night's dinner and the hour the four of them spent in the parlor after Isaiah and Michaela had gone to bed. The settee he and Tessa shared was hardly much larger than a wide chair. She'd been nestled to his side, distracting him.

When Chaim turned to respond to something she'd say, their faces were only inches apart. Her clean scent tickled his nose. Feeling the pressure from Tobit and Kathryn, who'd been holding hands, he'd taken Tessa's in his own. She readily complied, the contact causing warmth to creep up his arm and fill his chest. Theirs was a marriage of convenience. Tessa suggested it out of her love for Michaela. Her need to shelter his daughter's future. And, perhaps, a little out of her desire to finally have a last name. He commended her for the first two reasons and didn't fault her for the third. Every person desired to belong. The more he got to know her, the more his doubts over the unusual agreement faded. Especially when he'd been holding her small, warm hand.

"Again, I'll say it. The tall colt is a showstopper. I'll be surprised if you don't use him for breeding."

"That's what I'm thinking too, Chaim, but I appreciate you saying so with all your experience. He's sired by the McCutcheons' stallion." He pointed to a sorrel mare apart from the others, her sagging back and the graying around her eyes and muzzle apparent. "We won't get many more foals from his dam. She's nearing eighteen."

The three foals, curiosity shining in their dark, luminous eyes, approached the fence a few feet from the women.

Tessa did her best to hold Michaela high enough to see over the fence, but the baby still didn't have a clear view.

"Let me take her, Tessa," he offered, feeling very husbandly today. "She's getting much too large for you to lift for an extended time." Something about the warm sun on his back and the look in Tessa's eyes made feeling like a loving husband easy. Just as Emmeline had, he reminded himself. He'd never in a million years have thought his ex-fiancée would abandon their love so easily. Was he blind? Or had Emmeline been experienced at hoodwinking? He'd never know now, but that didn't mean he'd be blind to the future again. And that meant Tessa. He'd not let down his guard.

"Thank you," his wife said softly and handed the baby over.

But she stayed close, making his senses spring to life. When he held Michaela up so she could see over the top rail, he was surprised to feel Tessa's hand lightly on his back. The warmth from her palm quickly seeped through his shirt and branded his skin. He glanced down at her and smiled.

She answered him with questions in her eyes, as if asking permission. Hoping her show of affection wasn't offensive to him.

His thoughts at this moment, and his perception of her actions, were in complete opposition.

Chapter Thirty-Three

The party night finally arrived. Chaim lingered with the rest of his Texas family, hidden away in the back room of the Biscuit Barrel Café, waiting for his Uncle Flood, the unsuspecting guest of honor, to arrive to his surprise party. The group crowded together, quietly whispering in the dimly lit storeroom. Chaim's father silently stared at his boot tips, not having seen his brother for many years.

Tessa stood calmly at his side, holding Michaela.

His wife's clean, lemony scent was now familiar after several nights together in the upper bedroom of the Preece farm. He'd been amazed someone, namely one of his sisters, hadn't commented on the dark circles sagging beneath his eyes from lack of sleep.

"Should be any time," Madeline whispered. "I'll be so delighted to be free to explore the town and meet a few people once tonight is over. Staying hidden away in the Klinkner household has been challenging." She smiled at Becky and Wendy, close at her side. "Heather and Ina are very nice."

The three were gussied up for the party, looking extremely excited and happy. He'd not seen his sisters, or Miss Knutson, since they'd arrived. Or his parents and Dustin and Sidney, for that matter. For the past half hour, they'd exchanged stories and highlights of their short time in Y Knot.

"And you, John, must be chomping at the bit," Dustin added. "To be home and not be able to show yourself must be difficult. Tonight, we'll all be set free."

"True." John held Clara with Lily by his side. "But I've had a good few days catching up with my brothers. Luke's been over. As well as Matt and my mother. It'll be fantastic to finally see Father. And soon."

While keeping out of sight in the storeroom of the Biscuit Barrel, ranch hands and close friends who'd already arrived at the gazebo behind the café stuck their heads inside to briefly introduce themselves so there wouldn't be a need once the party started. Along with all the ranch hands from the Heart of the Mountains, Chaim and the rest had met numerous, happy-faced shop owners and townsfolk. Chaim felt right at home.

At the sound of the door opening, the whispering stopped.

A moment later, Charity stepped inside. Her face beamed, matching the golden fabric of her dress. "They're almost here," she said breathlessly. "They're arriving alone, everyone else having abandoned them earlier today with so much to do. Father thinks they're meeting the family at the Biscuit Barrel for pie and ice cream." She paused to laugh quietly. "You'll hear a lot of cheering once they arrive and Father reads the banner. He'll think the party is the *only* surprise. I'll send Roady, or whoever is closest, to fetch you all when we're ready for the *big* surprise. Just come on out and join us in the gazebo. The Twilight Singers are set up, but they don't take up much room."

"We'll be ready for you," Winston assured her, his deep voice steady and calm. "Now take a few calming breaths, Charity. You look ready to swoon."

She straightened and turned her head. "I hear the buggy. I'm sure Father's noticed the crowd by now and wonders what's happening. There's hardly a spot to tie a horse or park a wagon."

"Get going," Dustin prompted. "You don't want to miss anything. We're ready to get out there."

Chaim eyed his brother. He hadn't had more than a few moments alone with Dustin since arriving and wondered how he was doing staying with Luke. Chaim looked forward, as well, to meeting his legendary cousin.

Charity gave a small wave and disappeared out the door.

Their group listened intently. Charity must have been right, because it was only two or three minutes before they heard a roar of laughter and then applause. Music started, and they heard a crowd singing "For He's a Jolly Good Fellow."

When it was about to conclude, Francis stuck his head inside. "Time to go!"

A lump the size of Montana lodged in Flood's throat and refused to budge. He blinked and read the sign again. HAPPY 50th BIRTHDAY, FLOOD. YOU TRULY ARE THE HEART OF THE MOUNTAINS. The crowd was so large, it looked as if every living soul in Y Knot had turned out. The group stretched from the gazebo all the way back to the trees and then spilled around the edges. And for him? For his fiftieth birthday, if he was reading the sign correctly. Didn't they know his fiftieth was last year?

He glanced at Claire, stars shining in her eyes.

"I know what you're thinking, Husband," she said between her laughter. "We know how old you are. But last year, with all the snow and death, was just too tragic to celebrate anything. The family decided to wait a year and make it *really* special. We all want you to know just how much you mean to us, Jefferson Flood McCutcheon! You're the lifeblood of our family, and this town."

When Claire finished, his family, his sons, and his daughter, as well as all their spouses and children, rushed him on the stage. He didn't think he'd ever been so surprised or filled with emotion. The hugging and kissing went on for a good five minutes. They finally moved back so he could catch his breath. When he looked up, he thought he was seeing things.

Winston? Winston, his brother?

Winston stepped forward, his smile a mile wide.

Flood sucked in a great draught of air, undecided if he dare trust his senses.

Winston gripped his shoulders and pulled him into an embrace. "Good to see you, little brother."

The sound came out in an emotional croak next to his head.

"Far too many years have passed without us reuniting. We'll not let such a travesty happen again."

"You're right. We sure won't." Flood relished the feel of his brother's strong arms wrapped around him. His eyes welled. Everything else faded away, and he felt eight years old with Winston looking out for his hide from the schoolhouse bully. "I can't believe you've come all the way to Y Knot. I'm speechless."

Winston pulled back and wiped his own tears as they smiled at each other like two town fools. Winston gestured with the sweep of his arm. "Meet my family, Flood. We've had a chance to meet most everyone while waiting for you to arrive. We've been hidden away for the last few days, looking forward to shocking the stuffing out of you. I kind of like seeing you like this."

In disbelief, Flood listened as Winston introduced everyone. He knew Winnie, of course, but he hadn't seen her for years. She was still an attractive woman in every way. He met his two grown nephews and their wives, and his two nieces, as well as their friend from Rio Wells. Seeing Dustin and Chaim standing among his sons, talking and shaking hands, brought an extra meaningful moment to his heart. The new generation of McCutcheons were remarkable. The men presented a powerful force: tall and well-built. He couldn't have been prouder if he'd been elected president of the United States. Among them were Madeline and Becky and his Charity, all magnificent.

"That's not all, Husband," Claire said softly. "Turn around."

What more could there be? His mind was mush with all the surprises.

Turning, he found John Jake beaming. His eyes dancing with joy. At his side stood Lily, prettier than he imagined her, and Clara, his newest granddaughter, named for Claire. "John Jake!" Feeling as if he'd embarrass himself any second, he grasped John and tugged him into his arms. "John. John. You're home. I can't believe all this. I'm out of my mind with happiness seeing you, son. I've missed you every day."

"I know, Pa. And I you. It's incredible to be home. Back in Y Knot. It's been far too long, indeed."

Flood pulled away and turned to Lily. He held out his arms and they embraced, him being careful not to crush little Clara. "Welcome to Y Knot, and to your family. We're so happy to finally meet you." He looked down at the baby girl he'd heard all about in letters. "And Clara." He caressed her cheek, which was still damp. She must have been frightened by all the excitement but had just stopped crying.

"We were so happy to finally make the trip," Lily replied in a soft German accent. "John has told me all about the family and growing up in Montana. I feel incredibly welcomed."

Flood tickled the baby. "Of course, you are. You'll have a difficult time returning to Rio Wells because I don't think I'll let you go. There's plenty of room on the ranch for another household."

A hand on Flood's shoulder made him look up.

"Everyone's waiting patiently to greet you, Pa," Luke said. "No one is going anywhere for over two weeks, so you'll have plenty of time with John and Lily and everyone. Now you need to say hello to some of your guests."

Flood glanced again out to the crowd. "Doing so will take me all night."

"So be it." Luke nodded to the Twilight Singers, who lined up in formation. "Let's get this party underway."

Chapter Thirty-Four

Tessa stood on the fringe of the crowd, holding a sleepy Michaela in her arms. The meal had been eaten and the dance floor set up. The warm Montana air felt like velvet on her skin. Although Michaela was completely worn out by the hectic day, Tessa could tell she was struggling to stay awake as they watched the dancers waltz by.

At the moment, Chaim was off somewhere doing an errand for his mother.

Tessa noticed them speaking, and then he'd strode away around the building, and Tessa couldn't imagine where he'd gone. All the other McCutcheons were dancing, the men standing head and shoulders over most of the group. Several of the ranch hands from the Heart of the Mountains ventured over to where she stood watching and asked her to dance. She'd politely declined, saying she had no place to leave her daughter.

Two she knew were the Pettys, who'd driven the buggies and wagon the night they'd all arrived from Waterloo. As well as a weather-beaten fella named Smokey.

She'd also met the other two mail order brides before the big surprise. Evie, with her handsome husband, Chance Holcomb, and their darling son, Garth. And Heather and Hayden, the two Kathryn told her about who'd spurred Tobit on to send for her.

Luke and his wife, Faith, were making their way in her direction. They stopped before her. "Where's Chaim made off to?" Luke asked, tickling Michaela under her chin.

"Actually, I'm not sure."

"Well," Luke stated, "I've come to claim this dance. It's not right all the McCutcheon women are out there under the stars and not our newest." He put out his hand in invitation.

"I couldn't. Michaela is quite sleepy, and I don't have a place to leave her. I…"

"That's my job," Faith said with a smile. "I'll guarantee you I'll not let her get upset. I'm a professional baby talker." She laughed and glanced up into her husband's face. "Isn't that right, Luke?"

"I can vouch for her, Tessa. No baby can get the best of my wife and, if for some unfathomable reason she does, she'll be right here, and you can take over. I promise we'll not be out of sight for even one second."

Tessa was tempted. The mix of the nice evening, the talented singers, as well as the feel of the love of the group, she wanted to say yes.

"Come on. We don't have many chances to dance here in Y Knot. You've got to seize the day when you can."

How could she turn down Chaim's cousin? She'd heard his story from Chaim, how Claire was abducted and, when she was rescued, she was with child, making Luke the son of a Cheyenne warrior. The telling was remarkable, and Tessa came to the conclusion Claire McCutcheon was as tough as her children to survive such a trial. And to come out seemingly unaffected. The woman was nothing but kind and helpful to everyone. "If you're sure?"

"We are." Faith put her hands out to Michaela, who rested her head on Tessa's shoulder while listening to the conversation.

Since Luke's and Faith's arrival, the song, "Oh, My Darling Clementine," ended, and another tune began. It didn't look like this crowd was breaking up any time soon. Tessa kissed the top of Michaela's head and slowly passed her over, expecting the howl she knew would come. But, it didn't.

Dustin and Sidney smiled as they waltzed past.

Next came John and Lily, nodding their approval.

Mark and Amy, then Matt and Rachel soon joined the family, anxious to see the newest of the McCutcheon wives make her debut onto the dance floor.

Tessa remained several seconds as Michaela settled in on Faith's shoulder, her eyes drooping to half-mast.

"I think this'll work," Faith breathed softly. "Just don't dance out of our sight, and we'll be fine."

Tessa nodded and took Luke's proffered hand.

He held her left out and rested his other on her side, keeping a respectable distance.

Luke McCutcheon was an expert on the dance floor. He made more turns than normal to keep them in her sleepy baby's line of sight. As she relaxed, a small smile appeared on his lips.

"Let me say it again, Tessa," he said softly, over the music. "Welcome to the family. I know you've been in the family for quite some time."

He glanced at Michaela, under the mistaken impression she and Chaim had married and then conceived the baby, that taking at least nine months.

"How do you like Montana and the extended family?" He gave a conspiratorial wink. "And even your direct family?" He gestured to Dustin and Sidney with a tip of his head. "Must be daunting, meeting everyone at the same time."

She could tell he was teasing her and not really digging for information. Who wouldn't want such a large, loving family? A person would have to have their head examined if they had any objections with any small part.

She smiled up into Luke's face as he waited for her reply. "Any woman unhappy after the last few days would be considered extremely foolish. Every single person has been more than welcoming to Michaela and myself. This party is the perfect opportunity to meet the whole clan in one fell swoop." She smiled and nodded to Lily, who was passing in John's arms and watching her and Luke with interest. "Lily is undergoing my experience on a smaller scale. She's known her Texas family for some time and is just now meeting her in-laws. I'm sure you're all delighted to make her and baby Clara's acquaintance."

"I see you've skillfully turned the questions back to me. I respect a resourceful woman. Yes, we're gratified to finally have my younger brother home, along with his wife and daughter. We'd all really like them to stay."

She arched a brow. "Will they do that? I hear he's quite settled in Texas now. And Lily has her thriving business, as well."

They twirled once in front of Faith and the baby, bringing a smile to Michaela's lips.

"We all know their remaining when the rest of you go home is a lost cause, or should I say to your *new* home, but we can't help but dream."

Dustin and Sidney danced up close to their side.

"Good to see you on the dance floor, Tessa." He glanced at Luke. "Let me know if he doesn't behave himself." A half-teasing, half-watchdog smile split Dustin's face.

"No worries here, Cousin," Luke replied for her. "Your new sister-in-law is having a fine time under the Montana stars. You can let your guard down and relax—if doing so is possible. I won't carry her off, if that's what you think."

Such talk. What in the name of God would induce such a conversation? She knew how Luke was conceived. And she did see his darker hair, straight eyebrows, and high cheekbones. But bringing up any of that now seemed scandalous. Tessa's face scalded.

Luke turned her in the opposite direction. "He's been testing me ever since he arrived. Like everyone else at one time or another, he's curious about my Cheyenne blood. We're butting heads—in a nice way—so don't let our exchange worry you. He and Sidney are staying with us, but I believe they're planning to move to the large ranch house, since the surprise is over, for the remaining two weeks. I don't take offense. Actually, I'm used to it. When I was younger, I couldn't say the same. My brothers claimed I had a chip on my shoulder the size of a barn." He gave a deep rumbling laugh just as the music was ending. "I've come to learn to roll with the punches. The only thing in life worth fighting over is my family. And I won't be doing that here in Y Knot."

As the last notes faded, he delivered her back to Faith's side.

His wife had successfully taken a seat without upsetting Michaela.

The baby's eyes were closed as she slept on Faith's shoulder.

"She's such a sweetie pie," Faith whispered. "I can see the McCutcheon resemblance between her and Holly. Tall, rounded foreheads, wide-set eyes. She's beautiful, Tessa. I'm sure you and Chaim are enormously proud of her." She gently rubbed Michaela's back as they quietly talked. "You should dance again while she's sleeping. I don't mind."

Tessa felt a prick of panic. Where was Chaim? She didn't feel like dancing with anyone again. She wanted Chaim. "I just wonder where Chaim has made off to. I thought he'd be back by now," she stalled.

"You sit here with Faith," Luke suggested. "I'll fetch you both some punch, unless you'd rather have something stronger?"

Relief coursed through her as she sank into a chair. "Punch sounds delightful. Thank you."

Faith nodded, as well.

Luke strode away.

"It's not often a young mother gets time to herself, even sitting next to her child," Faith said. "I know. Enjoy it while you can."

"Truer words were never said." Tessa stretched back and studied the stars for a few moments.

"Do you have family in Arizona?" Faith asked offhandedly.

More to cover the silence than to be nosy, Tessa was sure. "Actually, I don't. I was there for my job. After I met Chaim, I gave up my position." What could she say now? She didn't want to lie to anyone, and especially not Faith.

Faith looked at her as if she expected her to go on, divulge where she was from, and about her family.

But the truth was too dangerous. Coming from the same town as Emmeline, anyone could make the connection. "Do you think I might sneak away and visit the…" She left the sentence unfinished. "Luke will be back with our punch in a few minutes."

"Of course. This little one won't even know you're gone. And if there's a line, don't worry. I can entertain her if she wakes up. When nature calls, there's little choice."

Feeling like the biggest deceiver ever, Tessa stood and hurried away, praying God would forgive her. Her mother-in-law smiled as she passed, the older woman in a conversation with Claire McCutcheon. Winnie had taken Tessa under her wing the moment they'd met in Waterloo. Would she feel the same if she knew Emmeline was her cousin, and the birthmother of Michaela? The thought made Tessa shudder. One little deceit led to another and another....

Chapter Thirty-Five

Chaim strode purposely along the fringe of the crowd, a small cradle in his arms. He spotted Tessa, her face flushed and her hair a bit out of place. He wondered where she'd gone off to as she made her way through the people back toward where he'd last left her. Surprisingly, Michaela wasn't anywhere in sight.

She pulled up when she saw him, questions in her eyes.

"I'm sorry," he said. "Ina offered us..." He lifted the woven basket he'd been sent away to retrieve. "This." It was large enough for an older baby and lined with a soft blanket. "So we can dance and enjoy the party. She's also offered to come sit with her, as well, so you won't worry. I didn't know fetching the contraption back from the mill would take quite this long. I intended to surprise you."

Her face lit up. "How kind of Ina. And thoughtful of you to make the effort. Is the mill close by?"

"Yes, actually. But getting the wagon free through all the other buggies and buckboards took me longer than driving to her place and back. As the saying goes, the best laid plans…"

The quip brought a slight smile to her lips.

He wanted her to be at ease with him. "You've been dancing?"

"How can you tell?"

"Your face is the color of roses."

She pressed a hand to her cheeks, and her eyes lit with pleasure. "Yes, I have. Your cousin, Luke, insisted. When I tried to refuse, Faith came forward and offered to hold Michaela."

"And Michaela didn't cry?"

Tessa shook her head. "I was surprised, too, but no. She's extremely tired." Tessa fingered the basket. "This is a fine idea. I think she'll fall asleep the moment we lay her down."

Chaim hid his disappointment. Even after his iron-clad decision not to let his heart run away with him, he'd been looking forward to holding Tessa in his arms. He'd wanted to be the first to dance with her. They hadn't had a wedding dance, and this would count as such. He didn't fault his cousin for asking, and he appreciated the fact others were looking out for her. Luke wanted to make her feel welcome. But Chaim hadn't even had the pleasure of watching. "Let's go see how Michaela likes this." He glanced around wondering why she was over here and not by the dance floor where he'd left her.

Tessa lifted a shoulder. "Nature called."

He grinned. "Happens to the best of us. Ina will be along any moment. If we're not in the intended spot when she arrives, she may wonder what happened."

"Are you sure she doesn't mind? I'd hate to keep her from enjoying the party."

"I can only go by what she told me. She's anxious for her own grandchild to coddle and will practice with ours. You know Heather is due in only a couple of months."

Tessa nodded. "I guess we shouldn't look a gift horse in the mouth," she replied, not meeting his gaze.

Was she as nervous as he was for their first dance? He'd promised himself he'd not be fooled again. Emmeline had pulled the rug from under his feet. *But I've been lonely so long.*

He could feel himself softening toward Tessa. Ever since their wedding in Waterloo, he'd begun to look at her in a different, softer light—a light that said she was the special someone he could entrust with his heart. Just like his father and mother, and Dustin with Sidney. And doing so felt right, not wrong. If only he could speak with his brother about the situation, but keeping Michaela's true maternity secret was vital. And his wife, who knew more than most on the subject, desired him to do so. "True enough," he said on a chuckle. He liked Tessa to make decisions and speak her mind. At least, his wife wasn't shy about that. "Lead the way, before this gift horse finds another baby to watch."

Tessa sucked in a deep breath. "Chaim!"

"I'm just teasing…"

Tessa turned and threaded her way through the people back toward the dance floor. She wore the same dress she'd worn to their wedding. She'd gathered some blooms from the farmyard flower garden and woven them into her hair. She looked beautiful. Young and willowy. She carried herself with poise, head up and shoulders back. Had her mother schooled her on such things, or did she pick them up from living with the Jordans? So much he still didn't know about his wife.

When she spotted their approach, Michaela's droopy eyes widened.

Luke was nowhere to be seen, but Dustin and the rest of his cousins were still on the dance floor, along with a mass of others. It looked as if this shindig would go into the wee hours of the night.

"What a good idea," Faith said, admiring the basket bed. She handed Michaela over to Tessa, who rocked her for a few moments and then laid her on her back into the bed.

For one instant, Michaela struggled to sit up.

But with gentle encouragement, and a whispered song close to her head from Tessa, she laid back and closed her eyes.

"It belongs to Mrs. Klinkner," Chaim explained. "She'll be along shortly, now that I'm back."

"Shall I watch her until Ina arrives?" Faith asked.

"Thank you, no. You've already done so much," Tessa replied. "Everyone has made us feel so at home. I can never thank you enough."

"You *are* at home, Tessa. You, too, Chaim. You're McCutcheons. We're all so delighted you came to help make this day perfect. We could never thank *you* enough."

Chaim smiled, feeling humbled. His gaze searched out Tessa's, wondering if she had the same deep ache in her heart.

"Well, I'm off to find Luke. I'm not sure where my husband went." She gestured to a cup of punch on the ground next to the chair. "That's yours, Tessa. He did return with our drinks, at least." With a small laugh, she was gone.

The moment Ina arrived, she shushed them out onto the dance floor without a word and sat next to the basket.

Chaim had wanted to say, "Mrs. McCutcheon, may I have this dance, our wedding dance?" But he didn't want to overplay his hand. The night felt sentimental. Tessa's position was clear. *In name only.* That may be true, but that didn't mean they couldn't enjoy their time together.

Chapter Thirty-Six

Tessa slipped into Chaim's arms, feeling small and desired, and timidly placed her hand on the strong ridge of his shoulder. Was it her imagination, or did his embrace feel extra caring, and the warmth in his eyes raw? The mind was strong and could create any condition it desired. Her mother was fooled to the detriment of her whole life, which affected Tessa, as well. She needed to keep a clear head and, more importantly, a clear heart.

She felt paralyzed to pull her gaze from his. He cocooned her hand within his own and placed it on his heart, drawing her closer. He laid his other on the small of her back, causing a rush of tingles to skitter up her spine. His chest was warm and the contact personal. Why was he holding her so closely? For the benefit of his family, his mother and father? For the story they'd created at the dinner in Waterloo and then again when they'd spoken their vows? She reminded herself not to read anything into his actions, but doing so was difficult with how handsome he looked under the stars, the music whispering in her soul, and the warmth of his hand around hers.

When she'd danced with Luke, she'd done her best not to miss a step, but doing so took total concentration. Living with the Jordans, she hadn't had much opportunity to dance or gather socially, although she'd learned much from Emmeline. At least, her cousin made sure she received a basic understanding of such things. But here feeling safe in Chaim's arms, she relaxed. No one was watching her but Chaim.

"What do you think of my family?" he asked as they glided in between the others.

His eyes searched hers in a way she'd yet to see before. She wanted to believe his attention was real, the close embrace, the care in his eyes, not some part of the pretense. When had she decided that?

"They're an interesting bunch," he went on with a chuckle when she didn't instantly reply. He gave a slight shrug and her hand on his shoulder rose and then lowered.

She smiled at Matt and Rachel as they waltzed past. "They're amazing. All of them." She cringed at the breathless quality of her voice. His nearness was heady. His masculine scent wrapped around her senses and didn't let go. As they turned, she saw Chaim's mother and father watching them from the side of the dance floor. Then they were next to the young ranch hand named Francis. He danced with his intended, both their young faces filled with happiness.

"They're your family now, too," he said. "I hope you can live with that."

Before she could reply, Dustin and Sidney swirled to their side.

"There you are," Dustin said. "I thought we lost you. Where've you been?"

For one second, Chaim released her hand, bringing a surge of disappointment.

He hooked his thumb over his shoulder toward Ina. "I went to the mill for a crib for Michaela. She's asleep over there."

Only a split second passed until he reclaimed her hand and pulled her back to his chest. Even Dustin and Sidney weren't dancing as close.

"The joys of fatherhood," Dustin quipped, and then a serious look entered his eyes. "It looks good on you, Brother. I'm envious as all get out. Congratulations. I'm delighted to be an uncle."

With that, Dustin and Sidney expertly twirled away, making Tessa wonder how many times they'd danced together throughout their married life. Many, she supposed, with a twinge of envy. When her stride faltered, Chaim pulled her closer.

"Relax. I've got you. And you're doing fine. No one here can tell this is our first dance together. I promise."

John and Lily were at their side. Lily looked pretty in John's arms.

"Evening, John." Chaim eased Tessa even closer. "How was your reunion with your father? He certainly looked surprised."

John's face clouded over. "I should never have waited so long to come home. Doing so was wrong. I was only thinking of myself." He took a deep breath, clearly disturbed. "But I can only learn from my mistakes. I'll return to Y Knot more often. The travel wasn't difficult."

"It wasn't the travel, John. It was your medical practice," Lily corrected softly. "You didn't want to leave your patients. That's commendable."

John shrugged and then smiled at Tessa. He tipped his head. "Either you remind me of someone, Tessa, or we've met before. No amount of talking will convince me otherwise. I just haven't figured out where, yet."

She fumbled a step.

Chaim's gaze found hers.

She hadn't mentioned she'd met John McCutcheon at the Jordans' home in Boston. So much had happened since their arrival, the incident had slipped her mind. Dread at the realization, and how the truth would tarnish her relationship with the rest of Chaim's family, blossomed. Since their arrival in Waterloo, no one mentioned Emmeline. Not one person. But they had to think something. If only she could keep John McCutcheon from remembering. Or maybe she could throw off his suspicions. But doing so seemed dishonest, too, even if she could figure out how. She didn't want to compound their duplicity.

"I can't imagine where," Chaim finally replied.

Tessa could see her husband was working something over in his mind.

"And neither can I. That's the problem. I've never been to Arizona—although I'd like to see the area, after everything Chaim has told me. The land sounds magical."

And hot! "I wish I could help you," Tessa said, giving a small shrug.

Lily laughed and patted John's shoulder. "You're imagining things. Let Tessa and Chaim enjoy the evening. The stars and the music. We've been anticipating the party for weeks." She glanced at Tessa and smiled.

Did Lily suspect she was keeping a secret? That was highly unlikely, and yet, the way she'd sought out her gaze made her think her question wasn't far from the truth.

Chapter Thirty-Seven

Thoroughly exhausted, Charity clung to Brandon's large hand, thankful for his support as they made their way down the street. The usually sleepy town of Y Knot still buzzed with after-party excitement. A half hour ago, the Twilight Singers packed up their instruments, and people began gathering their blankets and chairs, saying goodbyes or draining flasks. Amid chatter and laughter, partygoers returned to their homes. Before the party, the plan was her relatives were to pack their belongings and put them in the ranch buckboard in anticipation of their move to the homestead at the Heart of the Mountains. Except for her female cousins and Miss Wendy Knutson, who were staying at the Klinkner mill, everyone was moving into the main ranch house tonight to be closer to her mother and father.

"You wish you were going out to the ranch, as well?" Brandon asked quietly. His bootheels clomped the boardwalk, and laughter came from down the street. "I think you've been contemplating being left out for the last few days. I don't mind if you want to go stay with Rachel or Faith. Any of your brothers'll be happy to have you. With your girl cousins staying in town, your bedroom is available. If you want me to, I'll go, too. Justin can watch things in town."

She hugged his arm, loving Brandon all the more. Her husband became more considerate of her feelings as the years went on. "You know me so well," she replied, feeling grateful. "I *have* been thinking about that. But no, I'm not leaving you. I can ride out early and stay late. I like our calm sanctuary to return to after all the excitement. It feels like heaven on earth."

"Are you saying I'm not exciting?" He stopped and pulled her close, smiling down into her face.

She never knew what he was going to do next. They were in front of the mercantile, and Mr. Lichtenstein and Mr. Simpson had just disappeared inside only a few moments before. The golden glow emanating from the plate glass window as they approached winked out.

He was waiting.

"You already know my answer to such a silly question," she purred. "Even after being married for so long, I still count the moments until we're alone, Brandon. You're the mystery."

"*So* long? That's another statement I take umbrage with."

She laughed. Conversation was one thing, besides the obvious, that they never ran out of. He could arouse her anticipation with a cleverly placed phrase. He possessed a wicked ability to spin a double entendre, at least when they were alone. "You know I didn't mean, *so long*, as in boring. I'm fine staying in town, even with everyone else out at the ranch. I won't miss a thing."

Chance and Evie called out a goodnight as they jangled past in a buggy, followed by another driven by Roady with Sally and the baby by his side.

Morgan Standford and June Pittman walked along the opposite side of the street, arm-in-arm. Morgan gave a head nod but nothing more.

Mr. Tracy, the noticeably short telegraph operator, wasn't far behind them. He limped along dejectedly. On the dance floor, he'd caught a boot toe on something and fell face first, giving himself a bloody nose. The sight hadn't been pretty.

"You're making a scene," she whispered, enjoying his warm body against hers. "I can always count on you for that."

"Maybe I am, but you wouldn't have me any other way."

He was right. He always kept her guessing.

They separated and continued down the boardwalk.

"I was so happy to see Luke and Dustin getting along tonight," she said. "They were talking and laughing up a storm. You were right about them. I think they worked out the—"

"Competition between them?"

They were passing Cattlemen's Hotel and would be to their snug little home in one minute. She glanced up into Brandon's face. Was that it? Were her brother and oldest cousin in competition with each other? *"I* was going to say differences between them. The weird curiosity Dustin had about Luke when we were in Rio Wells."

"Of course, they're rivals. They both have strong leadership traits. Their only problem is they're *too much* alike. I noticed it when we were in Rio Wells. But I think that's in the past. We'll know more soon enough, I'm sure." At the jail, Brandon took one moment to give a scanning glance inside before they continued around back to the house.

"Oh my gosh, Brandon, you make them sound like bitter enemies."

He laughed and pulled her closer to his side as he reached into his pocket for the housekey. "You're such an innocent, darlin'. Not bitter enemies, just prideful cousins—and *that* can be a heck of a lot worse."

Chapter Thirty-Eight

Alone now with Michaela, Tessa marveled at the bedroom surrounding her. Even though it was well past midnight, Chaim had stepped out of the room to give her a moment to prepare. This was Mark McCutcheon's old room. The masculine decor matched the personality of the man she'd met. There was a sizeable pinewood bed, a large, brown-and-white steerhide on the shiny floorboards, a tall dresser with mirror and water pitcher, and two smoky-blue water glasses. A small vase held a single summer rose. A full-sized cradle, larger than the basket Ina had offered them at the party, sat on the far wall.

Dustin and Sidney were directly across the hall in Luke's old room.

Chaim's parents were given Matt's.

John, Lily, and Clara were, of course, in the room John had occupied as a boy, next to a vacant one belonging to Charity.

Tessa turned and glanced at Michaela sprawled out on the middle of the bed. She slept on her back with her arms stretched out like a bird in flight. The poor thing was exhausted. Tessa needed to change her diaper and dress her for bed. After everyone had retired to their own rooms, she and Chaim exchanged a knowing glance. The chair in the corner was not as large as the one at the Preece farm. Chaim would find little sleep there. The night of reckoning had arrived, and their marriage in name only would be put to the test.

Unsettled, Tessa went to the window and looked out into the darkness. Breathing deeply, she tried to calm the butterflies circling inside. Tonight, dancing in Chaim's arms, with her hand held firmly to his chest, she couldn't help but pretend he was holding her so close out of desire, not for any show for his family. Her heart warmed as he'd gazed into her eyes. The simple subjects they'd bantered about played second fiddle to her feelings, making her responses delayed and difficult. He was a skilled dancer, guiding her expertly along the dance floor.

Her husband was a handsome man. A virile man. Would he go back on his word of marriage in name only? Or would he honor their decision? The question was, what in the name of Heaven did she want him to do?

If only she had some experience with men. At her age, she should have been married for years. Every year at the Jordans', she'd planned to strike out on her own. They didn't own her, and if she'd gotten a job, perhaps she would have met an interesting young man. Someone to make a life with. But the days turned into years. Then, of course, Emmeline always said she counted on Tessa.

Tessa thought of the life her unwed mother had led in a man's world. Somewhere during her last year alive, when Tessa was thirteen and living with the Jordans for a year, her mother began to grow weak. Had she known she was dying? As Tessa prepared to leave from her last visit, her mother gave her a sealed envelope. To open later, she'd said. Somehow, Tessa understood she meant after she'd passed away. Upon her death, Tessa opened the letter with shaky hands.

My dearest Tessa, never despair. Somewhere out there is a man waiting to love you, marry you, make your life meaningful. Hope never disappoints. Don't spend your life working for people who don't care and appreciate you. I have little to give you on my death, only these simple words. Don't allow what happened to me to happen to you. Don't be fooled. Good men exist, but there are also tricksters. Be careful, but at the same time, don't harden your heart. If you do, you may miss the right one when he comes along.

Tessa closed her eyes, thinking of the well-memorized note with worn edges. She kept the cherished possession tucked away in her belongings, safe from prying eyes. Sometimes, she took it out just to gaze at her mother's handwriting. Well, she hadn't stayed at the Jordans' for life, but she'd remained much longer than she'd intended. And if Emmeline hadn't died, and the situation with Michaela hadn't presented itself, she most likely would still be there.

"I remember, Mother," she whispered, her fingers resting on the cold glass of the windowpane. Several stars winked as if in answer. "I'm unsure of what to do next. Give my heart, or guard it all the more? Is Chaim's attention for show, or does he genuinely care? He's a mystery to me, Mama, and I'm scared."

Quiet voices in the hallway made her turn. Was Chaim returning? Moments ticked by. Curious to know who was there, Tessa stepped silently to the door and placed her ear on the cool wood.

Chapter Thirty-Nine

"Chaim?"

Just as Chaim reached for his bedroom door, he turned to find Dustin quietly closing his door across the hall. The soft click sounded loud in the quiet house. The moment before, Chaim was contemplating whether or not Tessa would have yet fallen asleep. He'd stayed out in the ranch yard for as long as he could without causing suspicion.

Dustin came close. "I'm glad I caught you. You have a moment to talk?" he asked softly. "We've not had a private moment since arriving in Waterloo. Let's go out to the landing so we won't disturb anyone." He paused. "Or is Tessa waiting?"

Chaim did want some time alone with his brother and doing so now would give Tessa more time to fall asleep. "No, she won't mind. With such a houseful, who knows when we'll get another chance like this?" He started down the long hallway to the upstairs landing overlooking the great room downstairs.

Dustin followed.

For one moment, they both stood awkwardly looking at each other. They'd never struggled to talk before. Feeling uneasy, Chaim jumped right in. "Being back feels good. Mother and Father look healthy and happy, as well as everyone else. I'm grateful."

Dustin shifted, leaning his forearms on the railing to gaze at the serene room below. Stillness pervaded every corner. Everyone had gone to bed. Several lanterns burned, as well as the fireplace, even though the night was mild. He turned to Chaim. "Darned happy you had a change of heart. Stopped being so stubborn. You weren't meant to live in Arizona. You're a Texan with a capital T. Lone star state through and through." He grinned. "Just like me."

Chaim lifted his chin.

"Didn't mean to offend," Dustin went on quickly. "Don't take offense. But you've been obstinate," he said, giving Chaim a quick once-over. "The ranch hasn't been the same without you. You're an important part of our family operation. The men all miss you. I can't wait to get back to Rio Wells and get to know Tessa better."

Why's he rattling on? It's not like Dustin.

"And Michaela. If your aim was to shock us, you did. A wife and nine-month-old babe were the last things we expected to see in Waterloo."

Three heartbeats passed.

"But we couldn't be happier."

Was Dustin fishing for information? If not, this was the strangest welcome he'd ever experienced. Irritation crackled inside as Chaim thought of his wife—yes, Tessa was his legal wife—and his daughter—his true-blooded daughter—peacefully asleep in the room down the hall. "I could see they were happy. We all could. Tessa was nervous, meeting everyone at once, but she got through the introductions fine. And made me proud. I just wonder what your motive is to bring this up now. It's late. And I'm tired. Surely, this conversation could have waited."

Clearly surprised at his defiance, Dustin shifted his weight from foot to foot.

Chaim was always the peacekeeper, the first to cave to Dustin's whims. Being the younger brother, he had no reason not to. But that was before, when he only had himself to consider. Now his family came first. To protect. To love.

Dustin held up a palm in peace. "I didn't mean to put you off, Chaim." He glanced around. "Everything about you feels mysterious. Like now. What're you doing coming in so late? Out walking alone?"

"Getting some night air while Tessa puts Michaela down. Clearly, you've never lived with a baby. Michaela slept so much at the party, falling asleep now will prove difficult. One less distraction in the room helps." He tamped down his growing irritation at being questioned. "If she wakes up before morning and cries, I hope the clamor won't disturb you across the hall."

"Don't worry about us. Sidney and I enjoy the sound of little ones crying all night long. We've been traveling with Clara. She's not always quiet as a mouse."

Chaim smiled, letting go of the chip on his shoulder. He didn't want to be angry with Dustin. Maybe they'd just gotten off on the wrong foot. "That's right. I forgot you've been traveling with a baby, too."

Dustin scrubbed a hand over his face. "She's usually as good as gold, but she does have her moments. And we've been staying with Luke and Faith and their clan. It's a good bet someone is fussing over something right now."

When Dustin's face softened, Chaim thought his brother might be changing his approach.

"Your little one is cute as a bug. Why didn't you write? Knowing you'd married and were happy would have eased everyone's minds. Brick Paulson kept your secret. He never let on about Tessa, and actually fibbed, saying you were still overcome with grief over Emmeline and working yourself to the bone." He lifted a brotherly brow. "Falling into bed exhausted every night. I don't understand why he'd say that if it wasn't true?" His gaze pierced Chaim. "Ma and Pa were overwrought."

Heat surged to Chaim's face. He'd put his family through hell and should shoulder the responsibility. What Dustin said was true, but he didn't have the right to question Chaim's every move.

At his silence, Dustin's eyes narrowed. "I know you, Chaim, better than you know yourself. You're softhearted for the downtrodden. I just don't want to see you get taken advantage of—*again*. Spill the beans. What's *really* going on?"

Heat slammed up Chaim's spine, fueling an uncommon resentment towards his brother. "Back off, Dustin! I'm sorry I didn't write, but I'm not going to bare my soul to you." He worked to control his anger. Being older, Dustin never thought twice about questioning him about anything. And tonight, his brother was doing what he did best. "Either accept us or don't. I don't care which you choose."

Consternation replaced the suspicion on Dustin's face. His mouth grew taut. "Your story doesn't add up. The timing is off. Something's going on you're not sharing. If you're in trouble, I can help. But to do that, I have to know the truth." His tone rose from a whisper to a demand.

He thinks Tessa has taken advantage of me? He believes I'm weak! "Keep your voice down!" Chaim hissed. "You'll wake the household—and my *wife* and *daughter*. If that's the kind of concern you have, you can shovel it out with the manure."

"Chaim." Dustin reached for him.

But Chaim pulled back.

"You're taking this all wrong. We're delighted for you. Thankful you've found such a nice girl. Someone the total opposite of Emmeline Jordan. Marrying Emmeline would have ended in catastrophe. She would have cut and run, even after the wedding, perhaps leaving you with a young'un or two to raise on your own."

"I'm done here," Chaim growled and stormed off. If Dustin thought those things about him and Tessa, he'd bet everyone else did as well. Maybe they'd put Dustin up to do the dirty work. To dig for the truth. It hurt to think of his mother and father being suspicious of Tessa and Michaela.

"Chaim, wait!" Dustin called again.

Returning to the bedroom filled with anger was not his best choice. Chaim turned on his heel, passed Dustin without a word, descended the stairs, and headed for the door.

Chapter Forty

Tessa pressed her ear more firmly to the cool wood of the door. Dustin and Chaim. Outside in the hallway. She was almost sure. She heard her name, but not in what context. *They're discussing me? Why? Does Dustin have doubts?* Almost immediately, the voices faded, and she thought she heard their footsteps vanishing down the hallway.

She glanced at the bed where Michaela slept peacefully. Tessa wished for a thimbleful of her daughter's serenity. The McCutcheons were Michaela's true family. But Tessa was just a stand in, wife-in-name-only. Essentially, a fraud.

Dancing in Chaim's arms hadn't felt pretend. If she only knew what he was thinking. Was his attention only for show? Or were his feelings for her growing? In Waterloo, after their conversation over dinner, she should have no illusions about what this marriage was. They'd spelled out their terms clearly and rationally. A tangible business deal. Chaim wouldn't be pleased if he knew she was already reading things into his behavior. If she could only hear what he was saying to Dustin, then she'd know how to go forward without angering him or making herself a fool.

With her mind made up, and one more quick glance at Michaela to make sure the baby wouldn't wake up in the next few moments and crawl off the bed, she carefully cracked the door open the narrowest bit and waited. She'd not like to run into any of the McCutcheons. Finding a plausible explanation why she was sneaking down the hallway might be difficult. Feeling the way was clear, she slipped out on bare feet and tiptoed toward the stairs. She stopped just short of where the hallway turned. She could hear Dustin's deep voice. The two were talking softly, and she couldn't make out any words, but the agitation in his tone was unmistakable.

The voices rose. She glanced behind her, fearing someone else would hear and come to investigate.

"Keep your voice down!"

That was Chaim.

"You'll wake the household—and my wife and daughter. If that's the kind of concern you have, you can shovel it out with the manure!"

Her heart constricted. She didn't want to create problems for Chaim. With her heart in her throat, she turned. She heard movement. She must make it back to the room before she was caught eavesdropping.

Flood gathered Claire from the stool in front of her dressing table and kissed her tenderly. The bedroom felt quiet and peaceful after the exhilarating evening they'd had. He couldn't stop a smile from forming on his lips in the middle of the kiss. "Well, you got me, sweetheart, surprised the stuffing right out of me. How can I ever thank you for being such a thoughtful wife?"

She softly laughed, both her hands resting on his bare shoulders. "I'll think of something expensive. Maybe the trip to New York you've promised me for the last ten years. Oh, you'll pay, all right. Don't worry about that."

"Whatever, I'm game. Just tell me and it's yours. Bringing my brother and his family out is the best gift you could have given me. I'm still astounded. And now we all have some time together to get reacquainted. And those boys of his. Weren't they handsome, standing together with ours? Not to mention Madeline and Becky. I'm so happy to have them all here in Y Knot for the next couple of weeks. My head is spinning with all the possibilities."

"And John?" she asked softly.

He tightened his hold. "The greatest surprise of all. He looks fit and happy. The finest I've ever seen him. He's a man. Grown and mature. And I'm so happy to meet Lily and your namesake, little Clara. I guess Texas isn't so far away anymore with train travel. I've been a stubborn fool, not visiting. It'll be our turn to visit them next. I promise. I should have listened to you long ago."

"I was hoping you'd come around. It's been nice meeting everyone after so many years. Better late than never." She left his arms and pulled back the quilt, plumping the pillows first on Flood's side and then her own. She slipped into the bed and waited with a smile on her face. "Don't just stand there, come to bed, Husband. It's almost time to get up, and you'll be tired. The house is quiet, and everyone is asleep."

Nodding, he blew out the lantern on her dressing table, amid her creams and lotions, and started for the candle on the dresser when he heard something. Flood hesitated. Was that a door opening? Anyone could be getting up for a number of reasons. Nothing could be happening to worry over.

"What's wrong?" Claire asked.

"I heard something. Probably nothing, but I feel like checking."

"Don't. We have guests. I don't want them to think we're snooping."

"I'll just look out the door. Maybe Lily or Tessa need something for the babies and are hesitant to wake us." He gave her a husbandly nod and turned the knob slowly as not to make any noise. His and Claire's bedroom was at the end of the long hallway of the upper floor. The passage was dim, but he could make out a woman standing at the end as still as a statue. A second after spotting her, he heard angry male voices.

When she turned, he saw Tessa, not yet dressed for bed. She hurried for her room as if a swarm of bees was on her tail. Just as she reached for her doorknob, she glanced up, and their gazes met, him bare chested and in his sleep pants. He ducked his head and slowly closed the door.

"What was that?" Claire was sitting up, her long hair loose and flowing around her shoulders. "You look strange."

"Not sure. And I hesitate to speculate. Some trouble might be brewing with our Texas family we're not aware of."

"Oh?" She pulled back the cover as he climbed into bed.

"I hope it's nothing serious. Chaim and Tessa looked very lovey-dovey tonight at the party. I couldn't help watching them dance. As well as the others."

"They did look cute, didn't they?" Claire snuggled down beside Flood to rest her head between the crook of his arm and his chest. "I'm sure it's nothing. At least, nothing for us old folks to worry over. We're well past all that drama. You know how newlyweds are, there's always something occurring as they get to know each other. I'm sure Chaim and Tessa are no different."

"Newlyweds?"

"The first three years."

Flood grunted. "But who was Chaim speaking with out there? If I heard correctly, he sounded angry. And Tessa was sneaking. She'd been eavesdropping. There's no two ways about that. I know what I saw."

Claire reached up and placed a finger on his lips. "I'm sleepy, Flood. You can stay awake with your speculations if you want, but I'd like to be chipper in the morning. I'm no spring chicken anymore, and I need my rest. We have guests to entertain. I'm sure whatever's troubling them will be worked out before the rooster crows. That's how it works when people go to bed." She smiled sweetly.

Flood chuckled and pulled Claire closer, snuggling in. "Good night, sweetheart. I love you," he whispered, kissing her forehead. The glow of love he'd experienced tonight from his family and the townsfolk still had him feeling euphoric. He wouldn't sleep much before sunrise. "You *sure* know how to throw a surprise party, darlin'. Thank you again."

Chapter Forty-One

Morning dawned, and still no Chaim. Last night, when Tessa had rushed to the room in a panic to beat Chaim back, she'd hastily placed the baby in her crib without changing her or dressing her properly. Then she'd ripped off her dress, pulled on her nightgown, and jumped into bed herself, expecting Chaim to come through the door at any moment. But he hadn't. After his talk with Dustin, he must have gone outside again—or somewhere else. After her heart quieted and she felt sure he wasn't coming, she'd risen in the dark to carefully change Michaela's diaper. She carefully pulled the baby's nightgown over her sleepy head, and then completed her own toilette. The baby was so exhausted, she hadn't even roused.

Now, with little sleep, she felt tired and anxious. Had Dustin changed Chaim's mind? Did Chaim still want to be married? Did he still want his daughter? She was just about to go downstairs in search of coffee when the bedroom door opened.

Chaim stepped inside, looking rumpled and tired.

They stared at each other for several long moments and then his gaze cut to the crib.

"She's still asleep but should awaken any moment," Tessa whispered.

He nodded but didn't say anything.

"You stayed out all night? Did you find a place to sleep?" *Is the thought of sleeping in the same bed with me distasteful?*

"The loft in the barn. But, between the fussing chickens and a couple mice playing tag in the hay, I've not slept a wink." His gaze tracked to the bed.

Feeling uneasy, she fluffed her skirt. "I'm just on my way downstairs to find some coffee." *Why doesn't he mention anything about his talk with Dustin last night?* "If you'd like, I can bring you a cup."

"No, thanks. I think I'd rather try and get a few minutes of shuteye."

"Of course. I'd want too, as well." Should she mention last night? Mr. McCutcheon saw her in the hallway, darting back to her room. She'd better give Chaim a word of warning, so he didn't get caught off guard. Still, she hated to make him angry. "Chaim," she said softly.

He looked at her and waited.

"I heard you and Dustin last night."

His brows wrinkled together.

"Your brother doesn't like me."

"That's not true. He thinks I—well…"

"He thinks I tricked you or fooled you somehow. He thinks I was in trouble, and you rescued me."

Chaim lifted a shoulder. "He treats me like a kid. Has all his life. I was angry last night. I didn't want you or Michaela to pick up on my irritation, so I stayed out."

"It took you all night to cool down?"

He scrubbed a hand over his whiskered jaw. "Sorry. Thought you'd be asleep."

"When you didn't return, I thought you were angry with me."

"Over what? You've done nothing wrong."

"I didn't just eavesdrop through my door but followed you to the landing but kept out of sight."

His eyebrows shot up, but he didn't condemn her.

"And your uncle Flood saw me rushing back to the bedroom after the house was quiet and everyone had gone to bed. I can't imagine what he must think. Just wanted you to know."

"To warn me?"

She couldn't stop a small smile as she nodded slowly. A warm feeling spread through her blood. They were in this together. *Us against them*, if she could be indelicate. Her husband hadn't been upset with her or wasn't rethinking their situation. He'd argued with his brother, and from what he'd just said, Dustin was the one he was annoyed with—not her. "Climb into bed," she said softly. "When I return, I'll do my best to keep Michaela quiet when she awakens so you can get at least a little sleep. Is there anyone up downstairs?"

"The cook in the kitchen." Chaim toed off his boots. "Smelled like coffee's been brewed. I didn't see anyone else. And for a heads-up to you, the young boy, the one called Hickory, discovered *me* in the loft. I have no idea what he'll say, because I didn't give him any reason why I was there when a perfectly good, comfortable bed was in this room." He shook his head and took a tired breath.

"No matter. It doesn't make a difference what he says." Being bold, she took his arm and drew him to the side of the bed she hadn't slept in and pulled back the covers. She placed his hands on the buttons of his shirt. "You don't have much time before a big family breakfast will be served. Take advantage of the bed while you can."

He grunted and turned red, bloodshot eyes her way. "Thank you."

"My pleasure. Now, get in and pull the covers over your head. I plan to be back before Michaela wakes up."

Tessa had just brought a cup of strong coffee to her lips when Dustin walked into the kitchen. They both straightened when they saw each other. She felt like a fieldmouse facing the meanest cat in the barn. His dark hair was wet and combed. His pants and shirt looked fresh. A royal-blue bandanna was tied smartly around his neck.

Seeing him now, she was thankful she'd taken extra care with her morning toilette, which included brushing her hair one hundred strokes before pinning half up and letting the rest cascade down her back. She'd learned the style from Emmeline, and it was complimentary to Tessa's profile. Composing herself, she finished her sip and offered a gracious smile. "Good morning, Dustin." This was her new brother-in-law who believed she'd taken advantage of his younger brother. She'd like to win him over, if doing so were possible.

"Good morning, Tessa," he replied in a deep, congenial tone. "I hope you slept well." He glanced around the quiet kitchen. "Are we the first ones up?"

"We are. Esperanza is here somewhere. She just stepped out of the kitchen a moment ago. Other than her, it's just little ol' me." *Why did I say such a stupid thing?* "Esperanza said to help yourself to coffee and anything else." She gestured toward the work stand beside her and a platter filled with biscuits and cinnamon rolls. A stack of small plates sat to one side, with napkins and utensils. A crock of butter, and two more, one with honey and another of jam. "Breakfast won't be for about an hour. I guess Flood and Claire thought everyone would sleep quite late because of the late hour we went to bed." *What is wrong with my rambling mouth? I can't seem to stop.*

He smiled and tipped his head. "Looks good. Don't mind if I do." Walking closer, he filled a plate with three biscuits, a healthy daub of butter and jam each. Carrying the plate he proceeded to the stove, set his goodies on the sideboard, and poured a cup of coffee.

Tessa lifted a small earthenware pitcher at her side. "Cream?"

"No, thanks, I take my coffee black and strong." He put the cup to his nose and smelled. "This'll do me fine."

The conversation felt awkward. Should she walk into the dining room? Stay here? Or excuse herself, as she'd planned, and go back upstairs to await Michaela? There was no changing the baby's internal timeclock. She'd be awakening soon, and Tessa wanted to be there to keep her as quiet as possible. The thought of Chaim asleep in the bed brought a flutter of butterflies.

Flood McCutcheon walked into the room. "Good morning! I smelled coffee all the way upstairs. I see you two did, as well."

"Morning, Uncle," Dustin said.

Tessa felt a blush creep across her cheeks. Tall and powerfully built, Flood McCutcheon commanded a presence in the room. He was dressed nicely in denim, a cotton plaid shirt, and tan leather vest. He'd shaved and combed his thick brown hair peppered with gray. She prayed he wouldn't say anything about seeing her last night. Dustin wanted to save Chaim from her and Michaela. He was suspicious and wasn't holding back. "Good morning, Mr. McCutcheon."

"Flood. Please. Or Uncle Flood, if you like. We're all family." He gave a warm smile as he crossed the room and poured coffee into a cup. "This birthday is one I'll never forget."

He came close and placed his arm around her shoulders, bringing a surge of emotion to her throat. *Family*. Such a beautiful word.

Dustin followed.

"Claire sure surprised me with all this," he went on. "And the fact you all are staying on for a time. I'm delighted to have a chance to get to know you both."

His face clouded over and, for a moment, Tessa feared he might cry.

"We're happy to be here, as well, Uncle Flood. My father and mother have been giddy since the invitation arrived. I've enjoyed seeing the ranch, as much as we could while hidden away. You know me and my wife, Sidney, have been staying with Luke and Faith and their posse. They sure are a cheerful bunch."

When Flood took his arm from her shoulders and grasped one of Dustin's, Tessa felt a loss. "You remind me so much of Luke. You're both no-nonsense and commanding. It's good to have you here, Dustin. I can't say that enough. You'll always have a place at the Heart of the Mountains." He glanced at Tessa. "You and Chaim, as well."

Dustin exchanged a look with Tessa.

"I hope the girls will arrive in time to eat with us." Flood pulled a cinnamon roll in half and took a bite. He chewed and swallowed. "We're planning on them. Are your sisters early risers, Dustin? They were out late, as well, last night."

He nodded. "Just depends. They know how important this get-together is. And how upset my parents would be if they weren't here. They'll make it."

Feeling sentimental with all the family talk, Tessa sipped her coffee, willing her eyes not to fill. So, this is how others felt as part of a group. But now, she'd remained much longer in the kitchen than she'd anticipated and needed to get back upstairs. She took a napkin and wrapped up a biscuit.

"For my sleepy brother?" Dustin asked.

"Actually, no. For Michaela, to keep her quiet until breakfast."

Dustin looked at her as if he expected her to go on.

"What else do you need for our sweet little darlin', Tessa?" Flood glanced around the offerings. "Esperanza can fix you some hot cereal or toast to take up."

"Oh, no, this biscuit will do just fine to keep her happy until breakfast is served. But thank you. I really should get back upstairs before she awakens. I promised Chaim I would." She chanced another glance at Dustin, who watched her with interest. She wished he would stop that. Maybe she'd talk to him later, when they were alone.

Chapter Forty-Two

Chaim nestled deeper into the cool sheets when he heard another mouse squeaking in his ear. His kin needed a few more barn cats to take care of their rodent population. He hadn't had but snatches of sleep all night. He rolled over and stretched one arm over his head, his heavy-lidded eyes feeling scratchy and hot.

The squeaking came again, only louder. Next came a great howl, which sent him bolt up in bed. Realization dawned. He wasn't in the loft anymore. The cool quietness of the morning was interrupted by Michaela standing in the crib on the other side of the room, staring with watery eyes. As soon as she saw he was awake, and regarding her, two rivers gushed from her eyes. She began to sob.

"Shh, shh, shh," he said as he crawled over his covers toward the baby bed and lifted her from the crib. Her soggy diaper hung on her like a slab of curing beef. Every time she pumped her legs, the wet fabric slipped a little farther toward the floor and he feared she'd be naked before he made it to the bed. Seeing no other way, he placed his hand beneath the clammy cloth and carried her to the foot of the bed, holding her far from his body. Thankfully, a clean diaper was already laid out.

"Shh, shh, baby girl," he whispered into her stormy face. "Your daddy's sorry he slept past your waking. But he's here now, and everything'll be all right." He gently laid her down and, with a quick glance, searched the room for the duffle bag with all her necessities.

With his attention no longer on Michaela, her sobs returned. Her bottom lip shot out a good half inch, making his heart wrench. Determined to prevent her from waking the entire household, he leaned over and blew a loud kiss on one moist cheek and then the other. Next, he clucked like a chicken directly into her face.

Her sobs stopped as she studied his lips.

Unable to stop himself, he laughed at his own antics. "There you go," he said, feeling a sense of accomplishment. He made a wide smile and jumped his eyebrows up and down. "That's better, cutie pie. Everything's fine. You're just bogged down a little, like a calf in a mudhole." He didn't know children, but he did know livestock. Could they be so different? Realizing he couldn't wait forever hoping Tessa would rescue him, he worked the safety pins at each corner of the diaper and said a heartfelt prayer of gratitude it was only wet and not soiled.

Thoughts of Tessa reminded him of last night. The party and how she danced in his arms. Why had he held her so close? Was the warm night air to blame? The shining stars? The romantic music? The festive feel of the party and everyone's love, their faces filled with joy and happiness? Those things were true but weren't the reason he'd pulled her all the closer. The inviting sparkle in her eyes was irresistible. Or was the truth that she'd felt perfect in his arms? As if she'd been made just for him? And not to discount the way his embrace turned her soft cheeks a dusty rose.

When the door opened, he glanced over his shoulder, suddenly all too aware he was bent over the bed in only his light, warm-weather underwear that didn't hide a thing. Seeing Tessa, he straightened and grasped a displaced pillow, using it as a shield. Extremely exposed in his bare-chested state of undress, he felt his face flame hotter than any Arizona mid-day sun.

Tessa must have been just as embarrassed, because the color in her face instantly matched the watermelon slices they'd served last night at the party.

"I'm sorry. When I heard Michaela crying, I hurried up the steps, never thinking I should at least knock." She slowly turned around. The cup and saucer rattled in her hand.

"No need for apologies," he said, feeling like the biggest fool in the world. He held the baby in place with one hand and the pillow with the other.

Michaela struggled to sit up and play now that she'd been relieved of the heavy diaper.

To reach the shirt he'd so thoughtlessly tossed over the small chair in the corner he'd have to put the pillow down—or let go of his daughter. This was silly. Tessa was his wife. He shouldn't feel the slightest bit shy around her in his state of undress, and yet, he did.

He opted to release his daughter. As fast as roping a steer, he had the shirt on and worked the buttons. From the corner of his eye, he saw Michaela had crawled to the far side of the tall bed and was reaching for the front bed post. She leaned forward and, if she tumbled off, she'd surely be hurt. "Michaela, no!"

Tessa whirled, rushing forward just as he lunged across the bed. In the commotion, the cup she held crashed to the floor, and what looked like a biscuit went flying. The three of them ended up on the bed in a heap.

Michaela thought this a fun game and squealed with excitement.

Tessa was halfway on the bed.

He was stretched out like a steer caught by his hind legs.

"Oh!" Tessa exclaimed. As she struggled to right herself the bed jiggled.

Chaim felt Michaela's small hands as his daughter crawled onto his back.

A soft knock rapped the door.

Chaim rolled over, careful not to send his daughter off him and onto the floor. He sat up. "Yes?"

"Is everything all right in there?"

Aunt Claire.

Tessa stared, allowing him to take charge. She bent down to retrieve the cup and mouthed the cup had been empty.

"We're fine, Aunt Claire. Just a tiny mishap with Michaela. She's happy and not hurt, though. No need to worry."

Michaela let out another squeal of laughter, doing her darndest to climb back into his lap.

"That's good to hear. Breakfast is almost ready. I think we'll be sitting down in about twenty minutes. Oh, your sisters and their friend have arrived. They were asking for you."

"Thank you. We'll be right down. We're just about ready now." He glanced at Tessa, who was struggling not to laugh.

She hurried to the wardrobe, pulled out a small dress for Michaela, and shook the garment out.

At the sound of Aunt Claire walking away, he gave a sigh of relief.

"There's still clean water in the pitcher," Tessa said. "I only used a little."

"Thanks. If you'll see to this cutie pie, I'll wash up and dress."

"Of course."

He noted, as Tessa dressed and washed the baby, she kept her gaze far, far away from him on the other side of the room.

Chapter Forty-Three

The morning flashed by in the blink of an eye. Breakfast was a noisy affair with thirteen adults and two babies. Tessa was amazed at the amount of food Esperanza continued to place in the middle of the table. Platters of beef, fresh from the ranch's own stock were astonishing too. Back in Boston, she'd never seen steaks served at breakfast time. Several types of eggs, bacon, and sausage enticed. Nobody would go away hungry today. The serving dish of biscuits and cinnamon rolls was refilled several times. And the coffee. Pots and pots. The food just kept coming. With so many family members vying for the floor to speak, Tessa relaxed and listened to the stories keeping everyone entertained.

After breakfast, and in need of working off the huge amount of food consumed, the group decided to take a walk as Flood and Claire pointed out aspects of the ranch.

Ranch hands followed along, smiling and making small talk, staying close to Madeline, Becky, and Wendy, who looked to be having fun. The group circled behind the bunkhouse and the outdoor cooking area used in the hottest days of summer, they'd been told, where a nice view showcased the rolling vistas of the Heart of the Mountains. Cattle dotted the pastures, and massive clouds created scalloped shadows across the land.

The murmur of voices reached Tessa: Flood and Winston discussing cattle, John and Dustin comparing seasonal weather. Claire and Winnie, just standing together as they enjoyed the view. Later this afternoon, another family gathering was planned, but this time with all the brothers and their families, as well as Charity and Brandon. Thirteen additional people, if Tessa's calculations were correct and she wasn't leaving anyone out.

The place will be a madhouse. But a fun one. One she'd been pining for all her life. And what was she to think of her husband? Chaim stayed by her side every moment since sitting down to breakfast, sharing his thoughts and carrying Michaela whenever the opportunity arose. Acting like a real husband. Was he sticking to her to avoid Dustin after their angry confrontation last night, or did he truly enjoy being in her company? She dared not allow her thoughts to stray to this morning, when he'd been flustered. With his pillow-shield firmly in front and almost totally naked, he'd looked like a Viking marauder. Her face heated, recalling the moment. Even at her advanced age of twenty-four, she'd never seen the male body. Not even a glimpse. And especially not one as perfectly formed.

"Penny for your thoughts," Chaim said softly, for her ears only. "You have an odd look on your face. I don't think I've ever seen it before." They stood about thirty feet behind everyone else, and Michaela was playing in the grass.

She blinked and glanced at Michaela among the tiny buttercups dancing in the breeze. The baby's curls sparkled like sunshine as she tugged on a long green stem. She seemed totally happy. "My thoughts?"

"Uh-hum."

Tessa laughed, knowing she'd never in a thousand years tell him she'd been recalling this morning's mishap in the bedroom. Or how handsome he'd looked shirtless, shielding his privates with a feather cushion. She might be bold, but not *that* bold. "I'm sorry. I don't remember. Your question chased my thoughts away."

Chaim shrugged and folded his arms across his chest. He was hatless, since he'd sold his new cream-colored Stetson for the silver bell and stage passage.

Finished viewing the cattle pasture, the others moved on, leaving them to their privacy. Feeling as light as the clouds above, she smiled. "We should go, too. Shall I carry Michaela, or do you want to? She loves riding on your shoulders."

Chaim watched the others walk away. "We have time. Michaela's enjoying the flowers—and she's quiet. I think letting a contented baby stay put is wise." He looked at her. "What's your favorite flower, Tessa? Do you have one?"

Tessa blinked away several quick memories flowing through her mind. She'd never been asked such a question. Working for the Jordan household, few were concerned in her interests. Her likes and dislikes. But that didn't stop her from having a favorite and the remembered image brought a smile to her lips. "The mayflower. Have you ever seen one?"

"Not sure."

"They're a tiny spring flower that appears around March and April." She put both index fingers and thumbs together to show the tiny size. "They have delicate pale pink or white waxy petals and possess an exquisitely sweet scent." She couldn't stop twitching her nose at the memory. "And grow very close to the ground, so if you want a good look without picking one, you have to get down on your belly. I dirtied many a clean frock, much to my mother's dismay."

Chaim chuckled, an intriguing light in his eyes. "Did you have them at the Jordans'?"

She shook her head. "Oh, no. Their home is in the heart of the city. The mayflowers were at the house where I lived many years before working for the Jordans. A kind widow rented a room to my mother. The little square home had a rocky embankment behind where the mayflowers grew in the spring. The sweetness in the air always attracted bees. When I was five or six, I asked my mother if someone had sprinkled sugar all over the knoll. Every few weeks, while the hillside was in bloom, we would gather something to eat, usually some bread and cheese, and have a picnic without leaving home." She glanced up to find Chaim watching her intently. "It's a nice memory, one I enjoy thinking about."

"I'm not sure if I've ever seen a mayflower in Texas. But then, I'm not so aware of the flowers around me."

She gazed at him for a moment, thinking there wasn't much she really knew about her husband. "What's *your* favorite flower, Chaim?"

He grinned. "Trying to get to know me better?"

She nodded. "We shouldn't waste this golden opportunity. Everyone else is captivated by the view, and the flock of sparrows overhead are the only ones who will hear. Are you stalling?"

He tapped a finger on his chin. "Maybe." After a few moments, he said, "I don't have a favorite flower."

"No? That's a shame. Then what's your favorite meal?"

"That's easy. Steak and mashed potatoes—with plenty of gravy. You?"

Her mouth watered. "Breaded, deep-fried clams. Mind you, I've only eaten them three times in my life, but I'll never forget the experience. Just delicious."

He eyed her in such a way that said he couldn't imagine such a delicacy.

She laughed. "I know fried clams must sound horrible to a cattle rancher, especially if you've never experienced them, but I assure you, they're just the opposite. I hope you'll agree with me someday."

His gaze was different this midmorning day. It left her feeling fuzzy inside and a bit breathless. His eyes, shimmering with sunshine and mischief, filled her with something she couldn't decipher—or didn't dare to. But it seemed her heart could read them perfectly. "Color?"

He lifted a shoulder and then gazed down at his clothes. "I'd have to say, looking at my boots, pants, and shirt, brown or tan. I've never given it much thought." He lifted a brow. "I'd say yours is blue. Every time you wear blue, your eyes look like the surface of a lake on a clear day—like sapphires."

At his unexpected compliment, she glanced away, warmth pooling inside. "The others are almost out of sight," she said, her voice breathless. "We should go."

Chaim nodded and stepped over for Michaela but stopped and pointed. "Look, she's found her first ladybug."

They watched as Michaela touched a speckled orange beetle balancing on a buttercup. Before either of them knew what the child intended, Michaela grasped the insect in her small hand and brought it to her open mouth.

"No, no!" Chaim exclaimed and whisked the baby into his arms.

The little beetle flew away.

Startled by his sharp tone and quick move, she let out a shriek and began to cry.

Cuddling Michaela, Chaim gently rubbed her back until her cries died down to a whimper. "That could be poisonous, darlin'. We wouldn't want that."

In no time, Michaela was calm and watching the birds in the sky through watery eyes.

Chaim let out a deep breath and smiled at Tessa. "In the future, I'll have to be more observant."

Although he was correct about being watchful, Tessa didn't know whether a ladybug was poisonous or not. Either way, his actions and concerns warmed her. Such a good, loving father. Michaela was right where she belonged.

Ahead, Flood turned and glanced back, waving them on. She'd successfully passed the morning hours without inquisition from him about why she'd been lurking in the hallway the night before. Would her luck hold out? Or was Chaim's uncle just waiting to catch her alone?

Chapter Forty-Four

The five o'clock hour arrived with a bang. Tessa was upstairs, just finishing Michaela's bath, when a commotion in the ranch yard drew her attention. Placing her on her towel in the middle of the large bed with her doll, she told her to stay put and hurried to the window.

Matthew McCutcheon, driving a buckboard filled with his family of five, rolled to a stop below.

Rushing back to the bed, Tessa dried her, quickly pinned on a clean diaper, and proceeded to dress Michaela in a pretty pink dress, white tights—which she realized would be dirty in no time—and small leather shoes. "There! You're as pretty as a picture," she crooned. Leaning over, she kissed her soft cheek. "Mommy loves you very much." Well, it was true *now*. Marrying Michaela's biological father truly made her Michaela's mother— as she'd felt from the moment Emmeline had passed away.

She smiled into the cherub face regarding her. "One last thing, sweetie." She pulled Michaela to a sitting position and placed her bonnet on her head. "Now, leave this bow alone." Tying the ribbons stylishly on the side of Michaela's face, Tessa picked her up and walked to the window. "Ready for the party? There'll be many people, some you're not too familiar with. If they want to hold you, don't be frightened. They're your family." Tessa kissed the top of her head, the newly ironed bonnet smelling of warm cotton. "You're a very lucky girl, indeed."

The door opened and closed.

She turned to find Chaim. His boyish smile warmed her.

"You girls ready?" He stopped close to her side.

Michaela's face brightened, and she reached for her father.

Chaim laughed and took her from Tessa's arms.

A strong bond had grown between father and child in such a short amount of time. Much faster than Tessa anticipated. The transformation was truly remarkable.

"Because the reinforcements have arrived," he went on, pointing out the window.

The ruckus below was still happening. Between the family and number of ranch hands living here, the Heart of the Mountains was like a small town in and of itself. There was always something to do or someone to speak with. She was enjoying her stay very much. "We're both ready and waiting. I just finished tying her bonnet ribbons."

"And she looks like a princess."

Somewhere, Chaim had cleaned up, as well, and looked incredibly handsome. As was his practice, he'd given her privacy, as he did as often as he could without drawing undue attention. A bright indigo shirt with a matching bandanna made his sky-blue eyes stand out. His pants were clean, and boots buffed to a shine. She was hesitant to gaze into his face too long, frightened he'd see the truth. Gone was her ability to think of him as her friend. They might have delayed the inevitable by one night, but tonight they'd be in the same bed. Just his presence at her side brought a rush of skittering nerves pinging this way and that. Her face heated painfully.

Bouncing Michaela in his arms, he looked Tessa over and smiled. "You look beautiful. I've not seen that blue dress before." He lifted a brow. "Is your carpetbag magical? And dresses just appear at whim?"

She laughed, enjoying his attention.

He bounced Michaela harder, the baby laughing and patting his shoulder.

"You have an extremely generous family. It's Madeline's dress. This morning, she brought it along with her from the Klinkners' thinking the color would look pretty with my hair and eyes." She ran a hand on the soft, simple cotton. The light blue background was dotted with tiny golden flowers matching the color of her hair. The high-waisted dress accented her waist. It had a scalloped collar and three-quarter length sleeves. Tessa had fallen in love with the garment instantly and hoped for a reaction like this from Chaim. Still, she felt shy speaking about herself and his family so familiarly. Holding the skirt out, she did a quick twirl. She wasn't an old maid any longer.

"Madeline was right." His gaze caressed her face, bringing another embarrassing rush of heat to her cheeks. "I'll have to thank her when I see her. That is, if she can spare a moment away from the adoring ranch hands. Good thing we won't be staying long enough for her to fall in love. I don't think my parents would like her remaining behind."

"Oh?"

A knock came on the closed door.

Still holding Michaela, Chaim reached over and opened it.

"Chaim!" Madeline exclaimed. "I didn't expect you." She came into the room and looked Tessa up and down. "I *knew* the dress was perfect for you. If you like it, consider it a gift from your sister-in-law."

"I-I couldn't," Tessa sputtered.

"You most certainly can," Chaim responded, slinging an arm around his sister's shoulders. "That's awfully nice of you, Madeline. Thank you." He kissed her cheek. "The dress looks like it was made for my wife. And she looks absolutely charming. I'll have to keep an eye out some ranch hand doesn't try to steal her heart away."

Madeline extracted herself from his arm and reached for the baby. "We've missed you at the ranch. I'll do all I can to help with this little one once we get back to Rio Wells. She's adorable. And I see you both in her features." She buried her face in Michaela's neck, making the baby giggle with pleasure. "You know most everyone is downstairs?" Madeline asked when she straightened. "If you'd like, I can take Michaela so you can finish up getting ready."

Tessa's stomached tightened. Alone with Chaim while Michaela was sleeping in the room was one thing; being totally alone with him, with all these crazy feelings tumbling around inside, was quite another.

When no one objected, Madeline made for the door. "Don't be long. The party has begun." To punctuate her statement, a round of whooping from outside made them all look to the window.

"We won't be," Chaim assured her. "We're right on your heels." He winked at Tessa. "Right, Wife?"

"Yes, of course. And Madeline, thank you again for the dress. I truly love it."

"My pleasure." She quietly pulled the door closed, taking Michaela with her.

Feeling nervous, Tessa went to the mirror and began fussing with her hair. "Michaela has taken to everyone," she said, forcing the words through her lips. She moved a lock with trembling fingers, which caused her to drop a hairpin to the dresser top. Retrieving it, she re-pinned her hair.

"She sure has." He sat on the side of the bed to watch her as if the action was as normal as drinking a glass of water.

He didn't seem nervous in the least. As a matter of fact, the easy charm Emmeline had spoken of often was on full display today. Was he over Emmeline? Had he put his feelings for her to rest?

"She seems especially fond of my mother. Crawls to her every time she has a chance."

Through the mirror, Tessa watched the emotions crossing his face. He didn't seem to be one who wanted to hide things. "You're right. And your mother seems just as smitten with her. Between your mother and sisters, as well as your cousins and their wives, I barely get time with Michaela these days."

"Are you complaining?"

"Never. All I want is for Michaela to have a loving, supportive family. She has that now. I couldn't be happier."

He stood and was just about to reach for the door so they could go downstairs, but he stopped and turned to look back at her. A strange emotion shadowed his eyes but, in a moment, it was gone.

Laughter floated through the door as they stepped out into the sunlit yard. Chaim reached for her hand, and Tessa reminded herself this was all for show. His palm, rough and warm, sent flashes of desire up her arm and around her body. How could something as simple as a palm cause such a reaction? Sunshine warmed her face as she looked about, trying to appear relaxed when she was anything but.

Chairs were set about in groups, and a few blankets were laid out in the shade of several trees. Rachel, Matt's wife, sat with Amy, Mark's wife, watching their infant sons crawl slowly about. Lily joined them, laying little Clara onto the quilt.

A group of men, including Dustin, were lined up to toss horseshoes.

Dawn, the child Luke had delivered before he'd married Faith, was dressed like a little cowboy as she rode a small horse around in the corral.

Chaim leaned close. "Where shall we begin?" He gestured with their clasped hands. "My father and Uncle Flood over there? Or do you want to sit with the ladies by the babies? I don't see mother or Aunt Claire yet."

His warm, coffee-scented breath caressed her face. She felt small by his side. And even if the feeling was imagined, she felt cherished.

"Hmm?" He gave her hand a slight squeeze when she didn't respond. "I know. Too many choices. This way." He led her to the large fire pit where Lucky, the bunkhouse cook, was basting what looked to be a whole side of beef strung over a crackling fire.

Flood and Winston McCutcheon looked on, arms crossed over their chests in an identical look of satisfaction.

"Chaim," Winston called out when he saw their approach. "Was wondering when you and Tessa would join us." He welcomed them both with a hug. "I never get tired of doing that." He went from Chaim to Tessa and then grinned at Flood.

Chaim kept her close at his side. "This is some party, Uncle Flood. This meat smells delicious. I wonder if it'll taste any different from the beef we raise."

"Nothing's too good for my relatives," Flood responded with a chuckle. "Lucky and Esperanza are pulling out all the stops."

"Yer darn tootin', we are," Lucky said as he limped from one side of the beef to the other. "I've never seen this many McCutcheons in one spot, and my heart jist can't take doin' nothin' spotty. Tonight will be a feast." He glanced around quickly. "Where's your little half pint, Chaim? Surprised you let her out of your sight."

"I am, too," Winston agreed. "I wanted a chance to hold her."

The sound of Chaim's relaxed laughter was filled with love. Tessa was getting very used to this version of her new husband.

"She's around here somewhere with Madeline. She came and got her a little while ago from our room, and I haven't seen them since."

"No worries," Flood responded. "I saw Faith and some others walking toward her house. Faith must have forgotten something, and Madeline joined in on her walk. They're perfectly safe here on the ranch."

"You're right." Chaim nodded. "Where's Charity and Brandon? I haven't seen them yet today. They're coming, aren't they?"

Flood chuckled. "My daughter, miss a party? That's not possible. Especially here on the ranch. She and Brandon are just running a little late. They'll be along shortly."

Tessa tugged on Chaim's hand. No matter Mr. McCutcheon's proclamation Michaela was safe, she didn't like the child being out of her sight for such a long time.

He looked down at her.

"I think I'll go join the ladies on the blankets," she said. She didn't want Chaim to know what was bothering her. Without him at her side, she wouldn't have to be so careful about looking around. Before she realized what he was about to do, Chaim leaned forward and brushed a brief kiss across her forehead.

"Can't stay away from the babies, huh?" he said, his tone filled with humor. "All right. Go have some lady time. I'll stay with the men, or perhaps join Dustin at horseshoes." He leaned next to her ear. "Let him know I'm no longer irritated with his nosy questions. Back home, I'm the champ, and nobody can beat me. Not even Dustin." He looked over at his cousins. "I wonder if it's the same here."

Did Chaim really regret she was leaving him? Or was his attention and affection all for show in front of his father and uncle? The kiss on her forehead was still warm and special as she walked away, causing uncertainties and questions to swirl in her mind.

Dustin watched Chaim and Tessa from the opposite side of the ranch yard. After their contentious conversation the previous night on the upstairs landing, Chaim had avoided him all day. That hurt, especially since Chaim had been gone so long, the result of the beating his heart had taken from Emmeline Jordan. If he never heard *that* name again—it would be too soon.

At the rumble of wagon wheels, he turned to see Luke arriving with his family, as well as Madeline and baby Michaela. Blinking, he wondered if he was imagining things. Amazingly enough, Luke was dressed from head to toe in fringed buckskin breeches and shirt. A braided strip of his almost shoulder-length hair was adorned with an eagle feather. Dustin felt certain the

Indian attire was directed at him. Nobody but Dustin seemed surprised by this.

His family greeted them warmly, the ranch hands, too.

Aunt Claire ran her hand down the supple, honey-color leather, and made an appreciative sound in her throat. "You haven't worn your Cheyenne leathers for a long time, Luke. I'm so happy you did today. You look incredibly handsome."

Luke chuckled and searched the gathering until he found Dustin. Their gazes locked and then Luke smiled. "In celebration of John's homecoming. Just felt right." With a strong grip, he handed Faith and the others down. "I have nothing to hide about my heritage and everything to be proud of. Especially since meeting my Cheyenne sister, Fox Dancing."

When Aunt Claire took Holly from his arms, Luke spotted Dawn riding in the corral and waved.

Hickory led the now-empty buckboard toward the barn.

"Just the man I was looking for." Luke called Dustin over. "After our conversations the last few days, I thought you'd appreciate my native wear. They were given to me by an old friend, Eagle Gray, many years ago. I was married in them." He puffed out his chest and rubbed a hand down the soft leather. "What do you think?"

Luke's expression showed nothing, but Dustin didn't think his cousin was baiting him. Perhaps Luke was trying to win over his approval. Or find something to talk about. Everything he'd learned about Luke met Dustin's admiration, but the Indian heritage noticeable in his features—high cheekbones, deep, dark eyes, skin tone just a shade darker than the rest of the family—always brought a wave of shame. If only Dustin had stood up to the blacksmith's son when he had a chance, he wouldn't experience this inside turmoil.

Dustin stepped closer, felt the creamy soft leather, and a bit of his boyhood shame faded into the past. "I must admit, Luke, your native clothing is truly remarkable. You must be extremely proud. You have quite a friend to give you such an impressive gift." And he meant the words from his heart.

Luke nodded and smiled. "Remind me before you depart for Rio Wells, and I'll let you try them on. All my brothers have. They were a favorite of John's." He grinned and grasped Dustin's shoulder. "Nothing quite as comfortable as Cheyenne tanned leather. It's like wearing warm butter." He laughed, and his eyes sparkled with understanding. "You'll want a set of your own."

Chapter Forty-Five

"Look at 'em, Winston," Flood said quietly to his brother as they stood in the flickering light of the cookfire, watching their sons converse in the large group of men. The patriarchs each held a tumbler of good Kentucky bourbon while surveying the scene before them with proud and satisfied grins.

Luke, along with his brothers and cousins, had finished several games of horseshoes, Chaim victorious each match. Dinner had been served, eaten, and enjoyed, and then marionberry cobbler, one of Flood's favorites, with several dollops of sweet vanilla ice cream on top. Now their male progeny was gathered in a circle, along with Brandon, Roady, Francis, and several of the other ranch hands, exchanging stories and laughter.

"It's a sight to see, to be sure," Winston replied. "Our men. The men who will shape this country long after we're dead and buried. They're fine stock. Looking at these outstanding

specimens, I wish Winnie and I would've had two or three more."
He slung an arm around Flood's shoulders and pulled him close.
"Nothing like family, Flood. Nothing at all."

Flood nodded, feeling as if a pinecone was lodged in his
throat. "I know what you mean," he croaked out. "Seeing John
again after so many years, hearing his voice—it's a treasure. I
don't think I'll allow him to go back to Rio Wells when you all
depart. I can't. Having my youngest son home again is the best
present of all."

Winston turned to him, the flickering shadows of the flames
dancing on his face. "A man has to have a life of his own. John
has his medical practice in Texas. He'll not give that up easily. And
Lily operates her dress shop. They've built a life in Rio Wells.
That's a battle you won't win."

Flood huffed out his breath. "Don't I know all too well."

The fire popped, and Winston stepped away to crush a cinder
with the toe of his boot, his arm falling away. "*And* he has an
unhappy history here in Y Knot, too, lest you forget."

That was true. Bob Mackey. The merchant John accidently
killed when he was just a boy. Flood and Claire knew the horrific
mishap was one of the reasons John willingly left Y Knot for
medical school in the East. To get out of town. Away from prying
eyes—and memories. He'd not get John to stay home in
Montana, but a man could dream, couldn't he? "I'm sure the
accident is one of the reasons he might not feel at ease here, at
least for long. I wish it were different after all these years. Maybe
breathing is difficult for him in Y Knot. I wouldn't want him to
stay under those conditions."

"All you can do is love him," Winston said. "And know we're
looking after him for you. In all respects, I think of John as my
third son. Winnie and I both do."

They exchanged a knowing, sideways glance.

Laughter erupted from the group. Luke and Dustin were still at somewhat of a standoff. A friendly one, but a standoff all the same. Chaim nudged John with an elbow, and they laughed, including Matt and Mark.

Flood wondered what the conversation was about.

"And my Chaim," Winston went on. "Look at him. Such a handsome man. He's changed in the year and a half he's been gone. Matured. Maybe the time away was beneficial. He's grown up under an extremely influential older brother—sometimes finding the limelight was difficult. That couldn't have been easy. I can say that now, since he's promised to return to Texas and come back to the ranch. I don't know what I would've done if he was determined to return to Arizona. I sure like that sweet wife and baby he's bringing home. They're both such a revelation. I can't imagine why he never wrote to any of us, especially Winnie. He knows how much his mother has been pining for a grandbaby." He turned and studied Flood's face. "That's a mystery to me. One I'd like to figure out. Maybe, in some way, I could help him."

"A man's got to follow his—"

"I know. I know," Winston interrupted. "You don't have to remind me." He laughed at Flood's comical expression. "I guess you and me are in the same awkward boat. We still feel like the providers. Head of the households. We're old, with years of life under our belts. It's difficult to believe we can't control them anymore like when they were boys. We want to guide them, help make the right decisions clear, but that's not to their liking. The power pendulum has swung the other way."

Flood noticed Kyle Crittlestick marching his way, a huge grin splitting the preacher's face.

"Just returned from my two-week rounds to all the nearby churches to hear the news." The minister finger-combed his unruly, brown hair. "Happy birthday, my friend. I'm sorely put out I missed the big shindig. I hope you don't mind me crashing *this* party, but I just couldn't wait to offer my regards."

They shook hands and then Crittlestick pulled Flood into a hug.

"Not at all, Reverend, not at all. I'm happy you came out. Be sure and get a plate of food. Lucky'll help you. There's more than plenty left over. In the meantime, meet my older brother, Winston McCutcheon, all the way from Rio Wells, Texas. He was good enough to bring the whole Texas McCutcheon clan here to Montana. Claire and I are overjoyed with their presence and, they don't realize yet, I'm not allowing 'em to go home. And look, there's John! Home after all these years. He's here, along with his wife, Lily, and little girl, Clara, they named for Claire. Those other two tall, good-looking fellas are Winston's sons, Dustin and Chaim. He has two lovely daughters around here somewhere, as well. Just look for the muddled-headed ranch hands falling over themselves, and the young women won't be far away. Winston, this is Kyle Crittlestick, the reverend who's guided Y Knot and kept us all out of trouble for years."

"Good to meet you, Reverend," Winston said as they shook hands. "I'm glad my brother and his family have someone watching over their souls."

"I see the resemblance," Crittlestick said. "No one would ever question your relationship. The eyes. The smile. So good of you to make the long journey."

The reverend nodded his approval as Flood pointed out the wives and children who went with which son, as well as Madeline and Becky, and their friend, Wendy Knutson, being tailed by Nick and Tanner Petty. Since supper had been served, and appetites were appeased, the gathering had grown quiet.

Francis had driven Amy and Rachel home in the buckboard so they could put their little ones to bed. The older children would go home with their fathers when the party ended. Michaela was asleep in Tessa's arms, as was Clara in Lily's, as the two young women sat with Winnie, Claire, Charity, and Sally, cuddling her own little one. Shad Petty sat on the bunkhouse porch, strumming his guitar.

"The strangest thing," Reverend Crittlestick went on. "My last stop before returning to Y Knot was in Waterloo. They have a new preacher, so my services are no longer needed there, but since my route took me close, I decided to stop in and meet the new Shepherd. Offer my help, in case he was in need of clarification on any situation." He gave a nod. "Men of the flock must stick together, you know. Anyway, Reverend Pomeroy said he'd recently performed a wedding for a McCutcheon. You can imagine my surprise, since all your sons are already married, Flood. He mentioned this just as I was setting off. Being slightly absentminded, he'd already forgotten the bride's and groom's first names, and I didn't want to wait around for him to go to the rectory and find out. We'd been there earlier. The place was nearly unrecognizable with the clutter—which he said was the next item on his list of things to do. Finding the names might take all night, and I was in a hurry to get back to Y Knot." Crittlestick stopped talking and stared straight at Flood and Winston, waiting for a response.

What? Flood cut his gaze to Winston and then back at the reverend. No unattached McCutcheons could have gotten married in Waterloo. Had the new preacher lost his mind?

"The man must be confused," Flood ventured, speaking the only explanation that made any sense. "Chaim and his wife and daughter arrived on the train a day before Winston and his crew, but no single McCutcheons were among them. Being my family were in town, and many townsfolk are familiar with the McCutcheon name, folks could have been talking, as they do. The preacher friend of yours must have heard the name a time or two and gotten the names mixed up with the wedding couple. Maybe they're McPherson, McCrenshaw, or something other. There's no other explanation." He glanced again at Winston, who looked as if several confusing situations were running through his mind now, as well. "Right, Winston? Do you have any other idea to share?"

Winston shrugged. "I sure don't. The whole thing sounds mighty strange."

"Reverend Pomeroy said the fella was a strapping young man, handsome of face, with wide shoulders and honest eyes. The woman was a pretty thing, and she had a baby. A little girl." Crittlestick gave a nervous chuckle. "That description would fit any of your sons." He looked between them and then back over to the group of cousins. "Until I reached Y Knot and learned of the surprise party and your family traveling from Texas, I was confused as all get out. Once I heard that, I believed the ceremony Pomeroy spoke of must have been for one of your relatives. Although, traveling all the way from Texas to be married in a private ceremony in Waterloo before reaching Y Knot seems odd. But then I've had my share of curious requests before—it wouldn't be a first." He cleared his throat. "But, by the looks on your faces, you're just as bewildered." He grasped Flood's arm. "You must be right about Pomeroy mixing up the names of the wedding party with the names of a throng of McCutcheons invading Waterloo for a short amount of time." He glanced over his shoulder to the group and then back at the brothers. "Shall we keep this to ourselves for the time being? I believe that would be the prudent path to take."

Seeing Tessa in the hallway last night sprang into Flood's mind. She'd been sneaking. He'd seen her and was sure she'd seen him, too. Not to forget the strained, angry voices and the noise sparking him to look out into the hall in the first place. Claire said whatever was wrong between them would be worked out by the morning. Somehow, Flood didn't think that had occurred. Instead, another layer of mystery was added to the unknown.

"Flood? Winston?" Reverend Crittlestick ventured.

Winston was staring at Chaim in the group of men. "Agreed."

Flood nodded. Chaim and Tessa were the only possible choice, if the absentminded reverend could be believed. What was going on? And who really were Tessa and Michaela McCutcheon?

Chapter Forty-Six

Tessa wandered the party, feeling like an honored guest. In reality, the party was a reunion of the two McCutcheon families, but with how special she was treated by everyone, it felt as if the gathering was for her, Chaim, and Michaela. Everyone, without exception, were kind, interested, and loving. Even Dustin's suspicion seemed to have abated, and he addressed her with charm and wit, befitting a loving brother-in-law.

Every time she glanced up, she found Chaim's gaze following her. What did that mean? His interest produced a lightness to her step and made her breath come fast. She felt loved, even if she were reading her own feelings into it. Making his interest something more. For this one night, she'd enjoy herself. Allow herself to imagine what might be.

Watching at the horseshoe pit, Charity appeared at her side. She was carrying Michaela, who was all smiles. "Who's winning?" Charity asked quietly.

Roady was pitching against Chaim, and the two had quite a rivalry going.

"For the moment, Chaim, but he's just taken the lead. They've been going back and forth quite evenly." She took Michaela from Charity and settled the baby in her arms. Tessa appreciated the fact Charity treated her as if they'd been friends for years. No awkwardness between them. Tessa looked around. "And where's Brandon? I haven't seen him since supper was served."

"His deputy sent word a couple drifters were fighting in the saloon and he'd locked them up. Brandon went to town to make sure Justin had things under control. Justin's relatively new, and we don't have a lot of crime in Y Knot, so he's never really been tested. Brandon will take a second seat tonight, but make sure Justin has things in hand." Charity nudged her. "*And* because Brandon's a perfectionist. He likes things done by the book. He'll be back soon."

Tessa smiled. "I'm learning a lot about the family."

"*Your* family."

With a ringing clang, the men watching the horseshoe game burst into laughter. A few dollars exchanged hands.

Chaim appeared at her side and lifted Michaela from her arms. His forehead was shiny, and he'd just pushed his hair back from his face.

The baby snuggled into his neck, as comfortable as if she'd known him since birth.

Roady and the rest were laughing and setting up a new game.

"I lost to Roady, but that's fine. I was tired of playing. Wanted a little time with you and Michaela." He glanced at her now-empty hands. "Can I get you two something to drink?" He looked between her and Charity. "I think some of the women are sipping plum wine. I can get you a glass, if you'd like."

Tessa had never had an opportunity to drink liquor, but she'd seen the difference in Mr. and Mrs. Jordan when they imbibed a little too much. It was not uncommon for screaming matches and door slamming to follow. She wasn't sure she wanted to know.

"No, thank you." Charity smiled and shook her head.

"I'm fine too but thank you." Feeling his warm gaze, she nervously ran a hand down the front of her skirt. "I'm still quite full. I don't think I could take a drop."

He smiled as a sleepy Michaela played with the collar of his shirt. "I know what you mean. I overindulged in the meal, as well. My aunt and uncle do know how to throw a party." He winked at Charity then hitched his head. "Let's amble over toward the bunkhouse, where my sisters are. See what's keeping them smiling. Charity?"

She shook her head knowingly. "I'll just stay here and watch the next game."

Tessa marveled at the touch of her husband's free hand on the small of her back. Was this a dream, and she'd awaken to her small room at the Jordans' mansion, only to resume the drudgery of her life?

They were halfway to their destination when Brandon came riding back into the ranch yard. Charity greeted him and all looked to be fine. Tessa noticed Chaim's parents sitting with Flood and Claire, their curious gazes watching her and Chaim. Their interest was natural. They wanted to make sure their son was happy. That he hadn't married her on the rebound. If they only knew the truth, they'd be scandalized. "Do you think Hickory has told anyone he found you sleeping in the loft?" she whispered. "I've not heard anything or had questions about it."

"Not sure. If Dustin had heard, he'd surely ask me."

"Have you two made up?" she asked. "He's been very attentive and nice to me."

"We were never mad. I understand Dustin. He doesn't mean harm, even though sometimes he appears that way. He only wants what's best for me."

"And he doesn't think that's me."

Chaim tugged her to a stop. "I never said that. His suspicions are up, and, as we know, he has cause. He knows me well. There *is* a secret we're keeping. I think he feels that. He'll give up once he sees I'm committed."

Committed? Was Chaim committed? Would he stick with her through thick and thin? Now was easy, when every day was a party, and they had handfuls of family members supporting them. But what would happen later?

Chaim didn't know what was happening. A spell had come over him as he gazed at Tessa's face. She was the same woman he'd met only days ago and wore a dress she'd gotten from his sister. Her voice was just as lyrical as he remembered. Her demeanor unchanged. *Still,* something felt different. He hadn't had but one beer tonight, but lightheadedness made him giddy.

And the fact Tessa had attempted such an arduous journey alone, not knowing the outcome when she arrived, was astonishing. A love deeper than anything he'd ever felt before seeped into his blood and was now thrumming throughout his body. Tessa was his *wife.* He was the luckiest man in the world. Question was, would she ever feel the same? They'd agreed upon a marriage in name only. Would she ever want to change that? Would she be disgusted at his offer, or if he tried to kiss her? His life would be long and grudging, if she never wanted more.

"What?" asked Tessa softly. "You look odd." She pointed to Michaela and smiled.

The baby had lowered her head onto his chest and closed her eyes.

If she only knew what he'd been thinking the moment prior. He returned her smile. "I'm just admiring my beautiful wife here in the Montana moonlight."

She blinked and looked away.

"I mean it, Tessa." He gently turned her face back to him with a finger. He needed to get her thinking in the right direction.

"Chaim, please. You don't have to say those things. We both know where we stand. I like the honesty between us. As long as we're truthful with each other, no feelings will be hurt."

He was moving too fast. He'd work on being her best friend. Earn her trust. "Maybe you're right, but what I said is still true. Come on, let's go spend some time with Becky and Madeline. I've not had much chance since the big surprise."

They meandered over to the bunkhouse porch where Shad was playing his guitar and where his two younger brothers, as well as Smokey, stood in a circle with the unattached females.

"Chaim," Becky cried. "Just the person we're talking about."

"Oh?" He gave Tessa a knowing smile and winked. "What were you saying?"

"How pleased everyone is you're coming home to Rio Wells. And not only you, but Tessa and Michaela! Our nightmare has become a dream."

He'd been so confused in his misery he hadn't considered how his absence had affected his sisters. He'd make it up to them somehow. "I feel like it's a dream come true, as well, Becky." Now he only had to find a way to make his wife fall in love with him. Return his feelings. Idolization shone in his sister's eyes. He'd remember the look as long as he lived. "What do you think of Michaela?" he asked, to chase away the clog of emotion threatening to rob him of his voice.

"She's absolutely precious," Madeline replied. "I can only imagine what she'll look like when she's older."

Becky nodded. "Just like Tessa. I can see the resemblance. And you, as well, Chaim. Having a baby around the house will be so much fun."

Chaim felt Tessa straighten. He wished he could take away the hurt and fear she'd suffered as a child and young woman. Their fabrication was weighing on her, even if she didn't think so. Truth always wanted to be revealed. He wondered how long their secret would stay hidden.

Chapter Forty-Seven

Feeling shy, Tessa moved around the shadowy bedroom, making as little noise as possible. After all the goodnights at the conclusion of the party, she and Chaim had mounted the stairs together.

Michaela was fast asleep in her crib.

Tessa opened the wardrobe and stared at her nightgown. She dreaded undressing in front of her husband.

Chaim sat absorbed in the *Farmer's Almanac* he must have picked up somewhere downstairs. He looked relaxed in the chair, but maybe he felt as awkward as she did now. If that were so, he was a good actor.

She turned and faced him. "Anything interesting in there?" she asked, keeping her voice low.

His boyish grin said he'd been caught out. "Only the new moon and the coming rain. Supposed to be a wet year for

Montana and Texas, too. Let's hope the winter is milder than last."

"All things a rancher needs to know. Am I right?" She stepped over to the side of the bed and gingerly sat on the edge to face him. When she did, his eyes smiled.

"I think we should talk, Tessa," he said quietly. "I'm used to keeping my feelings and thoughts to myself, but now I'm married, I should change that. There's an edgy feel in the room. I think if we have a discussion why, it might go away."

A buzzy lightness zipped around her mind. Tonight had been lovely. She was getting to know his family and what it meant to be a rancher's wife. The women here were calm and delightful. Everyone looked out for each other. The iron-clad bond between these McCutcheon siblings and cousins was a testament, which was difficult to comprehend after spending so many years in the Jordan household. "I'm listening." She scooted back and made herself more comfortable on the bedside.

Chaim closed the *Almanac* and dangled the book in his fingers, as if in deep thought. After his statement, he seemed hesitant to begin.

Her breathing quickened. Had Dustin changed Chaim's mind? Was he rethinking their marriage? Nothing was forever. She knew that better than anyone.

He stood and stepped over, settling himself beside her on the bed. He took her hands in his own. "What did you think about tonight's shindig?"

Surprised, she was all too aware of his closeness. She glanced at their hands, almost overcome by the warmth. "I enjoyed the gathering very much. From the moment I met your family in Waterloo, they've been incredibly kind. And now I know your extended family, as well. They're truly a welcoming bunch."

"And?"

"And what?" What was he hinting at?

"What do you think about me?" When she didn't respond right away, he said, "Our being together. How I held your hand. Were you putting up with me for appearance's sake, or did you enjoy it?"

She felt a flush creep up her face. "I liked it, very much, but I believe the endearments were to make your mother and father happy. And to convince Dustin you're not hiding anything. I don't blame you in the least."

"What if I told you I wanted to feel your hand in mine? I wanted to kiss your forehead. Simple as that." Leaning forward slightly, he tucked a loose strand of her hair behind her ear and smiled. "I touched you, because I chose to. No—*needed* to." He held her gaze. "I've had a change of heart since our conversation in Waterloo. I hope you have, too."

A change of heart? What about Emmeline? Your true love you'll never forget?

"What kind of change?"

"About a marriage in name only."

A flicker of excitement raced through her. Still, she shouldn't jump to assumptions without giving him a chance to explain. "Because of Michaela?"

"Partly. I'd be a liar if I said I wasn't touched how tenderly you care for her. She loves you like a mother, and you love her as if she were your own. Your bond plays a part in my feelings, but that's not what I'm speaking about now."

His gaze roamed her face for several long seconds, intensifying the prickle of heat in her cheeks.

"You're always in my thoughts, Tessa. You've filled my mind. My heart. My world lights up when you walk into the room."

She took a trembling breath trying to believe this was truly happening.

"I'd like our marriage to be a real one," he went on. "And, if we're so blessed, give Michaela siblings." He studied her face as the importance of this moment sank in. At her silence, he brought her hands to his lips, and he kissed the backs of her fingers, never taking his gaze off hers. "Tessa, speak to me."

"I'm confused," she replied softly. "What you said so recently about always loving Emmeline is still fresh in my mind. I don't want to compete with my cousin who's passed away. Memories are strong. There'd be no way of winning that battle. And, too, thinking about a *real* marriage, I feel as if we hardly know each other. We've only just met." She dropped her gaze to the bed between them, her face burning with embarrassment.

"Tessa?"

She glanced up into his eyes. "I have little experience with men, Chaim. I've never been courted." Unable to hold his gaze any longer, she looked away. "I know that's shocking at my age," she whispered to the wall. "I'm embarrassed to even admit that aloud."

"Tessa, look at me."

She turned his way.

"Never be embarrassed about telling the truth. I didn't mean I wanted to consummate the marriage tonight. Or even in a week. If you're willing, I'd like to court you." He kissed her fingers again, letting his lips linger, their faces close. "Until being together is something you want as much as I do."

Such talk. "What about Emmeline?"

"I loved Emmeline. I meant what I said at the time. But I've changed. You've changed me. These days together, dancing with you in my arms, how you care so thoughtfully for my daughter…I'd be a crazy man to stay blind to the truth. Your sweet love has rescued me, Tessa. Pulled me out of a life of anger and bitterness. As well as the constant condemnation of myself for trusting Emmeline. I'm sorry for the position our rash actions put her in with the baby. Hiding the pregnancy must have been a frightening burden. I'll never understand why she didn't return. I know what you said about her family's finances, but we could have worked through that. I can't change the past. And given the chance, I'm not sure I'd want to. Because if I did, you and I would not meet, and we wouldn't have Michaela. I do feel a little guilty about the happiness I've found. All I can say is what I feel now. At this moment. And that's about you and me, not me and a memory."

He looked off to the window for several long moments and then shrugged. "But, to be perfectly honest, there's still an element of trust in you I'm wrestling with. I don't know if Rio Wells will suit you once we return to Texas. It's a long way from Boston and could be another planet, for all the differences. I'm more fearful than ever you'll grow tired of life in the West. Life is unpredictable. Your leaving would kill me. For those reasons, I'm cautious."

She contemplated her answer.

He rushed to go on. "I just want to be sure you feel the same. I know the most important thing to you is raising Michaela. If I'm pushing too much, or you want to stay with our prior agreement, just say so. I want you to want me for who I am. To *love* me. Not to be considerate of my feelings more than your own. I'd never want you to go against your sentiments."

The tremble began inside and worked outward to her hands.

He gave a steadying squeeze.

"I want to be a real wife to you, Chaim. I appreciate your patience, though, as well. And I think courting will be good for us both. Give us time to learn about each other. Sort out problems and discuss them…" Feeling dizzy from his words, she watched as he leaned closer, amazed he intended to kiss her.

Would he be able to tell their chaste peck at their wedding had been her first?

His lips touched hers. She stayed completely still as he lingered, pressed a bit more firmly. His lips were warm and dry, and tasted of coffee and the sweets they'd consumed at the party. Feeling heady and lightheaded, she resisted the urge to pull him closer.

He slowly leaned back, studying her gaze for a reaction.

"I'm sorry. I…"

"Shhh. It was nice. I'm going downstairs to put the *Almanac* back in the library and give you time to get into bed. I promise to stay on my side tonight. You don't have to worry about that."

Her face must be apple red. "Thank you, Chaim."

He stood and pulled her to her feet. "Nothing to thank me for." His eyes danced with anticipation. "Oh, we may need to disagree on occasion, like an old married couple, for appearance's sake. Just giving you a heads up."

She smiled. "I can do that." And she could. But what would happen to this plan if John remembered he'd seen her at the Jordans? When that truth came tumbling out, everyone would discover she'd taken Michaela without permission. She was a kidnapper, even though she'd acted to ensure Michaela's happiness. Could Chaim withstand the shock and dismay of his family? Or would he take Michaela and go on without her?

Chaim was halfway down the staircase when he met his uncle coming up. They both pulled up in surprise.

"Uncle Flood?" Chaim looked around. "The house was quiet. I thought I was the only one still up."

"I like to make one final pass around the place, especially when I have a house full of guests." He gave a wide smile and shook his head. "I'm pleased to have this opportunity to get to know you, Chaim. Thinking you're all here at the Heart of the Mountains all the way from Texas and Arizona is still hard to believe. I'm afraid I'll wake up and discover I've been dreaming."

With everything going on, Chaim hadn't had a good heart-to-heart talk with his uncle. The strong resemblance to his own father was uncanny. Chaim was a bit awestruck being in his presence.

"Is there anything I can help you with?" Flood asked, probably wondering what Chaim was doing in the semi-dark house.

He lifted the *Almanac*. "I picked this up in your library and mean to return it."

"Ahhh, I understand. Gives Tessa time to get your little one to sleep without any distractions. She sure is pretty and sweet. Actually, they both are. You're a lucky man."

Chaim got the distinct impression his uncle was curious about something and using small talk to prolong the conversation. Nothing he'd said directly, just a feeling inside the moment he'd mentioned Tessa and Michaela. If Tessa wasn't set on keeping Michaela's parenthood a secret, confiding in his uncle would be a relief. Someone who wouldn't be going home to Rio Wells. A good man who could listen with an open mind. Chaim still felt honesty was always the best policy. Keeping the truth back made him edgy. The next lie would always be needed to keep the story straight. "Thank you. I agree wholeheartedly. Sure was a nice evening tonight. Tessa and I enjoyed the party."

A few troubled lines appeared on Flood's brow. "Do you know what's between Luke and Dustin? I can't figure them out. A tension's there that shouldn't be."

"Between Luke and Dustin?"

"Like a simmering animosity whenever they're together."

Chaim leaned against the banister. How much should he say? He felt a loyalty to his brother but also to his extended family. "Not sure, exactly. Growing up, Dustin possessed a healthy curiosity about Luke. Other than that..." He shrugged.

"You're right. Probably nothing to worry over."

The way Flood was searching his gaze, Chaim wasn't quite sure his uncle believed what he'd just said.

"And how's Tessa getting along?" Flood eased his hip against the staircase balusters getting comfortable. "Is she enjoying herself here in Montana?"

A note of caution entered Chaim's mind. "Absolutely. She likes the fresh mountain air."

"Much cooler than Arizona, I'd suppose. A big change."

Chaim's face heated, even in the cool evening temperatures. "Definitely."

Uncle Flood rubbed his palms together and smiled. "I've not seen Arizona, but I'd like to someday. How did the two of you like Waterloo? You spent a night there before the others arrived. Do anything unusual?"

Unusual? What had Uncle Flood heard? A secret wedding could fall into the unusual category, as well as this conversation. Chaim hated to lie. "Unusual? In what way? Unusual as in rarely happening or unusual for a family with a small child? The two are quite different." He tried to smile, but the expression felt strained. Where was this line of questions coming from? The sooner he and Tessa made their marriage real, the sooner the others would stop picking up on their timidity with each other. Hopefully, after tonight's conversation, things would move in the right direction.

His uncle chuckled. "I guess my question was offhand. There's not much to do in Waterloo. I should stop being so nosy, or you'll think your uncle is an old busybody—which I'm anything but."

Chaim waved away his embarrassment.

Uncle Flood took the gesture as a signal to continue. "Your marital news took everyone by surprise. A delightful surprise, mind you, but still a surprise. Your father and mother can't stop talking about how amazing it is you've taken a wife. And you being a father, to boot." He grinned and gripped Chaim's shoulder, pulling him in for a brief hug. "Nothin' better than that, as you now know. They're so happy to have you back, son. I hope you don't mind me calling you son. You remind me so much of my boys right now, standing here discussing family matters, my heart is full to overflowing. I can't help but to think of you and Dustin as my own. Your sisters, too. If there's ever *anything* you need to talk about, Chaim, you know you can come to me." He searched Chaim's face intently. "I'm tightlipped when I need to be. *Anything* at all. Sometimes it's nice to toss ideas off someone who's not too close."

What's gotten into him? "Thanks, Uncle Flood. I'll keep that in mind." The jubilation he felt over the new development with Tessa only moments before was replaced with wariness. Uncle Flood knew something, but he was holding his cards close to his vest. Chaim couldn't understand how or what had happened exactly, but the pit in his stomach said the secret he and Tessa were keeping was out of the bag—at least, with his uncle.

Flood gripped his shoulder one last time and stepped past him on the stairs. "Goodnight, Chaim. Now go get some rest, and I'll see you at breakfast. Tomorrow's another busy day."

Chapter Forty-Eight

"You sure you want to make the ride?" Chaim slung his arm over the hip of the horse he'd use for the morning ride. He looked down at his wife and studied her face with concern. He worried about her. He wanted her to go, but not if she'd complied just to make him happy. Since they'd met, she'd displayed a hesitancy around horses. She hadn't said anything specific; he'd just picked up a few subtleties. "We won't be gone long. We'll return around midmorning and later head into Y Knot. You might be more comfortable staying here with Michaela." He noticed a few tiny freckles he'd never seen before as a gentle wind made wisps of her hair dance in her face. "I hear we're headed back to the Biscuit Barrel. They're famous around these parts for their pies."

They stood with the others at the bunkhouse hitching rail while the ranch hands saddled seven extra horses to outfit their guests for a ride around the Heart of the Mountains. Smokey was cinching up a roan for Dustin, and Nick Petty was doing the same to a docile chestnut for Tessa.

Chaim didn't trust Tessa's statement that she had enough experience on a horse if they stayed to a jog. She might have ridden, but he didn't want her to be scared. Once they reached Rio Wells, he could school her slowly and take the time needed to become a confident rider. One bad ride could sour a person forever.

Today, she'd borrowed clothes from Charity's closet and also from his Aunt Claire. He admitted to himself she looked fetching in a pair of trousers. In the bedroom, she'd questioned his decision to wear his gun, since she'd not seen it since arriving in Y Knot. He'd told her men didn't go into the unknown without the ability to fend off danger. Even on your own ranch. A bear or outlaw could always appear. Sure enough, every man there was armed.

"I'm *sure* about going, Chaim," she replied in a teasing tone. "Sidney and Lily are. I don't want to be left out."

He followed when she went to her chestnut and stroked the horse's silky muzzle. "You won't be lonely if you stay. Faith, Rachel, and Amy are coming over soon. And bringing the little ones. I just think you might worry about Michaela the whole time."

She turned to him, her eyes dancing with amusement.

"Don't be silly. Your mother and aunt promised to take extra care with Michaela and Clara. And, as you stated, the other women will be here any moment. Maybe Winnie and your aunt don't know, but Faith told me last night she and Holly planned to pick blackberries this morning. With such a large crowd, Esperanza needs them for her cobbler tomorrow evening, and Faith volunteered." Tessa gave a knowing smile. "I'd never consider leaving Michaela for a whole day. She'd be frightened.

But two or three hours will be fine. And I'm not the only beginner rider. Lily hasn't ridden much, either. This morning, at the breakfast table, she sounded excited for the tour."

She likes debating. Was she arguing with him because of his statement last night? He wasn't sure, but once she'd made up her mind, there was no changing it.

Dustin ambled up. "Lover's quarrel?"

The teasing light in his eyes asked for forgiveness, and Chaim didn't take offense. When he opened his mouth to reply, Dustin held up a hand. "Just kidding, little brother. You should hear Sidney and me go 'round and 'round when my opinion doesn't match up with hers. I rarely get the upper hand, but honestly, I'm glad you're coming along, Tessa. I think that's admirable, you bein' a city gal and all. We'll make a rancher out of you yet."

"That's what I'm hoping," Tessa replied. "Nothing like the present moment to begin…"

Chaim shrugged dubiously. "When she gets her mind set on something, I might as well toss in the reins. Anything else is a waste of breath."

Tessa blushed. "I'm not *that* bad."

"Not bad at all." Sidney had joined them at the hitching rail, dressed much like Tessa. "I couldn't help but hear the conversation. We women need to stick together. An easy morning ride will be perfect. The best view in the world is from the back of a horse. *And* we'll cover so much more ground. Your uncle is raring to go."

John and Lily arrived at the bunkhouse, Lily appearing hesitant, not nearly as confident as she'd been at the breakfast table. She reached out and touched the roan gelding with trembling fingers. "I've only ridden twice," she said in her soft German accent. Her long hair hung down her back in a thick blonde braid. "Once in the corral at the Rim Rock, and once around Rio Wells on John's horse, as he walked by my side." She gave a small laugh. "All before Clara, mind you. Every time John suggests I get more familiar with the idea of riding, I think of something more important that needs doing." She looked up at John, who had a smile from ear to ear. "Today, I don't want to be left out of the fun." She glanced around at the others.

Mark and Matt McCutcheon came out of the bunkhouse, the door slamming behind them. Both brothers carried an armful of yellow rain slickers. They began handing them around.

"We don't want to be caught off guard," Matt said, gesturing to the swaying treetops. "There's always a chance of rain this time of year. And with these slight winds, clouding can happen fast. I don't know about you all, but I don't want to get drenched before our trip into Y Knot. Tie these to the back of your saddles."

"You callin' me a tenderfoot, cousin?" Dustin asked jokingly. "You think just because I live in Texas, I don't know what to do with a slicker?"

"I'm speaking to the ladies, of course, Dustin." Matt grinned and shook his head. "My wife doesn't like getting caught in a downpour. The sky looks pretty clear now, but in Montana, storms gather quickly."

Dustin and Chaim exchanged a look. John slapped his cousins on the back. They were back on firm ground, and the fact felt good. Chaim never liked being in a disagreement with anyone.

While Sidney and Dustin rolled up their raingear to tie to their saddles, Tessa took her yellow slicker and slung the garment around her shoulders as if it was a shawl, catching Chaim's eye. She raised her brows playfully.

She's flirting with me. Sleeping next to her last night had taken every ounce of willpower he had. Under the covers was warm and enticing, and his wife only an arm's reach away. He longed for the time she'd fall asleep in his arms after making love. Chaim stepped close and whispered, "Remind me to buy you a slicker as soon as we reach Rio Wells. Looks good on you."

"No lovey-dovey stuff, now," Dustin quipped and then winked at Tessa. "My sister-in-law needs to keep her wits about her. Concentrate on her horse. She's not an experienced rider."

Luke rode into the ranch yard with Dawn at his side. The small, brown mare she rode yesterday was swaybacked and her muzzle, and the area around her eyes, frosty white. Chaim hadn't noticed before, but the tiny western saddle was equipped with everything a ranch hand might need. Hobbles, a lariat, a canteen, and even a bedroll. This little cowgirl took her job seriously. "Where're the older boys?" Chaim called as Luke and Dawn reined up beside the group. "Thought I'd heard they'd be riding along."

"Decided to go fishing. They've seen the ranch more times than they can count. With all the goings-on, they haven't had a chance for days, or at least, that's what they said." He lifted a shoulder. "I remember being their age and enjoying time away from adults. Can't say I blame 'em." He dismounted and handed his reins up to his daughter. "You can be sure they'll be back in time to go to the Biscuit Barrel. They'd never miss a chance at huckleberry pie."

The door across the ranch yard opened and closed, and Winston and Flood strode their way. All the horses were saddled, and the group waited.

Luke joined Chaim and the other men. "Look at 'em," Luke said. "I've never seen Flood so happy." He turned to his cousins. "I can't thank you enough for making this trip. You can be sure we'll return the favor. I'm anxious to see the Rim Rock firsthand."

Flood and Winston were of the exact same height. Both men were fit and walked with confidence and more than a smattering of pride. His pa was a bit grayer, but they both still sported a full head of hair. They were lucky that way. Uncle Flood's face was a bit more lined, especially around his eyes, but that added to his character. Who wouldn't get wrinkles having had his wife abducted by the Cheyenne all those years ago? "They sure present a powerful picture," Chaim mumbled. "An example for all of us."

"Amen to that," Matt replied. "I count myself lucky to have been born a McCutcheon. I don't know about the rest of you, young'uns," he chuckled, "but being the oldest McCutcheon here, besides our fathers, of course, makes me get a lump in my throat. I wouldn't want to be anyone else."

"Enough sentimentality," Chaim stated with a grin. He assisted Tessa into her saddle, patting her leg once she found her stirrups. "How does the length feel? If they're too short, you'll be sore for days. Stand up in your stirrups and let me see how much room you have between you and the saddle."

She looked askance.

He couldn't stop a chuckle. "What? All right, if you'd rather, stand up and look yourself to see. Should be about an inch, no more." He glanced away, giving her a moment.

"They're fine," she quickly replied, not catching his eye.

"Good." He gathered his reins and mounted his horse, excited for the coming day. A whole morning with Tessa touring the ranch and then a trip into town. They'd take in all the shops and then see if Montana pie could hold a candle to Boston. Or, that of Texas. His mouth watered thinking about the dried raisin pie at the Cheddar Box Restaurant in Rio Wells. Or the blueberry cobbler at the Lillian Russel Room in the Union Hotel. Surprised, Chaim realized he had missed his hometown. He smiled, catching Tessa's eye. So many things to look forward to. Chaim felt his life had taken a great big right-hand turn for the better and, with

Tessa thinking the way he was, it could only improve…and very soon to boot.

Chapter Forty-Nine

The beauty of the upper pastures, river, and bridge always created a homespun cozy feel inside Luke. The glittering rapids were peaceful, and the wildflowers in the springtime were filled with light—with no burdens at all. Growing up, he'd spent many, many hours in these grasslands. Flood made sure his sons worked alongside the ranch hands. The solid work ethic made all the McCutcheon brothers, and even Charity, tough as nails with a healthy dose of fortitude.

As Matt stated so heartfelt just this morning, he and his siblings and cousins were blessed to be McCutcheons. Luke wouldn't want to be anyone else. A few horses over, Dustin sat his horse as he looked over the view before them. He'd ridden close to Luke most of the morning and yet hadn't initiated any conversation. Didn't his cousin know your family—and the people who loved you and raised you—made you who you were. The blood flowing through your veins made no difference at all.

Glancing up, Luke contemplated the dark sky. His bandanna ends snapped around his neck. The storm had blown in over the past two hours, whipping the horses' manes and tails and any clothing that wasn't tightly tied on. At the last stop, they'd decided to cut the ride short for the day. After reaching the bridge, they'd head back. No one wanted the women to get drenched. For city girls like Lily and Tessa, that might be just enough aggravation to sour them on riding altogether.

"We completed the bridge five years ago," Flood called loudly over the sounds of the rushing river and howling wind. "Joe Brunn, you remember him, Winston, along with several men, built it." He puffed out his chest with pride.

"Looks sturdy," Winston commented.

"It'll be standing when we're long gone."

Mark twisted in his saddle to look at his uncle. "Has to be strong. We drive thousands of head over it several times a year. Saves us from swimming 'em each time, which they like about as much as being split up. There's always a chance to lose a few head to drowning."

Luke glanced down the row of horses lined up on the south bank of the river, listening to Flood. His heart squeezed, watching Dawn on Firefly. The little girl he'd delivered almost five years ago was his shadow and followed him everywhere. He considered her his own, even though he'd not sired her.

He grasped his hat when a strong gust of wind almost ripped it from his head. A bad feeling stirred in his bones. They should have left this ride for another day, but Flood was anxious to show off the ranch.

Another burst made the ladies laugh and reach for their flying braids.

Beneath Luke, Traveler snorted and the men along the bank exchanged an uneasy look.

"We should head back before the rain hits," he called over to Flood and Winston. "The sky looks..."

"I want to show Winston the far pasture first. We'll cross the bridge and ride to the top of the ridge. We won't go any farther. Only takes a couple minutes."

More like five.

"That's the best view of the valley," Flood went on. "We'll have time to get back before any of the women feel a drop of rain."

Flood and Winston nudged their horses forward, and the rest of the group followed amid excited chatter.

Luke glanced back to see Dawn chattering away with the ladies, ambling along with the rest. They crossed the wide bridge in a chorus of clomping hooves and the whistle of the wind. In a matter of minutes, the sky transformed from iron blue to a steely gray. He anticipated getting to the top of the ridge so they could turn around and head back. This storm seemed to be coming in fast from the Northwest, which was unusual. Once they got to the top of the ridge, they'd know exactly what to expect.

The horses pranced and pulled at their bits as they ascended the hill, frisky and raring to go. Luke held a tight rein on Traveler, who wanted to run.

Tessa and Lily looked frightened with saucer-wide eyes, but Chaim and John stayed close, talking quietly.

Sidney rode with the confidence of someone who worked cattle every day. Dustin was a lucky man with that. They had common ground between them.

Feeling antsy himself, he motioned for Dawn to ride forward and join him. Any tumbleweed could spook Firefly in this wind. He'd feel better with her at his side.

She nodded and squeezed Firefly into a trot.

Tessa's mare jumped forward, wanting to follow.

Chaim reached out and took one of Tessa's reins, snubbing her horse's head close to his knee.

When they reached the top of the bluff, anyone wearing a Stetson had to press their hat to their head to keep from losing it. The wind rushed in every direction. Leaves flew every which way, and the grass whipped back and forth.

Tessa's mare, probably picking up on her fear, spooked at nothing and crow-hopped several strides, even with Chaim's close attention.

Tessa screeched and grabbed for the saddle horn.

"Look!" The shout came from his brother, John, his arm pointing northeast.

Several miles away, the entire sky on the far horizon was as black as ink. The clouds churned in turbulence.

Traveler snorted and pulled on his bit.

All the horses danced in nervous energy, their manes and tails twisting violently in the wind.

"My God!" Flood shouted. "A twister! And headed this way." He looked down the line at the group. "Not much time. We've got to warn everyone. Get them to shelter." As his gaze riveted each son and nephew with purpose, his hat was ripped from his head and sailed away. "I'll take the new ranch. Judging by the trajectory, that monster may have already struck. Jonathan and Ike might be hurt and need help. As much as I want to ride home for Claire, I know you boys will get your mother, aunt, and the rest to the root cellar in the off chance the twister makes it all the way to the ranch."

"They're unpredictable as hell," Winston hollered back, clutching his hat to his head. "Two came near Rio Wells just last year."

Mark spun his horse, holding the gelding back with a firm hand. The horse reared and pulled at the bit. "I'm on my way to the ranch! That's where Amy and the children are. Don't worry about anyone there. I'll make sure they're safe."

Flood nodded.

Mark galloped away.

Winston grasped Flood's shoulder. "I'm going with you, Flood! Don't try to change my mind. I've seen a twister shift direction six or seven times, willy-nilly. You shouldn't go alone."

"The boys are at the fishing hole," Luke hollered over the roaring wind. "And Faith and Holly are out picking berries. Someone needs to round up the boys while I go find Faith and Holly." He glanced at Dawn, who was staring at the coming funnel cloud in horror. He spurred his horse closer, scooped her out of her saddle, and placed her in front of him.

"Firefly!" she cried.

"Matt'll remove her bridle, and she'll run home." He looked at his brother, who leaned from his saddle and did his bidding without even dismounting.

"I'll get the boys," Matt shouted, turning his horse. "I'll keep Colton with us, Luke. Don't worry about him." A second later, dust kicked up and he was gone.

Flood pointed at Dustin. "You and Sidney ride into Y Knot and warn the town. You know the way? Just pass the ranch and stay on the road. Look for the firehouse and ring the bell. Get going!"

The two wheeled around and galloped down the hill heading for the bridge.

Luke took a long look at the rest of the group. This could be the last time he saw any of them. With a heavy heart, he shot a quick prayer to the Almighty. Tightening his arm around Dawn's middle, he spun Traveler and raced away.

Firefly galloped on his horse's heels.

Chapter Fifty

Tessa couldn't tear her gaze away from the swirling, ominous darkness inching ever closer. Everything the funnel cloud touched was ripped from the ground, including large trees. She couldn't imagine anything living through such crushing force. She'd heard of tornadoes but had never seen a picture or heard any conversation about one. The unknown was terrifying.

"John, it's up to you and Chaim to get your wives safely home. We've got to go, *now*. You remember the shortcut to the ranch?"

"Of course," John hollered back. "There's no time to lose. Good luck, Pa. God speed to all of us."

Tessa saw fear in Flood's gaze, not just for the coming storm but for her and Lily, the two inexperienced riders.

Sidney had galloped off with the skill of a jockey. No one had any doubt she'd ride all the way to Y Knot just fine.

On the horse beside her, Lily cried out as her horse half-reared and then pawed the ground, anxious to be far away from the approaching blackness. A shower of stinging rain hit them in the face from a midnight-black sky.

Both husbands gripped the reins from their wives' mounts, fighting to keep the animals under control.

"We'll be fine," Chaim called to his uncle and father. "Just take care of each other. Don't be distracted thinking about us." He turned to read his wife's expression. "Hang onto the saddle horn, Tessa. We're going to lope."

Lope? The four horses in her group were prancing and pulling at their bits, wanting to race after Chaim's father and uncle who departed in a different direction than the others.

With a cry of alarm, her horse crashed into Chaim's mount and smashed her leg against his. Pain riveted through her knee.

The shrieking of the storm was deafening. Rain turned to hail, and the horses snorted in pain.

John and Lily went first, descending the hill at a lope, the gait she'd never dreamed she'd accomplish today.

Chaim moved forward and, with a tug on her horse, jogged a few strides, jarring her teeth mercilessly together. An instant later, the horse seemed to skip a beat, and the gait was more like a rocking chair. A *fast* rocking chair. She wished she was back at the ranch, rocking Michaela. The saddle, comfortable at a walk, now felt large and slippery. She struggled to keep her seat as she wobbled and tipped from side to side.

In front of them, John and Lily pulled away. Lily's long braid wagged on her back, and her legs flapped as she did her best to stay aboard. No one wanted to fall now and be gobbled up by the twister.

Thoughts of Michaela sluiced through Tessa's jumbled mind. Would she ever see her darling girl again? Would the twister hit the home ranch and kill everyone there? Or would her group die on the way going home? All the options were too devastating to even consider.

Dearest Lord, please deliver us from this storm...

"Lean forward and let your weight sink into your heels!" Chaim shouted over the howling wind. "Helps you balance." He sent her a tense smile. Their horses lunged forward, their hooves digging into the dirt. Soon, they were closer to John and Lily. As they approached the bridge, she prayed the men wouldn't gallop across. Now slick with rain, she feared her horse would fall and crush her.

Almost there, both men slowed.

Air pressure pushed wickedly on her eardrums and in her head. Hair stung her eyes. She dared a glance over her shoulder to the top of the hill they'd just descended.

The black, churning sky looked like something out of a nightmare, the first horrible image of the twister etched in her mind. Was it only last night she'd lain so still in the same bed with Chaim, dreaming about their future? Those moments of wonder felt like a year ago. Any second, they all could be dead.

"Hurry, hurry," she called, even though she knew Chaim and the others couldn't hear her. The two words were her mantra, playing over and over in her head. She gripped the saddle horn with white-knuckled fists. They crossed the bridge together in a clamor of hooves, not at a gallop but still faster than she'd have liked. The men's bandannas whipped around their necks and slapped them in the face. She leaned into the tempest, bending close to her horse's neck, the scent of sweat-soaked flesh cloying in her nose.

"Not much farther to a cave I know," John yelled at the top of his voice. "Ride like hell and don't lose me in the darkness."

A second later, they were galloping faster than before. The ground was flat and better suited for the horses. The rhythm of the four-beat stride felt good and bolstered her confidence. Leaning forward, she let go of the saddle horn and wound her hands in the long red mane, her gaze riveted to the ground in front of her mount's driving hooves. With the sound of a runaway train behind ready to crush them, she chanced another look to see the twister appear on the top of the hill and then descend in their direction as if hunting them down.

Swallowing a scream, she drummed her heels repeatedly into the side of her rain-soaked horse, and the animal jumped forward in a burst of speed, galloping neck and neck with Chaim.

It felt as if they were struggling through quicksand before they left the openness of the meadow to dart down a cattle path and through some blowing trees.

Chaim hated to give Tessa's mare more rein, but there was no help for it. They couldn't ride side by side any longer and she'd have to ride behind. He was surprised by his wife's bravery. And her ability to stay in the saddle. Brushes slapped around them in the tight quarters. He hoped Tessa was able to keep the worst from her face. Scratches and puncture wounds would heal. A trip up a twister could not. He felt helpless to keep her safe. The day had turned as black as night, and John and Lily were again pulling away.

Suddenly, John was there, waiting for them. "Here! Follow me." And with that, he rode off the beaten path, leading Lily's horse.

Chaim followed, cursing the slow pace. The rocky, uneven ground was dangerous. The rain and hail pelted the earth, leaving everything slick. A sheer granite wall appeared with a large, dark hole.

Dismounted now, John pulled Lily from the saddle.

Chaim did the same and whisked Tessa beside him. Grasping her hand, they ran into the murky darkness, watching for rocks and branches. Their sudden appearance startled a deer out of its safety, back out into the ferocious sound of the twister. "Stay here!" Chaim shouted and ran back for the horses but found them gone.

The surrounding rock gave relief from the brutal wind and noise. The respite was stunning. He pulled Tessa down and covered her with his body, praying they could ride this through. She was small, and he wrapped her with his arms and legs, wanting to protect her. The immense turmoil thundered as the monster passed. Cracking and splintering of trees and shrubs reverberated around the cave. Was this granite strong enough to shelter them through the chaos? He closed his eyes and held on.

At the sound of the mighty roar, Tessa huddled under the safety of Chaim's body as he shielded her. His warmth and scent guarded her thoughts, even too terrified to contemplate the cyclone beast just a few feet away. Any moment, they might be sucked out and flung miles, never to see Michaela again. Never again to feel Chaim's arms around her. As the thunderous roaring outside increased, she knew the tempest would be on them at any moment. She closed her eyes and prayed for deliverance.

Jagged memories of her mother pierced Tessa's mind. First, she was five, and then ten, her mind settled on twelve. Visiting for her mama's birthday. The handkerchief she'd embroidered with her mother's initials and a little blue mayflower. Her mother at the sink washing two teacups. Tessa on a stool beside her, drying as she admired the beauty of her mother's hands.

"Will I ever fall in love? Will he stay with me always?"

When Tessa went to work at the Jordans', her mother had revealed the whole truth about her birth and who Tessa really was. She was not just a housemaid or servant, but the daughter of one of the Jordan brothers. Important in her own right.

"You will, absolutely. And your husband will love you always, and the two of you will grow old together. I promise you that."

"But what if he doesn't love me enough? What if he thinks he does and then later decides he wants to leave? What if I end up alone, like you? How will I know the difference?"

Her mother had stilled for a moment before she'd resumed the chore. She turned to Tessa and smiled.

Tessa hadn't meant to hurt her mother's feelings and wished she could take back her question, even though she wanted to know the answer. Before her mother could reply, she asked, *"Is it better for my beau to love me more than I him, or for me to love him more than he loves me?"*

Finished with the dishes, Tessa's mama dried her hands and ushered Tessa out back into the coolness of the evening air. When they sat, she picked up Tessa's hand and caressed it with her own.

"You mustn't worry so much about this, my love. You're only a girl. What happened in my life will not happen in yours. Your question is one many have pondered for all time. All I can tell you is what I think is the best. What was best for me, over my life.

If I could have a wish, it would be for you to love your husband the most. When a person is truly in love, wholly and completely, their heart is happy. A joyous heart wants to do and be everything for the other. It stays happy, for the most part, even when the love that's returned is not as ardent. But, the wonder is, not responding to an all-consuming love is difficult. St. Augustine said, better to have loved and lost, than to have never loved at all. I loved your father, Tessa. Even after he hurt me. I never begrudged him because he brought me the greatest aspect of my life. You. My prayer is, someday, some miracle will bring the two of you together."

Chapter Fifty-One

Dustin and Sidney galloped into Y Knot side by side, not slowing even when a group of men hanging out in front of the Hitching Post Saloon stopped talking to take notice of the fierce, blustery weather. The storm had increased to a tirade as the day descended into darkness. Foreboding black clouds swirled low, just over the building tops, promising a drenching rain, if nothing else.

Dustin slid his horse to a halt, turning a half circle as he scanned the area for the building Uncle Flood had called the volunteer firehouse and the bell they were supposed to ring to alert the town.

Sidney shouted over the wind and pointed. "There!" A small, barn-shaped building where the town's buckets, shovels, and water wagon must be stored away was just down the street. On the fast ride into Y Knot, strands of Sidney's hair had worked loose of the braid and now whipped around her face like the cyclone itself.

With only a nudge of encouragement, his horse bolted off with Sidney close on their heels.

True enough, a steeple was built on the top of the red, two-story building containing a medium-sized bronze bell. The fierce winds had blown the rope out of the tower and onto the adjoining building, which was Lou and Drit's Boardinghouse, and had gotten entangled on the chimney. Even on his horse, grasping the task would be impossible. Dismounting to run up the stairs would take too much time. With no other option, he pulled his gun, aimed at the bell, and pulled the trigger.

The roaring wind swallowed the sound. Impatiently, he waited for a small break then squeezed off three more shots. This time, the bell made a statement most residents of Y Knot would hear.

Doors opened and townsfolk appeared, holding their hats to their heads and dresses flat to their legs.

Brandon and Charity ran down the street toward them.

"What is it? What's going on?" Brandon hollered into the wind.

Charity grasped the reins of Sidney's flighty horse, making dismounting possible.

"Twister!" Dustin shouted, stepping out of his saddle. "Spotted in the high pasturelands of the Heart of the Mountains by the upper bridge. It's right behind us."

A cluster of people gathered around to hear the warning.

Some Dustin recognized from the surprise party the night before last. Old Mr. Herrick held his son's arm, looking frail and shaky. Mr. Simpson, his hand behind his ear, leaned forward, trying to hear the important news. The female livery owner, June Pittman, and her beau, Morgan Standford, stood in the front row, lines marring their brows. Everyone was frantically looking around as if the swirling black monster would descend on them at any moment.

Charity's expression sliced his gut. "How soon?" she asked. She must be thinking of the ranch, her folks, and everyone else. This could be catastrophic.

"Hard to tell," Sidney replied.

Dustin didn't miss she and Charity were holding hands. In the short amount of time they'd known each other, the two had formed a close bond. "We have twisters in Texas," he shouted. "And there's never been one we could predict. Round up your families and get them into a basement. Anyone have a large cellar that can take people in need?"

A blast of wind buffeted his back, forcing him several steps forward.

Lenore Saffelberg, the waitress who worked at Cattlemen's restaurant, cried out when a board sailed out of the alley and struck her in the back. She crumpled to the ground.

Women rushed forward, their skirts flapping this way and that, and pulled her to her feet.

"I'll ride to some homes to warn them," Dustin shouted to Brandon. "But not Sidney. She needs to stay here in town."

"Everyone, come to my basement!" the German proprietor of Lichtenstein's called in a loud voice. "It's large and strong. All are welcome. You will be safe there."

"Charity, you and Sidney go to Lichtenstein's," Brandon commanded. "No argument."

"No!" both Charity and Sidney said in unison. They turned to each other and smiled.

Brandon took Charity's hand and pulled her close. "You're staying," he said directly into her face. "You haven't felt well for days. Sidney's staying, too." He gave Dustin's wife a hard stare then took the reins to her horse and mounted up. "Everyone else, get to safety *now*."

The blackened sky burst. Drenching rain swiftly turned to hail. People cried out and shielded their heads the best they could with their arms, but warding off the walnut-sized chunks of ice hurled with the strength of Zeus was impossible.

The crowd ran toward Lichtenstein's and were gone.

Dustin remounted the roan gelding, thankful his cousins had given him such a substantial horse. The animal snorted as hail pelted them both. In Texas, twisters could pass without so much as a blade of grass being displaced, and other times whole towns were destroyed. Y Knot was in peril.

His last glimpse, as he headed toward Klinkner's Mill, was Sidney and Charity disappearing into Lichtenstein's Provisions with a large group of people. He knew how stubborn both his wife and cousin could be and hoped they weren't planning to exit right out the back door.

Chapter Fifty-Two

Outside the cave, Tessa took a huge, gulping breath, happy to be alive. She turned a circle with her arms wide. The path leading through the trees to the granite cave was nowhere to be found. Instead, a wide strip of land void of all vegetation stretched in both directions. Broken trunks, previously majestic oaks and pines only minutes before, were either crushed and jagged or stripped of all limbs and stood pointing to the sky like arrows embedded into the earth. Parts of trees rested in the canopies of others untouched. The sky was clear and blue. If not for the soggy ground beneath their boots, and the startling change of the landscape, no one would even think a storm had passed through.

The foursome stood speechless on the damp earth, taking in the devastation. A flock of birds swooped overhead, seemingly undaunted by the turn in the weather, happy to be alive.

"Look!" John pointed to a tree some fifteen feet way. A large beam of lumber hung in its branches, uneven and waiting to fall.

"What is it?" Lily asked, her shaky voice void of its usual lilting quality. She trembled uncontrollably.

"Part of the bridge," Chaim replied in disbelief. "The one Uncle Flood was just showing us with such pride." He turned to look at his cousin. "That's a shame. Looks like they'll have some work to do."

Somber, John nodded. "Undoubtedly. We're extremely lucky we weren't pitched ten miles away ourselves. Or decapitated by flying debris. The horses are long gone. We have no choice but to start walking."

"How far?" Chaim asked.

"Seven to eight miles."

The hike back to the ranch gave Tessa time to brood over Michaela and what might have transpired. Not only now horseless, leaving them on foot, but Lily had sprained her ankle at the first rocky slope, and John was carrying her. The earth was deceivingly wet and slippery. They trudged along in silence, resting often.

Despite the passing of the tornado, the robin-egg blue sky was devoid of clouds. As long as Tessa didn't recall the devastation outside the cave, and the wide swath of land resembling a swerving road they'd left behind, she could have convinced herself she'd dreamed the whole frightening scene.

Chaim held her hand tightly as they splashed through a new inlet of water dividing the meadow.

John and Lily were several feet ahead.

"You're awfully quiet," Chaim said softly. "Michaela's all right. John figures we'll be back to the ranch in less than an hour, and you can see for yourself. Stay strong."

Tessa tried to stifle her shivers but doing so was impossible. They were all wet to their core from the hellbent ride they'd made to outrun the twister. But she didn't care. Nothing mattered to her except Michaela and if the tornado had hit the ranch. "I'm trying to be," she replied, thankful for his firm grasp on her hand. "I keep my mind filled with anything but her—

but it's difficult. The loud wind would terrify her." Feeling the hot sting of tears, she glanced away, not wanting Chaim to see the magnitude of her fear.

Ahead, John stopped by an outcropping of rocks and set a shivering Lily down. "Getting close," he stated, red faced. "Won't be long now." He turned and stroked Lily's cheek. "And you'll be able to warm up, and I'll wrap your ankle for support. Thank God, nothing is broken."

"I don't care about my ankle," she replied, her blue lips pressed in a firm, hard line. "Except for the time it's cost us. I'm so angry with myself for slipping. We could have been back by now, if not for me."

"Stop worrying, sweetheart. The Heart of the Mountains has a deep, strong root cellar. If, by some slim chance, the tornado did make the ranch, everyone is safe. And that means Clara and Michaela. And…we came through the tornado and lived to talk about it."

Tessa, resting on the rock next to Lily, didn't miss the silent exchange between John and her husband. The men exuded confidence, but they were worried, as well. Deep down, a fear of doom passed through her, making her shiver again.

Chaim pulled her into his embrace, rubbing her arms briskly, unaware he could do nothing to chase the bad feeling away. Something more was bearing down on them. Something her husband couldn't stop.

Chapter Fifty-Three

The expanse of the wide-open horizon stretched out before Flood and Winston like a huge patchwork quilt, dampened and laid flat by the storm. The sight was always a mystery and always a draw. It pulled at Flood like a dying man grasping for his last breath. The fact they'd lived through a twister, and the reality Winston rode silently at his side, seemed inconceivable. The thought took him back to Texas, when they were boys, and then again as young men.

"Thank God, Jonathan and Ike weathered the storm," he said, relaxing in the saddle. Ace's sides heaved for air as his gelding ambled along. They'd galloped all the way to the new ranch, checked in on the ranch hands, who'd be setting out soon for home, as well, and then turned straight around. As anxious as he was to get home and check on Claire and the rest, he'd not run his horses into the ground. They needed a breather.

"Amazing how the twister took everything except the earthen passageway from the root cellar to the other small chamber." Winston shook his hatless head.

"Isn't it, though? A miracle, really."

Winston chuckled mirthlessly. "Too bad the house and barn are gone. From all you've said these last few days, I was looking forward to seeing the place. Your ranch hands are lucky to be alive. Unhurt except for a small knot on Ike's head from a flying cup. Good thing it was tin and not ceramic."

"He'll have quite the headache for a while," Flood added. "Was clever to hunker down in the passage. It saved 'em. And praise be to God for that. They'll have some bunkhouse fodder for years to come and be champions with such a tale to share. I'm anxious to hear it again myself." He quieted, thinking, and praying everything was fine at the ranch. In town, too. The unknown was unbearable.

The afternoon was now calm. Neither one of them seemed inclined to talk. Had the time come for Flood to share something that had weighed on his soul for years? Reveal a secret he'd never told anyone? The real reason he'd left Texas all those years ago and never returned, except for the time Claire was abducted and held captive, and he needed to leave his boys with kin. Seeing his brother's patient profile, still strong and handsome, even for his fifty-four years, Flood knew he needed to spill his guts. Time was still left before they reached the Heart of the Mountains. This chance might never present itself again.

"Just you and me," Winston said, breaking the silence. The horses walked along at a comfortable stride after their hard run. "Just like old times."

"I second that, Brother. I'm still having a difficult time believing you're here in Montana." He glanced over and returned Winston's knowing smile. Winston could always sense Flood's moods. He was waiting for whatever Flood had to say. "So, you like the new ranch, even if the house and barn are gone?" Flood was stalling for a few more moments what was really on his heart. "Think the land was a good purchase?"

"I do. It's a fine addition to yours. I'd say you got the best end of the deal. You can rebuild a homestead, if that's what you want."

Flood nodded. "I tried to make the deal good for Mrs. Lambert. She planned to leave Montana no matter what and would have settled for far less than we offered. I've never been a thief, though, and paid her the land's worth."

Winston grunted.

"I wanted you to see the skeleton, though," Flood said, disappointment within. "That fella's now scattered from here to Texas. Been thinking long and hard why the fella's death, seemingly trapped in his root cellar, caught my attention so firmly. Wasn't the rickety old bones or ragged clothes. Or the fact he most likely died alone."

"Oh? Why then, do you think?"

Flood wiped a hand over his face, one last-ditch chance to change his mind. Did he really want to go back to those hurtful times? Revisit them after all these years? They'd been dead and buried for thirty-five years.

"Well?" Winston turned. "You gonna tell me or not? Claire shared with Winnie her concerns about you and the Lambert place. The iron-clad draw it had over you. Must be more than a change of scenery, Flood. She's worried about you. Even worried about your relationship."

Shocked, Flood cut him a look.

"Spill your guts so I can help work the demons out," Winston said.

"You might not want to help me when you hear what I have to say." Ace eyed a large hole dug into the embankment almost hidden in shadow by several large trees on the opposite side of the trail. A den of some sort, Flood supposed.

"Go on," Winston encouraged.

"It's about Gideon."

"Our little brother? I think of him from time to time."

Flood nodded. "Not knowing where he went or what happened after he left Texas makes me think of the poor fellow in the root cellar. So many unknowns. Has Gideon suffered a similar fate? I don't like to think it." Flood felt the intensity of Winston's gaze on the side of his face. His big brother was waiting for him to continue.

"You don't think those old bones were Gideon's, do you? That possibility didn't even cross my mind."

"No, no, those bones were aged far beyond sixty or seventy years. It's just the loneliness I felt when I looked at them. The unknown about Gideon. So many questions. Sometimes makes finding sleep difficult."

A hawk, startled from a tall pine, sailed out into the sky. The bird's cry, a cross between a hiss and high-pitched whistle, rent the quietness. The mate flew from the tree, as well, the two birds effortlessly gliding out a few hundred yards or so like dandelion fluff on the spring breeze. They circled back.

Flood pointed. "They nest up there every year."

"Why do you think Gideon never sent word?" Winston asked. "A letter? A telegram? You know, Flood? Does this obsession with the new ranch have anything to do with why you've never come home to Texas for a visit? I understand the years pass quickly as we get older, but I've wondered. Pondered if your absence had anything to do with me."

They were almost home. They'd forded the river some time back, discovering the bridge gone. Flood reined up and relaxed to the squeak of his saddle.

Winston reined up beside him.

"Do I know for sure about Gideon?" Flood asked, running his fingers through his hair. "No. I think that's a mystery none of us will ever know. Do I know why I'm drawn to the new ranch? I think I do, anyway. It's something I've never told a soul."

"It's about time you did then. Whatever happened, you need to get it off your chest. I can see in your face you believe you caused our brother's departure."

Flood sat his horse, contemplating his next words.

"Spit it out. Can't be as bad as you think. Thirty-some-odd years has made the incident larger in your mind."

Flood let loose a breath trapped in his lungs. "We had an argument. A fight. About a girl. Emmy Lynn Davis. You remember her?"

"Indeed, I do. Her eyes talked without words. Pretty, too. We speaking about the same person?"

Flood nodded.

Winston stood in his stirrups and stretched his back. "I think every young man in Rio Wells was sick with love of her. As far as I can remember, neither you nor Gideon was courting her. Or, at least, if you were, I didn't know about it. Heck, you were young, fifteen or sixteen."

"Sixteen and old enough to fall in love with Emmy Lynn Davis. She and Gideon were both fifteen. Anyway, I found some hidden notes between them. Only two, I think, but those were enough for me to feel completely betrayed by my brother. When I learned the way of it, that she was sweeter on Gideon than she was on me, even though she led me to believe she and I would marry, I saw red. Accused Gideon of sneaking behind my back.

Brought up every way he'd ever let me down, Pa down, and you. Claiming his laziness got Harvey Sterns killed, when I knew better. I claimed Pa thought as well, too. I had no right to say such a thing. That man's death was an accident."

Flood scrubbed a hand over his face, recollecting all the hateful words he'd flung at his younger brother, not letting up even when he'd seen his words hit their mark time and time again. "I was mad with rage. Even though I outweighed him by twenty pounds, we went to fisticuffs. I cringe with shame when I think of it."

"And?"

"The day after we fought, he was gone. Packed a few items and lit out for places unknown. It's haunted me all these years."

"That's a shame. I know Ma and Pa were never the same after." Winston gazed up at a few early stars in the late afternoon sky. "He shouldn't have done that, run away without word. As much as his leaving might have been inspired by your actions, every man is responsible for his own decisions. You're not to blame for him staying away without word."

"But he never returned." Flood's throat was tight and achy.

"Sometimes, a man stays away so long he feels it's impossible for him to return. I think that's what happened. Many young men—*brothers, too*—fight over a woman. His staying gone was his choice, not yours. Ease up on this guilt that's been pushing you."

Flood shifted in his saddle; his gelding's hoof now cocked in rest. "I think he got himself killed. That's why he didn't cool off and come home. And that *would* be my fault. His life wasted because of a woman and my hot temper."

Winston side-stepped his horse close enough to grasp Flood's shoulder. "You've carried this pain long enough. We might never learn what happened to Gideon. Let your culpability go. Just remember the good times."

Flood felt a rush of relief. Perhaps more reasons could be counted for Winston's surprise visit besides his birthday party.

"As I recall, you didn't hang around much longer after Gideon left. You and Joe Brunn set off to find your own destinies. Where's Joe now?"

"Settled in Priest's Crossing, a town not so far from here. Luke and Colton went to his wedding."

"That's right. Luke got himself locked up, and worse."

Flood slowly shook his head, remembering. "I don't like to recall those days. He almost died in the jailhouse fire. Faith and Claire couldn't have stood it."

They sat silently for a few moments in thought. Finally, Flood asked, "Whatever happened to Emmy Lynn Davis? You know?"

Winston rubbed his chin. "Vaguely. I didn't pay much attention because I didn't know she meant anything to our family."

"And?"

"I think she ran off. Not when Gideon did, or when you left. But later. Like six or seven months, if I'm remembering right. That's all I know, except her leaving caused her ma to take to her bed. Her family tried to find her but gave up after some time."

Flood pulled his gaze from the trail ahead, knowing they needed to get moving, and stared at Winston. "Maybe they're together. Somewhere happily living their life. I hope that's the case."

"I do, too—and better than the alternative." Winston shifted in his saddle. "In many ways, Emmy Lynn was a lot like Emmeline Jordan. Emmeline came to Rio Wells to marry John, *your* son, but fell in love with Chaim. At least there's no bad blood between the cousins because of her—but there could've been."

"True," Flood agreed.

"She ripped out Chaim's heart when she left and didn't return. I can't think too kindly of her for that. He's been gone for a mighty long time, trying to get over her memory. I'm so thankful to have him back."

"But look what happened. If Emmeline hadn't hurt him, he'd never have gone to Arizona to meet and marry Tessa. You wouldn't have that cute-as-a-pin granddaughter. I guess things do have a way of working out for the best, just like Claire always says."

"I thank God Tessa healed Chaim's heart. I don't think Chaim could survive another heartbreak like the one he went through with Emmeline."

For a moment, they both stared at each other.

Flood wondered if Winston was also recalling the strange news they'd gotten from Reverend Crittlestick the night before about a McCutcheon wedding taking place in Waterloo only a few days ago. One where the couple had a darling baby girl. Chaim and Tessa were the only plausible explanation.

"Tessa McCutcheon is a welcome addition to the family," Winston went on, as if the thought hadn't just passed between them like smoke. "Her and my granddaughter. Have you ever seen anything more precious, Flood? I could sit and stare at Michaela from sunup to sundown and never get bored. She's the apple of my eye."

Winston's eyes fairly glowed, making Flood realize just how much he'd missed his brother. Talking over problems. Listening to his sage advice. "No, Brother, I haven't," he said, although he had his own granddaughters who hung the moon in every way possible. He'd not say so to Winston. "You've been bitten by the grandbaby bug. The most potent love sickness on earth. And the love only gets stronger as the years pass. Believe me, I know."

Winston withdrew a handkerchief from his pocket and wiped his eyes. "I'm pleased as punch with both of 'em," he said through a thick, choppy voice. "And *so* happy for Chaim. I'm certainly looking forward to getting to know Tessa and Michaela better. They'll be a bright spot in Rio Wells when we return. We'll put together some sort of celebration to commemorate their marriage, and Chaim's return—and as an introduction to the townsfolk. Just like Chaim's leaving meant he found Tessa, *your* leaving Texas was the reason you found Claire. Can you imagine your life without *her*? Or the family the two of you have produced? Your five children and all the grandbabies since? I'm proud of you, Flood. You've built yourself a dynasty here in Y Knot, without any help from your family. A lesser man couldn't have done the same."

Flood couldn't hide the joy his brother's words created. "Nope. I can't imagine it—and I don't want to. Claire's the light of my life. That first, silly love that pounded a wedge between me and Gideon pales in comparison. But I didn't find Claire, it's the other way around. She found me. And just when I needed her the most."

"So, you've never told her you were suffering a broken heart when the two of you met?"

Flood shook his head. "And I never intend to. That part of my history feels better left unsaid and forgotten. As far as Claire knows, she's been my only love—and part of that is true, because she's my only *true* love, and that means more to me than anything else."

Winston searched his face. "Feeling better?"

"Indeed. I've needed this talk for a long time. I'm awfully grateful you made the trip to Montana, Winston. I can't ever repay you."

"Good. I like having you in my debt." He laughed as his grin split his face. "Now, we best get moving. These horses are rested and fit to go. And I'm anxious to make sure the twister didn't come near our loved ones."

Flood nodded and gathered his reins. The two galloped off.

Chapter Fifty-Four

Relief flooded through Tessa as they approached the quiet ranch house. Besides a horse and buggy out front, the place seemed deserted, although messy with leaves and small branches that had been blown into the yard. Still, the tranquility buoyed her heart. Nothing mattered except that the house stood untouched. As well as the bunkhouse, fencing, and corrals. The buckboard Luke always used was parked in its usual place, waiting to be hitched up. The twister hadn't come this way. The scent of drenched earth coiled around.

Excitement at reuniting with Michaela chased away the discomfort of being cold for hours. Her chilled skin would be warmed soon inside by the fire, and she'd change into dry clothing. The feeling of disaster weighting each of her steps on this arduous journey was no more than a memory.

Hickory ran from the barn to meet them. One strap of his small overalls dangled undone in front. Long, honey-blond hair, usually tied at the nape of his neck, swung around his shoulders, reminding Tessa of a wheat field in the wind. His crystal-clear blue eyes inquisitive.

"Where's everyone?" John asked as he set Lily on her feet. He kept a supporting arm around her ribs to keep her from resting any weight on her injured ankle. "The place looks deserted."

"Most of the family's inside. The ranch hands are out looking for you, since your horses returned wild-eyed and covered in sweat. Must've run the whole way from wherever you left 'em. That was near on three hours ago."

"That's big country to cover," Chaim said. "And we've been going slow."

John nodded. "I guess we should have just stayed put. The ranch hands would have found us. I took us through the trees." He glanced at Lily. "The women were anxious to see the children, so we set out. I can't blame 'em much."

Tessa smiled to herself and nodded to the boy. *Yes, we're anxious to hold our darlings.* One more second without Michaela was one second too long.

"Well, the fellas will be darn glad ta see the twister didn't take you. They've been back a time or two to check," the boy remarked. "Dustin and his wife only showed up a short while ago from Y Knot. They stayed around to help clean up the mess from the powerful wind. They said the twister barely missed town, but it hit part of the mill outside of town boundaries. Just the lumber shed. Klinkner house got missed."

Chaim straightened. "What about Madeline, Becky, and Wendy?"

"All fine."

"And my father and uncle?" John asked. "Any sign of them?"

"Not yet. But Mark, he's the one who came with the alarm, said not to worry until nightfall. Lambert place is the farthest out.

He expects they wouldn't stay over unless circumstances forced 'em." The boy's face clouded up. He looked off toward the corral for a second or two. "Like if Jonathan or Ike was hurt."

Tessa tugged on Chaim's hand. Her empathy for the ranch hands' possible plight didn't overshadow her burning need to get inside to see Michaela.

He smiled down at her, understanding written in his eyes. "Let's get inside by the fire," he said. "These women are cold and wet and dying to see their babies. And so am I. Thanks for catching us up, Hickory."

John, nearest to Hickory, touched the boy's shoulder. "And don't you worry about Jonathan and Ike. I'm sure those fellas are fine. They're tough, like you." He lifted Lily back into his arms and followed Tessa and Chaim through the ranch yard to the house. "Whose buggy?" John called over his shoulder to Hickory. "You know? I can't imagine anyone out visiting on a day like this."

If Hickory answered, Tessa didn't hear him because she was intent on the moments to come. At least, she knew now the ranch hadn't been hit by the twister and looked perfectly fine. The only anxiety Michaela might have suffered was the separation for so many hours.

With the excitement of Christmas roiling within, she went through the door hand in hand with Chaim to a room filled with the others. Dustin and Sidney were there, as well as many of Chaim's cousins and their wives. The only ones missing were the middle-aged boys, Chaim's father and uncle, and his sisters and their friend, Wendy. A quick sweep of the room told her Michaela and Clara were nowhere in sight.

Conversation stopped and exclamations of relief broke out, filling the room with noise.

Claire McCutcheon waved them over to the warmth of the crackling fire. "Thank God, you're back." She first rubbed Tessa's damp arms, and then Chaim's. Relief flushed her face. Her smile widened at the sight of John and Lily. "Come warm yourselves by the fire. We've been praying you'd return soon. Oh, Lily, you're hurt!"

"It's just a sprain," Lily responded, hobbling along with John's help. "I'll be fine in a few days."

Something was wrong. For all the happiness at their return, everyone else was silent. As quiet as death. Tessa felt Dustin's gaze on her, as well as Luke's. "Where's Michaela?" she asked tentatively. "And baby Clara?" She tried to keep the tremors from her voice but failed.

"No worries about the children," Winnie answered, her voice tight and high, a change from her usual warmness. "Both little girls are upstairs sleeping. They played so hard they wore themselves out. Drifted off to sleep about an hour ago, and we carried them up to their beds. They should be awake soon, though. It's been their missing parents we've all been worried over."

A loud harrumph sounded…

When Charity and Faith stepped forward to give them hugs, the ways parted, and the other side of the room was visible. Shocked, Tessa sucked in a jab of breath.

Chaim turned at her sound of distress. "Tessa?" When she didn't reply, his gaze followed hers to an unknown older couple.

In that instant Tessa noticed Brandon Crawford, Y Knot's sheriff, standing by their side.

At Tessa's stricken look, Chaim instantly stepped in front of his wife, blocking her view to the strangers. Judging by their fine clothes, the couple who looked to be in their fifties were not from around here by any stretch of the imagination. The man wore a black suit coat over fine slacks and expensive leather shoes that must cost a ranch hand's yearly salary. The woman was tall and straight and wore a black dress and hat. Ashy blond curls framed her face. Their sudden appearance explained the buggy outside.

"John *McCutcheon,*" the man said sternly.

John, who was making Lily comfortable by the hearth, snapped around. He blinked a few times and then glanced at Tessa, as if just realizing something important. "Mr. Jordan? Mrs. Jordan?"

Chaim straightened and took a step back. Emmeline's parents? The same people he'd damned in his thoughts ever since Tessa explained why Emmeline hadn't returned to him a year and a half ago. All the way from Boston? And Brandon, standing at their side, his expression unreadable. He was here on business, not as family. Now Chaim understood Tessa's stricken face. It hadn't made sense before.

John crossed the room and shook the man's hand. John had known his future in-laws as he'd courted Emmeline when he'd been studying medicine in Boston. Had he seen Tessa at the Jordans' home? And the reason he'd felt a recognition as soon as they'd met? Tessa never said anything about previously meeting John. Were there other things he'd learn today about his wife?

Dead silence filled the room. What had been discussed before he and Tessa arrived? Here stood her beloved aunt and uncle, the same two who refused to acknowledge her relationship to the family and paid her as a servant.

"What brings you to Y Knot?" John asked again looking between them. "I can't imagine."

Mrs. Jordan pointed at Tessa. "That young woman, *Miss Webb,* has kidnapped our granddaughter! We've come to take her home. I want to see Michaela this instant. I need to make sure she's unharmed and has been properly cared for, but these women won't let me." She gestured to his mother and Aunt Claire.

Mr. Jordan put his arm around his wife's shoulders and said, "Sheriff Crawford has looked over our paperwork and will take her to jail."

At the words kidnapped and jail, Chaim felt an invisible punch to his gut. Panic scaled down his spine and he reached for Tessa's hand.

During Mrs. Jordan's weighty speech, the door had opened, and Chaim's father and uncle stepped inside. They were as rumpled and wet as the rest of them, but at least they were alive. They'd heard the accusation leveled at his wife.

Chapter Fifty-Five

"The Heart of the Mountains is my home!" Uncle Flood exclaimed forcefully, stabbing a finger at the Jordans. "No one barges in and accuses a McCutcheon of wrongdoing. Chaim and Tessa, I suggest you and the Jordans take this conversation into the library, where you can have some privacy to work through the details of this misunderstanding."

Chaim fisted his free hand. As angry as he was, a feeling of gratitude at seeing his father and uncle alive passed through him.

The others murmured thankfully.

He cut his gaze back to the Jordans, anticipating the coming storm. He was ready for this fight. No one would take his wife or daughter!

"This is *no* misunderstanding," Mrs. Jordan proclaimed hotly. "I'm Michaela's grandmother. I won't take a step anywhere until I see her. We've endured a long trip, horrible food, and now a tornado. I won't be prevented a moment longer."

Mother, being Michaela's other grandmother, took a step to the side and crossed her arms, planting herself in front of the staircase like a guard. "You'll have some time to wait then, because we'll not awaken *my* granddaughter from her peaceful nap. She's had a trying day, as well. One filled with nervousness and fear. And one without Tessa." Winnie pulled back her shoulders. "You'll see her when she awakens and not a minute before."

It was a standoff. Chaim felt a rush of love for his mother and her show of protection.

"Thanks, Uncle Flood," Chaim said. "We'll be glad to take this conversation elsewhere."

Flood glanced around at the quiet spectators, all shocked into silence. "The rest of you, go home. Or rest in your rooms until supper. I think everyone can do with some time to reflect over the events of the day and give thanks to the Lord none of us were killed." He dragged a hand over his ragged face. His already stained chaps appeared soaked through.

Luke and Dustin exchanged a glance.

John and Lily still appeared stunned.

"If you'd like your father and me to join you, Chaim," Flood went on, "I think Winston and I could be a calming influence. But that's up to you and Tessa."

Chaim glanced at Tessa. He knew he'd appreciate including his father and uncle, but the decision was hers because of what she'd need to reveal.

She nodded.

"And *we* will bring the sheriff, since he has our formal complaint and is a man of the law," Mrs. Jordan said gravely, casting a dubious glance at Brandon.

Brandon straightened and held Chaim's gaze, giving nothing away.

"I can't imagine this will take any length of time," Mrs. Jordan said. "I don't want to spend a minute longer than we have to in these backwoods."

Everyone else filed quietly for the door.

"Supper back here at seven," Flood announced in a loud, commanding tone. "This reunion isn't over yet. I expect to see each and every one of you."

There were nods of acknowledgement.

"Tessa needs to change out of her wet clothing." Chaim glanced at his father and uncle. "And so do they. We'll meet in fifteen minutes." The steel in his voice brooked no argument. This was war. He'd not let Tessa down.

Outside, amid the downed branches and leaves scattered everywhere, Luke ushered his family to the buckboard and handed Faith and the children up.

Colton ran into the barn for the horse and quickly hitched him up.

"I'll be home in a bit," Luke said to Faith. "I feel the need to stand by." He searched her gaze. "Never know what might happen next. With Brandon involved, I think this is more dire than I first thought."

"I completely understand." She glanced back at the quiet house. "I'd like to stay, too, but these little ones are worn out. Holly needs a nap so she won't be cranky at dinner. If you want to stay until then, do. No need for you to rush home. Colton can easily bring us back at seven."

He climbed up and gave her a quick kiss. "Thanks."

Mark and Matt, with their families, refused a ride and set off on foot.

Only Dustin remained, standing by the corrals.

Feeling a need to talk the current dilemma through with another man, Luke approached. He couldn't lie to himself; through the days, he'd felt a simmering animosity from Dustin. With no other explanation to blame, Luke assumed his Cheyenne blood was the cause. Thing was, Luke didn't care. He was sure his cousin could use some moral support at this moment. If John was in there, or another of his brothers, Luke would be half crazy.

"Luke," Dustin said as he approached.

The sun was to Dustin's back, shrouding his expression in obscurity. He still wore the damp clothing from his wild ride into Y Knot.

Sidney must have gone up into their room to change. Any sane person would. Luke, being back for some time, had borrowed dry clothing from his father. "Dustin. You and Sidney make Y Knot with no problems?" He'd already heard the news from them earlier, right before the Jordans' arrival. Fortunate for everyone, the twister had come full-bore at the town but at the last moment took a quick turn, nicking only one building to continue out into open land, dissipating a short time later. He'd asked the question to break the ice. Other things were on both their minds.

"Yeah, no problems." He glanced at the house.

Luke swiped a hand across his mouth and rested an elbow on the corral fence. "First twister I've seen up close. And the last, if I have anything to say about it. That's an experience I never want to go through again."

"I've seen a few," Dustin mumbled, leaning back against the fence.

Luke eyed him again. "You need to get into some dry clothes."

"I'm fine," he shot back. "Just can't figure out what kind of tangle Chaim's in. I felt something was off since we met up." He kicked at a small branch close to his boot. "Damn. I wish I'd pressed him harder." He looked at Luke. "Is Michaela not his?"

"I'm sure we'll learn soon enough. I assume you know; my son, Colton, and my daughter, Dawn, are not my natural children. We don't try and keep that a secret. It's just a fact we seldom discuss."

Dustin kept his gaze on the house.

He and Dustin were incredibly close in size and build, and even looked somewhat alike, despite Luke's darker skin. They could have passed for brothers.

"And why did they call Tessa Miss Webb?" Dustin said, breaking the silence of the afternoon. "I'd hoped the best for Chaim's return. He'd been gone so long, we weren't sure he'd ever return to Texas. Now I see he's been mixed up in some charade." He shook his head. "Thing is, I like Tessa. A whole lot. And I believe Chaim does, as well. No, he loves her. What now?"

"Don't write anything off just yet. We need to hear all the facts. Those people might have only part of the story." He reached out and placed a hand on Dustin's shoulder.

At the same time, the ranch house door opened, and Charity stepped out. She spotted them right away. Instead of coming over, she stood a few lingering moments and then slowly turned. She went back inside and closed the door.

Dustin chuckled. "She's been keeping an eye on us. Worries we'll get into a fight."

Luke had noticed the same thing. As soon as his cousins arrived to stay with him and Faith before the party, Charity was out several times for no good reason other than to say hello. "Really? And I thought she just liked our company."

They both laughed, bringing a feeling of well-being to Luke. Maybe all he and Dustin needed was a common problem to ponder. Except for the unknown matter going on in the house, this felt kinda nice. "You know I have a Cheyenne half-sister? Fox Dancing must be sixteen or seventeen by now. I met her when she showed up unannounced and wounded to meet her half-white brother." He grinned. "That would be me. I'm a blessed man."

The lingering smile Dustin wore from their revelation about Charity melted away. "Yes, I did know that."

"Her being here was tough for my mother and Flood, to relive the nightmare they'd gone through when my ma was abducted. But they got through it. I have to say, I was surprised. At first, I worried more about how my mother would react to seeing Fox Dancing. Being reminded of all the days she'd spent in captivity. In reality, my father suffered more…"

Dustin listened carefully.

Seemed he was having an inner conversation with himself about something. "If we'd let it," Luke went on, "Fox Dancing's arrival could've driven a wedge between Flood and me. I'm thankful that didn't happen." Leaning back against the fence he looked up at the clear sky, thinking.

"Luke…"

Having let his gaze wander to the bunkhouse, Luke cut back to his cousin's serious tone. He waited for Dustin to continue.

"I'd like to apologize."

"For what?"

"I think you've noticed my attitude, at times, hasn't been as friendly as it should."

Luke smirked. "I've noticed. And I've wondered. I've concluded my Cheyenne blood is to blame. You're not the first. And I'm sure you won't be the last."

Dustin shook his head. "I was wrong—"

"No explanation needed. Thing is, now that I'm older, I've come to believe I'm blessed being half Cheyenne. I'm proud of my heritage, and I wouldn't change a drop of my blood if I could. I'm comfortable in my skin, Dustin. Happy with my life."

Dustin stroked his chin and a small smile curled his lips. "That's easy to see. But I'd like to explain what happened. I didn't disdain you because of who you were, but because I'd allowed myself to be bullied. I didn't stand up when I should have and bloodied a nose, and it's always made me feel shame. It started out about you but ended up about me. Any mention of you reminded me of my cowardice. I've never shared this part of my past with another living soul, and it feels damn good to get it off my chest."

"Understood." Luke reached forward for Dustin's hand. "I'm glad we've cleared the air. We might have bigger issues to consider in the not-so-distant future." He glanced back at the house. "And Chaim and Tessa will appreciate a united front."

Chapter Fifty-Six

Minutes later, Chaim and the others filed into the library in stone-cold silence. The *Farmer's Almanac* he'd returned the night before was still in the bookshelf covering the wall. A fire crackled in the hearth. He made sure his and Tessa's chair were close to the warmth. Even with dry clothes and a heavy cardigan from Aunt Claire, she shivered like a tree in the wind, making him wonder if it was caused from cold or fear. She'd faced these two hard-eyed people alone for her whole life. Well, that was about to change. *Nobody* was taking his daughter away. She belonged with him and Tessa, and no others.

Once everyone was seated, Chaim looked to Brandon, who stood by the closed library door with his hands clasped in front of him, his expression dark. "Brandon?" Chaim asked. Although he had a fairly good idea, he still wanted to know how much the Jordans understood. Upstairs in the bedroom, he'd stared at Michaela sleeping in her crib while Tessa changed. When she'd finished, he'd tried to ask a few questions, but the despair in her eyes stopped him. He'd know everything soon enough.

Brandon began, "The Jordans claim Michaela is their granddaughter, the daughter of Emmeline Jordan, your first intended who recently passed away, and a man she married named Jason Whitmore."

Seated in one of the upholstered wingback chairs next to her husband, Mrs. Jordan moaned and dabbed her eyes.

A coffee table divided the long room between them and chairs by the fireplace on the far wall. Two straight-backed chairs had been brought in for his uncle and father, who sat to the side, out of direct line between Tessa and her relatives.

"We've had hardly a second to mourn our daughter properly before this calamity befell us," she went on.

Brandon waited a moment, and then continued, "They allege Miss Webb, a member of their household staff who was Michaela's nanny, was hired to travel with Mr. Whitmore to Georgia after Emmeline's death, where he planned to start anew. One day, at a train stop, Tessa departed the train with the child and never returned."

"That's all correct." Mrs. Jordan nodded as she twisted the handkerchief in her hands. "She kidnapped her. I just want to see Michaela. Has she awakened yet?"

"No," Chaim replied. "She's still asleep."

Tessa looked stricken as she listened to the charges lodged against her.

Both his father and uncle waited to hear what she'd say. Strangely though, they didn't look surprised in the least.

"Tessa," Chaim said softly, wishing he could do this for her but knew the story must come from her. "Tell everyone what you told me."

Sitting forward in his chair, Mr. Jordan frowned. "Whatever she claims will be a lie. To cover her crime."

Chaim, Flood, and Winston all bolted to their feet.

"No one calls my daughter-in-law a liar," Winston barked.

Mr. Jordan shrank backward, pressing his back into the fabric.

Brandon held out a calming hand. "Settle down, everyone, and take your seats. We'll figure this out."

Chaim narrowed his gaze at Emmeline's parents. "Before Tessa speaks, why don't you tell everyone Tessa's *true* identity? Even after all the years she's worked in your house, you still refuse to accept it."

Mr. Jordan looked as if he'd been struck in the face with a wet towel.

Mrs. Jordan averted her gaze to the ceiling.

When neither of them responded, he addressed his father and uncle. "Tessa is Emmeline's cousin. She was with Emmeline when Michaela was born. The Jordan family don't recognize Tessa as a niece because her father, Mr. Jordan's brother, never married Tessa's mother. But they did employ Tessa in their home, as a way to help."

"I don't see how those facts change anything," Mr. Jordan stated. "Kidnapping is against—"

"What neither of you know is, *I'm* Michaela's father, not Jason Whitmore. Tessa brought the baby to me to fulfill a promise she made to Emmeline on her deathbed." Anger and pent-up energy propelled Chaim to his feet. He stalked across the room, wishing he could punch Mr. Jordan in the nose. Exact some of the pain he'd caused so many others. "Your scheme to keep Emmeline from marrying me has blown up in your face, Mr. Jordan." He stopped in front of Emmeline's parents and drilled them with a hot stare. "You're the lowest form of human beings. I can't imagine how you sleep at night." Mr. Jordan had the decency to turn red. Seemed he didn't appreciate his whole money-making scheme aired to the world. How he'd used his own daughter to save their family fortune.

Mrs. Jordan frowned and shook her head, as if, just maybe, she didn't know her husband's wicked deeds. "I have no idea what you're talking about." She stared hard at her husband for explanation. "Jason Whitmore is Michaela's father," she insisted, turning from her husband to Chaim. "Emmeline and Jason were married. The wedding was glorious. At this moment, he and his mother are sick with worry over what's become of Michaela. He telegrammed us just as soon as they realized Miss Webb was not returning with the baby."

"Her name is *Tessa*. Your niece. I want to hear you say it. *Tessa McCutcheon*."

Winston stood and came to Chaim's side where he continued to glare down at Emmeline's parents. "Settle down, son. We'll get to the bottom of this. Nobody is taking my granddaughter. Not now, not ever." He encouraged Chaim back to his chair next to Tessa's. Before returning to his own seat, he rubbed Tessa's arm in a show of support.

Until then, Chaim hadn't been sure what everyone else would think of the Jordans' claim.

"Mrs. McCutcheon," Brandon said respectfully, "why don't you tell us, in your own words, what happened?"

"That's a good idea," Chaim agreed. "But first, let me say, in no uncertain terms, before Emmeline boarded the train in San Antonio to return to her dear ailing father's side in Boston, we stayed the night together. I'm sorry if you're embarrassed to hear that, Mr. and Mrs. Jordan, but it's the truth. Our wedding was set for the next month. After that, I never heard from her again. She didn't tell me we'd conceived. Like it or not, those are the facts. Michaela is *my* daughter. Michaela is the name Emmeline and I talked about in San Antonio, on the off-chance we had a baby, and it was a girl." He glanced at Tessa, proud to see her head held high as she gazed at him with warmth. "Go on, Tessa," he encouraged. "Tell them what happened."

Tessa took strength from the expression deep in Chaim's eyes. His intensity stirred her courage and righteousness. A stab of anger chased away her fear. "How shameful." She looked between the Jordans. "To come here and accuse me without knowing any of the facts. It's disgraceful, but not surprising. When my mother needed your help, you turned her away. I don't care for me, and the years of toil I spent in your home serving you, but for her and how she scrimped and scratched to stay alive." She took a deep breath, "On the night prior to Emmeline's wedding, she realized she was carrying Chaim's child. She confided in me about San Antonio. She cried because she felt obligated to marry the man her father wanted to save her family's finances."

Flood and Winston murmured angrily between themselves, looking large and menacing. Brandon straightened and cut a disgusted glance at the ceiling.

"Distraught and frightened, Emmeline was compelled to go through with the wedding. The event cost a fortune, and she said her lot was cast. Afterwards, she did her best to hide the pregnancy, eating tiny portions, staying secluded, but as the months passed and she was showing much too soon, her mother-in-law became increasingly suspicious and even confronted Emmeline with her misgivings. After the baby came early, Emmeline feared the woman would tell Mr. Whitmore."

"Oh, my poor baby," Mrs. Jordan whispered, her ashen face stricken with the story Tessa had laid out.

Mr. Jordan sniffed indignantly. He listened to Tessa with narrowed eyes. "We don't know the truth of it yet, Constance."

All four men glared.

"I'll let your remark pass, for now," Chaim commented. "To keep things hospitable for Tessa and Michaela. No other reason than that." He glanced at her to continue.

"Life went on, and Michaela thrived. All seemed fine until Emmeline became ill. The doctors didn't seem worried until she failed to recover. Her fever continued to increase." Tessa knew her words must be hurting Chaim, so she reached over and took his hand in her own.

"Yes," Mrs. Jordan said, her face drawn in sorrow. "We came several times and stayed for days. I should have done more. Demanded to take her home. Seen a different doctor. Perhaps the outcome would have been different. We just didn't know she was so sick."

Tessa remembered the stressful times well. She'd been tending Michaela exclusively and was instructed to keep the baby far away. Those days were the first Tessa could remember seeing her authoritative aunt with sagging shoulders and a drawn countenance. The sight stirred her compassion and, if she'd been able, she would have offered a comforting word. But doing so would not have been welcome.

"When Emmeline realized she might die, she made me promise I'd make sure Michaela reached Chaim. She implored me to tell him the truth and beg him to accept Michaela as his own. Emmeline admired the McCutcheons. Their close family. Their strength of character. She felt her daughter would have a better life growing up on the ranch, away from the rigors of society in Boston. She also feared if her parents discovered Michaela was illegitimate—and they *would* at some point, from her vengeful mother-in-law—they'd treat her the way they'd treated me."

A murmur of disquiet came from Emmeline's parents.

Tessa hurried on. She wanted this whole ugly mess behind her as soon as possible so she'd know where she stood with everyone—*especially* Chaim. They might be married, but that didn't mean he'd want to stay that way if she was arrested for kidnapping. "After Emmeline's death, as I was formulating a strategy to somehow take Michaela to Chaim, I learned Mr. Whitmore was planning to move to Georgia. Through the grapevine, it was believed he'd met someone else and planned to marry her. Very soon after that, the maid who worked for Emmeline's mother-in-law came to me in tears. She'd overheard a plan to leave Michaela at an orphanage along the way under a false name and allege she'd died. Without a way to disprove the claim, I was compelled to act as if what she'd told me was the truth. I assumed Emmeline's mother-in-law relayed to her son the truth about Michaela's paternity. After Emmeline's death, I presumed he didn't want to raise another man's child. Or risk the chance of such scandalous news getting out and marring his reputation. Once they reached Georgia, they'd planned to send a telegram to the Jordans."

Mrs. Jordan gasped. "The scoundrel."

Winston, Flood, and Brandon scowled.

Mr. Jordan raised an eyebrow. "If what you say is true, Miss Webb, why didn't Jason send the telegram stating the baby had died? Instead, they sent a telegram as soon as you didn't return with her. They let us know the baby was gone so we could begin a search. He could have stayed with the plot you described—if it were true."

"*Mrs. McCutcheon*," Chaim corrected sternly.

Mr. Jordan conceded with a dip of his head. "Forgive my slip."

"I'd assume because they didn't know what I planned to do with her. They could hardly claim she'd died if I returned her to you in Boston. No one knew my intention. I don't know how you found us."

"We searched your room at the Whitmores' home that has yet to sell," Mr. Jordan replied. "Under the bed was a scrap of notepaper with the name Chaim McCutcheon, among other things. We supposed you fled to Texas with Michaela."

"Did you go to Texas?" Chaim asked.

Mr. Jordan nodded. "We did. That's why we look so weary. We've been traveling for days on end through this God-forsaken country."

"I don't think I can give her up," Mrs. Jordan proclaimed, as if she and her husband were the only ones in the room. She resumed dabbing at her eyes. "She's my granddaughter and all we have left of Emmeline." Her lips wobbled slightly, and she let out a loud sigh as she looked around the room. "How can we be *sure* of any of this story? Maybe this is Miss Webb's—*Mrs. McCutcheon's*," she quickly corrected, "way of punishing us. Releasing her pent-up frustrations. I wouldn't put anything past her."

Hurt and disappointment swamped Tessa. Would the Jordans ever think well of her? They were her family. Her aunt and uncle. They were supposed to love her. Cherish her. She was nothing to them but a lamentable person who might ruin their respectability if her true identity were ever known. Perhaps they even feared her. All the interactions with her aunt throughout the years came rushing back. The condescending tone. The expressionless stare and exasperated flutter of lashes. And the time she'd slapped

Tessa for accidently breaking an expensive china teapot when she'd first arrived.

"Everything sounds so far-fetched," Mrs. Jordan said. "I won't leave Michaela here, Alfred. It's our word against theirs. She is *our* granddaughter. Our first and only." She crossed her arms over her chest and glared.

"There *is* a way to prove Tessa's story and Michaela's paternity," Flood stated forcefully. He stood and looked around the room. "My son, John, is a doctor. He knows all about women in a delicate condition—and the timing thereof. I say we call him in here and see what he has to say. Chaim, have you shared any of this with him before this?"

"No, sir."

"Well, it's time we did."

Chapter Fifty-Seven

John followed Brandon into the room and waited by the bookshelf while Brandon quietly closed the door.

Not a word had been spoken after the sheriff left in search of his cousin. Filled with nervous energy, Chaim leaned over and whispered into Tessa's ear, "Things'll be all right. Michaela isn't going anywhere except to Rio Wells with us." Tessa's aunt and uncle were a formidable pair, but he'd not allow them to take his daughter from her rightful place in *his* family and from under *his* protective roof. He was her father. That ace trumped a king and a queen all day long. He held the winning hand.

John stood straight and tall and steadfastly confident.

"John," Chaim began. "Mr. and Mrs. Jordan need proof Michaela was conceived in San Antonio, the night before Emmeline departed for Boston. We need your medical opinion about her birth."

"Understood," John replied.

"Emmeline and I spent the night together, the first of November 1886," Chaim said clearly, unemotionally, surprised at how little pain the statement caused him. Only a month ago, that wouldn't be the case. Important matters rode on getting this right. "From that day on, I never heard from her again. From what I've learned from Tessa and the Jordans, Emmeline went home, and her father introduced her to a man named Jason Whitmore. A wealthy fellow her father desperately needed her to marry to shore up their family's accounts."

Mrs. Jordan twisted in her chair and glared at her husband.

"Emmeline agreed, and the two married in February." Chaim recalled he'd just settled in Arizona, still agonizing over losing Emmeline, her lack of communication, and his indecision whether to go to Boston himself. Maybe, if he had, things would be different now. He had no way to know. And the way she'd so quickly abandoned their love, he figured perhaps things turned out the way they were meant to.

"Emmeline gave birth August eighteenth," Mrs. Jordan whispered, as if she was just now beginning to see the whole picture. "Extremely early. I was frightened to death for them both."

John rubbed a hand over his jaw, thinking. He withdrew a pencil and paper from his pocket and scratched a few notes.

The fire crackled and flared up.

John straightened and confidently lifted his head. "If Emmeline conceived in February, after she'd married, she'd be around twenty-four weeks along when she delivered. Michaela would have been extremely tiny. Few babies survive such an early birth. Imagine a newborn puppy and how small they are." He looked from Mrs. Jordan over to Tessa.

"Michaela was small, but not abnormally so," Tessa said. "About five pounds. She was strong. No problems with eating or sleeping."

"That's all true," Mrs. Jordan agreed, looking long at Tessa.

"Emmeline was very disciplined during her confinement," Tessa went on. "Eating very little to keep the truth from being discovered when the baby was born."

"If she conceived in November, as Tessa and Chaim have said, the birth would be perfectly on time with an August birthday. Taking into consideration the baby's weight, and the fact she had no extenuating problems with breathing or eating, I have no doubt Michaela McCutcheon is Chaim's daughter."

Mr. Jordan jumped to his feet. "This gibberish proves nothing. We need another doctor's opinion. Someone without a vested interest."

In the impending silence after Mr. Jordan's outburst, a baby's cries wafted downstairs from the bedroom above.

"She's awake," Mr. Jordan barked. "You can't keep us away any longer. Whatever comes to be, we are her grandparents." He glared at Brandon. "Sheriff?"

At the first sound coming from the upper rooms Tessa stood. "I'll go get her, but it'll take a moment for her to awaken properly."

Chaim followed out into the living room, but she stopped him at the stairs.

"Please, do you mind if I have some time with her alone? It's been her and me for the last month, and pretty much since her birth, as well. I'd like to hold her for a few moments since I haven't all day…" Her lips turned down and giant tears spilled down her face.

"Shh, shh," he crooned, pulling her into his arms to stroke her back. "Of course you can. Everything will work out, Tessa.

You'll see. You can't keep truth hidden under a pillow, like I tried yesterday morning." His comment to make her smile failed miserably.

Winnie looked down from the upstairs landing. "Michaela's awake. I didn't know if you wanted me to get her, or…"

"Let Tessa, Ma."

Winnie nodded, a sad smile pulling her lips.

Everyone was worried about the outcome of today, unsure of how the day would end.

Chapter Fifty-Eight

Michaela stood at the side of her crib, red-faced and crying.

Tessa was usually at her side the moment she awakened, taking time for her to rouse slowly. Gently. Today was strange for the baby, as well. "Shh, shh my little love." Tessa lifted Michaela into her arms and cuddled her close, singing softly as she nuzzled the top of her warm, damp head. "As soon as we go downstairs, my darling, I'll get you some milk."

At the sound of her voice, Michaela stilled.

Michaela was so good at settling down, even without Emmeline here to nurse her. She wanted to be good. Her actions said nothing less. Tessa rubbed her small back as they rocked back and forth, memorizing the feel of her.

Now quiet, she rested her head on Tessa's shoulder, her breathing slowing as she settled into awareness.

Was there still a chance she'd be arrested for kidnapping? She'd taken Michaela for the right reasons, but the law was the law. Not only that, now all the McCutcheons knew she was a fraud. She couldn't even guess what they must think of her now, or she might cry. And there was no time for tears. Or regrets. She needed to change this angel and get her dressed in something fresh. The Jordans were waiting…

"There we go, sweetheart. Let's get you ready. Someone special is waiting to see you. Your grandmother and grandfather from Boston," she said in a happy tone, eliciting a sleepy smile from the baby. "They've missed you terribly and have come all this way to make sure you're safe and sound." Tessa laid Michaela on the bed.

The baby smiled up at her in anticipation of having her diaper removed. Her eyes twinkled with mischief and her dimple appeared, making her look just like Emmeline.

"I've done my best to do what you asked, Emmeline," Tessa whispered, all the while adoring the darling face before her. "I've fulfilled your request to the best of my abilities. I hope you don't mind too much that I married Chaim, as well…"

A quiet knock came on the door.

She turned.

Chaim leaned in, a crooked smile on his lips. "How is she?"

Now naked, and hearing her daddy's voice, Michaela kicked with gusto.

"Come see for yourself."

Chaim came into the room and stopped at her side. He smiled down at his daughter for a few moments and then took Tessa's hand. "And how are you? Facing them must be difficult."

"I'd be lying if I said I was fine. I'm scared. I know truth is on our side, but Mr. Jordan has a way of making things work out for his benefit. I've witnessed how he twists the truth just so." She glanced down at Michaela, who listened to them intently as if she could understand each word. Tessa couldn't resist and leaned over to kiss her sweet neck. The scent brought to mind the days when Michaela was a small baby.

"Mr. Jordan and his power don't matter one whit. I'm Michaela's father. I won't let anything happen." He searched her eyes once she straightened. "I promise."

"I needed to hear those words," she replied.

"Now I have a favor I'd like to ask. You know the little dresses and bonnets Faith made for Michaela and Clara?"

"Yes."

"I'd like you to…" He leaned close. His warm breath created a flurry of shivers inside as he laid out his plan.

She nodded with a smile. "But what about Lily's sprained ankle?"

"I've already spoken with her. John's wrapped it, and she feels much better. She'll take it slow."

Trepidation sizzled inside. "You're sure? I don't want to anger the Jordans any more than they already are."

"Do you trust me?"

She'd trust Chaim with her life, and she had, earlier today. "I do."

Smiling, he surprised her with a quick kiss. Then he left the room.

When Tessa and Lily appeared at the top of the stairs, the room quieted. Each held a baby girl wearing identical dresses and bonnets. Everyone who'd not left to go home milled around in the living room, quite aware Tessa was retrieving Michaela, and the Jordans hadn't seen their granddaughter since arriving earlier today.

Flood and Winston stood with Claire and Winnie.

John stood with Luke, Dustin, Brandon, and Charity.

"Here she is," Chaim said quietly to the Jordans, who hadn't said more than a handful of words to him since he'd come to stand by their side.

Emmeline's parents weren't overjoyed at the way things were turning out. Mrs. Jordan seemed more inclined to look at him and give a grudging smile as he expounded on the things they'd done since arriving in Montana. Stubborn Mr. Jordan only scowled.

Mrs. Jordan clasped her hands over her heart. "Please, bring her down so I can hold her. I've been overwrought with worry."

The babies' matching pink dresses had cream-colored bows on each mid-length sleeve and another at the center of the scalloped neckline. A white eyelet pinafore with starched cap sleeves that shot up, reminding Chaim of angel wings, was layered overtop. The babies looked adorable and wiggled excitedly upon hearing the enthusiasm in Mrs. Jordan's voice, just as he'd hoped they would.

Michaela's blonde hair gently curled where Clara's, the same color, was straighter. But the matching bonnets covered everything. With the matching dresses, and both babies very close in age and size, their faces looked remarkably the same. They could pass as twins.

Mrs. Jordan met Tessa and Lily at the bottom of the staircase and held out her arms to the baby in Tessa's arms.

Chaim cleared his throat. "You sure that's Michaela?"

Mrs. Jordan leaned closer peering back and forth between their faces. Finally, making up her mind, she reached for the baby in Tessa's arms at the exact time the baby in Lily's arms stretched forward for her.

"This is Michaela," Lily said softly, handing the baby over. "Here is your granddaughter."

Humbled, Mrs. Jordan took Michaela, who appeared delighted to see her grandma.

She bounced and wiggled, smiling at all the spectators as if she knew this hubbub was all about her.

Tessa handed Clara back to Lily and headed for the kitchen. "She won't be happy for long if I don't warm some milk."

"It's on the stove, dear," Winnie said, following. "I got busy as soon as I came downstairs. I've also cut up some bread and some oatmeal cookies. Enough for both the babies."

"From what Tessa's told me, Jason Whitmore was quite dark," Chaim said as Tessa hurried away. "Dark hair, brown eyes, much like Emmeline. His skin was tinted olive because of his mother's Italian blood. Michaela favors me with her blue eyes and light hair." Untying the bonnet strings beneath her tiny chin, all to her amusement, Chaim removed the headpiece and ruffled her hair, still warm and damp from her nap. "You see how much she resembles her Texas cousin, as well, don't you? Of course, you do. You could hardly tell them apart." He raised an eyebrow in question at Mrs. Jordan. The way to winning this war, and removing all doubt who'd sired Michaela, was through her.

"I do, Mr. McCutcheon," Mrs. Jordan admitted as Michaela cuddled on her chest. "And Alfred does, as well, but he's too obstinate to admit it." She glanced at the man standing silent and unforgiving at her side. "Alfred, tell Mr. McCutcheon you see the family resemblance. We're extended family now, and you might as well concede." Her voice was firm. "But don't think I'm finished with you. We still have matters to discuss later, like how you manipulated our daughter for *your own* good."

"And *your* good, too."

"Don't you dare lay this travesty at my doorstep."

Chaim cleared his throat again and tipped his head at the baby. He didn't want an angry argument to frighten her. "So, now that you know the truth, you will drop the kidnapping charges," he stated with an iron-clad tone. He wanted this to be the end of every little obstruction to their happiness as a family.

"I assure you, we will." Mrs. Jordan gazed lovingly at Michaela. "Whatever is best for the child."

Brandon nodded.

"And that she's to live with her father and Emmeline's cousin as her new mommy." Chaim didn't miss Dustin's and everyone else's expressions of amazement, having yet to be filled in with the details of Tessa's true identity. That would come later, in private.

Tessa was back with the warm milk.

When Michaela saw the small cup, she began to squirm with anticipation.

"Would you like to do the honors, Mrs. Jordan?"

Mrs. Jordan couldn't meet Tessa's eyes but nodded.

"Good. I thought as much," Tessa replied. "The highchair is in the kitchen." She led Mrs. Jordan across the room. "You and Michaela can get reacquainted…"

Chapter Fifty-Nine

Flood paced the lengthy dining room table, taking in every detail. This was the largest group they'd ever seated at the ranch. Twenty-seven, not counting the four infants. They kept two highchairs here for his two new grandsons and rounded up two more for Michaela and Clara. One they'd borrowed from Roady and Sally. The other he'd pulled out of the storage room in the hayloft where the one he'd built many years before for his children had been gathering dust. He'd cleaned the keepsake with olive oil and buffed the wood to a high sheen. The carving of flowers on the front of the seat looked as sweet as the day he'd etched them. Since the table had limited seating, the highchairs were positioned between and a little behind where their parents would sit.

His heart warmed. He didn't believe in having a separate table for the small children, either. They were the best entertainment a party could have.

Smokey and Nick delivered the stored table extension, which added ten feet. The section of boards was rustic, but well sanded, and when covered with an ivory tablecloth, nobody could tell the difference.

He nodded, taking in the finery but contemplating the evening to come with a pinch of anxiety. After the unpleasantness in the library concerning Chaim and Tessa, Brandon and Charity rode back to town with the Jordans to Cattlemen's Hotel, but only after Flood insisted the two return and join them for supper. They *were* Michaela's grandparents, after all, *and* Tessa's aunt and uncle. *Family.* The best option now would be to win them over. Flood had weighed the alternatives carefully and felt he could do nothing else but extend an olive branch. Doing so was the Montana way.

Soon after the Jordans' departure, Chaim tracked him down for a private talk. He and Tessa had decided, under the circumstances, and since much of the story was already revealed, they wanted *all* the truth to follow. Chaim requested Flood spread the word so, by the time the rest of the family returned for dinner, Tessa's identity and the circumstances surrounding their marriage would be known. His nephew emphasized the reasons for his and Tessa's actions. To protect Michaela from harsh judgment from others through no fault of her own. Proud of their decision, Flood caught Luke in the barn, saddling up to go home, and asked him to take the message to Matt's and Mark's homes, as well as the bunkhouse. Chaim had already spoken with his parents and brother.

The mystery of Waterloo was solved.

Claire emerged from the kitchen, wiping her hands on her apron. "Everything's about ready. I'm running upstairs to freshen up, put on a clean dress, and fix this rat's nest."

He smiled down into her flushed face. She'd never been prettier. "And Winnie?"

"She went up fifteen minutes ago."

The clock on the mantel chimed once. It was already six forty-five.

"You best hurry, woman. Your guests will be arriving any time."

"And I'm sure you can handle things until I'm down. Am I correct?"

Taking her chin in his fingers, he leaned down and gently kissed her lips. "And you'd be correct." He shook his head in wonder. "Can you believe all that's happened in the last few days? Surprise reunion, tornado barreling down on Y Knot, and now a secret wedding and baby?" He gave a chuckle. "My wife sure knows how to stir things up."

"I wouldn't want you to get bored with your life, Flood McCutcheon," she said sassily, smiling up into his face.

He didn't see her wrinkles or the gray hair gradually appearing at her temples these last few years, but a beautiful fifteen-year-old love of his life who had stolen his heart. The moment she'd opened her cabin door, him covered in snow and seeking shelter, flooded back. The memory was his favorite and one he never intended to forget. Filled with concern, and no stronger than a forest fairy—but a thousand times prettier—she'd dragged him inside by his snow-covered bearskin sleeve and brought him to a big leather chair in front of a roaring fire. From there, she proceeded to treat him like a lost puppy, filling him with food and hot cocoa. Checking his feet for frostbite, drying his clothes. Her father, a preacher, watched with an arched brow, not knowing the extent of his daughter's involvement—or Flood's. He'd said his daughter made a habit of finding needy creatures and helping them. From the first second, Flood decided he'd never let her go.

She was the woman for him, then and always. "Get bored?" he repeated. "That wouldn't be possible with a woman like you and a family like ours!"

Laughing, she tried to slip out of his arms he had around her waist, but he held her tight.

"I need to go this instant," she insisted. "Or I'll frighten everyone upon arrival." She poked and prodded at the messy bun on the back of her head. "They're stirring upstairs. I heard them while I worked in the kitchen. I hope everyone is rested. We'll need every ounce of patience to face those Easterners again. My word, Flood. Can you imagine what they did to their daughter? And our sweet Chaim? And Tessa, too. For years. It's unconscionable."

Flood cocked his head. "I'm surprised to hear you say that. Aren't you the one who preaches everything happens for a reason?"

Caught by his words, her face pinked.

He turned to the table. "Anything over there catch your eye?"

"Flood," she gasped. "The highchair." She rushed over to caress the carvings on the now-gleaming wood. "We should have pulled this out years ago. I forgot all about it." Her eyes overflowed with affection and memories.

Dustin and Sidney appeared at the top of the stairs.

"Oh, my. My time's run out," she said on a breath. "Flood, entertain our guests, and I'll be down in a few minutes. Dinner is almost ready, Dustin. I'm sure you and Sidney are starving after such an ominous day."

"Absolutely." Dustin's voice rang out. "I could smell tonight's feast all the way up the stairs." He and Sidney descended the staircase hand in hand. "After all the events, my stomach's doing summersaults in anticipation."

Tessa contemplated the full room below. No one noticed her appearance on the landing as they chatted excitedly in small groups. She'd chosen the light blue dress with tiny golden flowers Madeline had gifted her. The first time she'd worn the garment, she'd felt pretty. Tonight, a deep pit of nerves gnawed at her insides. The evening to come would be a trial. She'd been antsy since the moment she and Chaim closed their bedroom door two hours earlier.

She could just imagine the topic of conversation. Although they were goodhearted and meant well, the revelations of this afternoon would be too much to ignore. What must the McCutcheons think of her? A kidnapper. A liar. No matter the reason, she was still the illegitimate daughter of Theodore Jordan. She'd worked as a servant most of her life. They would believe she'd lied and schemed to marry Chaim, their beloved son, cousin, brother, and nephew.

Below, Faith was in conversation with Rachel and Amy, the two latter holding their infant sons. The babies squirmed and cried to get down and crawl. Their gazes locked on where two-year-old Holly, along with Dawn, who was almost five, and a great little babysitter to her younger sister and cousins, played with blocks on the large wooden coffee table in the middle of the room. The furniture also held several small dolls, a toy puppy, and a variety of children's books. The McCutcheons knew how to keep a room of children happy during a family gathering.

Dustin and Sidney chatted with John, Lily, Luke, and Faith.

Mark and Matt belted out a laugh at something Winston had just said.

Winnie and Claire circled the table, helping Esperanza fill the water glasses and wine goblets.

Two months ago, she'd been alone in the world. Besides Emmeline, she had few friends and zero relatives. At least, ones who acknowledged her existence. Now, by marrying Chaim, essentially everyone in the crowded room was her new family. She took a deep, unbelieving breath.

Chaim appeared at her side holding Michaela, who she'd redressed in the darling dress and pinafore made by Faith. Her soft baby curls framed her face and tumbled halfway to her little shoulders in waves of gold. She looked like a princess.

"You ready to go down?" Chaim asked, his tone heavy with worry.

She'd been quiet since leaving the library. She hadn't meant to worry him; she just didn't have anything to say. She'd played with Michaela on the bed, the baby bright-eyed after her long nap, while Chaim sat in the chair. Then, after an hour, she'd gotten up and slowly prepared herself for the upcoming dinner. Doing so was disconcerting with Chaim in the room, but asking him to leave didn't feel right now that everyone knew everything about them. So, she pressed on, stripping down to her slip and washing with the clean water in her pitcher. When she glanced at him through the mirror, his attention was always on Michaela. What could possibly be said to fix the situation, the one everyone— including the ranch hands—now knew? "As ready as I'll ever be," she replied softly, noticing the chatter downstairs dying away. They'd been noticed. "At least, the Jordans have yet to arrive."

If possible, would she turn back the hands of time? What else could she have possibly done to save Michaela besides what she did? They'd married to keep Michaela's circumstances secret. Now, the situation was common knowledge to all, but Chaim was tied to her in a marriage she'd suggested. With the union still unconsummated, should she offer to let him off the hook?

Lifting her chin, she started for the stairs with Chaim's supportive hand on the small of her back. Only a few hours ago, the women below were her friends and considered her family. What did they think of her now?

Chapter Sixty

Laughter, talking, and eating reverberated around the room.

Tessa sat to Chaim's right, bringing a rush of pride at her beauty and poise.

Michaela's highchair was situated behind and between them, and either he or Tessa checked on her often.

The Jordans arrived at ten past seven.

As soon as they'd said their hellos, the group promptly sat, and the banquet was brought to the table.

Platters of beef and gravy boats filled to the top. Potatoes and vegetables piled high on serving dishes. Three different casseroles loaded the table—one chili, one chicken and rice, and the last with green vegetables. A delicious oven dish Chaim couldn't identify but wanted to try was right in front of his face. There were baskets of biscuits and several types of bread, some with seeds and nuts, others white with a hard, crinkly white crust.

Not to leave out corn bread and even a platter of tortillas. Crocks of honey butter were set every few feet to make passing easy.

Flood offered a brief but meaningful prayer, thanking God for the best possible outcome for such a large tornado. So far, no reports of any deaths in town or the surrounding area had surfaced. The aftermath could have been a catastrophe.

Beside him, Tessa's anxiety was like a living, breathing thing. Unless she was asked a direct question, she sat quietly eating, tending to Michaela, or smiling at the conversation. Knowing what she must be feeling, he did his best to calm her fears and make her feel comfortable.

Both his sisters, as well as Miss Knutson, commented how pretty she looked tonight, which was an understatement.

Dustin asked how she'd liked this morning's ride before the storm hit. And if she intended to continue riding once they all returned to Rio Wells.

Before they'd been seated, most everyone came by for a quick touch, a kiss to Michaela's cheek, or a gentle hug.

Curious, though, all the women at the table, his sisters, cousin, mother, and aunt, and all his cousins' wives seemed overly animated tonight. They were excited about something, but he couldn't imagine what. Exchanged glances, a raised eyebrow here, a whisper there, and all the peculiarities were followed by a deepening in their complexions. Chaim wondered what was going on. They'd all heard his and Tessa's story. Was that the reason they were twittering like schoolgirls?

Mrs. Jordan was a bit more approachable than she'd been earlier, but the old man sat as rigid as ever, still holding onto his prejudices, eating forkful after forkful and drinking a tumbler of bourbon.

Luke sat back in his chair and looked down the table. "Mr. Jordan, all night you've listened to what we do for enjoyment around the ranch: hunt, fish, whittle, play horseshoes, break mustangs, target practice, and camping. I'm curious what you do for relaxation in Boston. I've never been." He glanced across the table at John and winked. "Although, my younger brother has."

Mr. Jordan set his tumbler back to the tabletop. "I remember clearly John visiting our home." He lowered his brows, a slight scowl pulling his mouth.

The reference to John courting Emmeline hadn't been Luke's intention when he'd asked the question, Chaim was sure, but he could imagine how the comment might affect Tessa.

"We go to the opera or a play," he said, after clearing his throat. "We have several world-renowned theater groups. Sumptuous house parties." He glanced around as if this dinner party wouldn't be counted as such. "In the summertime, we sail."

"And you have your *men's club*," Mrs. Jordan said, none too sweetly.

Tessa turned in her chair to attend to Michaela, who was eating her carrots with delight.

She must fear what comment might come next here in front of everyone. Didn't she know his family would stand behind her, no matter what took place?

Luke's troubled gaze snagged Chaim's, having realized his mistake.

Chaim dipped his chin in acknowledgement.

"Speaking of fishing," Mark jumped in on a laugh. He held his two hands out at least three feet apart. "I was shocked at the size of the trout Billy snagged this morning. The coming twister must have brought him luck. I'm surprised the whale didn't snap his line." He glanced down the table where Billy sat, his brother, Adam, on one side and Colton, on the other.

At hearing Billy's name spoken, the boys' chins snapped up and the whispers humming between them stopped.

"Isn't that right, son? Caught on the far end of the creek by the small pasture. What were you using for bait?"

"That spot used to be one of my favorite holes when I was about your age," John said. "I caught many a trout there. I'm curious about your bait, as well."

Billy's face turned bright red. He glanced at Colton, who ducked his head. "Bread dough balls," he coughed into his hand.

Rachel's head whipped around from checking on Heath. "Is that what happened to my second loaf?" she said in mock outrage. "I'd prepared several pans of dough which were resting by the fire early this morning," she explained to the group. "I didn't like to think it, but I assumed a rather large mouse must have gotten inside and helped himself to one end. Now I learn *the mouse* is my *son*." She glanced at Billy and then smiled. "Next time, please ask."

Everyone laughed.

Under the table, Chaim took Tessa's hand and brought it to his lap, rubbing his thumb across the top.

"I expect you to share your catch with us, Billy," Flood said, his fork raised halfway to his mouth. "Sounds like the one I've been stalking for years. He's cagey. I should've been the one to hook him."

"I will, Grandpa," Billy said. "I'll bring him over in the morning."

"Maybe you boys can show Winston and me the fishing hole tomorrow," Flood went on. "But only if your mother can whip up some more of the magic bread dough. Nothing on the calendar for us to do, as long as Y Knot doesn't need us for clean-up. Fishing sounds like a nice, calm day after today's excitement." He glanced down the table at Brandon. "Are we needed in Y Knot?"

Beside her husband, Charity, who looked a little wilted, straightened.

Chaim could hardly blame her from the events of the day.

"No, sir," Brandon replied. "As earlier stated, the tornado veered at the last second, only damaging the lumber shed at Klinkner's Mill. The Lord surely held Y Knot in His hands today. No one was hurt and the house untouched. Hayden has already recruited all the help he needs for the job." A wide grin appeared. "Norman Klinkner claims the structure was a small price to pay for the wide path the twister created to the river. Harvesting his logs won't be as challenging from here on out."

"Excellent," Flood replied. "Be sure to send word if anything changes and they need more manpower. We'll be happy to help." He narrowed his gaze on Mr. Jordan. "Now that that's decided, back to fishing. How about you, Alfred? Care to join us? Seems only fitting *all* the grandpas go fishing together. You have another day to spare?"

Mr. Jordan just stared.

After the seconds that passed made it quite apparent Mr. Jordan didn't intend to take up the invitation, Flood harrumphed. "I'd hoped you'd soften. For Chaim's and Tessa's sake. Your granddaughter's, too. But I can see you're about as stubborn as the old, retired mule I keep in my pasture. If we weren't trying to extend a nice Montana welcome to Tessa's family, after hearing about your shenanigans in the library, I'd take you behind the barn and teach you some manners." He was holding back his temper, but still he thumped a fist, rattling his water glass. "Lucky for you, the olive branch is still out there, and you better think long and hard about refusing it." He took a deep breath. "I've said my piece."

Mrs. Jordan elbowed his side, and he dipped his chin.

"Good. Good, I'm glad to hear it." Flood turned his attention to Winston at the other end of the long table. "You have fish that size in Rio Wells?"

"Bigger," Winston responded. "You'll have to come see for yourself."

"That's a wonderful idea, Winston," Claire sang out, her face strained from the showdown a moment before. "I promise we will. And tomorrow, we grandmas will have fun, as well. Constance, I'm taking Winnie around the ranch to see all our wildflowers this time of year. It's a pleasant walk and not far. Would you please consider joining us? I'm sure you'd like as much time as possible with your granddaughter before you head back to Boston and she goes to Texas, since everything's been settled."

Chaim liked how his aunt threw in that last part.

"And after our walk," Claire went on, "who knows? With Charity, all my daughters-in-law, my nieces, and friend"—she winked at Wendy—"and my nephews' wives, I'm sure our day can be as full as we'd like it."

"And me, Grandma! And me." Dawn, almost five, had wandered back from the toy-filled coffee table where she and her girl cousins played after being excused. She stood between her grandma and grandpa, listening to the adult conversation. "And me. I can think of fun things, too."

"Of course, you can, Dawn." Claire circled the child with her free arm and kissed Dawn's cheek. "Nobody would dream of leaving you out."

At the coffee table, Cinder, Beth, and Holly had stopped what they were doing and listened intently with long faces to the sound of their grandma's voice.

"*All* my darling granddaughters are welcome, as usual," Claire amended quickly. "You're all resourceful helpers, each and every one of you. No one will be left out."

Mrs. Jordan blinked several times, a look of amazement in her eyes. "I'd like that very much, Claire. Thank you for the invitation."

When Michaela began to fuss, Chaim released Tessa's hand and, after gently wiping the baby's face with his napkin, brought her to his lap and gave her a crust of bread to keep her quiet. She was warm and smelled like carrots and potatoes, and his heart squeezed at the goodness of it all.

Michaela turned in his lap and looked up into his face. As if just remembering something, her mouth moved around and then she said, "Da da" loud and clear. Her eyes sparkled, and she said it again.

The hum of chatter and the sound of forks and knives tapping the china plates stopped. Everyone looked at them.

"Good girl," Faith was the first to say. "You remembered. All morning, while we were babysitting, we were teaching her to say da da, hoping she'd say it for you. That was before we knew anything about stormy weather or a twister."

"We never dreamed she'd pick up on it so soon, Chaim," Amy added. "We kept repeating da da over and over, laughing and having fun, hoping she'd catch on." She glanced at Clara. "With Clara, too."

Chaim gazed back at Michaela, a wonderous gaiety stripping him of all other feeling. "Yes, *Da da*." He grinned like a fool. "I'm Da da." Glancing at Tessa, he felt his eyes fill. A little over two weeks ago, he didn't even know he was a father, and now here was Michaela, the most incredible girl in the world.

Not to be outshone, John scooted back from the long table, gathered Clara from her highchair, and brought her onto his lap.

She brightened with a smile with everyone now looking at her.

"Say Da da," John said in a funny voice and brought her close to kiss both cheeks. "Say Da da, my little angel. Come on, sweetie. Your cousin Michaela can say it…" He glanced at Chaim and grinned. "I can see us in Rio Wells. It'll be nothing but competition between cousins—friendly, of course."

Little Heath's and Zach's highchairs were side by side. The two toddlers, both just over a year and a half, had food smooshed over their bibs and faces. Zach, the younger of the two by a month, possessed a thick swath of brown hair that resembled something scalped from a bear. Their mothers encouraged them, waiting for some words to pop out, too.

Mrs. Jordan appeared delighted. The lines Chaim had noticed earlier today around her eyes and on her forehead, had softened considerably with the conversation and went completely away when she smiled. And she was smiling a lot right now.

Mr. Jordan, not so much.

"Horsy ride," Heath blurted proudly.

Everyone clapped.

His face was greasy with foodstuffs. "Giddyup. Giddyup," he called enthusiastically.

Zach fisted a carrot slice and threw it at Heath, smacking his cousin on the forehead.

Heath's face screwed up tight, and he howled like a wounded dog.

"Uh oh. Here we go," Mark said with a chuckle. "No food fights at Grandma's, young man. She'll set you in the corner."

Claire stood and went to Zach. She wiped him down and then lifted him from his highchair. "I'll do no such thing, Mark, and you know it. Zachie only wants some attention, too. It's all going to the girls. Come here, little man, Grandmama'll hold you so you don't get into trouble." She smiled at Heath, who'd stopped crying, but storm clouds were swirling in his eyes. "You're next, big boy. Don't you worry."

Esperanza and another helper set about clearing the table.

"Da da," Michaela babbled again, getting another roaring round of approval. "Da da."

Moved beyond measure, Chaim leaned close and whispered in Tessa's ear, "You made all this possible, Tessa. Only you, Tessa Webb McCutcheon. I'm so grateful you're so brave. Not many women would have attempted what you did. I'm so lucky. I *love* you, Tessa. I hope you can feel it. Believe it."

Not wanting to embarrass himself, he leaned back, cuddling Michaela close. Something incredible had happened today. What Tessa feared the most had transpired—the Jordans had arrived with condemning words. But, in doing so, the truth had set them free…

Chapter Sixty-One

The supper dishes were cleared, and slices of pie and cake were being distributed around the table.

If Tessa could just get through a bit longer, the party would break up soon, and she'd be able to retreat to her room. No sharp looks or off-color questions were spoken. Everyone smiled, allowing her to sit quietly, just listening. The Jordans hadn't said anything embarrassing, either, except for the one time speaking with Luke.

Rachel and Amy took their toddlers into the kitchen for a quick cleanup, and some of the others stood to stretch their legs before the last round.

It was eight thirty, and even with her long nap today, Michaela's eyes sagged.

Tessa was incredibly proud of her for being so good and entertaining. And saying Da da right to Chaim's face. She couldn't help but feel a little proud, thinking of Emmeline. Her cousin would be so happy to know how loved Michaela was already. Her daughter's future with the McCutcheons was as bright as the stars.

A knock sounded on the door.

"Who knocks here?" Flood said from his seat, his fork hovering above a large slice of walnut cake drizzled with chocolate frosting. "Come in."

Roady and Sally stepped inside. They glanced around. "All finished up?" Roady asked.

"Your timing's impeccable." Luke chuckled. "I knew you wouldn't miss dessert. Pull up a chair."

Roady grinned. "I wouldn't want to let you down, Luke," he responded with a wink.

Sally, holding Gillian, took a vacant seat offered by Matthew.

Most of the older children were eating their dessert at the toy table in the living room while the adults enjoyed coffee and more tumblers of bourbon.

After introductions, an evident hush swirled around the room, making Tessa wonder what was happening. Something, because all the women had stars in their eyes, and the men wore silly grins. Just as she began to relax, an interior warning flashed alarm bells.

John tapped his water glass several times with his knife. "Since I live in Rio Wells now with our Texas family"—he looked at Chaim and then at Tessa—"and you will soon, as well, I've been selected to do the honors."

Frightened, Tessa reached under the table for Chaim's hand.

Still holding Michaela, he looked at her in question but enfolded her hand into his without saying a word.

"We've all come to learn congratulations are in order," John went on. "That the two of you are newlyweds, having only married last Wednesday. Since then, the three of you have been crowded together in that bedroom upstairs."

Tessa's face burned with embarrassment. She never considered they would speak of the doings of the last two weeks. She wanted to dash up the stairs and close out the world. She kept her gaze riveted to the button on John's shirt just under his chin, praying he would hurry up and spit out what he was about to say before she got sick on the table.

Faith gave a sigh. "John, do you mind if I take it from here?"

John looked relieved. "Please do."

"What John, and all of us, are trying to say is, Roady and Sally have a darling little cabin very close by. It's the original ranch house. They're offering the place to you for however long you'd like. For a *proper* honeymoon. And…we won't take no for an answer."

Sally smiled kindly at Tessa. "We come and stay with Flood and Claire often, Tessa. Since the big house is usually too quiet with just the two of them. At least, that's what Claire tells me all the time." She laughed and exchanged a look with Claire. "We bring Gillian to stir things up. We consider staying over a treat."

"We couldn't," Tessa eked out. "It's your home…"

"Nonsense," Sally prodded. "Consider the cabin yours. It's been cleaned and polished from top to bottom by all these ladies just this afternoon."

"We would have set up the honeymoon suite at the hotel in Y Knot where Brandon and I spent our wedding night, but we thought you'd rather be closer to Michaela," Charity piped in.

At the mention of leaving Michaela, Tessa intended to put her foot down. Put a stop to all this foolishness. "Your thoughts and actions are incredibly sweet, and we would never be able to thank you enough, but we couldn't possibly leave Michaela," Tessa said softly. "She'd be frightened. She and I haven't spent a night apart since…"

Chaim studied her face. "Since Emmeline passed away," he finished for her.

Uncertainty hummed around the room; the only sound came from the children playing at the coffee table.

"She'll be fine, Tessa," Claire replied kindly. She'd risen and approached Tessa's side. "She's nine months old and, from what you've said, sleeps through the night. She was extremely good this morning with all these aunties and cousins to play with. I don't think she even cried once. And if *you* put her down for the night, she won't even know you're gone. She can sleep side by side with Clara. They're already fast friends. But, if for some odd reason she awakens and cries, you and Chaim are extremely close by. Only a short ride away. I promise, we'd alert you immediately. You have nothing to worry about." She smiled into Tessa's eyes. "You and Chaim deserve some time away—*alone*."

How could this be happening? And in front of the Jordans, of all people. From the corner of her eye, she could see her uncle watching. Listening. What was he thinking?

Refusing would be rude. The women had prepared all afternoon. She'd hurt, and maybe even anger, all these amazing people who were, for the time being, her new family. To her horror, she felt her eyes fill, and she turned her face away.

Instantly, Chaim scooted back his chair.

"Da da," Michaela said happily.

He stood and helped Tessa to her feet. "We're heading upstairs to discuss the situation," Chaim said evenly. "We're grateful for your thoughtfulness."

The three of them proceeded to the stairs, the room behind them left in utter silence.

Once in the bedroom, Tessa took Michaela from Chaim and paced to the darkened window, trying to calm her rattled nerves. Claire McCutcheon's words kept reverberating through her mind.

She'll be fine, Tessa.

She won't even know you're gone.

She and Clara are already fast friends.

She doesn't need you anymore.

Tessa didn't want to talk. Or think. She just wanted to stand here and look out into the darkness. There always was the possibility the Jordans would somehow find her. She hadn't thought so, but the chance did exist. Because of them, the truth had come out and all the McCutcheons knew the truth.

"Please don't suffer this by yourself, Tessa," Chaim said from behind her. "Tell me what you're thinking. That's the only way I can help." He stood quietly. "Tessa?"

When she didn't respond, he put a hand on her shoulder and gently turned her around.

She didn't care the tears that had threatened downstairs were slipping down her cheeks. She couldn't do anything about them now. If she didn't cry, she felt like she'd explode. The genie was out of the bottle, and he wasn't going back in.

Chaim's face was overcome with concern as he gently wiped her tears away with his thumb. "We don't have to go anywhere if you don't want to," he said. "We'll stay right here. It's worked out fine so far. I'll just tell them no."

Michaela reached for him; her new favorite pastime was going from one to the other.

Tessa reluctantly let her go.

"I'll go down right now and put this to rest."

"No," she gasped and caught his arm. Her sharp tone made Michaela sit back, and her eyes got large. "Please. You can't do that. I'm sorry, but you can't tell them no. What they did was thoughtful and kind. They'll think I'm ungrateful. Just like the Jordans do and always will. That's just a fact."

"They won't, I promise you. I know them, Tessa. They love you, even now. Even after knowing you such a short time. No one thinks anything bad."

She sniffed and took the handkerchief he offered.

"Why, though?" he asked. "Why don't you want to go? We'll still have the same arrangement we agreed upon, if that's what has you worried. I won't expect any different."

She looked at him, thinking how to make him understand. "I don't want to leave her. Although I know it's not true, I feel like everyone downstairs wants to take her from me. That Michaela is fine without me, which I know she would be, but I wouldn't be fine without her." She looked down to the floor. "I'm being selfish."

He tipped up her chin. "Stop talking nonsense. You're *not* selfish. You're the least selfish person I know. No more talking bad about yourself. I mean it. We'll work through this, but I'll not let you condemn yourself after everything you've done."

A soft knock sounded. She felt her eyes go wide.

He leaned in and said quietly, "If we go to the cabin, we'll have a little privacy…"

She couldn't stop a small smile from slipping out.

"Chaim. Tessa. May we come in? Please. We'll only take a moment of your time."

"My mother," Chaim whispered.

Tessa frantically scrubbed away her tears. "And who?"

"I'd guess my father? I'll send them away."

"Please, no." She gripped his arm again. "We can't. Doing so would be impolite. We should at least hear what they have to say."

His brows pulled down. He placed his warm hand over top hers, the one that held his arm. "You're sure?"

She nodded.

Chaim opened the door and stepped back so his parents could come inside. They looked pensive and unsure.

Tessa sniffed quietly, wishing she'd thought to blow her nose.

"We're sorry to intrude," Winnie began softly, her hands clasped tightly in front of her skirt.

When Michaela saw Winston, her face lit with pleasure. She extended her arms out to him. "Da da da."

She was the perfect tonic. Tessa couldn't help but smile, which caused a few more tears to fall.

A tiny smile appeared on Winnie, and her mother-in-law's troubled brow softened. She rubbed Winston's arm as he gathered the baby from Chaim. "She's just the sweetest thing," Winnie said, adoring her granddaughter with her gaze.

"Winnie, tell Tessa why we're here," Winston said, his deep voice making Michaela smile. He tickled her belly. "This young lady needs to hit the hay soon. It's way past her bedtime."

Tessa couldn't imagine what would bring them to their bedroom at a time like this, other than to repeat the plea Claire had just voiced downstairs.

"Go on, Ma," Chaim said.

"Yes, well," Winnie began. "Tessa, Winston and I just wanted to tell you what a wonderful, brave young woman you are. We're delighted you and Chaim have married. Ever since—"

Tessa touched Winnie's arm before she could go on. "May I explain how that occurred, please? And why. Since the truth has come out, I want you to know—"

"You don't have to tell or explain anything," Winnie interrupted in a soft voice. "Nothing you could say would make us think any better of you, or *love* you more, than we already do now. You're not only a sweet young woman who has captured Chaim's heart, and I mean that in all the right ways, but you also saved Michaela. You, all alone. Think about that. None of us would have known she existed, if not for you. And you took on the difficult task, even though you could have landed in trouble. Or worse. The uncertain journey you made was not easy. And who knows what would have become of Michaela in the orphanage? Or the life she might have had if she'd been adopted into a harsh family." Her eyes filled and she dashed away a tear that escaped. "The possibilities are difficult to even contemplate. Tessa, our beloved Tessa"—she took both of Tessa's hands— "we're so sorry for the hardships you've lived through. We're just beyond delight you've joined our family. You're a McCutcheon now—*now and forever more*. Please, don't ever have any doubts about that."

Winston nodded, his eyes glassy, too. "That's all true. We love you, sweetheart. We all do. Everyone downstairs feels the same. We don't want to see you cry."

Chapter Sixty-Two

Chaim sank into a creaky chair on the Gutheries' cabin porch, the cool air seeping into his clothing and chilling his skin. Glancing up into the darkness, he welcomed the happiness easing though his veins. If possible, the stars seemed brighter here than in Texas. Millions of glittering pinpoints spanned the sky, so much so the sight took his breath. He was pleased the truth was out in the open. As much as Tessa wanted to protect Michaela from the unhappiness and shame she'd felt as a young girl, she'd soon come to realize their daughter's experience, with the loving support of the family, would be much different.

He smiled into the darkness. Yes, *their* daughter. Michaela belonged to Tessa just as much, if not more, than she belonged to him. He swallowed down an unfamiliar emotion. Life had a way of changing up without warning. Like sitting an angry broomtail determined to throw you. Chaim hadn't anticipated this trip to Montana would bring such life-altering transformation. His life back in Arizona was a vague memory.

He turned his head, listening. Every now and then, he heard a small sound coming from inside where Tessa was settling in— whatever that was, he couldn't imagine. The cabin was tiny. One room with a loft. The four windows, adorned with cheery yellow curtains, must keep the place bright during the day. The cabin had a water pump at the sink, a pie safe, and a small, cloth-covered table with four chairs. A vase of flowers sat in the middle. An old rifle was displayed over the fireplace. A knitted blanket hung in the corner of the room opposite the four-poster bed, partitioning the sections off for privacy. Behind, a crib and set of drawers were arranged just so in the tiny nook. Two little dolls sat side by side on the bedcover. The place was cozy and sweet.

Was Tessa anxious at being completely alone with him for the very first time? When he'd talked her into accepting the Gutheries' generous offer, at least for one night, he'd hoped she'd relax and enjoy a little solitude. Something she had little of these days since meeting him and now his family.

When they'd arrived, if Tessa was nervous, she was hiding it well. And, in actuality, he was the one feeling a bit shy. Nothing would happen between them tonight, because he was bound and determined to give Tessa the time she'd asked for. Time enough to warm to him. To want him.

A coyote yipped from a hilltop and was answered from across the meadow. When a wolf howled, he took notice of the direction.

Before starting out for the cabin, and while the women were busy helping Tessa gather a few necessities and put the baby to bed, Dustin and Luke, along with his other male cousins and Roady, insisted he have a bourbon or two in celebration. The men could hear the women's laughter upstairs as they re-filled his glass and thumped his back with each new toast.

"Chaim? What're you doing?"

He felt a little woozy when he turned to look at her.

She stood in the doorway with the lamplight behind her.

She looked small. In the darkness, he couldn't see her face but already knew every inch by heart. His pulse kicked up a notch, and he looked away. "Just sitting out here and waitin' on you."

"You are?"

"Yep. And hoping for a shooting star."

"Any luck?"

The coyote yipped several times and was followed by an owl.

"Nope," he responded, looking up into the sky.

"Did you hear that deep howl a few moments ago? Different from the coyotes."

"I did. It's a wolf. He won't bother us though." He chuckled to ease her fears. "He's more interested in the bunnies trying to hide from him. Been quite a few animals singing their songs." He heard her come closer but didn't look around. "Another chair's right here. Would you care to join me?"

She sat on the edge of the chair. "It feels wilder here than even at your uncle's. And dark. Much darker than Boston."

He chuckled. "I'd imagine so. Roady said, if we're awake at dawn, to look out the window by the sink. A young doe has been showing up most mornings to nibble the sweet grass on the east side of the cabin."

"I'll be sure to look," she said softly.

By the sound of her voice, he could tell she was looking off over the pasture toward the sliver of moon. Not too far out, the river sparkled in the moonlight as it wound its way through the meadow.

She relaxed back into the chair, and the sounds of the night drifted around. "Would you like a glass of water?" she asked suddenly, as if she'd just remembered something.

"No, thank you. I had enough to drink at the ranch." He shook his head, angry at himself for not being more forceful with the men. Just the sound of her voice made shivers, and more. "Would you like one? I'll be happy to fetch you a glass."

She laughed.

But he knew she wasn't used to being waited on. She was the one expected to serve. He'd noticed her tendency toward pleasing him.

"I should have asked you sooner, Tessa. Or something else? Sally told me there's some nice apple wine."

"No, thank you," she replied. "I'm still full after the large supper."

We're so polite. "Why're we whispering?"

"It's so quiet and dark out here. Just feels right."

"Takes some getting used to, living away from town. It's the same out at the Rim Rock. Dark nights. Quiet days. Miles and miles of solitude." He'd let that sink in so she could begin to adjust to her new life. "I hope you're going to like it. How'd Michaela do going to bed in the new room? Did you have any problems?"

"I thought there might be trouble at first, but she surprised me. She instantly knew she wasn't in her old room when we moved everything to Lily's." A tremor of laughter colored her voice. "She looked around, taking everything in, and then began saying da da da at everything. It's her favorite word."

"It's her only word."

Tessa laughed again.

Chaim's heart thumped at the sound.

"I know she knows you're her da da, but I think she also likes the way the sound feels in her mouth. And the way we all react. There's no two ways about it, she's bright. I rocked her on the bed for a few minutes and sang her bedtime lullaby until her eyelids drooped. You can always tell when she's almost ready to fall asleep because her eyes become glassy, and she can't keep them open. Then, fighting it off, she begins to blink." She laughed softly under her breath. "I have to hide my smile because it looks so cute. If she sees me, she'll wake up right away and want to play. But tonight, because she was so tired, she snuggled right in, and I transferred her to her crib." Tessa gave a deep sigh. "I hope she stayed asleep and isn't crying."

"I'm sure she's fine." He stood, realizing he was a little unsteady on his feet. Faith and the other mothers warned him Tessa might begin to worry and want to return to the ranch to check on Michaela. They'd assured him the baby would be fine.

"Where're you going?" she asked.

"Inside, for a lamp. You'll be more comfortable with a little light. I guess, once a city girl, always a city girl, or so I've been told." He glanced at her in the darkness. "I'll be right back."

Tessa waited patiently for Chaim to return. Every time she was tempted to become frightened, she took a deep breath. The small cabin sat on the edge of nowhere, backed by a dense forest where a plethora of animal sounds emanated, and the pine trees whispered in the slight breeze. The place in whole seemed like something out of a fairytale more than a home where the Gutheries lived. And to think Flood built the home all those years ago for Claire and his growing family. The thought was amazing.

Chaim appeared. He hooked the lamp on a nail on the side of the wall and then draped the woolen shawl his mother gave her over her shoulders. He resumed his seat. "You looked a little chilly."

"Thank you. This does feel nice." She shrugged into the softness. "I didn't realize how chilly the night had become." Aware he was watching her, she glanced around at everything except him. Had he meant what he'd said about his expectations tonight? They'd never experienced such privacy before. The circumstances put her on edge.

"Thought you might like that. Saw it laid over the chair inside and decided to bring it out."

Small talk. Would they ever get past it? Daring to turn in his direction, she took in his handsome profile, where now, he was politely looking at the stars. He must have anticipated her glance in his direction.

Strong jaw, straight nose, and the abundance of hair she'd admired since the day they'd met when he'd sold his new Stetson for the silver bell. Even after a combing, it appeared a bit disheveled and in need of tending. The memory stirred a covey of warm feelings inside. He'd done so much for her. And for Michaela. In actuality, he didn't seem to mind they were married. He never gave her the impression he regretted their decision. Not like herself, who continually second guessed everything, since she'd been the one to propose. Her cheeks heated at the thought, and she was thankful for the darkness. At the time, getting married felt like the right thing to do...*but now?* Now that everyone and their mother knew the truth, where did they go from here? She took a deep breath, trying to relax.

The *hoot hoot* of an owl brought her mind back from wandering. She smiled into the night sky, thinking how funny they must look. Newlyweds sitting outside in silence, tiptoeing around each other like strangers. Chaim had shown his true colors since they'd met. And today he'd shielded her from harm, and perhaps death, with his own body.

We might be silent, but we're not strangers.

"Tell me about your travels." She fidgeted with the dangly ends of the shawl. "About the time after you left Texas. You've made reference several times but haven't said much."

He straightened in his chair and was silent, as if recalling all those pain-filled months. Moving slowly, he reached over and took her hand into his large, warm one. "All right," he said, nodding his head. "If you really want me to. There's not much to tell."

"I do. Very much."

"Like I mentioned before, a ranch hand, as well as a friend, named Brick Paulson, came with me. You'll meet him in Rio Wells. He's a good man. Anyway, Brick was not only a fast friend but an excellent trail companion. He left me to my suffering, for the most part. Just rode along in silence, keeping an eye out. Feeling my pain. The majority of towns we passed through weren't much. One thing we could always count on, though, was a saloon, or cantina, or even a hole in the wall selling whiskey. Brick didn't complain when I drank. He just stayed sober and then carted me off to our room, or our saddle blankets, whichever the case may be, so I could sleep it off. In the morning, he'd put on a pot of coffee and made sure I drank enough to sober up." Chaim shook his head and gazed up at the stars. "I'm not proud of myself for my behavior. No, sir, not in the least. We traveled south and soon came to the gulf and an island, a sand-barrier, called Galveston. Have you heard of it?"

She shook her head.

"The Gulf of Mexico. Now that's a sight to see. Water everywhere—as well as bright sunshine, even in the winter. If a man didn't believe in God before arriving in Galveston, after contemplating the amount of water and wondering what's beneath, I think he just might. We kept hearing about the place as we rode south, so we set our course, thinking it'd be a shame riding this far and not seeing it with our own eyes."

He gave her hand a gentle squeeze. "It's one of the most amazing places I've ever been, Tessa. Here's this large city built right down there at sea level. Oh, it's a few feet up, they say. Something like seven or eight." He shook his head. "Felt like a sandbar to me. In reality, the island is twenty-seven miles long and less than three miles wide. A railroad connects it to the mainland. I'm not too proud to admit, the ride over tested my nerve. Feels like the train skims across the top of the water like a stone and sways back and forth something fierce." He chuckled. "I thought more than once we'd end up in Davy Jones' locker."

She listened, loving the sound of his voice, and began to relax.

"An amusement park and countless restaurants line the pier. A large bath house comprised of two round buildings in the middle of a long pier is built some six or seven feet above the tide. Tall poles, buried in the water, have chains the swimmers hold on to." He chuckled. "They bob up and down in the waves like corks."

"Did you swim?"

"No, it wasn't even spring yet. But some hearty souls were out there a time or two. By strolling through the shops, I *did* see the outlandish swimming costumes the women wear." He playfully looked her over in the lamplight. "Actually, I'd like to see you in one."

Her mouth dropped open.

He shook his head again and laughed. "Well, it's true. But getting back to the topic, Galveston's a sight to behold. I enjoyed myself. But I'll enjoy myself more if it's the three of us. We'll go together sometime. Make it a holiday."

The warmth in his voice made her think he was picturing the three of them walking on the beach hand in hand, the toasty sand squishing between their toes and the salty water heady. She'd never felt so close to him as she did at this moment.

"To be honest, I don't know how the people live there. Any little storm could bring the waves right over the town. But they go on like nothing. I guess I'm a rancher through and through. Need the land and rock beneath my feet. Some nights, I'd awaken to the sound of crashing waves. If I wasn't sleeping off a bender, I'd get up, go out to the beach, and sit until the sun crested the horizon."

Thinking of Emmeline.

"But, after a few weeks, I decided enough was enough and stopped drinking myself to an early grave. Such behavior wasn't right. Not fitting for a McCutcheon. My family raised me proper. I knew they were worried. Wasn't right to do to Brick, either. He deserved better. I haven't drunk myself unconscious since. I've actually had very little, until tonight."

She glanced up. The light on the wall created a halo around his head. "What happened then?" She'd been enjoying the sound of his voice and wanted him to go on. "Did you stay long in Galveston?"

"About three more weeks, I'd say. Long enough to write home with a little news. Ease my family's worries. Got to know the place good and well—mostly because I didn't have the nerve to ride the rickety train back across the water. I was stalling." His thumb traced circles across her fingers. "From there, we headed west through Las Cruces, New Mexico, and then hit Tucson. Las Cruces is a wild place. A man could get himself killed faster than blinking an eye. Not much law and too much lawlessness. We killed a few days there, playing cards and keeping a close watch on each other's backs, but something just kept pushing me. Something I can't describe. I needed to forget—"

"Emmeline?"

He paused and looked up at the stars. "Yes. But forgetting was impossible. I warred with myself, thinking I should have followed her to Boston. Forced her to tell me face to face why she didn't want me anymore." He grew quiet again. "I don't know," he finally went on. "At the time, her not writing or sending word said everything she hadn't. My pride was like quicksand, always pulling me deeper. Maybe I didn't want to know the truth. If I didn't hear it, I could pretend her betrayal wasn't true. Maybe she'd still be alive if I'd gone after her. That's a hard pill to swallow."

Was he asking for her forgiveness? She hurt to think of his suffering then and now.

Snapping out of his thoughts, he brought her hand to his lips and softly kissed her fingers. "I've come to realize something during these last few nights."

"You have?"

He nodded. "I know Emmeline's father pressured her, and she thought she was doing right by her family by marrying Whitmore. But when she learned she was carrying my child, she should have at least let me know. A telegram or letter. If she'd truly loved me like I thought she did, she would have. She was resourceful. She could have found a way." He glanced up at the moon, thinking. "I don't share any of this to hurt you. I know speaking about Emmeline is difficult for you, as well. You're torn. She's your family. You loved her. You made a pledge to fulfill her dying wish."

"I did—and still do."

"Of course, you do. Emmeline is Michaela's birthmother and, at some point, if we think she's ready, she should be told the truth. I want to be able to mention Emmeline without worry of either of us being hurt or offended. What you need to know is speaking about Emmeline, discussing matters over with you, doesn't hurt anymore inside here." He thumped his chest with the hand that wasn't holding hers. "*You* took the hurt away. You and Michaela." He slowly leaned forward and kissed her in the light of the moon. "I love you, Tessa McCutcheon," he breathed out on a sigh. "I've told you that tonight, but I don't think you believe me. It's the God's honest truth—I can't imagine a day of my life without you."

Awash with turbulent feeling, Tessa let his words flow over her like a warm balm. He loved her, truly loved her, and she loved him, and would for the rest of her life. Something magical had transpired on this trip. Something she'd thank God for every day she walked this earth. His lips still close, she leaned closer wanting more.

Chapter Sixty-Three

Chaim came awake slowly to the sound of chirping birds. Unsure of his whereabouts after the months of travels, he stretched a leg, marveling at the softness of the goose-down mattress. Had he gotten any sleep? Didn't feel so. But how could that be true?

Rolling to his side, he came face to face with Tessa, warm and still blissfully asleep, her breath coming out in quiet little puffs. At the magical sight, the night before rushed back with force.

The kiss.

Tessa's eyes darkening with passion.

Tessa tugging him to his feet.

He was tempted to stay here all day, just staring. But his face was chilly, which meant the rest of the cabin was, as well. He needed to start the fire, warm things up for her before she awakened. The fire had gone out sometime early in the morning, and the barest hint of light was lining the edges of the hills outside the window next to the bed.

Tessa was more gorgeous than an exquisite painting. Abundant lashes rested on her peachy soft cheek. A lush tendril of wavy hair looked like spun gold. It swirled down along her neck and disappeared under the cover. Judging by her neckline, or absence of one, she appeared to be naked.

If he didn't leave now, he wouldn't at all. His wife deserved coffee, a fire, and whatever else was in the picnic basket Aunt Claire and his mother placed in the buggy the night before.

Filled with an achy feeling in his chest that made him want to scoop her up and never let her go, he rolled carefully away and lifted the blankets and quilt, going quickly so as not to let any cold air into the warm cocoon. He hunted down his clothes that were scattered around the room. Pulling on his pants and shirt, he worked the buttons quickly, glancing every few moments at the bed. *Last night was a revelation*, he thought, his cheeks warming. If he looked in the mirror, he knew they'd be pink.

Quietly splashing his face with frigid water and brushing his teeth, he set about in the Gutheries' cabin like a stealthy madman, lighting both fires—one in the hearth and one in the stove. He filled the coffeepot with water and placed it on the stove while he hunted for coffee. Delighted to find a canister with already ground beans, he scooped several heaping spoonfuls into the upper section of the coffeepot and then filled another pot with water for Tessa's toilette, setting that on the warming stovetop, as well.

He wanted hot coffee and something to eat ready as soon as she opened her eyes. Finished setting the contents of the basket on the table, and enjoying the rich scent of the boiling brew, he lowered himself into a comfortable chair by the crackling fire, feeling as if Christmas morning had just arrived.

Tessa didn't need to open her eyes to know where she was. Heat prickled her face as she recalled her actions of the night before. After Chaim's declaration of love, and his kiss, she hadn't wanted to wait a moment longer before becoming a true wife, regardless of her words about slowing down for time to court properly. To get to know each other better. Hadn't she thought the same during the close call with the tornado? She knew everything she'd ever need to know about her husband. He was kind, thoughtful, and possessed the ability to set her blood singing through her body. Still, what must he think of her brazenness this morning?

Keeping her eyes closed as much as possible, she gazed around the dim cabin until she spotted Chaim. He sat by the hearth, contemplating the crackling fire. At least one of them was relaxed this morning, if his demeanor was any indication. Her insides were tangled like a wet sheet in the wind. Her thoughts blushed with each recollection of the previous night. How on earth could she face him?

"Good morning," he said from his chair, traces of humor in his voice.

With no other choice, she sat up, being careful to keep the bedding pulled up to her throat. "How could you tell I was awake?"

"Your blankets stopped moving. Either you were awake or dead, and I didn't think the latter was a true choice." He stood but didn't come toward her. "Would you like a cup of coffee? It's ready."

"Oh, yes, I've been smelling it…"

His brows lifted.

She smiled. "No, really. I've only been awake mere moments. If you'll allow me to…" She glanced around for her clothing which, to her utter embarrassment, was littered around the cabin. Her dress across the back of a chair. Her petticoat on the floor by the bed. Was that her chemise on the headboard? No, she could look no farther! What on earth had she been thinking, her mind wanted to scream at her—but she knew. She'd been enjoying her husband in a way only a wife could, and she'd loved every second.

"You stay right where you are, and I'll bring you some."

He was already dressed and stood at the sideboard, looking rakishly handsome. Using a folded towel, he carefully lifted the sizzling coffeepot and filled two mugs. She watched as he stirred in not one, but two spoons of sugar to one cup and then added some milk. He must have noticed she had a sweet tooth. He added nothing to his.

He glanced in her direction. "The milk came over in the picnic basket, and the sugar was here. You should see all the fancy foodstuffs they sent. You'd think we planned to stay for a week. For now," he said walking toward her with the two cups in his hands, "coffee will do."

Oh, my. She didn't know *this* Chaim, but the look in his eyes sent a warm thrill zipping up her spine. She needed to think of something to say. She glanced at the window beside the bed. "Was the doe here this morning when you woke up? Like Roady said?" She needed to stop trembling, or he'd think her a ninny. She'd been the one to instigate last night, and he hadn't seemed to mind. She felt a whole lot shyer in the morning light.

"She was. For a short time."

"You should have awakened me."

He raised one eyebrow in question. "Not a chance of that. What do you always say about *our* sleeping baby?"

"Not to wake her."

"So, there you go. I was only following your direction."

She smiled and carefully took the cup he offered. "Thank you."

He sat on the edge of the bed, gazing at her. "Be careful, it's hot."

"I'm not used to such treatment," she eked out, feeling his contemplation all the way down to her toes. She never knew toes could be so sensitive.

"Well, get used to it. I intend to spoil you for the rest of your life."

When he lifted the cup to his lips, she did the same, enjoying the heady, sweet taste of the coffee. They sipped along in silence for a few minutes, just enjoying the bliss of each other's company. When their gazes happened to meet, her face prickled with heat, and a small smile played at the corner of his lips. No doubt about it, Chaim McCutcheon was tremendously proud of himself this morning, and with good reason.

Chapter Sixty-Four

Feeling as conspicuous as a drunkard at Sunday service, Tessa cringed when she saw all the men milling around the ranch yard of the Heart of the Mountains, as if waiting for the honeymooners to return. To her embarrassment, it was already two o'clock in the afternoon. She and Chaim *meant* to return first thing in the morning, both agreeing wholeheartedly doing so was the only way to quell their curiosity about their daughter. How she'd passed the night? Was she happy or sad missing them? But soon, their good intentions were forgotten. One thing led to another, and another, and another. Then she'd needed to bathe and tidy the cabin.

After that, Chaim insisted on getting some fresh air and seeing their surroundings in the light of day so, hand in hand, they strolled through the meadow and shared a number of kisses under the shade of a tree, the soft spring grass cushioning her back. What she'd felt inside was pure magic. A chubby, yellow-breasted meadowlark, high in the branches above, serenaded them with a song which created a storm of feeling she'd been unable to control. Her eyes filled and spilled over. Noticing immediately, Chaim had been alarmed until she explained her reasons.

"I'm sick with love, my darling," she'd responded as he gently wiped the tears away with the pad of his thumb. "And happy beyond all measure. I didn't know love could feel this way. I lived through a frightening tornado yesterday morning and another tornado of passion last night. I'm a mess of emotion today. I'm sorry."

That proclamation produced a tender look, followed by another round of kisses. The lazy morning slowly slipped by, marked by the warmth of the sunshine and the heat of their desire, to where they were now.

Tessa denounced herself as the worst mother in the world for staying away for so long. Where was Michaela? She could hardly wait for the buggy to come to a stop.

Luke and his brothers stood at the corral, speaking with Dustin. They'd been admiring several horses inside only moments before but, hearing the buggy, looked up and smiled at their approach.

"Good afternoon," Dustin called, waving them in. A smile played around his mouth.

Winston, Flood and *Mr. Jordan*— Tessa couldn't get used to thinking of her uncle by his first name—stood by the barn holding fishing poles. Dressed in comfortable clothing, they grinned, as well, everyone besides her uncle and Winston held up a long line of fish.

"The dough balls must have worked like a charm," Chaim remarked, pulling one rein. The horse came around and stopped next to an unhitched buggy.

Chaim didn't seem embarrassed in the least, and perhaps, even the opposite. He appeared as comfortable and confident as if they'd just returned from church. Her face warmed as she took in the speculative gazes of the onlookers. "Must have."

The group gathered around as Chaim helped Tessa down and reached for the food basket.

"Welcome back," Dustin said, fighting to keep a straight face. He came over and gave her a big, brotherly hug.

If she wasn't embarrassed enough before, she wished now she could evaporate into a mist and float away. The men looked expectant and admiring at Chaim as if he were a knight just returned from battle—or from defrocking his bride. Back at the cabin, she'd found clean linen in a bottom drawer of Sally's dresser and prayed Roady's wife wouldn't mind her snooping. Chaim helped her make the bed, keeping his thoughts to himself. Their one-night honeymoon had been a dream. Nothing would ever compare.

"Mrs. McCutcheon," a deep voice called out.

They all turned toward the bunkhouse.

The tall cowboy named Shad Petty was striding their way. What on earth could he have to say to her? She felt Chaim's possessive hand on the small of her back as they waited. Shad's cheeks were actually pink, as if he also knew where they'd been. "Yes?"

"I'm sorry to interrupt your arrival, ma'am, but I was in town this morning and ran into Norman Klinkner. He asked me to give you this." He held out a small package wrapped in brown, wrinkled paper.

All at once, she remembered. "Thank you so much, Mr. Petty! I appreciate your kindness."

"My pleasure. Wasn't any trouble at all."

As she expected, all the men were overly curious, including Chaim. They gazed at the bundle with a tinge of excitement and smiles—everyone except her uncle. He just looked bored. Mark, Matthew, and John stood back with the older men, giving her room, but Dustin and Luke stood next to Chaim, one to each side.

She handed the gift to her husband, still reveling at the heady thought this handsome man, now seen in a brand-new light as of last night, was her husband 'til death did they part. "For you, Chaim. A wedding present."

Chaim's face grew bright red.

She'd never seen him speechless since they'd met, even after all the revelations about Emmeline and Michaela.

"What?" he finally said.

"A wedding present," she repeated. "Go on, open it. Hurry up, before everyone dies of curiosity."

Shad, who had yet to walk away, nodded his agreement. "I've been pondering the contents all day. They rattle."

The contents clinked softly together as Chaim carefully unwrapped the rumpled gift. Inside was the money clip and pocket watch he'd sold to the pawn broker in Waterloo. His mouth dropped open. "How?"

She'd never seen the money clip up close until now. An *MC* was fashioned on the top in a fancy cursive scrawl. "I watched you through the window in Waterloo. At the surprise party for Flood, Ina Klinkner mentioned her husband was going to Waterloo to deliver some lumber. That got me thinking, so I asked if he might inquire about your items, the money clip, and what I believed was your pocket watch since I hadn't seen it since. If they were still there, I asked him to buy them back at any cost. I'll reimburse the Klinkners before we leave for Texas. Ina said Norman would consider the task an honor."

"Norman had just pulled into town when I ran into him," Shad said. "The timin' couldn't have been better."

The stunned look of delight on Chaim's face made her smile.

"Thought I'd never see these again. Thank you, Tessa."

"What's this about?" Dustin asked. "Why'd you sell your money clip and watch, Chaim?"

"Traveling to Montana, I was a little short on funds—"

She gazed up at her brother-in-law. "He used the money for diapers, Dustin, and rooms in the hotel. Meals and whatever else we needed. He made sure we didn't go without."

Chaim's brows pulled together. "But I don't have a wedding present for you."

Tessa smiled, not even caring Mr. Jordan would hear her response. "You already gave me the most precious gifts of all, Chaim. You gave me your name. And, along with that, you gave me Michaela."

The men seemed dumbstruck, and if she wasn't mistaken, teary-eyed, too.

Giving a parting glance to them all, she headed for her daughter, feeling as light as air.

Chapter Sixty-Five

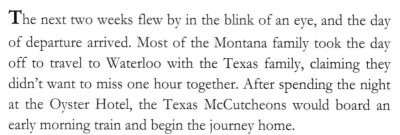

The next two weeks flew by in the blink of an eye, and the day of departure arrived. Most of the Montana family took the day off to travel to Waterloo with the Texas family, claiming they didn't want to miss one hour together. After spending the night at the Oyster Hotel, the Texas McCutcheons would board an early morning train and begin the journey home.

The prior day, Brandon and Charity departed for Waterloo themselves, claiming the need of a getaway, but Tessa noticed a look of worry cross Claire's face when Charity announced their intentions. Tonight, Brandon and Charity promised to meet the group at the Oyster for one last family meal.

Flood had gone out of his way to make their journey to Waterloo eventful by borrowing a fancy surrey from the Klinkners. The carriage, driven by Francis, seated eight adults comfortably, with the three babies riding on their mamas' laps. Tall, white wheels were polished to perfection, and the plush brown upholstered seats were comfortable. A sun canopy provided shade on this last day of May. Long golden tassels fringed the edge of the canopy top and jiggled with each step the horses took, keeping Michaela, Clara, and Gillian enraptured during the long trip.

Claire and Winnie rode in a buggy driven by Shad.

The men rode horseback alongside the conveyance, as did Sidney. The ranch buckboard, guided by Smokey, transported the luggage and two wooden crates filled with parting gifts they weren't supposed to open until Christmas.

With the two infants and other small children, the trip would be challenging, so Faith, Rachel, and Amy said their goodbyes at the ranch.

Taking the menagerie of tiny people on such a long trip, only to turn around and return the very next day, would have been as easy as herding a colony of prairie dogs, Luke proclaimed colorfully.

Billy, Adam, and Colton were disappointed when Flood asked them to stay behind and help their mothers, but a smile appeared when their grandpa promised them a ranch hand's pay for their effort, which made staying home a bit more palatable.

The lively group turned heads as the surrey, buggy, and buckboard, surrounded by a group of ten riders, entered Waterloo in the late afternoon. When people recognized the McCutcheons, they called out friendly welcomes. The air hummed with excitement.

Stiff from the bumpy miles traveled, they unloaded in front of the Oyster Hotel, delighted to have arrived in one piece.

Tessa looked up at the white, two-story clapboard building with the pretty yellow curtains in every window and the weathervane topped with a flying seagull. Whoever built the establishment must have been missing their beach home somewhere. Looking at it now, she enjoyed a plethora of memories flowing through her like a waltz. She and Chaim at dinner, her proposal, his surprise, and then his reply. Waterloo would always be special.

"Penny for your thoughts," Chaim said over her shoulder, his warm, peppermint scented breath tickling her ear. "I have another mint in my chest pocket, if you'd dare to dig it out."

She smiled.

He held a suitcase in each hand and was tromping from the buckboard to the boardwalk unloading the wagon.

"Why, thank you, sir. Don't mind if I do." His gaze followed her every move as she reached into his pocket and fished around with her fingers.

"Be sure to check it for fluff before putting it in your mouth."

Her face heated. Everything he said these days caused a flutter in her belly. Didn't matter what subject it was. Finding the sweet, she did as he instructed and then popped the candy into her mouth. She'd enjoyed the pleasure of watching him during the trip to Waterloo, under the pretense of talking with the women. He and his cousins and brother cut up the whole way. Their laughter kept the babies smiling. Chaim's boyish grin melted her faster than butter on the stovetop. The McCutcheons were a magnificent sight. And especially Chaim. *Her* Chaim. Here was the Chaim McCutcheon Emmeline had fallen in love with, too.

She followed him to the boardwalk and waited as he set the bags down. "You want to know what I was thinking while taking in the hotel?"

He ran his arm across his moist brow then nodded.

"Just how blessed I am. How much has happened since we traveled through those doors the first time—not all that long ago." She blinked away a sudden rush of tears. "I'm just amazed how everything turned out." The expression he got whenever he was thinking of her in *that* special way appeared in his eyes. Her body flushed.

"Don't be amazed. I'm not. What else could I do but fall in love with you?" He traced a heart across the left side of his chest and then glanced around. "Where's Michaela? Where's my little girl?"

"Your mother took her inside to show her the grandfather clock at the foot of the stairs. It should be donging anytime."

"Oh, she'll like that."

Tessa nodded. "Madeline and Becky held her much of the way here, you know."

He nodded. "Don't go thinking I wasn't watching you, because I was. I hope you don't mind all the help you'll have now with Michaela, holding and carrying. Between my sisters and mother, sister-in-law, and my cousin's wife, you might have to fight for time with her."

With the buckboard unloaded, Luke and Dustin headed to the livery with the wagon and whatever horses hadn't already been taken down to be stabled overnight.

Chaim picked up her hand and, for a moment, studied her fingers. "Mrs. Jordan will want her fair share of Michaela, too. I'm glad the two of you reconciled. You didn't have to, after all the hurt they caused you over the years, but you did. You're a good woman, Tessa McCutcheon, and I'm one lucky man to love you."

The Jordans departed two days after her and Chaim's night in Roady and Sally's cabin. Before they caught a stage to Waterloo, Mrs. Jordan came out to the ranch without her husband and asked to speak with Tessa alone. She apologized for not taking Tessa into the family when she was a child. She saw clearly now just how wrong they'd been. She also intended to have a discussion with Tessa's father and set him straight on a few things.

The woman seemed truly contrite, which was a new side to her aunt Tessa didn't know. The most incredible part was, she actually approved of her and Chaim raising Michaela in Rio Wells. Said after all the goodness she'd witnessed from the McCutcheons, she didn't have any hard feelings toward Emmeline for the final wishes her daughter made. She and Mr. Jordan intended to have words with Jason Whitmore. Without any proof of what Tessa alleged about putting Michaela into an orphanage, they couldn't bring charges, but she assured Tessa she believed every word.

Mrs. Jordan also promised she'd work on Alfred, and the two would come to Texas at least twice a year. She didn't want her granddaughter to grow up unaware of her Boston grandparents. Or, if Tessa and Chaim decided to keep her parentage hidden, they would be content in being Michaela's great auntie and uncle from Boston. They just wanted to be included in her life. Her aunt finished by thanking Tessa profusely for taking action and saving her granddaughter. They would always be eternally grateful.

"I'm the lucky one," Tessa replied, remembering the kiss her aunt had placed on her cheek. She slipped her hand in the crook of Chaim's arm as they made their way to the hotel door where Winnie was waving them in.

Michaela cuddled in her grandmother's arms, as if they'd known each other since birth.

"Do you think we can sneak off and say goodbye to Mary Margaret? I would feel bad if we didn't," Tessa asked under her breath.

"The train leaves early tomorrow morning, so we'll have to do that before supper. I was thinking the exact same thing. If we hurry and get settled in our room, there should be plenty of time."

Chapter Sixty-Six

With his spoon, Flood tapped the side of his wine goblet, and the conversations quieted along the large rectangle table inside the Oyster Hotel. Their group of eighteen adults, along with the three babies, in the middle of the dining room, was loud with everyone in a cheerful mood. Dinner of steak and potatoes was excellent, followed by warm chocolate cake. A sated, lethargic bliss seeped through Flood's body like warm honey. If there was a way to feel happier than he did right now, he didn't know what that could be. He looked at Claire's expectant face and smiled.

"It's time I said some words, this last evening of our first annual McCutcheon Family Reunion." His throat tightened, and he hoped to make it through without embarrassing himself. His sons and daughter all gazed at him with their heart in their eyes.

Claire reached over and rubbed his arm.

How he hated to see his brother and the rest go. He'd known this time would come, but he wasn't ready. "The first thank you goes to my wife, for thinking I was worthy of such a significant celebration. My life would be empty without you, sweetheart. I think you know how much I love you."

Claire nodded. "Only slightly."

Laughter rippled around the table.

"My boys. And my daughter." He glanced at Matthew, Mark, Luke, John, and then Charity and Brandon. "My daughter-in-law here," he smiled at Lily, "and the ones left back at the ranch. And my son-in-law sheriff." He twice thumped his chest with a closed fist, working out the lump threatening to close his vocal cords. "Not to forget all my grandbabies. I don't deserve such a family. No man could love his family more."

"The feeling's mutual, Pa," Luke called, sitting between his brothers, John and Matt. "Never question that."

Flood nodded and wiped his eyes. Looking down the long table, he smiled at his older brother, dreading the arrival of the morning. Winston and his family would be gone on the early train. He didn't want to see them go. "And you, Winston. I couldn't have been more shocked to see you and your family. I'm still flabbergasted. Thank you for making the long trip. I can't tell you how meeting your sons and daughters has soothed my soul. Dustin and Sidney. Chaim, Tessa, and little Michaela. Madeline, Becky—*and* Miss Knutson. Claire feels the very same. I give my word: we'll return the favor next year. Nothing could keep us away. It'll be good to be back in Rio Wells."

"We're counting on it," Winston said. "May first. We'll see you in San Antonio!"

Flood nodded and then realized he'd left out Roady and Sally, sitting quietly down at the other end of the table by Winston and Dustin. That jolted a memory. What about their announcement? Surely, Sally had shared the good news with Roady by now that she was expecting. She was keeping the secret too long. "I realized

I didn't say a word of thanks to Roady and Sally. They're like another son and daughter to us. We couldn't love you two anymore than we already do." What better time or place to share their good news, with everyone together for the last time? He'd give a little help along. They were probably holding off because they didn't want to draw attention away from him and his birthday. Poppycock! Nothing was better news than a new baby.

At the mention of their names, both Roady and Sally looked surprised. They sat straighter and smiled down at Flood.

"Speaking of Roady and Sally," he began again. He paused and waved the waiter over. "We'd like champagne, enough for a toast."

The man hurried away.

"What's this about, Flood?" Claire asked, touching his arm.

"Just hold on. Wait for the champagne. We don't get chances like this every day, dear wife."

The waiter was back with a helper, and the two men had the bottles opened quickly and refilled the wineglasses around the table.

Funny thing was, Roady and Sally were not giving a thing away. They looked as curious as the rest. Flood stood and lifted his glass. "To Roady and Sally—and the new little cowboy or cowgirl on the way. Gillian is soon to have a sibling to play with. Cheers!"

Everyone clapped and cheered, calling out their good wishes. They drank down their glasses.

Sally gasped.

Roady reared back in his chair, staring at his wife as if he'd never seen her before. A moment later, he pulled her into his arms and kissed her with conviction in front of everyone.

When they finally came up for air, Sally was sputtering.

"Why didn't you tell me, sweetheart?" Roady gaped around at the others, the silly grin stretching his lips, looking like the town fool. "I'm the happiest man in the world."

They all waited for Sally's response.

Flood adored Sally. She was the perfect wife for Roady and made his top hand's life better in every way.

"I-I," she began.

Her face was so red it looked painful.

"I didn't say anything because it's not true. I have no idea what you're talking about, Flood." She turned and stroked Roady's cheek. "And I'm sorry to disappoint you, my love."

Thunderstruck, Flood felt his face flush. He slowly turned to Charity with narrowed eyes. "Daughter? Do you have something to say?"

Charity's eyes were huge over the hand that covered her mouth. "Well, uh…"

Brandon stood and brought Charity up with a gentle pull of her hand.

Charity put an appeasing hand out to Sally. "I'm so sorry, Sally. I fibbed when Father got too close to the truth about the party. All I could think to say was the secret I was keeping was you were expecting and hadn't yet told Roady. I swore Father to secrecy and forgot to tell him the truth once the party was over. Roady, Sally, can you ever forgive me?"

Everyone laughed heartly and Roady kissed Sally again. "False alarm again. I guess it'll happen when it happens, and not a moment before. I better get workin' on that."

More laughter.

Brandon and Charity remained standing. "But Brandon and I have some *news* to share." She took Brandon's hand, gazing up into his eyes. "Brandon and I came to Waterloo a day early to see a doctor. I wondered why I hadn't yet conceived."

"I didn't know it, but Charity's been worried," Brandon said, emotion deepening his voice. "She should have let me know. We men can be so dense…"

"And?" Claire said on a whisper.

Charity's face brightened to match the sun. "The doctor said not to worry about a thing. Nothing is wrong. And…Brandon and I are expecting!" She began jumping up and down with excitement. "I've been feeling a little off these last few weeks, and now I know why. Brandon should be a daddy by next April!"

"Brandon's a daddy now," Flood corrected, feeling a little like the town fool Roady resembled only moments before. He waved over the waiter. "We're needing a few more bottles of champagne." Scooting out of his chair, he went to Charity and wrapped her in his arms. Giving way to her brothers, cousins, and the rest, Flood called out. "Anyone else? Now would be the time to speak up."

Chapter Sixty-Seven

Tessa huddled under Chaim's arm on the platform of the train station, Michaela still sleepy-eyed from being awakened so early, tight in her arms. Rainfall overnight gave the air a sharp bite, and mist rose around the legs of the individuals waiting for the five o'clock train. All the McCutcheons were present, the smiles from the night before gone now that half the family would soon depart for Texas. They stood around in small groups, murmuring quietly, as if their talk might wake up the town.

She took a deep breath, gazing east where the sun illuminated the mountain peaks and splashed golds and pinks onto puffy, flat-bottomed clouds. The sight stole her breath. She stared, longing to remember this morning forever. She was a part of a family. A real, bonded-of-steel family. The concept felt magical.

"Warm enough?" Chaim asked quietly, tightening his hold around her shoulders. "You shivered."

She smiled up into his face, so handsome in the new, cream-colored Stetson he'd bought yesterday after borrowing money from his brother. "I'm fine. Just taking in all this beauty." In reality, she wanted to turn in his arms and profess her love again and again. She never knew life could be so sweet.

"How about Michaela? We don't want her to catch a cold."

"She'd let us know if she wasn't warm. She's still drowsy. She didn't sleep much last night."

"I remember."

Waterloo, the town Tessa thought so small and peaceful, had been alive throughout the darkest hours. The sounds of riders and a few loud voices made Tessa wonder what was happening outside on the street. Once, a gunshot sounded, followed by laughter. She hadn't worried. Not with Chaim sleeping at her side and the rest of the McCutcheons all together under one roof. The feeling of security was heady.

From the opposite side of the platform, Sidney glanced over and smiled. She stood under Dustin's arm, as well.

Luke and Mark talked with them and John and Lily.

Claire held Clara, with Flood and the older McCutcheons in another small grouping, getting in her last few snuggles until next year. Claire's eyes were rimmed in red when they'd said good morning in the lobby over a fast cup of coffee. Seeing her loved ones depart must be soul wrenching. Especially her youngest son. So much love here, and so much heartbreak.

Last night, when the men went to the saloon for one final drink together, Sidney, Lily, and the rest of the women appeared at Tessa's door. They'd sat around the room on whatever surface was available, or the floor, sharing their hopes and dreams. For the first time, Tessa felt very included. The three baby girls, who were supposed to be getting sleepy and going down, rallied and were passed from one woman to the next, as if they didn't want to miss any of the party.

Tessa wished she could bottle up the laughter and love. Take it to Texas and experience it again later. She never wanted to forget the feeling. "I'm so happy we were able to visit Mrs. Mary Margaret yesterday," Tessa commented to Chaim. "Did you see her face when she opened the door? We were the last people she expected."

Chaim agreed with a sound in his throat. "Her eyes were saucers. What surprised me was that Michaela remembered her. My daughter is teaching me so much about children."

Chaim had glanced away, staring into the distance.

"Go on and join the men, Chaim, you don't have to babysit us. We'll go see how Charity's feeling this morning. She and Brandon sure look happy."

He breathed out in a great gust of air. "I will, but there's something I'd like to give you first." Reaching into his pocket, he pulled out a white handkerchief.

"What's this?" Her hands were full of the baby.

He slowly unwrapped the corners. On the white linen, in the center of his palm, was a golden band. "It's not new. Aunt Claire offered it to me yesterday. It was her grandmother's and has been in her jewelry box for years." He picked it up so she could see it better. "If you'd rather wait until we get to Texas, I'll get you a new one. Or, I can have this one engraved with our wedding date."

"Oh, Chaim!" Heat flushed her body. "I want this one." She couldn't get any more words past the lump in her throat.

Chaim leaned forward and kissed her lips. "I sort of thought you would." He picked up her left hand and slipped it on. The ring fit perfectly and glimmered like new.

"Chaim. Tessa," Luke called, waving them over. "You'll have enough together time on the train."

"Go on," Tessa whispered. "I need two seconds to control my runaway emotions." She put out her hand and gazed at the ring, her eyes watery. "We'll be right over. I promise."

"You're sure?"

"Absolutely. There's not much time left."

Nodding, he leaned down and kissed her cheek.

She and Michaela watched him walk away.

"Da da," Michaela called out softly.

Chaim turned and winked, looking more attractive than any man had a right to. At the men's group, he jumped into the middle of the conversation, saying something to Dustin and elbowing Luke in the side at the same time.

The group burst into laughter.

Her husband was good medicine for everyone. He had a gift.

She kissed Michaela on the temple, rocking her from side to side then a loud whistle split the air. Turning, she saw the approaching train still a good way down the tracks. Black smoke billowed from the dusky gray smokestack and mingled with white steam from a vent. The lot trailed out behind like a tail on a kite.

The rumbling rails brought a tremble of expectation swirling within her for the life God had blessed her with. "You're going home, sweetie," she whispered to Michaela. "And so am I."

Read on for an excerpt of Heart of Eden.

USA Today bestselling author Caroline Fyffe's sweeping
saga about five sisters finding love and forging new
lives on the Colorado frontier.

Books by Caroline Fyffe

McCutcheon Family Series
Montana Dawn
Texas Twilight
Mail-Order Brides of the West: Evie
Mail-Order Brides of the West: Heather
Moon Over Montana
Mail-Order Brides of the West: Kathryn
Montana Snowfall
Texas Lonesome
Montana Courage
Montana Promise
Montana Reunion
~~~*~~~

Prairie Hearts Series
Where The Wind Blows
Before The Larkspur Blooms
West Winds of Wyoming
Under a Falling Star
Whispers on the Wind
Where Wind Meets Wave
Winter Winds of Wyoming
~~~*~~~

Colorado Hearts Series
Heart of Eden
True Heart's Desire
Heart of Mine
An American Duchess (Spin-off title)
Heart of Dreams
~~~*~~~

Stand Alone Western Historical
Sourdough Creek
~~~*~~~

Stand Alone Contemporary Women's Fiction
Three And A Half Minutes
~~~*~~~

All titles in AUDIO!
Take your reading experience to the next level!
Caroline's Books @ Audible.com

Join Caroline's Facebook Readers Group
https://www.facebook.com/groups/234877343243183/
for fun, giveaways, and book news.

Don't miss a single title!
Sign up for Caroline's Newsletter
http://www.carolinefyffe.com/

Acknowledgements

What a joy for me to be back in Y Knot, Montana, with the McCutcheons, as well as with the McCutcheons from Rio Wells, Texas, visiting all the people I've come to love! *Montana Dawn*, book one of the McCutcheon Family series, was the second novel I'd ever written, and that was way back in 2009. It's difficult for me to believe *Montana Reunion* is book eleven—and five years have passed since the last book of the McCutcheon Family series was released.

Research is the best part of writing historical fiction. I'm thankful for all the caretakers, owners, and business proprietors of the authentic ghost town of Goldfield, Arizona, established 1893, who have kept the gem of history so true to its original form. I enjoyed wandering the streets, soaking up the landscape and feel of the gritty environment. All of it helped me to understand Chaim McCutcheon and what he'd gone through living in Arizona. Stepping into the Mammoth Saloon, I took a step back in time. What fun it was!

A huge thank you to my editing team and beta readers. They make my writing shine far better than I could alone. The ending result is always lightyears superior to the original. Thank you!

Much gratitude and love to my family for their unending support when I'm shut away in my office for hours on end. To my husband Michael (my first reader, who catches my big potholes and storyline booboos), sons Matthew and Adam (who assist with marketing and graphics), my daughters-in-law Rachel and

Misti (who give unending womanly support in ways only a woman can do), and grandchildren Evelyn and Hudson—the apples of my eye, and growing faster than I could ever believe possible—*thank you*!

Tons of love to my dear sisters and their spouses, reminding me very much of the Brinkman sisters and their husbands of my Colorado Hearts series. They always have my back. They answer questions, brainstorm, cheer me on, and improve my work in every way possible. I possess the best family a person could conceivably want! I love them all dearly.

Much love and gratitude also go to my faithful readers! Without each and every one of you, I couldn't do what I love to do day in and day out. Your love and support mean more to me than you could ever know. Thank you!

And last but not least, thank you to our wonderful God, who has blessed me mightily with a career I never dreamed I'd have.

About The Author

Caroline Fyffe was born in Waco, Texas, the first of many towns she would call home during her father's career with the US Air Force. A horse aficionado from an early age, she earned a Bachelor of Arts in communications from California State University-Chico before launching what would become a twenty-year career as an equine photographer. She began writing fiction to pass the time during long days in the show arena, channeling her love of horses and the Old West into a series of Western historicals. Her debut novel, *Where the Wind Blows*, won the Romance Writers of America's prestigious Golden Heart Award as well as the Wisconsin RWA's Write Touch Readers' Award. She and her husband have two grown sons and live in the Pacific Northwest.

Want news on releases, giveaways, and bonus reads? Sign up for Caroline's newsletter at: www.carolinefyffe.com
LIKE her Facebook Author Page: Facebook.com/CarolineFyffe
JOIN her Facebook Reader Group at https://bit.ly/3HizITd
Twitter: @carolinefyffe
Write to her at: caroline@carolinefyffe.com

Excerpt from

Heart of Eden

By
Caroline Fyffe

Chapter One

Eden, Colorado, 1880

From atop a small rise, Blake Harding sat on his horse as he surveyed the north pasture of the Five Sisters Ranch. Large, puffy clouds hung motionless in the indigo sky. If not for the movement of the bald eagle that had appeared from the west, he'd think he was looking at a painting. A crisp breeze ruffled Banjo's mane, and all seemed right with the world.

Everything here and now, anyway.

Blake sighed and relaxed his tense shoulders, letting a hard-earned peace push back the agitation that was never far from his mind. He missed John. For the last eighteen years, his boss had been so much more than his mentor—he'd taken the place of the parents he didn't remember and the brother he'd lost in the Civil

War. John Brinkman had been Blake's whole family wrapped up in one honorable man.

From his position on the rise, he spotted Trevor Hill cutting through the herd. The cowboy's lips moved slowly as he spoke to the cattle in an effort not to rile them as they grazed. At the base of the slope, he waved and then loped to the top of the knoll.

"Trevor, what brings you out this way?" Blake called once the ranch hand was within hearing distance. Trevor had worked for the Five Sisters for three years. "Thought you were in Eden today, picking up supplies."

"Was, boss, but came back as soon as Henry gave me this." He held out a folded note.

So it's actually going to happen.

Still not used to the men calling him "boss," Blake took the paper. Henry had sent a telegram two days ago. Upon hearing of their father's death, John's daughters had apparently responded right away. *Imagine that.* He opened the note and scanned the missive, anger twisting his gut. There was only one thing worse than having to contend with John dying—that would be confronting his five selfish, self-centered daughters. Blake stared at the words in front of his face. *Well, miracles do happen.* The Brinkman sisters would be arriving within the month, after all the years John's pleas had fallen upon deaf ears. He fisted the note in his hand.

"Boss...?" Trevor said, a bit cautiously. "They comin' to Eden?"

"Yeah, they are. Too bad it took John dying to get the deed done."

"Why now, do you think?" Trevor lifted his hat and scratched his head, then gazed lovingly up at the morning sun. "Seems a bit late."

"Doesn't take a genius to figure what they're after." He remembered two little girls, two toddlers, and one infant. The eldest, Mavis, had been almost five to his ten the last time he'd seen her.

"Money?"

"What else?"

Chapter Two

Philadelphia, Pennsylvania

Belle Brinkman hurried down the sidewalk toward her older sister's apartment holding the folds of her black mourning dress, lest she catch her toe and fall. The blustery wind pulled persistently at the ribbons that kept her headpiece from tumbling into the rain-soaked street. Lesley had surprised her with the gift last week, and she'd not let it spill into the mud.

She wrinkled her nose at the puddles, horse manure, and garbage that lined the road. Passing the slaughterhouse, she pinched her nose closed. *How I despise this part of town.* She'd begged Mavis not to move there when she and Darvid wed, one year ago last month. Unfortunately, both Mavis and her sister's late husband earned little at the department store, where they worked in accounting. Compassion stirred in Belle's chest for her sister's plight. A month ago, Darvid had taken ill with pneumonia and died—but only after racking up a bill with the doctor to add to their other debts. *Where will Mavis find the money to pay?* As far as Belle knew, she had little put away for emergencies. The pittance Belle had wouldn't go far to help.

Belle sighed, ashamed at how coldhearted she'd become. Instead of thinking of her brother-in-law, who was now gone to his just rewards, she was worried about money. *The lack of money is the root of all evil.*

Appalled at herself, she thought of her mother, dead for fifteen years. "I know, Mother, it's the *love* of money that's the root of all evil, but sometimes it doesn't feel that way at all. Scrimping by gets old." Belle's mother had been the kindest, most loving woman—at least that was what her six-year-old self remembered. Left orphans for all intents and purposes after her death, Belle and her sisters owed everything to Vernon and Velma Crowdaire, friends who took their mother in after she fled their unstable father and the untamed wilderness called Eden. Her mother's death, three years after arriving at the Crowdaires', had been a shock. The couple the girls now called "Aunt and Uncle" took them in permanently, providing room, board, and even the clothes on their backs.

Still, Vernon Crowdaire has no right to make us feel so indebted every second, Belle thought as her disgust for him surfaced. The way he flaunted his generosity like a badge of honor made them all feel like beggars. *It's not right.*

Gathering her skirt again, Belle stepped over a wide puddle and then sidestepped a lump of refuse in her path. The bedroom she shared with her three younger sisters in the Crowdaire home was a bit less crowded since Mavis had married. And two years before that, their guardians had moved to a more upscale area of town as well, giving them a larger bedroom—but still just one.

434   C a r o l i n e   F y f f e

That was something. *I should work on my charity. Not harbor such dislike for Vernon. Try to be more grateful.* She knew she should, but she hadn't after all these years.

As often as the Crowdaires expounded on what good catches she and her sisters were, only Mavis, the eldest, had received an official offer of marriage, and that from a man who had little more than two nickels to rub together. Even though Belle had liked Darvid, she'd been against the marriage from the first, feeling Mavis was settling because of Velma's constant harping to accept the proposal. It had almost seemed like the Crowdaires wanted Mavis out in order to relieve the burden of expenses. It was understandable, she supposed. They *had* done so much over the years.

In reality, what did Belle or any of her sisters have to offer a husband, besides love? Each year the tiny stipend their guardians gave each girl grew by only a few coins. As soon as they were out of school, each of them had found work to help pay their expenses and supplement their wardrobes. They had all long passed the age where only hand-me-downs would do. Katie was the exception. The youngest Brinkman sister had taken a loan from Uncle Vernon to attend a normal school in Massachusetts and train to become a teacher. She'd graduated three months ago and was in the process of looking for a position.

Finally arriving at the tall brownstone, Belle ascended the crumbling brick steps, opened the door, and proceeded to the first apartment at the back of the lobby. She rapped several times.

"Who's there?"

"It's me. Belle."

Mavis opened the door dressed in widow's attire. Her wavy mahogany hair was swept on top of her head, and she wore the wrist-length gloves she never went without to hide her disfigurement. Her blue, wide-set eyes gave away that she'd been crying, bringing an ache to Belle's heart.

They embraced.

"How're you?" Belle asked stepping back, knowing well her sister was taking Darvid's death extremely hard.

"Getting by. Everything still seems so surreal." She glanced around the room. "Everywhere I look, I see Darvid's face. I don't know how I'll get through this."

Belle looked her up and down. "Mavis Brinkman Applebee, you're resilient. The strongest woman I know." She laid a gentle hand on her older sister's arm. If she could take away her pain, she would, in a heartbeat. Mavis had always been Belle's best friend. Loyal to a fault.

She glanced at Mavis's left hand, and the abominable gloves hiding her missing pinkie. Belle's guilt was ever-present. Before they'd moved from the river area to a nicer neighborhood, Mavis had gotten her hand caught in some tangled fishing line. Cleaning up the litter in the alley beside their uncle's home had been Belle's chore, but she'd put the distasteful task off that day. Mavis, wanting to spare her sister a tongue-lashing from Aunt Velma, had come out to help. A passing carriage caught the line in its spinning wheels. In an instant, Mavis's finger popped off at the knuckle as easily as a pea snaps in half.

Belle would never forget the sound.

Or the look on Mavis's face.

Because of her mutilation, Mavis hid herself away at her accounting job at Thornton House department store. Until Darvid joined. In less than three months, she'd said yes to his proposal—even though she'd confided to Belle that the most she felt for him was a deep, abiding friendship. Darvid was a nice, considerate, mild-mannered man who smiled and laughed at every chance. And indeed, until now, that had seemed enough. Although they'd had little, they'd appeared happy.

"Do you have a moment to talk?" Belle asked.

Mavis closed the door. "All right. My manager has been quite understanding. If we hurry, I won't be too late."

She directed them to the secondhand settee in front of the fireplace, resting her hand over a small tear in its arm as she sat down. "What's on your mind, Belle? I know you don't enjoy coming to this part of town."

"You don't either, if you're honest."

Mavis ignored the comment. "Whatever you have to say must be important."

"Actually, you're right. It *is* important. I've received a telegram from Eden."

Mavis's eyes grew so wide that Belle could almost read her thoughts right through them. *Eden.* Where Mother and Father met and married. Where all five sisters were conceived and born. A place Belle wondered about all the time. Her memories of their departure when she was almost four were foggy. Her clearest image was of Mother stuffing clothes into a large trunk as a man, who must have been Father, stood back, taller than any tree, watching in disbelief. Belle thought she remembered a need to run to him, lay her small hand upon his cheek, but the tears on Mother's face had fastened her feet to the floor. Belle convinced herself that must be a dream, something her mind had conjured up, distorting the truth for want of a father's love. She'd been too young to know the kinds of questions to ask her mother. It was only after Mother died that Uncle Vernon told them—with unseemly glee—that their father had been a violent man, disrespectful and coarse. That their mother fled out of fear of what he might do to her or the children. The story each of the sisters carried inside was that John Brinkman had been a despicable character. And hadn't he proved as much? He'd never come to see them or sought them out in any way. He'd turned his back on his family, pretending they never existed.

No point tiptoeing around the news. "Father has passed."

The color drained from Mavis's face. For a moment, they sat in silence.

"This feels like a pointed arrow through my heart," Mavis whispered. "Somehow, some way, I always believed we'd get a chance to be reunited." She looked at the floor. "I was wrong."

"Oh pooh," Belle said. Mavis was too much of a romantic for her. "Why would you want to? He didn't want us. Why should we despair now?"

Mavis's lips wobbled. "He was our *father*. Regardless of how he treated Mother or us, we should show a little respect."

"He never gave this family a moment's thought. We were *nothing* to him, Mavis. And actually, saying that aloud *does* break my heart." A strange image of a man stirred inside her. His scent, the rumble of his voice—she felt a faint longing for his gentle touch, a kiss good night... She blinked and looked away from Mavis's censorious scrutiny.

"When did you receive word?"

"Last week."

Mavis's eyes widened again. "Why didn't you tell me sooner?"

If Belle didn't explain quickly, they'd have an argument on their hands. "I know you don't like being kept in the dark, Mavis, but I was sheltering you. Darvid passed barely a month ago."

"And the others? Do they know?"

Belle nodded. "You've gone through so much. I wanted to spare you for a little while—*we* wanted to spare you. Emma, Lavinia, and Katie agreed." *Well, sort of. Two out of three.* "You'd do exactly the same for one of us. Aren't you glad you've had this week to yourself, without it being more complicated?"

"Father shouldn't be thought of as a complication."

Time to change the subject. "Everyone is packed and ready to travel, as am I. Strangely enough, we've been summoned for the reading of Father's will. Mr. Glass, an attorney in Eden, sent enough fare to cover our travel."

Mavis pushed to her feet, her lips pulled into a frown. Belle knew all too well that her oldest sister didn't like being left out of the decision making. She considered herself substitute mother and protector of them all. But her irritation lasted only a moment. She walked slowly to a window overlooking the gray day outside.

"What happened? Do you know? How did he die?"

"His horse fell, and he broke his leg. Infection set in."

"How horrible."

"I agree. And that's all I know—except that the will can't be read unless all five of us are present."

Mavis turned, a wistful expression on her face. "I remember sitting in tall, green grass with you, Emma, and baby Lavinia. Katie wasn't yet born. Someone was singing. A man's voice. Father must have changed greatly." She slowly shook her head. "I don't think I have the energy to travel west. From what Uncle Vernon has told us, the little Father had has been lost over the years. A broken-down house on a small patch of land with a handful of cattle."

"Then I guess we'll have to go without you." Belle gazed innocently at her hands, folded in her lap. "Though the telegram *did* say we *all* had to be present…"

Mavis returned to the sofa. "You can't go without me." Alarm tinged her voice. "Who'll make sure Katie doesn't become turned around in some station and get left behind? And Emma needs her cup of warm milk before bed. You know she can't sleep in a strange place without one. Don't get me started on Lavinia. She's liable to be run over by a team of horses if a pretty bonnet catches her eye. I swear, I don't think I want any children of my own after raising the four of you."

Irritation rippled inside Belle. *Mavis doesn't have to act like she's the only one with a brain in her head.*

"What about me? You're not the only one capable of looking after Katie and the others."

A silly smile pulled at Mavis's lips. "You're right. I meant no offense. I worry, is all. You know you can be impulsive, Belle. When you get angry, you pay little attention to what's happening around you. A train ride has dangers. Bad weather, outlaws, Indians. Snakes!"

Belle shuddered. "That's plenty of peril to worry over." She hesitated. *She's not going to like this.* "The train doesn't go all the way to Eden. We'll have to take a stagecoach from Pueblo for the last three hundred miles."

Mavis's hand flew to her chest. "What about Katie's claustrophobia? No, absolutely not. We'll wire and tell Mr. Glass a trip like this is impossible. He can come to us."

Belle's patience vanished. "For heaven's sake. She can sit by the window or up top with the driver."

"You're heartless, Belle."

"Pack your things. We have tickets for tomorrow and will arrive in Eden in about a week and a half. We'll stay long enough to hear what the lawyer has to say, pay our respects to Father's grave, and get back on the train. Think about it, Mavis. *Why* does the reading have to be so formal?" She lifted a brow and let that thought simmer. "What if Father *did* have at least a little something set aside to leave to us? Any amount will help with Darvid's medical bills, and more. We *must* go."

Mavis's mouth was still set in a stubborn line. "I can't. I'll lose my job. Being a widow, I depend on that income."

"Your manager has already offered you time off, which you didn't take. And he thought very highly of Darvid. He'll understand, I'm sure. Especially when you tell him why you need the time away." Belle stood. "Discoveries await."

"Really, Belle, you sound like a novelist. What about Lesley?" Mavis tipped her head. "I can't imagine your fine young gentleman is just letting you waltz off to Colorado. Not when the two of you are so close to making your relationship binding."

Belle smiled at the mention of her sweetheart. "You're right about that. He's coming with us. To keep us safe. I thought that exceedingly kind."

"You're wiping away my objections like they're ice in the sun," Mavis said, her brow still lined with worry. "And Uncle Vernon? What does he think about the whole situation? He never had one nice thing to say about Eden—or our father."

At the mention of their uncle's name, Belle cut her gaze to the window, squelching her immature desire to make a face. How she loathed that man. "Actually, he's been very strange since the telegram arrived. When I told him we'd been called back to Eden, his face turned white as chalk and he said little, which confounded us because we've all heard him go on and on about Father. Anyway, the next morning, he announced that Aunt Velma would be accompanying him on a long-planned business trip. They packed that day, wished us well, and departed."

Mavis cocked her head, confused. Their aunt and uncle had been orchestrating their lives for years and didn't give power away without a fight. "Not one protest or complaint?"

"No. It was the strangest thing. I'm still trying to figure out why."

"How curious," Mavis whispered. "Where'd they go?"

"I have no idea. Uncle Vernon hadn't mentioned the trip until that moment."